# *Tomorrow's Promise:*
## *Survival on the Plains*

D.L. Rogers

D.L. Rogers – Author
June 2008 Release
All Rights Reserved;
Any similarity to any living person is strictly coincidental.
This is a work of fiction; based on historical fact.

**THE WHITE OAKS SERIES:** by D.L. Rogers

***Tomorrow's Promise: Survival on the Plains*** – Book 1 in the original trilogy, released 2008
**Brothers by Blood** – Book 2 in the original trilogy, released 2008
**Ghost Dancers** – Book 3 in the original trilogy, released 2007
**Caleb** – Book 4 in the continuation of the series, released 2010
**Amy** – Book 5 in the continuation of the series, released 2011
**Maggie** – Book 6 in the continuation of the series, released 2012
**Beginnings: Into the Unknown** – Book 7 (and prequel) in the continuation of the series, released 2013

Other Books by D.L. Rogers

**Elizabeth's War: Missouri 1863** – Released 2014
**The Journey** – Released 2009
**Echoes in the Dark** – Released 2009

Cover design by Delle Jacobs & Glen Dixon

DLRogersBooks
www.dlrogersbooks.com

## Dedication

This book is dedicated to my mother, Leah Paugh, my "biggest fan," who passed away in June of 2006 from cancer. She believed in Ben and Sarah from the first revision to the last.

Here's to you, Mom.

I miss you,
Dee

## Acknowledgements

I'd like to thank all those who have helped me to never give up on my dream of seeing this book in print. First to Chris McLain, my first editor who "bloodied" me mercilessly, but made my book better with each stroke of her red pen.

I'd also like to thank my friends and family who read version after version and never gave up on me. And finally to Jim Beckner, former teacher and Civil War expert who has taken the time to review *PROMISE* to ensure all the history contained herein to be as correct as possible through research and historical confirmation. Thank you to each and every one of you.

## FOREWORD

War is ugly! And the American Civil War is the ugliest of all wars! Before a cannon shot was fired at Fort Sumter, Missourians and Kansans had been at war for seven bitter years. *Both* sides had evil men, doing evil things, mostly for personal gain and fame.

As a lover of, researcher of, and living historian of Civil War history, I have not purchased a fiction book in twenty years. However, I was recently compelled to read a few and discovered that I have been missing some great stories. Two examples are *TOMORROW'S PROMISE: SURVIVAL ON THE PLAINS* and *GHOST DANCERS*, both titles by Diane Rogers. *TOMORROW'S PROMISE: SURVIVAL ON THE PLAINS* is as historically accurate as many history books. It is evident Ms. Rogers has taken great pride in the historical accuracy of the works. Therefore, if you enjoy reading about the Oregon Trail, Indians, survival, romance, adventure, Kansas City history, Border War, Civil War and stories with a happy ending? You can find it all in this one novel. I highly recommend it.

History strips itself of personalities, of individual struggles, of great stories of survival, and we soon forget that people make history. This book refreshingly reminds us and brings us back to that fact of human survival. It makes this struggle real to us once again. Congratulations!

Jim Beckner
Civil War Historian

## Prologue

Sarah stared down at the package in her hand, at the delicate bow tied around the brown paper that concealed the box inside.

"Go on. Open it." Ben pushed her hand closer.

Sarah glanced at her husband of six months, his face silhouetted in the light of the fire. Dark eyes that matched his dark hair reflected hope and happiness as he snuggled next to her in front of the hearth. The flames of the fire popped and crackled to cast vibrant streaks of light across the room.

"Come on." He nudged her. "I'd like you to see what's inside before we're both old and gray."

Sarah smiled and tore at the paper, slowly at first then faster, curious of what lay hidden inside the long, rectangle package. Once exposed, she traced her fingers over the black, velvet cover.

Ben hissed an impatient noise. "Sarah..."

But Sarah wanted to savor the moment. To remember forever their first Christmas together.

Ben Walters was all Sarah Reynolds ever hoped for or dreamed of in a husband. Not like the dandies her father had tried to marry her off to.

Roger Reynolds, Sarah's father and one of the largest landowners in the state of Pennsylvania, had tried for years to marry his only daughter to any one of the sons of rich men who resided in the same county. But she'd resisted and chosen the one man who made her heart soar and her blood rush like an open floodgate. Ben Walters, the newly hired foreman of her father's vast ranch, was that man. Ben was real with the strength and character of a good man, yet gentle and loving.

Sarah's heart swelled with love for her husband who lay next to her on the floor in the front room of the tiny home they called their own.

"Go on," Ben said again.

Sarah raised the lid—and gasped. She lifted the necklace from inside. Light exploded around the little room from the golden oval locket like hundreds of shooting stars when the light from the fire struck it. It danced and swirled in the firelight as though alive. Sarah could only stare through blurred eyes at so precious a gift.

She put it back in the box and threw her arms around her husband. She kissed every visible part of his face, ears and neck and thanked him over and over again.

Ben laughed and squeezed her tighter. "It's only a small token of how much I love you," he said, his voice gruff with emotion.

Tears streamed down Sarah's cheeks and it took several minutes to regain her composure. She sat back on her heels, lifted the box and gazed down at the locket inside.

"This is beautiful, Ben. The most beautiful gift I've ever received."

Ben raised an eyebrow and pursed his lips. "You know that's not true. Your father's given you hundreds of beautiful gifts." He paused and smiled. "But I like the fact you'd say so."

"No matter what you think, Ben Walters, as far as I'm concerned this is the most beautiful gift I've ever gotten." She scooted away from him. "Certainly Father's given me many lovely things, but none compare to this. I can imagine what it must have cost. Now I know why you spent all those long hours at the Harris ranch these past months." She stared into the fire while her fingers slid back and forth across the box containing the locket. A single tear clung to the corner of her eye. It slipped to her cheek when she turned back to her husband.

"Father loves me and he's only interested in what's best for me. That's why he's made things so difficult for us." She looked away. "And because we're going to go to what he considers the ends of the earth," she added.

Before she'd thought her actions through, Sarah had mentioned Ben's dream of going west to her father, and from then on, he'd done his best to separate them any way he could. He'd gone so far as to fire Ben from his position as ranch foreman and even tried to discredit him. But the other ranchers knew what was really in Roger Reynolds' heart, and the Harrises had snatched Ben up in a heartbeat.

Sarah remained thoughtful about where her life was headed. Toward a place where the unknown ruled. Where its beauty was beyond compare, yet death was commonplace as the struggle for triumph over the elements too often became all consuming. Where life was lived, or lost, according to the world around you.

Ben turned Sarah's face back to his. "Sarah, we're going to have a good life. We'll have a ranch of our own, one we'll build with our own sweat and blood. A ranch we can be proud of. We'll be happy. And no one will take that away."

Sarah forced a smile. She and Ben had spoken of this often. He called the journey they'd soon take along the Oregon Trail *their adventure.* She couldn't help but smile when she recalled how he'd spread fliers all over the floor in his attempt to convince her how safe it was to travel west. "We'll be trailblazers. We'll open up new country," he'd said, his voice proud and full of awe.

"Sarah?" Ben's voice broke into her thoughts. "Are you all right?"

She covered his hand with hers. Yes, she was all right. She was with the man she loved and no one would drive them apart. And she would do what made him happy. And that was to go west, to find their destiny.

"You know your father's tried to drive a wedge between us since the day he found out about us," Ben continued. "Even before he knew about our plans to leave. I'm just plain not good enough for his little girl."

Sarah frowned. "You know why. I'm his only child and he's been mother and father to me since Mama died when I was so young. He's a bit protective, that's all."

"A bit protective?" Ben snorted. "He's more protective than a mother bear over her cub. He would've been happy to marry you off to any one of the sons of those rich dandies and let you be miserable the rest of your life. I didn't measure up, even though he knew I made you happy." He sighed.

Sarah poked him.

"You're good enough for me. Better than good enough." She leaned over and kissed him on the lips. "Ummmm. Much better," she murmured with a giggle when they parted.

She sat back and used the hem of her dress to shine the locket and again let the necklace dangle from her hand, the lights refracting around the room.

"Here." Ben sat up. "There's something else I want to show you." He took the locket, pushed a tiny clasp at the top and it opened. Etched into the gold on the left side were their initials.

Tears welled again in Sarah's eyes as Ben placed the necklace around her neck.

Her fingers caressed the golden surface. "I'll never take it off. I promise."

Another kiss sealed her vow.

# PART I

## THE INDIANS

*I am a fox*
*I am supposed to die*
*If there is anything difficult*
*If there is anything dangerous*
*That is mine to do.*

*Oglala Kit Fox Society Song*

# Chapter One

The scream was so shrill and laced with foreboding Sarah Walters jerked upright at the sound. She dropped her laundry into the river without a thought as her breath caught and her stomach clenched into knots of fear. The hair on her neck bristled and a shiver ran up and down her spine. She whirled around from the river's edge. A colorfully painted Indian dressed in ankle-high moccasins and a loincloth stood in front of the women of the wagon train. A breastplate of bones and beads covered his wide chest. Cold, black, hooded eyes glared at Sarah and the other women as they stood in silent fear.

Almost a dozen Indians joined the first and Sarah's heart hammered in her chest. A hand came down on her shoulder and she jerked around, fists balled, ready to fight for her life. But it was Ben who stood beside her.

"What do they want?" she managed through a tightened throat.

"I don't know. We'll have to wait and see." Ben pointed. "Andrews is on his way to talk to them."

A short, stocky Indian emerged from the center of the group. His greased black hair was adorned with feathers and beads and stood straight on end. He appeared to be the leader and waited, motionless, as Andrews, the wagon master, pushed through the gathered crowd of emigrants on shore.

Through sign and a few words, Andrews and the Indian parleyed for several minutes.

"They want a toll for passage over their land," Andrews finally told the men and women gathered at the edge of the river. "They want coffee and tobacco."

Sarah imagined they'd take whatever they wanted one way or another.

Sarah, Ben and the rest of the members of the train hurried back to their wagons to gather the requested goods as the Indians wandered through camp.

One brave came around the side of the Walters wagon

## Tomorrow's Promise: Survival on the Plains    D.L. Rogers

and stopped to gaze at Midnight, Ben's horse, tethered there. Concealed on the other side of the wagon, Sarah gaped at the Indian's missing right ear. She stared at the small opening surrounded by white, thick scar tissue as the Indian ran his hand over the animal's firm haunches.

One Ear was admiring Midnight's fine lines just as Ben poked his head out of the wagon. His back stiffened and his jaw ticked in anger at the sight of the Indian and his horse. He jumped down and stepped toward the brave, but Andrews stopped him in mid-stride.

One Ear pointed Midnight out to several braves who nodded their approval. His hand slid up the animal's neck, over his head and he grabbed the bridle.

Ben surged toward the Indian and horse, but Andrews held firm.

"Don't Ben. It's not worth it. It's only an animal. He's not worth your life."

Ben yanked his arm, but Andrews wouldn't release him. "If he wants that horse, he'll take it. Don't give him cause to try and kill you. We don't want any trouble," Andrews hissed.

One Ear glared at Ben from the corner of his eye. The brave seemed to dare Ben as he continued to stroke Midnight's silky coat. Slowly, he removed the bridle from the horse's head, dropped it to the ground and replaced it with a length of rope. The Indian looked over at Ben, a smile of satisfaction on his face.

Ben lunged, but Andrews was a strong man with big hands and his grip held Ben in place. Unable to watch her husband trying to get himself killed, Sarah stepped forward and grabbed Ben's other arm.

"Stop it, Ben! It's only a horse for God's sake. He's not worth your life. That Indian has murder in his eyes. Can't you see that? He'd love to challenge you for possession of that animal." She paused and her voice softened. "I know you love him, but he isn't worth your life."

One Ear stared gape-mouthed at Sarah and his hand dropped from the horse. He stepped toward Sarah, his hand stretched out in front of him to touch her.

*Tomorrow's Promise: Survival on the Plains*     *D.L. Rogers*

Ben tore free of Andrews' grip and jumped between Sarah and the brave who was only five feet from her.

"You're damn well out of your mind if you think you're going anywhere near my wife."

Ben stood his ground and One Ear stepped closer, their heavy breathing the only thing heard.

They faced off ready to do battle until the gruff, guttural voice of another Indian shattered the quiet. One Ear's back stiffened and he whirled to face his leader. He shouted and pointed at Midnight. The chief crossed his arms over his chest and spoke, his voice hard and controlled. One Ear shouted at him again, but the other Indian turned his back and walked away. One Ear spun back to Ben, a look that would chill the devil's soul on his face, before he stalked away.

Several minutes later, with bags of coffee, flour and tobacco tied to their horses, the party of Indians rode off. Save one.

With dread sharp in the pit of her belly Sarah recognized One Ear. He sat atop his pony scanning the camp and stopped only when his eyes settled on Ben and Sarah. He jerked his horse's reins. The animal reared up, its hooves slashing the air, its head flinging back and forth. The Indian raised his lance high above his head and his shrill cry resounded throughout camp. Sarah's skin bubbled with gooseflesh.

One Ear swung his mount around and raced away with the others, his challenge hanging on the air long after their departure.

A bad feeling overwhelmed Sarah. She held tight to Ben. They hadn't seen the last of the one-eared Indian.

"Storm's blowing in!" Ben yelled over the howling night wind, clutching his hat to keep it from flying away across the plains. "Coming in fast! We've got to secure the wagon and get these animals tied off!"

Sarah forced herself from the safety of the wagon and raced to help her husband. Her hair whipped and snapped painfully around her face and into her eyes and mouth. She ran from one side of the wagon to the other tying off every loose bucket and lantern. Her skirt stung her ankles and legs in the frenzied wind as Ben fought to tether the animals before the full rage of the storm hit. The wagon swayed. Raging wind shook everything in its path. Thunder rolled toward them; the ground rumbled beneath Sarah's feet to echo like hundreds of stampeding horses. Mean black clouds stretched the length of the night sky until bright, white streaks of lightning split the inky darkness to momentarily blind. Animals bellowed and lashed their tails in fear. Children cried in terror and men and women shouted orders as they braced for the storm's fury.

Ben shoved Sarah inside the wagon only moments before the wind hit again, bawling like a calf at branding time. Shivers ran down Sarah's back. The sky turned black as tar and the air grew icy cold. Hailstones the size of silver dollars battered and slashed at the dusty canvas, Ben and Sarah's only protection against the mounting storm.

The hail subsided its furious tirade within a few minutes, but on its tail came a torrential downpour of rain, more thunder and lightning. The sky glowed eerily as crooked fingers of light reached out across the blackened earth to strike and tear at the helpless wagons. The ground shook with each roll of thunder and pots and pans that hung from the wagon beam rattled wildly. Sarah covered her ears and curled into a ball as the wind wailed by like a banshee warning her next victim.

The rumbling mounted again and Sarah waited for the explosion of sound then light. She closed her eyes against it, pushed her hands tighter around her ears. She was in the middle of a war of the elements, unarmed and helpless.

Strong, warm arms encircled her and she fell into Ben's welcome embrace. But Ben's warmth didn't change her thoughts. Doubt overwhelmed her. *Why had she come on this foolish quest? For fortune? To tame the wilderness?* Fear of the unknown threatened to rise to the surface of her mind and consume her, but she forced it back. *What else would they find along the trail, alone, without benefit of civilization? More Indians? More hardships? More storms?* She started to shake and Ben's arms tightened around her shoulders.

"Shhh," Ben whispered before he kissed her ear. "It'll be

fine. We just have to wait it out, but we'll be fine. I promise."

But would they be fine? she wondered again. If they survived this storm, what would they find further along the trail? She had read the publications heralding the vast beauty of the plains. But all she had seen so far was grit and mud and sweat. And Indians. She'd read of the bounteous grasses that grew six feet tall and waved in the warm, gentle breezes. About the beautiful flowers spread out across the plains and the wild buffalo that trod there. Of the land waiting to be claimed and turned into the ranch she and Ben dreamed of. But where were those lush grasses and beautiful flowers now?

"It'll be all right, Sarah," Ben soothed.

"Will it?" She jerked out of his arms. "How do we know that? This is the second violent storm we've encountered since we left Westport. Everything about the trail looks the same. Flat, desolate, few trees and wide-open, and either covered with dust or mud. And what about the Indians? Will we see more of them? And if we do, will they be friendly or more hostile than the ones we just met? What if their chief hadn't stopped that brave from fighting you? What might have happened then?"

"What are you saying, Sarah? Have you changed your mind about our going west? I thought it was something we both wanted." Ben's face took on a stricken look in the dim wagon. "We talked about this for days. Weeks. We agreed the only way for us to survive was away from your father. You knew there were dangers. I thought you wanted this as much as I did. To build a new life for ourselves on a ranch that might someday rival any back East. Even your father's. One we can pass on to our children."

Sadness washed over Sarah like a wave. He'd said the dreaded word. Children. They'd been married for eight months and had planned for children immediately, but there was no sign. Sometimes Sarah's stomach hurt enough to make her think she was carrying, but she was always disappointed. Tears filled her eyes and Ben pulled her back into his arms.

"Oh, Sarah. We'll have children, and if we don't, there are worse things than going through life childless." He paused and stroked her face with his forefinger. "Like life without you."

She lifted her eyes to his. He loved her, she knew that, and she loved him with all her heart. Staring at his eyes, she recalled the first time she saw them. She had just rounded the barn of her father's ranch, smelling of horses and hay after a long hard ride on her favorite horse, Jezebel, when she'd run smack into the man. They collided, nearly knocking each other down. He had to reach out and grab her to keep her from landing on the ground. Their eyes met and she'd been lost from that day on.

She touched his face; conjured in her mind all the arguments as to why they shouldn't go on, but she stopped at the one reason why she would. Because she loved this man with every ounce of her being and what he wanted, she wanted. Why had she come on this journey?

She had come for him.

The night seemed endless. Rain pounded the earth and soaked everything and everyone on it. It wasn't long before the oiled canvas of the wagon offered little protection from the downpour. Water dripped slow, yet constant. It seeped in through the sides, soaked the floor beneath them. Cloaked in as many blankets as they could find to ward off the bone-chilling moisture in the air, Ben and Sarah still grew wet and cold. But the elements continued to unleash their beastly fury around them. It rocked the wagon on its axles as it sank deeper and deeper into the mud.

Hours later the storm rumbled into the darkness and Sarah drifted into sleep. Ben looked down at her slumbering form and a smile came to his face. He searched the contours of her heart-shaped face, the high cheekbones, the small, crooked nose, and the lips that were soft, moist and sweet when he kissed them. She was his. Forever. He gazed down at the long, dark lashes that were closed in sleep and imagined the brilliant, blue eyes hidden beneath them, eyes that seemed to have a life of their own, always smiling and happy. He reached down and touched a lock of her wheat-colored hair; wanted to roll his hand in it and pull her lips to his in a passionate kiss. Instead, he let her sleep. His eyes slid down from her narrow chin to her silky neck where the golden locket rose and fell with each breath. He smiled, lay down beside her and remembered her words.

"I'll never take it off," she'd said as she caressed the locket. "I promise."

Ben smiled in the dark. He couldn't remember a day since that Christmas morning she hadn't worn the necklace proudly. He was a lucky man. A lucky man indeed.

The following day the wagon bogged down in the mud every time they tried to move. Only when the sun had been out for hours and the wind blew constantly, did they make any headway.

When the wagon got stuck just before sundown, Ben dug them out one last time then announced they'd camp there, an uncomfortable distance from the rest of the train.

Ben ate a quick meal then curled up in the bedroll at the rear of the wagon. He was asleep within minutes of his head finding the pillow.

Snuggled beside him in the glow of lamplight, Sarah put the final stitches in a dress she'd been working on. Midnight snorted outside, drawing her attention. She listened, but all remained quiet. Midnight snorted again and moved restlessly. Not wanting to disturb Ben's much needed rest, she put her sewing aside and waited. God how she wished they'd camped closer to the rest of the wagon train.

"Who's there?" she asked. Silence. She leaned out and found herself looking into a pair of familiar, hard black eyes. She started to scream, but One Ear's hand clapped over her mouth in an instant.

Midnight stamped and snorted and she prayed the horse's noise would waken Ben. She tried to bite the Indian's hand, but couldn't grab any skin with her teeth. He dragged her out of the wagon like a rag doll.

She fought with every ounce of strength she had, but One Ear was too strong, solid like a wall. He pulled her up against his chest. His eyes danced with evil in the moonlight. Sarah's mind raced. Her feet dangled helplessly in mid-air. She kicked at him, but only managed to make him grunt. His grip never wavered. Desperate, she went limp in his arms hoping to make him believe she'd fainted.

His grip lessened, only slightly, but enough. With raw fear gripping her senses, she tore her mouth free and screamed with every breath she had.

"Ben! Help me! Ben!"

Ben stumbled out of the wagon. One Ear dropped Sarah, untied Midnight and flung himself onto the horse's back. Ben pulled a knife from his boot and ran toward the Indian. He grabbed for One Ear's leg as Midnight reared in the commotion. He caught and held on, his feet dragging in the dirt as the horse hit the ground and tried to run. Ben yanked the brave from the animal's back and the two crashed to the ground.

They jumped up and faced each other. One Ear drew his knife to match Ben's. They moved in a circle. Both blades flashed in the moonlight and Sarah thought she'd be sick at the sight of the two men facing off before her. The Indian lunged forward. Ben jumped aside. The blade missed his stomach by mere inches. One Ear whirled and smiled, as though pleased for a worthy opponent.

Each time Ben jumped, Sarah jumped. Unable to stand and do nothing, she ran to the wagon to look for something she could use to hit the Indian. She scrambled inside and threw aside anything that wouldn't help her in her quest. She finally looked up and spotted a heavy cast-iron skillet above her. She grabbed it with both hands and scooted back outside the wagon in time to see the brave dive toward Ben with his knife ready for the kill. But Ben kicked the knife out of his hand and swung his own knife toward One Ear's belly. The Indian grabbed Ben's wrist and the two struggled for control. One Ear shoved his knee into Ben's gut. Air exploded from his lungs and he staggered. The knife clattered down beside him and One Ear leaped to retrieve it.

Fear tore through Sarah. She ran up behind the brave and swung the pan with all her might. But the Indian must have heard her coming, because he jerked aside and the pan merely glanced off his shoulder. He grabbed the knife from the ground and swung back around.

"Ben!" Sarah screamed as she ran away. "He's got your knife!" The knife glinted in One Ear's hand as he stood back up to his full height, an evil glint in his eyes.

Ben's hands were on his knees and he was gasping for air, but he looked up in time to dive away from the slashing blade.

"Come on you bastard," Ben yelled as he refilled his burning lungs. "Let's finish this. Now!"

The Indian's face became hard. He charged. The knife narrowly missed Ben's neck when he rushed past. Ben swung his leg and kicked One Ear in the back as the brave ran by. He stumbled, but didn't fall and he turned back to Ben, a murderous scowl on his face. He charged again. The two met, chest-to-chest, the knife poised above Ben's back, ready for the kill.

Ben struggled to keep One Ear's arm suspended above his head. In a burst of effort, he plunged his knee into the brave's stomach. One Ear doubled over. Ben punched the Indian in the face, knocking him to the ground. The knife flew out of One Ear's hand and skittered away. The brave scrambled toward the knife, Ben at his heels. They rolled and tumbled, each man trying to gain the advantage.

Sarah had never seen such stamina. Ben was a strong man, but this Indian seemed invincible. She ran to the front of the wagon and screamed. She screamed at the top of her lungs for someone to come and help them. It was then she remembered the gun. She ran to the wagon seat, lifted the lid and reached inside, her mind a whirl. *Where were the others? Why didn't they hear her? Why didn't someone come and help them?* Unable to see inside the seat in the darkness, she fumbled around until her fingers finally touched on the smooth wood of the box that contained the Colt Ben had told her about over and over again. She pulled out the box, ripped it open, grabbed the gun and ran back to where the two men struggled.

One Ear had broken away from Ben and was clawing his way toward the knife that lay in front of them. Ben, right behind him, grabbed at his heels. The Indian reached the knife, rolled and jumped upright. He landed on his feet as easily as a cat. Ben was still on the ground, defenseless. One Ear muttered something and settled the knife in his hand. He raised his arm to plunge the knife into Ben's heart.

Gunfire tore through the night air and the Indian's arm stopped in mid-thrust. His body jerked, his knees buckled and he fell to the ground, his face in the mud.

Ben jumped to his feet and ran to Sarah. He pried the smoking gun from her trembling hands, just as the others from the train reached them. She muttered, incoherent, as she looked down at the fallen brave's body.

"What happened?" Andrews yelled over the voices of the other emigrants. "What the hell happened?"

"I had to kill him," Sarah said over and over again. "I had no choice." Her hands trembled and her face was as white as parchment.

Ben jerked his chin toward the dead Indian. "I guess coffee and sugar weren't enough for him." He put his arm around Sarah's shoulders and led her toward the wagon.

"I had to. I had no choice," Sarah continued to mumble as she and Ben disappeared into the darkness of the wagon.

## Chapter Two

The wagon ground to a halt at the top of a ridge. Sarah stared down at the vast wilderness below, neither beautiful nor picturesque as the fliers had touted in their efforts to entice people west. Instead the wilderness looked desolate and wild. The land was brown, foreboding, and nothing moved except the lizards and grasshoppers darting across the dusty earth where dried prairie grass and prickly pear cactus grew.

Unable to stand the constant jarring of her teeth and body, Sarah handed Ben the reins and jumped off the wagon to continue on foot. She walked mindlessly and neither saw nor felt the terrain around her. She didn't see the wildflowers that grew in huge clumps and splashed yellow and purple hues across the landscape. She didn't smell the sweet aroma of sagebrush as the bushes were crushed under the wagon's wheels. Nor did she notice the clear blue sky with its patches of white, puffy clouds that floated like ships across a vast blue ocean. All she saw were her feet, dust, and the hundreds of grasshoppers that skittered away in clusters as they hopped to safety from each step she took, each step more difficult than the last. All around, deep ravines made travel difficult and hazardous for the stock and wagons.

At least there were a few trees here, she thought. Evergreens and ash she'd heard Ben say. But she didn't care. After a long, endurance-testing month on the trail, in which she'd killed a man and survived all manner of weather, all she wanted was to sleep in a real bed, bathe in a real tub and eat without benefit of bugs crawling all over her. To spend one day without the sun burning every inch of her exposed skin. She was tired of the drudgery of the constantly moving wagon train that never stopped, not even to birth a baby or tend a wounded man. She walked endlessly, mindlessly forward, following the wagon in front of her.

The wagon creaked to a stop at the crest of the next steep hill and Sarah joined Ben beside the front of the wagon. She wanted to cry over what was below. Nothing but more ravines and more hills.

Ben grabbed her around the waist and lifted her off the ground. "It's incredible, isn't it?" His face was aglow with childlike excitement.

Words couldn't express what Sarah felt. She managed to force a smile, for Ben's sake, as he touched her feet back to the ground. He gave her a squeeze and led her to the back of the wagon where he tied off the rear wheels to the wagon box to keep the vehicle from rolling freely down the hill. A hill that seemed more like a mountain in her estimation. Sarah's heart pounded. All she could envision was the wagon careening out of control and watching all their earthly belongings smashed and destroyed before it crashed to the bottom.

"Don't worry, Sarah. We'll be fine. Just like everybody else." He pointed at the other wagons already at the bottom of the hill then double-checked the wheels before he led Sarah back up front. She turned her face into the cool breeze and stared out over the terrain they had yet to cross. All she could see were hills, hills and more hills. Not grassy, rolling hills, but steep, rocky, treacherous hills that stretched all the way into tomorrow and beyond.

"Our turn." Ben's voice drew her from her temporary musing. He kissed her forehead, reached out and grabbed the lead mule's harness to begin the decent.

Sarah's heart stuck in her throat as she watched Ben lead the mules forward over the crest. After several minutes of prodding the reluctant animals, down they went. The wagon slipped and slid with each mule's step. But Ben was patient as he guided them downward, talking softly as they went. Behind them, dust and loosened rocks swirled around Sarah's ankles as she tried to avoid walking in the already deep ruts cut into the hillside. Slowly, she picked her way down until they were both at the bottom of the hollow. Ben untied the rear wheels and led the team away so the next wagon down didn't slide into them. He stopped the mules a short distance away and Sarah flopped down beside one of the wheels.

"That's it. I can't go any farther," she mumbled. "I'll never make it. I'm not strong enough. I can't make it. I just can't. I never should have come," she muttered over and over again until Ben's voice penetrated her mumbling.

"Sarah!"

She stopped and looked up into his face. His eyes were wild with fear, his mouth tight.

"Stop it, Sarah. Stop it right now!" he commanded.

"Stop what? I've stated a simple fact. I can't go on. I'm not strong enough. I thought I could do this, but apparently I can't. No more rivers or prairies; not another hill or ravine. I don't have the strength." She gazed at everything around her. "I know there's nothing here to sustain us if we stopped right here, but I just don't have the energy to keep going right now. I'm tired of the desolation, the dust or mud, whichever it happens to be at the time, the heat, the bugs and the constant, burning sun. I can't do it, Ben. I simply can't go on."

"Sarah! Listen to me. You have to. You have no choice."

She threw her hands into the air. "Why did I agree to this lunacy?" she yelled to the sky. "Why did I give up a comfortable life with everything I could have possibly ever wanted to blindly follow you to this—this Promised Land? I can't take much more, I tell you. I can't." She clamped her hands down over her face. "I can't go on, Ben. I won't."

Her mind slipped back to the past, to a life that had been easy and carefree. Where her every desire needed only be spoken and it was granted. Where people took care of her, pampered her, loved her. She imagined herself in a hot tub of water as warm liquid sluiced over her body. A towel brought to her by Cassie, the free black woman who'd been in their household as long as she could remember. She could hear the ranch hands shouting outside, hear carriages arriving for another of her father's famous parties.

She was abruptly drawn from her musing when Ben grabbed both her wrists and yanked them away from her face.

"Sarah. Listen to me." His words penetrated her sullen state. "You can go on, and you will. You have no choice and neither do I. Look around you. There's nothing here. Nothing to sustain us even if we did stop. There's no water and no shelter. We have no choice, Sarah. We have to keep going."

Sarah searched Ben's face then looked around. A few trees stood like sentinels over the open expanse of land, but nothing else was visible to sustain life. No water, no shelter. Only rocks, grass and dirt. Ben was right, there was nothing here. Even if they did stop they would die within days without water or protection from the elements other than the wagon. And they'd be alone, for the wagon train would move on without them. She forced back an overwhelming desire to scream. To vent her rage for being here in the middle of nothing, going only God knew where. But she had to go on and she knew it, even though her mind begged for respite.

She looked at Ben's face and noticed new lines etched around his eyes. Those hadn't been there a few weeks ago. The strain of this journey was wearing on him, too.

Rest. That was all she needed. Just a few days rest and then she could go on. But they didn't have a few days. The train waited for no one. They were already falling behind. She remembered hearing something about Fort Laramie. Hadn't someone said they were only a few days away? If only she could reach the fort, then she could rest.

"Sarah? Are you all right?" Ben touched her face.

She nodded and forced herself to speak. "Yes, just give me a minute." She looked up at Ben and guilt washed over her. "I'm so sorry, Ben. You're right. We don't have a choice. It's just that...everything closed in on me all at once. The Indians, the constant grueling pace, the heat one minute and the bitter cold the next. It got to me. If I can just rest a few minutes, I'll be fine, then we can catch up. Please," she added in desperation. "Just a few minutes."

Ben's relief was obvious. "A few minutes, that's all. We're already behind. We'll have to hurry to catch up as it is."

Sarah closed her eyes and nodded, thankful for the respite, however short it might be.

Only two day's ride from Fort Laramie, Sarah allowed herself to think of the few luxuries she would avail herself of when they arrived. She would languish in a hot tub for hours, wash her hair and scrub her skin till it turned bright red. She would sleep in a real bed and eat at a real table.

The reins dangled loose in her hands and her eyes closed as the mules followed the wagon ahead. She dozed.

Shouts of warning rent the air and jerked her from her slumber.

A strangled cry of pure terror caused the hair on Sarah's neck to stand on end. She pulled the wagon to a stop and slipped the reins around the brake. Fear rose sharp and quick in her throat as she reached below the seat for the box that contained the Colt handgun, the same gun she'd used to kill One Ear. Who'd have thought she'd have to pick it up again so soon? The weapon tight in her grip, she waited for Ben to come and tell her what was happening.

He raced toward her a few seconds later. Clumps of dirt and grass flew out from Midnight's hooves as they sped toward her. Ben jerked the animal to a skidding stop, jumped off the horse and quickly tethered him to the wagon. He climbed onto the seat beside Sarah and grabbed the reins off the brake.

"What's happening?" Sarah managed, her throat dry, nerves tight.

Reins slapped against the mule's backsides. "We've got to get this wagon into a circle with the others. Indians have been spotted over the rise behind us, in full war paint!" The mules pulled the wagon into formation with the others.

Sarah's heart pounded. *Were they here because she'd killed One Ear? Were the Indians going to attack all these people because of her?*

Ben seemed to know her thoughts. "We don't know why they're here, Sarah. We don't know if they're even from the same tribe as that Indian you killed and we don't know for sure if they're going to attack. But we'll be ready, just in case." Ben again slapped the reins against the rumps of the mules.

As the wagon swung around, Sarah saw them. Dozens of riders sat atop painted horses at the crest of the rise, their faces a blur of colors. Feathers stuck out from their long, straight black hair. Their ponies pranced with anticipation as the riders waited. Sarah's body went cold and guilt overwhelmed her at the thought that good people of this wagon train might be killed because of her. But it had been either Ben or One Ear and that was no choice.

The wagons formed a circle. Men and women scrambled from their seats and hurried for cover. Sarah dropped to the ground. She peeked out from behind the wagon where she hid and searched the painted men lined up in front of her. She thought she'd jump right out of her skin when Ben came up beside her and placed his hand protectively on her waist.

Sarah opened her mouth to speak, but the words were choked off when the line of Indians began to move.

In one motion they started forward. Their speed increased with each horses' step. Faster and faster they came. Closer and closer. War cries, high and shrill, laced with the promise of death, reverberated through the mass of approaching Indians and pierced Sarah to her very core.

The Indians raced toward the wagon train. Their long black hair flew wildly around their shoulders. Reins dangled from the Indians' teeth, which allowed bows, arrows and war lances to be gripped and ready in their hands.

Ben shoved Sarah under the wagon. He jumped into its bed, grabbed the rifle and extra ammunition then scrambled under the wagon beside her. He checked the load on his rifle, took the Colt from Sarah, and checked its load.

The Indians thundered to within about a hundred yards of the wagons—and stopped. They sat motionless for what seemed like an eternity as they looked over the wagon train and its inhabitants. Sarah felt like a chicken in a henhouse, gathered with the others for slaughter, as the hard glare of the braves slid over the wagon train. Her chest heaved, her heart pounded wildly and blood surged through her ears.

With a loud, high-pitched yell, the Indians broke formation and raced toward the emigrants. They shouted and waved their bows, lances and war clubs. Within moments, the wagons were surrounded. Arrows were unleashed and guns exploded. Women and children screamed and cried. Men shouted orders.

Sarah gripped the Colt, unable to fire, while Ben aimed the rifle at an approaching brave. The Indian fell fifteen feet from the wagon, his neck twisted unnaturally. Shots echoed from beneath and behind every wagon as the settlers tried desperately to ward off the attack.

In the distance Sarah heard Andrews' familiar voice cursing a blue streak. She turned and focused on the screaming man.

"You son-of-a-bitch red bastard!" he yelled. He stepped away from the wagon and shook his fist in the air. "You stole my horse. They hang people for that where I come from you no account, thieving red devil!"

Sarah scanned the Indians and spotted a young brave riding Andrews' prized dapple-gray mare that had disappeared the night before. The Indian waved his bow in open defiance of the raging man. Sarah watched in stark terror as the Indian brought his bow to chest level.

She turned in time to see Andrews step completely out from cover to fire at the brave who had stolen his horse. Another man tried to coax Andrews back, but he'd have no part of it. He was blind with rage.

An arrow tore through the air and ripped into the wagon master's chest. He fell to his knees, still yelling.

"You...stole...my..." His voice faded and he slumped to the ground.

Sarah stifled the sob that threatened to explode from her throat. Would she and Ben end up like Andrews?

Ben's voice broke through her terror. "Pass the Colt. Reload the rifle!" he yelled. He threw the rifle in her direction and grabbed the Colt out of her shaking hands.

Sarah took the rifle and tried to reload, but couldn't see through her tears. The more she tried to push her fear away, the more the tears came. She turned the rifle around and around in her hands and tried desperately to crush the wetness from her eyes. The Colt exploded beside her and she found herself looking into the dead eyes of a half-naked Indian, his body contorted in death. She screamed.

Shooting continued all around her, but the firing beside her stopped.

"Sarah, pass me the rifle!"

She stared through tear-filled eyes at Ben.

"Sarah!" he yelled. He rolled onto his side and grabbed her by the shoulders.

"It's not loaded Ben. I can't do it. I just can't do it!" she screamed. Her hands and body shook with her fear.

"Sarah, listen to me. If you want to live through this day, you have to get control of yourself. I need you. I need your wits about you or else we won't live to see tomorrow. Now reload the Colt." He shoved the spent handgun into her hands, grabbed the rifle and reloaded it.

The sound of pounding hooves drew Sarah's attention. An Indian jumped from his horse and landed in front of them.

"Ben!" Sarah pointed at the stocky brave who peered under the wagon at them. The Indian grabbed Ben by the shirt and dragged him out into the open. Ben managed to cling to the rifle as he was hauled to his feet.

A tomahawk swung out with incredible speed once Ben was on his feet, but he managed to deflect the blow with the rifle. Sarah screamed and watched in horror as the two men clashed. The Indian struck out again and again until Ben finally lost his grip on the rifle and it fell from his hands. The Indian walked forward. A sneer curled his lips before he hurled himself at Ben.

Sarah's mind raced. The handgun. Reload. She grabbed the pouch with the ammo for the Colt. But her eyes were so blurred she couldn't see. The bag fell out of her shaking hands and the tiny packages of lead balls and wadding spilled onto the ground. This is our lives! she screamed at herself. She had to reload the gun. She took a deep breath, crushed the tears from her eyes with a fist, retrieved the fallen ammunition and jammed one of the balls inside.

As she worked, Ben struggled for his life with the powerful Indian. The two men fell to the ground and rolled back and forth in an effort to gain possession of the tomahawk. Ben freed himself from the Indian's grip and scrambled away. The Indian lunged after him. The tomahawk slashed through the air and barely missed Ben's back. He rolled to the side, just as the weapon embedded itself in the ground where his body had been.

Panting with exhaustion, Ben forced himself off the ground and, at the same time, pulled his knife from his boot.

"Now," he growled, "it's a little more even." Ben moved from foot to foot like a nervous cat, the knife tight in his right hand. The Indian stopped his forward movement when he saw Ben's knife and drew his back up straight.

Sarah watched in abject horror, the reloading of the Colt forgotten, as the two men faced off. The tomahawk whizzed through the air and narrowly missed Ben's shoulder. Ben hurled himself at the Indian, who easily sidestepped his knife. Ben pulled back in time to miss being slashed by the blade of a knife the Indian had drawn. He yelled like a savage himself and threw his body at the brave. His blade slid into the Indian's side. Blood saturated the buckskin shirt, turned it deep red, stunning the Indian because Ben had drawn first blood.

Ben stepped back to regain his balance and gasped for breath. The Indian muttered something then charged. He narrowly missed Ben's stomach before Ben jumped to the side, whirled and flung his knife out. The knife sliced the Indian's arm. With an angry yell, the Indian swung around and dove toward Ben, his eyes pinched almost closed in his rage. Ben flipped the knife to his other hand, thrust it forward and at the same time jumped sideways. He jammed the knife into the brave's belly and ripped upward. The Indian's blade dropped from his hand and a look of disbelief swept across his face. He grabbed Ben's shoulder, mumbled then slumped to the ground, his face in the dirt, his blood dripping from Ben's knife onto his boot.

Ben stared at the dead Indian. Sarah screamed his name and he jumped aside to miss being impaled by an arrow. He scrambled back under the wagon.

Sarah now realized if she wanted to survive this day, she had to keep her wits. She jammed the wadding and ball into the chamber, placed the firing cap on the nipple and the weapon was ready to fire. Ben slid out from under the wagon long enough to retrieve the rifle then scurried back under cover. The handgun reloaded, Ben fired. Sarah, her mind now sharp and intent on her task, reloaded the rifle. As Ben fired one weapon, she reloaded the other.

Sarah tried to keep her mind off the sounds echoing around her. The terrorized cries of women and children. The constant explosion of rifles and handguns. The agonized cries and moans of those who had been hit by a well-aimed arrow. The smell of spent powder and ball. The scent of death as it searched for its next victim.

She reached for another pouch of ammo for the Colt and her eyes flew open. There were none! She reached for ammunition for the rifle. It, too, was gone.

"Ben! It's gone! It's all gone!" She held out the empty boxes in front of her. "What do we do now?"

Ben looked into her eyes and she saw the sorrow etched on his face, saw the regret.

"Sarah, I'm sorry. So sorry," he managed before he pulled her into his embrace and held on tight.

Within moments, the Indians were on them. They were everywhere, came from all directions. Ben crawled out from under the wagon and waved his knife as a burly, heavy-set brave approached. Ben lunged his strong, six-foot frame at the Indian. The two met, chest-to-chest and fell to the ground as each tried to gain the advantage. They rolled and thrashed and, although Ben was strong, Sarah could see he was beginning to weaken. His breath was short and labored as he struggled with the Indian. He managed to free himself from the brave's grip and sprang to his feet, ready for the next attack.

It never came.

Ben staggered forward from the blow to his head and tried to keep from falling. Blood soaked the back of his head.

Sarah screamed. She knew she had to get to him and scrambled out from under the wagon. She ran toward her husband, but was jerked to a stop in mid-stride. Grabbed from behind, she used her broken nails on the bronzed hands that held her and pounded the arms with her fists.

She screamed Ben's name as she struggled to get out of the iron hold the brave had on her. She watched Ben try to stay conscious. Watched him try to force himself to his feet, only to fall back to his knees.

"Ben!" Sarah clawed at the Indian's arms but his grip only tightened. "Let me go! Let me go to him! I have to help him," she raged. She struggled like a mad woman, but the more she struggled, the tighter the faceless Indian's grip became.

She stopped in stupefied horror as the scene unfolded in seemingly slow motion. As Ben tried to drag himself to his feet, an arrow ripped through the air and into his back. He jerked upright then fell forward onto his hands. He raised his head and looked at Sarah, regret plain in his eyes. He tried to speak, but fell face down onto the dirt.

"No! Ben, no!" Again Sarah tried to wrench herself from her captor's grip, but to no avail.

She watched Ben's blood soak his shirt. She screamed and cried until she had no breath left. She kicked and scratched and pummeled, but nothing lessened the grip of the faceless Indian.

The Indian grabbed her like a sack of wheat and threw her over the back of a horse. She kicked her feet and hands, tried to slide off. The Indian mounted behind her and drove his heels into the animal's sides to send it racing away.

Sarah was beyond reason. Beyond caring what happened to her. She continued her tirade, unable to stop, unable to get the sight of Ben's lifeless body out of her mind. The Indian yelled at her. She struggled harder. Finally, she managed to slide free.

Her feet hit the ground and jarred every bone and tooth in her head as she rolled and tumbled crazily. Her arms and legs were scratched and torn by rocks and sticks. She felt like a tumbleweed bush tossed about in the wind as she careened out of control. Her head hit something solid. Lights exploded in her brain. She rolled to a stop and tried to focus her eyes, but everything was still spinning. Finally, unable to stop the blackness from coming, she closed her eyes and allowed the darkness to claim her.

## Chapter Three

Sarah bounced. Up and down. Up and down. Where was she? She couldn't remember and struggled to regain consciousness. Daylight pushed its way through her closed eyelids. She came awake with a start and realized she was astride a galloping horse. Her head pounded, her vision was blurred. She touched the back of her head and felt a huge knot there. She remembered falling, rolling, hitting her head. Darkness.

Images cleared in her mind. She blinked her eyes and searched the landscape. Ahead lay the plains, but behind her... Her head snapped around, causing bright lights to flash behind her eyes as everything rushed back with astonishing clarity. The wagon train! It was engulfed in black smoke that billowed high into the sky. Faint wailing cries carried on the breeze.

Ben! Her mind screamed. Where was Ben? She recalled the arrow, Ben falling. She gulped for air, felt as though a rope were being tightened around her lungs. She tried to slide out of the saddle again, but the faceless Indian's grip grew tighter each time she moved, squeezing the breath out of her.

Harsh words rang in her ear and hot breath floated across her cheek. The more she struggled the tighter his hold became. Finally, unable to believe everything that had happened, she relaxed against the Indian's chest and wept. She wept for Ben. Wept for the senseless slaughter of the wagon train. And in fear for what was to come.

Hours later, her eyes puffed nearly closed and her brain numb, Sarah and her captor rode into a camp nestled beside a river. Dark-skinned women and children poked and jabbed at her exposed legs, laughed and spat at her.

Overwhelmed, she watched them through a haze but felt little of their torment. Ben was gone. The man she had loved with her entire being was dead. More riders entered camp, but she saw no other captives. Was she the only one still alive?

Fresh tears formed in the corners of her eyes; eyes already so swollen she could barely see. High-pitched laughter rang out around her. She felt pricks and pokes on her legs from the women and children, but ignored them.

The horse stopped before a round lodge and the Indian dropped her to the ground. Weak with exhaustion, fear and disbelief, she dropped to her knees. The Indian slid down behind her. She turned and for the first time stared into the face of her captor.

He was taller than most of the other braves. Long, straight hair fell just above his waist, hair as black as tar with several feathers woven into it. His face was smooth and sun-darkened with eyes as black as his hair. High cheekbones angled upward and a straight nose and squared chin gave him a look of strength and intimidation. Thick scars over each breast accentuated a powerful-looking chest that was painted yellow with red lightning bolt stripes on it. Only a loincloth covered his lower body. Bone bracelets adorned well-muscled arms.

Fear and hate consumed Sarah at the same time when she looked into the hard eyes of the man who had captured her. The man who had taken her away from Ben and her people. She glared into his expressionless face and anger overwhelmed her. With strength borne of fear, rage and desperation, she attacked him. She pounded his chest with her fists and kicked his legs. He didn't move.

Her rage poured out as she continued her assault. She screamed and scratched him. Still, he didn't move.

"Murderer!" she shrieked again and again until her voice cracked and she fell to her knees, exhausted.

"Why don't you just kill me and get it over with?" she gasped. "I don't want to live any longer. Not with you! Animals! Savages!" Her voice resounded throughout the camp and she heard laughter. But not from her captor. His eyes remained fixed on her, unyielding, unblinking and unfeeling.

She fell silent, her energy spent, her tears exhausted. Without warning, the Indian reached down, grabbed a handful of her hair and dragged her into the lodge. She tried to resist, but his strength was too great and her exhaustion too much. Pain exploded in her brain as she scrambled to keep up behind him.

He shoved her inside the tipi and onto a bed of furs then turned around and left her alone. Sarah didn't move. She couldn't, paralyzed by pain and fear. She scanned the lodge through tear-filled eyes. In the center of the tipi was a pit with the embers of a dead fire. Furs and buffalo hides made the bed she sat down on. On the opposite side of the lodge stood an odd arrangement of items, possibly weapons or cooking utensils, and several piles of wood. On the walls were pictures of Indians and buffalo and horses. All she needed was something sharp to cut her way out. But outside, the Indians were chanting and laughing. How could she escape when everyone in the village was right outside the door? She needed rest. Yes, once rested and in the darkness of night, she would escape.

Her mind spent in the day's ordeal, she could function no more and withdrew into unconsciousness...

Sarah woke with a start. Drums pounded and shrill chanting rang in her ears. She pushed herself up from the furs and noticed a fire had been lit. How long had she been asleep? An hour, two, twenty? She had no concept of time.

Still groggy, Sarah stumbled to the opening of the tipi and pushed the flap up enough to peek out. Her throat constricted and her hand flew to her mouth, unable to stifle the scream that exploded from her chest. The villagers danced drunkenly around a huge fire, long, thin poles gripped in their hands. And from those poles human scalps flapped and dangled. The women sang high-pitched songs and the men seemed to be telling stories of the attack on the wagon train while they stuffed their mouths with food. The braves laughed and pushed each other playfully. They drank. Sarah stared, mesmerized, as their faces took on ghostly forms in the eerie glow of the fire.

Sarah was paralyzed. Her skin crawled and bile rose in her throat. With a will of their own, her eyes followed the scalps as they swayed from the poles carried by the celebrating Indians. A horrible thought seeped into her mind. One of those scalps could be Ben's. She gagged and stumbled backwards into the lodge.

Horror and revulsion welled up inside her and she screamed out her anger, helplessness and fear. She groped her way back to the bed and fell onto the furs, pounding their softness, crying.

"Why, God? Why? Why am I alive? How could you do this?"

The flap swung open and the Indian stepped inside.

"Kill me and get it over with!" she shrieked. "I don't want to be raped or beaten or be your slave. Do you understand? I'd rather die than be here with you!"

He walked toward her, his gait slow and deliberate, and knelt beside her. He reached for her hair, but she jerked away.

"Don't touch me," she said in a low, controlled voice. "Don't you ever touch me."

He watched her in questioning silence, his eyes almost gentle. If she hadn't known better, she'd think he felt pity or remorse.

He said something Sarah didn't understand, but it was gentle. Again, he leaned toward her and reached for her hair. She slid as far away from him as she could until her back was against the hide wall of the lodge. She was trapped. There was nowhere she could go.

His hand slid into her hair then stroked the skin on her face. His hand was rough and she recoiled. His dark eyes moved from her face down her neck to her body and he touched the tattered material of her dress.

The Indian stood and strode to the opening of the lodge. He spoke to someone then walked back to Sarah. Again she tried to pull as far away from him as she could, trying to make herself smaller. A few moments later a woman appeared, handed the Indian a bowl, then left. He in turn offered the bowl to Sarah.

Her stomach churned. She was sickened by what she'd seen outside and pushed the bowl away. The Indian offered it several times, but she pushed it away again and again. Finally with a grunt, he put it beside her and left the lodge.

Outside, the noise rose to a frenzy. She couldn't imagine people laughing and joking about the slaughter she'd witnessed. How could human beings be so evil and heartless?

Alone in the lodge with her exhaustion and fear, she fell into a troubled sleep. Tall, bronzed demons with long black hair chased her. She ran and ran, but got nowhere. They were always behind her. She cried out for help, but none came. In the distance she saw a vague form. Ben. He beckoned her from across the prairie. She ran faster, but couldn't reach him. Finally, he faded away into the darkness.

It was nearly daylight when her eyes opened again. She sat bolt upright. The motion caused her head to spin and pound. The cuts and scratches and dried blood on her body pulled and ached. Her eyes flew open when she saw the Indian asleep beside her and she scrambled away, clutching the fur blanket to her chest. He woke and black hooded eyes stared back at her. He flung off his fur and stood to his full, naked form. He picked up his loincloth, wrapped it around him and strode from the lodge, a slight smile curling his lips.

Sarah stared after him. Her heart pounded. He had slept with her. Beside her. She felt invaded and shivered with revulsion. Thank God he hadn't raped her. She closed her eyes and said a prayer of thanks.

Gathering her composure, she scanned the lodge. The bowl of stew was still beside her. Although it had been almost a full day since she'd last eaten, her stomach did flip-flops at the thought of eating. She wouldn't give in, she promised herself. She would die of starvation before she took nourishment from these people.

She needed to relieve herself. If she tried to leave the lodge, what would happen? To the point of soiling herself, she had to find out.

Sarah lifted the flap and peeked out. It was quiet. No one was in sight. Maybe they were so hung over from their celebration, they wouldn't notice if she just walked out of here. Hope flickered. Perhaps she was no more than an oddity to be gawked at for a short time until interest was lost. She swung the buffalo hide away from the door, stepped outside and headed toward a clump of bushes not far away.

Her task completed, she surveyed the area around her. Still no one had appeared. She could hardly believe her good fortune. She crept toward the sounds of horses. If the Indians were too hung over to follow her, maybe she could ride off before anyone knew she was gone. Then she remembered her captor was awake somewhere, but nowhere in sight. She had to try. She'd heard what Indians did to captive white women. With a last glance around her, she stole toward the horses as quickly as she could.

Inside a makeshift corral with fifty or so other horses, Sarah spotted Midnight, who must have been taken in the attack. She said a prayer of thanks and headed toward the animal. The black snorted when he sensed her presence. When she reached him she stroked his nose to quiet him.

The other horses were becoming agitated so she quickly led Midnight through the makeshift gate into the open. She grabbed the horse's mane to pull herself onto his back. But he was too tall and she was too weak. Spotting a protruding stump, she led Midnight to it and flung herself onto his back.

"We're getting out of here, boy. Now," she whispered into his ear.

She pointed him out of camp. Once outside the circle of lodges, she prompted Midnight into a gallop. The camp fell away behind her and excitement coursed through her.

Only moments away, she heard the pounding of hooves behind her. She turned around and cold fear washed over her. Her heels slammed into Midnight's flank. The Indian was in pursuit, and gaining.

Midnight's nostrils flared and his head bobbed with each stride as he sucked air in and out of his powerful body. Sarah slid down on his back and held on. Afraid she might slow the animal down, she dared not look behind her again. They raced toward some woods two hundred yards away.

*If we can make it to those woods, maybe we can lose him*, she hoped as she clung to the heavily muscled animal with her legs and arms.

Midnight thundered on as though he understood the desperation of her situation.

They reached the trees and the horse slowed only enough to leap between two towering oaks, almost unseating his rider, before he thundered into the woods' interior.

Sarah's hopes rose with each stride of the animal under her. She guided him between the trees, hoping to gain some time. Searching for a hiding place, she heard the other horse and rider crash into the woods. Leaves and branches crackled and she looked over her shoulder to see exactly how far away the Indian was. His horse leapt over a fallen tree and headed in her direction.

"Damn! Go, Midnight. Go!" She thrust her heels into the horse's sides, her hope for an easy escape crushed.

The pounding of hooves grew louder behind her. How could he be gaining so fast? Then it dawned on her. He probably knew every inch of every tree and bush that grew here. This might as well be his backyard.

Her heels again slammed into Midnight's sides and the horse surged forward. He leapt over bushes and squeezed between trees, scraping and banging Sarah's legs. Ahead, she spotted bright light. The end of the tree line. If she could reach it, maybe she could outrun her pursuer.

Intent on getting through the trees, Sarah realized she no longer heard the horse and rider behind her. She turned and hope surged through her. The Indian was nowhere in sight, but she dared not slow down. Not yet. She guided Midnight around a huge tree and ran right into the Indian and his pony.

The brave's dark eyes bore into hers. Not ready to give up the fight, she yanked Midnight's mane and turned him around. The horse jumped into action. But the Indian was right beside them this time. She noticed a looped rope dangling from his hand. They broke through the tree line and he angled his horse right next to Sarah. With a triumphant shout, he threw the rope over Midnight's head.

"No!" Sarah shouted as the rope slid into place.

The brave reined his mount to a stop and Midnight stopped behind him. Unwilling to give up, Sarah slid off his back and ran on foot back into the trees. She grabbed her skirt and hiked it up above her knees to keep it from tangling in her legs.

But she was a split second too late. The fabric snagged on some briars and it jerked out of her hands. She tumbled to the ground in a heap. Seconds later, the Indian was above her. He bent and offered his hand, a triumphant smirk on his face. She slapped the hand away.

The Indian backed away and Sarah untangled herself. He

pointed toward Midnight, who stood with the rope still hanging from his neck. She grabbed up her skirt and returned to her horse.

Her arms circled the horse's neck. "We gave it one hell of a try didn't we, fella?"

The Indian grunted and pointed again at Midnight. Now angrier than frightened, Sarah grabbed the horse's mane and tried to pull herself onto his back, but couldn't. She tried several times, but was unable to pull herself over. The Indian watched with an unconcealed grin of superiority before he walked over and placed his hands on her waist. She whirled on him as though burned.

"I told you once, don't touch me! I can damn well do it myself. I certainly don't need your help to mount a horse!"

The Indian's eyes grew hard and angry. He shouted at her. She turned her back to him and looked for a rock or stump to help her. But, although trees surrounded them, there was nothing at hand to use as a stepping block.

Filled with despair, she tried again to pull herself onto Midnight's back. Again she failed. She rested her head against the horse's belly and drew in deep breaths.

The Indian grabbed her waist and threw her onto Midnight's back. She grabbed his mane to steady herself then turned and glared at the man who stood beside her. She couldn't read the odd look in his eyes.

Sarah remembered the rope around Midnight's neck. Was it still there, dangling loose? Damn. The Indian had it in his hand.

"Damn you," she hissed.

The brave grabbed his own horse's reins but, much to Sarah's horror, he mounted behind her. His breath bore down on her neck and she squirmed in rebellion when his arm slipped around her waist and he headed Midnight back in the direction of camp. She tried to push his arm away, but his grip remained tight.

Bristling with resentment and filled with hate for the man who held her prisoner, Sarah sat stock still atop Midnight when the Indian finally slid out from behind her. He led

Midnight and his unwilling rider back through camp, which had come alive during their absence.

It seemed to Sarah as though he returned for the first time with his prize all over again. The women poked and prodded and the children pointed and snickered. But this time Sarah sat proud and tall. She'd no longer cower in front of them.

When they stopped in front of his lodge, he reached up to pull her from Midnight's back.

She slapped his hand. "I don't need your help."

He spoke, his voice deep and harsh, then grabbed her by the wrist and dragged her off Midnight's back. She hit the ground hard, but managed to stay on her feet.

"Let go of me you savage! I won't be your slave. And I won't do as you say! Leave me alone!" She tried to jerk away from him, but couldn't.

He hauled her up into his arms. She kicked and screamed and pounded him with her fists. She heard laughter from those who watched. He carried her into the lodge and dropped her heavily onto the bed of furs.

He hovered over her, his hands on his hips. He just looked at her, as though trying to decide what to do with her now. After a minute or two of silence, he pointed at her and then at the dead fire in the center of the lodge.

"If you want a fire, Indian, I suggest you build it yourself." She sneered the words. "I told you I won't be your slave." Fire of her own burned in her belly.

He yanked her up by her wrists and led her to a pile of kindling wood. He forced her hands around several pieces of the small, dry tinder then led her back to the blackened fire pit. He pointed and spoke.

"No, I told you. I won't." She let the wood drop to the dirt floor far from the fire pit.

Muttering more to himself than to Sarah, the Indian picked up the kindling that littered the floor and placed it back in her hands. He shoved them over the pit and forced her to drop the wood into it. Then, as if leading a dull-witted child, he led her back to the pile of wood, from which he gathered several larger pieces. He tried to load them into her arms, but they, too, tumbled to the ground with a crash. For an instant, anger exploded in his eyes, but then he grinned and nodded.

He grabbed the logs at his feet and again tried to pile them into her arms. Again she let them fall. He tried for several minutes before he grew weary. Sarah couldn't help but smile when he struck the flint rock to start the kindling afire before he added the larger pieces.

He looked up at her. His lips were pinched tight and his eyes snapped with anger. He turned and strode from the lodge but returned several minutes later with a pot filled with a stew of some kind. He placed the pot over the fire then left again.

Sarah sat down on the bed and thought hard. *What next? How do I get out of here? Can I get out of here?* Her mind was spinning when the Indian returned with bread and bowls. *Did he believe she would eat?* He left again then returned with what looked like a dress draped across his arm. He threw it on her lap, and spoke.

Sarah didn't understand the words, but she picked up the dress. Its softness surprised her. Light tan in color, she supposed it was made from the hide of a deer. The workmanship was detailed and precise. He pointed at the dress, then at her.

She shook her head. "Oh no. No. I will not put this on." She threw the dress back at him and shook her head. "I'm no Indian squaw. I'm a white woman and I will wear my own clothes. I won't wear it."

He scooped the dress off the floor and leaned toward her. His muscular form threatened, but she continued to defy him. She was beyond reason. Beyond knowing she should be afraid of him instead of defying him.

"I will not put it on, I tell you." She scooted back against the wall of the lodge as he inched toward her.

He reached for her tattered dress. She slapped his hand away. He reached with the other hand. She slapped it away, too. He stood to his full height, dominating and demanding and chills ran down her back.

He spoke again, his voice deep and hard. He grabbed her by the shoulders and pulled her to her feet.

"No!" She pushed at his unyielding chest. "It stinks."

His face moved to within an inch of hers and his hot breath seemed to suffocate her. Again he spoke, but this time his voice was soft. A smile grew on his lips and crept up into his eyes.

Without warning he grabbed Sarah's dress and tore it away in two strokes. She screamed and tried to cover herself with her hands, although the Indian's eyes never wavered from her face. He spoke again.

"No!" she screamed. "I'm not an Indian. I'm Sarah Walters. Not some squaw!"

He reached for her, but she jerked away. He dropped the dress at her feet and scooped up the remains of what had been her dress. He turned to leave the lodge, but not before Sarah saw the satisfaction in his face.

She wanted to kill him. Wanted to disappear from the face of the earth and the life that now claimed her. A cold chill passed over her. She had to put the dress on. There was nothing else she could do. She picked it up and its softness again surprised her. Once over her head, it slid easily over her body and molded to her form, its musky smell only slightly offensive.

She examined the porcupine quill beads that decorated the bodice and waist that ran in neat, circular patterns, one inside the other. It was a fine piece of work, she thought, remembering the time and effort spent making her own dress, now a shredded rag. Defeated, she slumped down onto the furs.

A delicious aroma wafted through the air to interrupt her thoughts. The stew bubbled in the pot and she got up and walked toward it. The smell set her stomach rolling. She'd never been so hungry in her life. She lifted the bone utensil and stirred the stew. Again her stomach rolled. Angrily, she threw the spoon back into the pot. She wouldn't eat! Not now. Not ever.

The hide door burst open and the Indian stood in its arch. He entered, pointed at the food then to her.

"Yuta."

Sarah scrambled away from the towering Indian and shook her head.

"I'm not hungry," she lied. "Not for your food."

He stepped toward her. She slid backwards. Again he

pointed and shouted, "Yuta."

Again she shook her head. In two strides he was over her, his eyes dark with anger. He grabbed her arm and dragged her to the fire.

"No. I don't want any. I'd rather die than eat your food or live with you," she screamed. She dug her heels into the dirt floor, but it did little to stop her from being dragged to where he wanted her.

He shoved her down onto the furs then scooped out a bowl of stew.

"I'm not going to eat that." Their eyes met. Sarah gritted her teeth. "You can't make me eat."

The Indian smiled.

Sarah's skin crawled.

Her cheeks hurt from the pressure of his hand on her chin when he forced her mouth open. She tried to shake free, but his grip was firm and unwavering.

"No," she ground out through clenched teeth. "I won't."

Within seconds of her denial her mouth was full of stew and his hand was clamped tight over her lips. She tried to spit it out, but he wouldn't let her. Unable to help herself, she swallowed. Her stomach churned violently and she threw it all back up.

He tried to jump away, but wasn't fast enough and stew dripped from his chest. He glared at Sarah with eyes so hard and black he looked like the devil himself. But Sarah's resolve was strong.

The Indian muttered to himself, wiped off the food and tried again. He clamped her chin and forced another spoonful of food into her mouth. Again, it was ejected.

Shaking with anger, Sarah glared at him. He could not make her eat. She would die first, she promised herself.

She forced her teeth together against his next assault, but he merely exerted more pressure on her cheeks and jaw. This time she intentionally spit the food back at him.

His anger exploded. He grabbed her by the shoulders and squeezed her so tight she could already feel the bruises his grip would leave. But she threw her head back in defiance. He lifted her off the floor and shook her till her teeth rattled. Lines of anger and frustration formed on the Indian's face as he stared at Sarah. He yelled at her, his nose nearly touching hers, but she didn't cry out.

He threw her onto the pallet where she landed with a grunt. He stepped toward her, a menacing look on his face. She took a deep breath, forced her back straight and squared her shoulders. She shook her head. She would not eat.

Again he made her open her mouth and again she gagged on the food he shoved inside. Tears stung her eyes, but she would not eat, could not.

The Indian finally gave up. With a vicious glare he stood up, shouted at her one last time, then stalked out of the lodge.

Sarah sighed in relief. She had won this battle, but there would be more. Of that she was certain. She pulled her knees up to her chin, circled them with her arms and closed her eyes. She would escape. Even if she had to die to do so.

Her head snapped up and she realized she didn't want to die. But she didn't want to live among these people as a slave or God only knew what? A shiver ran up her back. Her only hope was to escape. Her mind started to whirl. That was the answer, the only answer. Escape. She'd live with them long enough to gain their trust in order gain her freedom. She would live—to escape.

## Chapter Four

Four days passed, each more a blur than the one before. The Indian took care of Sarah. He came to her several times a day, sat with her, spoke to her and made her eat. But he never tried to hurt her. It was as though he felt guilty for his earlier ill treatment of her, even though he was well within his rights to do whatever he wanted according to his people's ways. She felt a strange closeness to him, but still remained his prisoner. She woke each morning knowing he'd slept beside her, but she never saw nor felt him there in her exhausted state. Each morning there was only a bowl of stew and water beside her.

Her plan for escape in mind, Sarah began to eat of her own accord. Slowly at first, she allowed her stomach to adjust without throwing up everything she ate. She had little to do, so her mind began to wander within the memories of her past.

She was back in Pittsburgh, in her and Ben's little house, snuggled in front of the fire on Christmas morning. Ben had just given her the locket.

Sarah touched the naked spot on her neck where it no longer rested.

"I'm sorry, Ben," she whispered.

She felt as though it had been years since Ben died and she prayed each day for strength to help find a way to stay strong and eventually free herself.

It was early morning, but already hot when the Indian came for her. He spoke in a stern voice then led her outside. Since her first escape attempt, she'd only been allowed to leave the lodge to attend to personal needs, and then only in the early morning before the heat of the day and later at night. So now as she emerged into the full sun, her eyes hurt and watered.

The Indian grabbed her hand and led her away from the lodge. She pushed several locks of stray hair from her face and shielded her sensitive eyes in order to see the village around her.

People milled between lodges, chatted and played, just as the white man did in his towns. Dogs barked at the heels of playful children and mothers prepared food or stitched clothing from animal hides. Fathers worked with their sons, showed them how to handle a bow and arrow or make a flute from the branch of a tree. It was so different, Sarah mused, yet it was the same.

Sarah continued to scan the village as she walked beside the Indian. There were many drawings on the lodges, an almost living chronicle of their hardships and joys they'd endured through the years. Several women spat as she walked by, others eyed her with great scrutiny, and some just looked at her with curiosity. She slowed her step and stared at a man who sang a soulful song, whose hands were raised to the sky in prayer. Did these people pray to one god, much the same as we do? she wondered.

She jumped when a group of ten to fifteen well-armed braves on horseback raced by and she hoped they sought animal prey and not human. They passed in a flurry of dust and racing hooves and she took the brief moment to study them. Their long black hair, worn loosely or in braids, whipped in the breeze. Bows were looped around their upper torsos and quivers filled with arrows bounced up and down on their bare backs. Only a loincloth covered most of the men, their muscled bodies deep brown, some almost black, from the rays of the sun, with feet covered by deerskin moccasins. The warriors' dark eyes stared ahead. They barely glanced at Sarah, as though she didn't even exist.

Sioux, she heard herself whisper as the dust settled and the riders disappeared. These were Sioux warriors. Her captor shoved her to draw her from her musing, and led her from the village into the trees along the river. Birds sang in the trees and shafts of sunlight filtered down to warm her face and body. Leaves glistened and blew in the wind while squirrels and other small animals darted in and out of the bushes. She breathed deeply of the fresh, clean air she'd been deprived of for so many days and she reveled in the warm sunlight on her face.

They stopped at the river's sandy bank. She understood and hesitated only a moment before she stepped into the cool water. It surrounded her toes and her feet tingled. Again she sucked in the air around her, thankful to be outside the confines of the stuffy, cramped lodge.

The Indian came up beside her and, through hand signs, let her know he wanted her to bathe.

"I'll bathe if you leave me alone." Her throat felt hoarse and weak. She waved her hand toward the trees.

He nodded and walked back toward the village. Sarah removed the deerskin dress, now soiled and smelly after so many days of wear, and laid it on the riverbank.

With only her chemise to cover her, she waded into the cool, inviting water and let it surround her. She closed her eyes and languished in the feel of it. There was a splash beside her. A blob of something thick and gooey-looking bobbed up and down in front of her. She realized the Indian was close by and dipped her shoulders under the water. When she looked up he was on the bank making washing gestures. She took the glob into her hands. It was soft and creamy like the face lotions she'd used so thoughtlessly as a young girl back in Pittsburgh. She applied it to her soiled body, then to her hair, and washed away the days of grime and sweat.

Sarah was allowed to enjoy her bath for nearly an hour before the brave returned for her with another dress in his hands. He stood on the bank and beckoned her to come to him.

She refused to come out of the water as long as he watched. Finally, he draped the dress over a bush and walked away.

Sarah emerged from the river and climbed the bank to where the dress was left. She worked her way out of her wet chemise and slipped the dress over her head. Her hand smoothed it to her body and she, again, appreciated the quality of the garment. She picked up the discarded dress and chemise and headed back toward the lodge, at the same time trying to smooth the tangles from her hair with her fingers.

Not far along the path the Indian emerged from behind a tree and fell into step beside her. Refreshed and rejuvenated, Sarah didn't protest.

At the lodge, he pushed open the buffalo hide door flap for her to enter then walked away. He returned several minutes later and gently prompted Sarah to sit on the bed of furs. She sat down, her legs crossed in front of her. Once settled, he sat down behind her, his legs crossed in the same fashion. Her back stiffened at his initial touch, but she relaxed when she realized his intent. With a bone-toothed comb he worked out the snarls in Sarah's tangled hair.

While he worked, Sarah tried to comprehend his savage ways. In a moment, he could ruthlessly murder a man, scalp him and leave him for the buzzards of the plains, and in the next, he patiently combed the tangles from a woman's hair. It made no sense to her no matter how she tried to understand.

Once finished, her hair soft, silky and nearly dry, he slid away. He turned her to face him so they sat cross-legged across from each other. He laid down the comb and touched his chest then uttered several words Sarah couldn't understand. She shook her head and he spoke again in halting English.

"Man-Who-Runs." He touched his chest then touched Sarah's shoulder.

Sarah stared.

He tried again, touched his chest.

"Man-Who-Runs." He pointed at Sarah.

Ben's face exploded into her mind's eye and she couldn't answer. How could she sit here and be nice to this savage when he'd made her watch Ben die and his people had massacred those of her wagon train?

His eyes grew hard and he pounded his chest. "Man-Who-Runs." Again, he pointed to Sarah.

Sarah looked into his hard black eyes. He was frightening, intimidating. She lowered her eyes to the furs on which she sat. She could invite his anger all she wanted by not answering him, but it wouldn't bring Ben or the others back. She raised tear-filled eyes to his.

"Sarah," she whispered.

In a heartbeat his face softened and changed his appearance from frightening to handsome. She watched him try to form her name with his mouth.

"Sar..ah." He smiled after he said the name then touched his chest for her to say his name.

"Man-Who?" She shook her head and shrugged her shoulders.

"Man-Who-Runs."

"Man-Who-Runs," she repeated.

"Sarah." He touched her shoulder and a smile lit his face.

For the first time, Sarah studied the strong lines of his face. Only the pitch-colored hair that fell about his features softened his square jaw and high cheekbones, but the hardness she had seen in his eyes was gone.

She pointed at him, careful not to touch him. "Man-Who-Runs." She pointed back to herself. "Sarah."

He nodded and his smile grew. This time Sarah allowed herself to smile, too. Man-Who-Runs indeed. No wonder he caught her so easily when she'd tried to escape. He was probably the fastest warrior in the tribe.

For the moment Sarah was not afraid. They'd broken the barrier of communication. At least now he had a name. He was Man-Who-Runs. An odd name she thought, but they were an odd breed of mankind.

Later that day he came and again led her from the lodge. He took her to a place where many women worked. Some weaved baskets, others pounded dried animal meat, while others scraped and sewed clothing from buffalo and deer hides. She was taken to an old, wrinkled woman and put to work. She pounded meat then blended it and crushed berries together, covering them with a layer of fat, Sarah supposed, to keep the mixture fresh. It was already hot and after several hours of constant pounding the bone mallet began to grow heavy in Sarah's hand. She stopped, took a breath, pushed her wilted, sweat-soaked hair off her forehead and leaned back on her heels. Within seconds the sting of a switch bit into her shoulder. She swung around and stared into the face of the old woman, bent and wrinkled, wielding the switch like a saber. The woman spoke and threatened Sarah again. Sarah started to protest, but the woman raised the switch higher. Sarah resumed pounding the dried meat.

Unused to the strenuous work, Sarah stopped and turned to the old woman. Hoping to improve her status, she spoke.

"What is this?" She pointed to the concoction she was

shoving into a rawhide container.

The old woman shrugged. Sarah tried again. "What is this?" Again Sarah pointed to the container and its contents.

"Wasna." The answer was short and curt.

"Wasna."

"Wasna," responded the old woman before she pointed to the container. "Parfleche."

Sarah also pointed to the container and repeated the word. "Parfleche."

The old woman nodded then waved her hand for Sarah to continue her work. Sarah leaned back to her task, but felt as though a wall, no matter how small, had been breached.

Sarah worked until her hands cracked and bled, but she didn't complain. She wouldn't give the old woman, or the others, the satisfaction.

While she worked, the other women continued to poke at her, tried to arouse her fury. Instead, she forced herself to ignore them, working in a blank haze. For the first time since her capture, she didn't think. She only worked.

## Chapter Five

Pitiful, woeful cries woke Sarah with a start the morning of the fifth day of her capture. She looked out of the lodge and watched the villagers crying openly as they walked toward a hill in the distance. Man-Who-Runs was nowhere in sight. Her curiosity piqued, she stepped outside into the mass of Indians and fell in step with them.

She walked quickly, anxious to discover the cause of so much grief. She crested the hill. There the tide of villagers flowed down to the grassy knoll below where a corpse, wrapped in colorful woven blankets, rested on a raised scaffold. Weapons lay beside the body and a buffalo skull sat on top of it. A long, flowing headdress was tied to one of the scaffold poles and billowed in the gentle breeze.

Sarah watched the men, women, and children openly show their grief for this person's death. They raised their hands to the sky and cried to the heavens. Men and women alike cried out like wounded animals. Who was this person? Curiosity drove her forward.

Sharp pain tore up Sarah's arm from her elbow. She jerked around to find Man-Who-Runs glaring down at her. His eyes were hard and cold as he squeezed her arm again. She opened her mouth to protest his harshness, but snapped it shut when she saw the brutal look on his face. He pushed her back to the top of the hill and stopped. They turned around and Sarah focused on the procession of villagers who ringed the scaffold and watched as a horse was led beneath the corpse-laden structure. Sarah stared, captivated by the unfolding ceremony.

Sarah gasped and vomit rose in her throat when the horse's neck was slit from side to side. The animal tried to cry out, but instead there was only a gurgled noise as it slumped to the ground, feet slashing, before it stilled in death. But the scene played on. She tried to pull away, to run back to the safety of the lodge, but Man-Who-Runs held her tight in his grip, forcing her to face the display. She searched his expression, tried to find anger, sorrow, something, but could read nothing in his face.

Sarah turned back to the scaffold and watched a woman walk beneath it. She began a chorus of melodious, almost feral songs whose notes pierced Sarah to her very being. The woman danced drunkenly then fell onto the dead horse. From a sheath in the horse's saddle she withdrew a knife. Sarah held her breath and her hand went to her throat.

She wanted to understand what was happening, but when she turned to question Man-Who-Runs, hard, expressionless eyes met hers. She turned back and watched in horror as the woman stood up, squared her shoulders and again began her feral song of sorrow to the countryside.

The chorus suddenly stopped. In her right hand the woman clasped the knife and in the other she held her long ebony hair. The knife slashed through the air and separated the chunk of hair from the rest of its bulk.

Sarah released the breath she'd been holding. She turned to Man-Who-Runs and was now met by eyes full of haunting pain.

"Who was he?" She pointed to the scaffold.

Man-Who-Runs didn't look at her.

"My chief." His voice was gruff, controlled as he stared out over the platform. "Killed. Many soldiers," he said in broken English.

"He killed many soldiers?" she repeated.

Man-Who-Runs jerked her around and pushed her toward the lodge. He shoved her through the door and onto the fur bed, then stalked back outside.

Frustration and curiosity threatened to suffocate Sarah if she didn't get some answers. She stormed out of the lodge after him.

"Please! I only want answers to my questions." The air heaved in and out of her lungs and her chest rose and fell with each painful breath. "What happened to your chief, Man-Who-Runs? I want to know." Man-Who-Runs seemed neither to understand, nor care, about what she wanted.

He turned to her, his arms crossed tightly over his chest, and looked down with vacant, angry eyes.

Although his face was a mask, Sarah was determined.

"What happened to him?" she asked again.

Man-Who-Runs' features hardened. He reached out and grabbed her shoulders, pushed her through the door and toward the bed of furs.

"Man-Who-Runs," she stammered, "I don't know what happened to your chief, but I am sorry." What had she expected to happen by chasing after him and demanding answers? Fear tightened in a knot in her stomach and she bowed to him several times to show her conciliation, but he continued his advance.

"Please, Man-Who-Runs. I'm sorry. I won't demand answers again. Please..." Her words stopped as his large hands grabbed her wrists.

"Soldiers—bad hearts," he spat, his face only inches from hers.

"Why? What did they do? What happened to your chief?" She was unsure of how much he could understand. Or how much she could press him.

As though he hadn't heard her words, he stepped back and stared at her. Both remained silent for several moments before he spoke.

"Chief Conquering Bear. My chief. Great chief. Soldiers...came..." He stumbled for the words.

Sarah nodded to show she understood, hoping he would continue.

"White soldiers came to our village. Killed my chief."

Sarah let out her breath. Soldiers had killed his chief, the opposite of what she had chosen to believe on the hill.

"Kill Shining Star, Little Deer." His pained voice drifted off.

"Shining Star? Little Deer?"

"Wife," he said then fumbled for another word before he put his arms in front of him in a cradling motion.

"A baby?" Sarah gasped.

Man-Who-Runs looked down into the face of an invisible child as he rocked it in his arms, pain obvious on his face.

Sarah's heart caught in her throat. Bits and pieces began to fall into place. Was that the reason their wagon train had been attacked five days ago? As revenge for the soldiers attacking the Indians' village, killing Chief Conquering Bear and others? Not because she'd killed One Ear as she'd believed? And because of the army's attack, Ben and all those other innocent people had died? Man-Who-Runs' wife and child had died?

She looked into the bronzed, agonized face of her captor and anger consumed her.

"And because the soldiers killed, you killed? More women, more children were murdered?" She felt heat in her face. "I understand the need for revenge, Man-Who-Runs. I understand it very well, because I wanted it. I wanted it so bad I could taste it, feel it. Here!" She pounded her chest. Man-Who-Runs looked on, a curious expression now on his face.

Her hands encompassed everything around her. Including him. "I wanted you and everyone else in your damned village dead. Dead, Man-Who-Runs, because you murdered Ben and all those innocent people on my train. You murdered men, women and children who never did anything to you or your people. We only wanted to be left alone to find our way..." Anger gave way to choking sobs and she hid her face in her hands. Revenge. Ben and all those others were dead because of the need for revenge!

She felt Man-Who-Runs' hands on her shoulders and she jerked away.

"Don't touch me. You killed my husband and all those other people in retaliation for something they didn't do! Revenge is taken upon those who exact the crime," she raged. "Not the innocent!" Her voice sounded high and shrill in her ears and she knew she was becoming hysterical.

"'Vengeance is mine, sayeth the Lord.' You have taken the Lord's work into your own hands." She stood up and walked to the lodge door, but was stopped by Man-Who-Runs' powerful grip on her arm.

She felt frighteningly calm. She glanced down at his hand then up at him. "Let go of me." Her words were clipped, controlled.

He held firm.

Her composure dissipated like mist in the morning. She

pawed and scratched at him, but he held on. He forced her to the bed and pushed her down. She scrambled to get up and he shoved her back.

"Let me go," she raged through her tears. All she wanted was to get away from him. To get away from all of them.

She kicked and pounded his face and chest, but he wouldn't let her up. The more she struggled, the angrier he became.

He spoke harsh words to her. Words she couldn't understand, which frustrated her more.

"I want to go home! Let go of me!" She was beyond reason now. "Ben. I want Ben," she sobbed. Tears streamed down her cheeks and her husband's face exploded in her brain.

Foreign words bounced around inside her head. Words she didn't heed. She continued to kick and scream Ben's name.

The Indian's grip tightened around her wrists and became even more painful, but she ignored it. She wanted to go home!

His nose suddenly touched hers; his dark eyes bore into her like a lance. "Inila!" he shouted.

His voice echoed in the lodge. She jerked to a stop and stared into his face. His chest heaved with each ragged breath.

He was above her; the length of his body covered her. Raw terror ripped through her.

"Please," she whimpered, cognizant of her hysteria. "Don't."

The brave stared down at her. He released one of her wrists and raised his hand.

She turned her head aside to avoid the blow.

Instead, he stroked the side of her face. In a gentle stroke he wiped away the tears that wet her cheeks.

"Inila." His voice was now a whisper, a caress.

She had no idea what the word meant, but his tone soothed. Her heart stopped racing and her breathing became regular.

He released her other arm and she felt his body stir. She started to struggle again, but he quickly silenced her with a finger across her lips.

"Hiya. No." Again, his voice was gentle. It possessed none of the anger she'd heard earlier.

He smoothed her tear-soaked hair from her face and rolled away. Like a sleek cat he stood. Sarah lay there, uncertain, frozen.

The Indian stared down at her a few moments then turned and strode from the lodge.

Sarah gazed after him, amazed. She felt a new respect for her captor, well aware that as his prisoner, he could take her at any time. But he hadn't.

She curled up into a ball on the fur bed, her mind spinning. Why had he taken her from the wagon train in the first place? And why, when it was his right, did he allow her to remain unspoiled by him? Could it be that he mourned the loss of his wife and child as much as she mourned Ben?

Ben's face floated in her mind, called to her. His name was on her lips when she finally fell asleep, alone and very lonely.

Sarah woke the next morning beside a well-tended fire, her arms and wrists sore from the struggle with Man-Who-Runs. She felt drained of life and emotion and totally alone. She didn't want to be in this prison that held her. She wanted Ben and what they'd shared.

The events of the night before rushed into her mind and guilt washed over her. Although the Indian hadn't claimed her, she knew deep inside, feelings for him were stirring. How could she care for him? A savage! Even in a small way? She couldn't betray the memory of her beloved Ben!

She looked around the room and her heart sank. There was nothing for her here with this man and these people. Tears filled her already puffy eyes. She made up her mind.

In the burial ritual where the Indian woman had failed to join her husband in death, Sarah would not.

She sat up in the quiet lodge and took a deep breath. Slowly, she stood. Her legs shook as she searched for something sharp. On the opposite side of the lodge she found several arrowheads in a pile waiting to be attached to the shaft of an arrow. Vessels of death. She grabbed one of the stone pieces and slipped back to the bed.

"Oh, Ben. I miss you so much," she whispered as she felt for the soft place on her wrist. "I won't be long. I hate this place. I hate my life and what it's become. I'm too impatient to try and gain their trust so I can someday escape. I miss you so much and I'm so scared."

She found the tender spot and summoned the strength to do what she must. She smiled sadly and shoved the arrowhead deep into her wrist. She clamped her mouth shut so she wouldn't cry out. Tears streaked her cheeks, but she couldn't stop now. She found the second spot on her other wrist and ground her teeth when the pain almost forced her to cry out. Red droplets of blood spattered the furs. She closed her eyes and lay down.

"I'm coming Ben. Soon."

## Chapter Six

Unfamiliar sounds echoed and reverberated through Sarah's brain. What was it? Singing? Crying? She drifted in and out of the comforting darkness trying to distinguish the sounds, but couldn't. She stretched out her hand, but no one took it.

She continued to drift, without form, without destination and without meaning. She floated for an eternity until a cool, soft cloth touched her forehead. She tried to sit up but her head burst with pain. The coolness of the cloth soothed her brow and she tried to focus on where she was. Her eyes opened and, with the full force of a hammer blow, it hit her. She was still in the Indian's lodge, still a prisoner, and still alive. Her heart sank. She had failed.

Sarah managed to lift her head and Man-Who-Runs' muscled form came into view. In his eyes she thought she saw concern.

He touched her face. A caress. Sarah shuddered, but didn't pull away. She stiffened against his touch, which brought a smile to his face and a nod to his head. He seemed pleased.

"What are you smiling at?" she managed to croak.

He took her chin into his hand. "Good." He nodded again, a grin on his face.

She closed her eyes in amazement, at a loss to understand this man.

Memories of Ben assaulted her senses. Memories of the day they'd met, been married and that Christmas morning she'd been so happy when he'd given the locket to her. The day they'd made plans to come west and that fateful day the wagon train was attacked. The black smoke in the air and the stench was so real in her mind she could almost smell it now. With great pain in her heart she envisioned the arrow that ended Ben's life and her desperate struggle to reach him.

But now, as she breathed in the sweet breath of life, she was glad she had failed in her attempt to kill herself. She would escape, some day, she swore. But for now she would just live.

She touched her chest, neck, then her face, glad to be

able to feel, see, hear and taste. She was still alive and she was glad. For now, she would live with these people and learn from them to some day escape. Now she knew no matter how much she longed to be with Ben, she was happy just to be alive.

Her eyes opened and she again surveyed the interior of the lodge. For the time being, this was her home. She would work hard and long and do whatever it took to stay alive and gain their trust. For one day, she would be free. Free of all of them.

She turned her eyes back to the Indian. "You may have won this round, but in the end, I'll be free," she promised him, but most especially she promised herself.

It didn't take Sarah long to recover, and within days she ate heartily. Her strength regained, she was brought each morning to the place the women worked and each day she pounded, scraped and sewed beside them. Her hands grew rough and calloused, her skin darkened and her hair lightened.

Glad to be alive and accepting of her fate, she began to study the Sioux and their ways. Each morning she sat quietly while Man-Who-Runs greeted the day with prayers and songs to Wakan Tanka, the Great Spirit. He taught her about the four winds and how their spirits helped The People to find their way in the wilderness, to place their lodges, and begin their sacred ceremonies. She learned all of nature was revered: The animals were thanked for giving their lives to The People for food.

Sarah marveled at the complexity of these people. They were mere savages to many, but as diverse in their ways as the white man.

The days passed and she found herself beginning to understand more and more about these strange people she had become a part of. One thing she learned quickly was if she did as she was told, Man-Who-Runs did not punish her. However, each day was a test of endurance from the continued abuse by the women of the tribe. They still poked, pushed and antagonized. They openly mocked her and threw stones at her while she tried to do her work. Each night she fell into bed physically and mentally exhausted. Thoughts of Ben were always with her and loneliness for him consumed her.

One morning while Sarah washed clothes on a rock at the river's edge, several of the women approached. They jabbed her with sticks and pulled at her hair as they passed. She forced herself to ignore them, although she wanted nothing more than to fight back. She kept her back to them, continued at her task and grit her teeth against the pain and humiliation they inflicted.

Someone stepped up behind her and shoved her, hard. A woman's voice challenged. Sarah remained silent. Laughter reverberated in her ears, fingers poked and pushed at her. Unable to tolerate their hostility any longer, she balled her fists and whirled, ready to unleash her anger. She opened her mouth to scream at her abusers, but the words died in her throat. Around the neck of the woman closest to Sarah was a gold oval locket. Sarah's locket. Her resolve snapped like a dead twig in winter.

"Where did you get that?" Sarah's throat was so tight she could barely breathe. "That's *my* locket." She stepped toward the squaw, her hand stretched toward the locket, her body shaking with controlled rage.

The woman backed away and covered the locket with her hand. A smile of contempt covered her face. She shook her head. "Mitawa."

Sarah stepped closer and the woman's smile disappeared. She shook her head again and clutched the locket at her throat.

"Give it to me," Sarah ground out. She reached for the locket again. "It's mine."

The woman backed further away and held tight to the locket.

The last of Sarah's control vanished. Like a wild animal, she dove at her, pounding wildly at the one who held such an important part of her life away from her. All her well-controlled emotions were now free. They rolled in and out of the water along the sandy bank. They sputtered, spit and screamed.

"I've had enough of you. All of you!" she shouted. "That's my locket and I want it back!" Sarah slapped the woman and knocked her into the water. She came up thrashing and gulping for air.

Another of the women jumped onto Sarah's back.

"You want to play, too?" Sarah bent over in half and deposited the woman head first into the river.

"Anybody else?" she yelled. Her fists rolled in and out of tight little balls, her wet hair splayed wildly around her head and shoulders, and her eyes were like that of a cornered animal. "Come on! I'm ready for you!" She waited for the next onslaught. Her chest heaved and her heart pounded.

A third woman rushed from shore and pushed Sarah back into the water. They broke the surface spitting and gasping for air. Sarah grabbed the woman's tangled mass of black hair and pulled. The woman cried out and fell back. But Sarah wasn't through. She grabbed the woman by the front of her dress and punched her square in the jaw then pushed her into the water. The woman scrambled away, her lip bloody.

"Have you all had enough?" She stood in the shallows, her feet apart, hands still in tight fists, her hair a wild, wet mass around her head, and scanned the bank where the three women stood.

She swung around and jerked to a stop when she spotted Man-Who-Runs on shore upstream a short distance watching.

The fury went out of her, but she remained alert. Her body was tight as a bowstring.

He strode toward her. Water splashed around his ankles as he entered the water. She steeled herself for his punishment.

"No, Sarah. No." He placed his hands over hers. She relaxed her fists and dropped her hands. She smoothed her dress then threw her matted, sopping-wet hair off her face and walked to the woman who wore her locket.

The woman stared at her, first with fear, then confusion. Sarah stepped forward and reached for the locket, but the woman placed her hand over it.

The Indian's face softened. "Nitaya le?" she asked.

Sarah shook her head. "I don't understand."

"Nitaya le?" The woman touched the locket.

Sarah nodded and pointed to herself. "Yes. It's mine."

The Indian fondled the locket a moment then reached behind her neck, unclasped it and held it toward Sarah. Her eyes glistened with respect. She nodded.

"Nitaya. Icu." The woman offered the locket to Sarah.

Sarah's hand shook and her eyes welled with tears as she reached for her treasured necklace.

"Thank you," she whispered. "Thank you." She stared down at the locket in her hand and her heart broke with the memories it evoked. She looked up with tear-filled eyes and nodded at the women in front of her.

All three inclined their heads.

Sarah turned and walked to the pile of laundry that lay in a heap. She scooped it up and headed toward camp, her back straight, her head high, her locket clasped in her hand.

Sarah heard the women and Man-Who-Runs behind her. A gentle touch on her elbow brought her to a stop.

Man-Who-Runs stepped up beside her. "Wi Tapeta Yuha Win." He touched her shoulder.

Sarah stared at him. He smiled. The light of the sun sparkled in his eyes and his hair glistened blue-black in its reflection.

"Wi Tapeta Yuha Win."

Sarah continued to stare, puzzled.

"Woman With Fire Like the Sun," he said, his words clipped. He touched her shoulder again then walked away, a smile on his face, his head shaking.

She watched him walk down the path toward camp. The women followed. Each nodded as they passed. A name, she thought with pride. She'd been given a name. A name of respect. Her shoulders squared, she walked back to the lodge unescorted.

In the days after the fight at the river, Sarah began to notice a change among The People. The women took time to speak with her and show her how things were done. They no longer poked or prodded or tried to anger her. Instead, they tried to help her.

As she walked to the river's edge one morning to do her daily washing, a young woman ran up beside her. A wide smile broke across the woman's face when Sarah looked over at her.

"Tokiya la hwo?" the woman asked.

Sarah stopped and shrugged her shoulders. "I don't understand."

The woman pointed all around. "Tokiya la hwo?" She then pointed to Sarah's basket, filled with dirty clothing.

Sarah shook her head.

The woman joined Sarah. She smiled again, pointed to the river and repeated her words.

Sarah concentrated on the woman's actions a moment then decided she was asking where she was going. Sarah pointed to the river and made washing motions with her hands.

The woman nodded her head and smiled.

In that silent moment Sarah heard a deadly rattle. She stopped with a jerk and threw her arm across the chest of the young woman and brought her to an abrupt halt.

Surprised, frightened eyes turned to Sarah.

"Shhh." She looked down at a small outcropping of rocks just off the trail. A rattlesnake lay on one of the boulders, coiled and ready to strike only a few feet from the two women. It rattled again.

Both women froze. The snake's tongue flicked in and out of its mouth. Sarah barely breathed, afraid any movement would cause the creature to strike. Her arm across the woman's chest grew heavier with each passing second.

Sarah began to panic. What could she do? The woman beside her wore a long dress, but low moccasins exposed her ankles. Sarah, on the other hand, had on knee-high moccasins. If the snake attacked, would her moccasins be enough to protect her from its fangs? Or if it attacked the other woman, would it strike at her exposed flesh and sink deep to fill her full of poison that could eventually kill her?

The snake shook its tail again to remind Sarah of their predicament. Her heart pounded and sweat beaded on her brow. What could she do?

The basket under her arm weighed heavily and she realized it was her only weapon against the serpent. She took a deep breath and turned to the woman. She gave her a stern look, said a quick prayer then in one motion, heaved the basket at the snake and pushed the woman backwards.

The snake lunged forward and sank its teeth into the basket. The young woman scrambled up from the ground where she'd landed and the two ran in the opposite direction. Several seconds later they were met by several braves who'd heard their frightened cries as they ran back toward camp. The young woman related what had happened and the men ran off to dispose of the snake.

Sarah was still shaking when Man-Who-Runs came toward her. A huge smile covered his face and his step was proud and tall.

"I'm glad you're having such a good day," Sarah grumbled, irked by his good cheer.

He grabbed her and hugged her then pushed her back to look her over.

"Wi Tapeta Yuha Win, suta!" he shouted. He raised his fist in the air.

Sarah had no idea what he was yelling. She recognized her name but not the rest. Others came and spoke with him. He motioned toward her and his words continued. After several minutes of watching and listening, Sarah realized he was proud of her!

The young woman walked up to Sarah and took both hands into hers.

"Pilamaya."

Sarah had learned this word meant thank you. She inclined her head. "You're welcome."

The woman touched her chest and said, "Hinhannah Wahcha Win." She touched Sarah's shoulder. "Wi Tapeta Yuha Win."

Sarah smiled and tried to say the woman's name. The woman laughed and repeated the words several times and after several tries, Sarah could say the woman's name easily.

She turned to a grinning Man-Who-Runs.

"Hinhannah Wahcha Win." Sarah pointed to the woman.

Man-Who-Runs nodded. "Morning Flower Woman, sister-by-marriage," he said.

"Sister-in-law?" Sarah turned back to Morning Flower Woman who inclined her head, her face now serious.

She again took Sarah's hands. "Pilamaya. Mitakola."

Sarah looked to Man-Who-Runs for help. He leaned over and whispered, "Thank you. My friend."

Morning Flower Woman called for Sarah the next day.

"Hiyu, come." Morning Flower Woman waved her hand for Sarah to follow. Reluctant, Sarah followed her new friend to where many women worked and talked as they made baskets from the long buffalo grasses that grew in abundance on the plains.

Morning Flower Woman pointed for Sarah to sit down, plopped a pile of grass in her lap then sat down beside her.

"Psawognaka." Morning Flower Woman pointed at the baskets the other women made.

Sarah nodded and lifted the mass of grass and leaves in front of her. She crinkled her nose and let the pile fall to her lap.

"I have no idea what to do."

Morning Flower Woman giggled then slid closer. She pulled several strands of grass out of the heap and began to weave. Sarah stared, held rapt by the agility with which her friend wended the pieces together to form the bottom of what would become a basket.

Morning Flower Woman showed her work to Sarah, then placed it on Sarah's lap.

"Iyuta." She held out several strands for Sarah to try.

Sarah took the grass and tried to weave it the way Morning Flower Woman had, but only succeeded in making a big, ugly knot.

She noticed her friend trying not to laugh out loud, but she was failing miserably.

"Then you do it." Sarah shoved the barely started basket back at Morning Flower Woman, while trying to keep a straight face.

Both women's eyes met and they burst out laughing. Sarah glanced around at the other women and noticed they were laughing, too. Her heart warmed and, for the first time in months, she felt at peace, accepted.

Warming to her task, determined to defeat the uncooperative basket, she leaned toward Morning Flower

Woman and took the unfinished basket from her friend's hands.

"Show me again."

The lesson lasted several hours before Morning Flower Woman pulled Sarah to her feet and led her away from the circle, jabbering as they walked between the lodges. They stopped at a clearing at the edge of the village where many women clustered with their children.

She followed her friend into the clearing. Children ran around Morning Flower's legs, laughing and shouting. Women chatted in groups amongst themselves.

Sarah hung back. She watched Morning Flower Woman scoop a little girl into her arms and swing her around. The child laughed with delight.

The younger woman waved for Sarah to come closer. Caught in a bout of self-pity Sarah shook her head no. Her friend frowned, but before she could do anything, she was dragged away by a persistent little boy.

Sarah stood alone. She watched the children play and laugh and felt as though her heart would break for the children she and Ben would never have, whether he were alive or dead. Her eyes watered and she wiped her tears.

Several women drifted toward her, even spoke to her. But she'd mastered so little of their language she couldn't talk to them yet.

So she stood alone and listened to the children's laughter while their mothers scolded and called their names.

Unable to stand the ache in her heart, Sarah decided to go back to her own lodge. She turned to find herself looking down into the huge dark eyes of a beautiful little girl. The child didn't move. Neither did Sarah. The child gazed up, her head cocked to one side as if in a question.

Sarah knelt down in front of the little girl who remained still. She sat back on her heels and put her hand out to the child. The girl studied it several moments before she stepped forward and touched it.

Sarah waited.

Then, as gently as a summer breeze, the child slid onto Sarah's lap and placed the flat part of her small hand on Sarah's cheek. A jolt of emotion surged through her. Uncertain what she should do she remained silent and didn't move. She just stared down at the little girl and smiled.

Morning Flower Woman stepped up beside Sarah. "Wikmunke," she whispered into her ear.

Sarah looked up at her friend and smiled.

Assuming the word Morning Flower Woman spoke was the child's name, she bent over and whispered in her ear, "Wikmunke."

The smile that came to the child's face warmed Sarah's heart. Slowly, Wikmunke removed her hand and touched Sarah's lips, nose, eyes and ears before she wound her fingers into Sarah's hair. The child giggled and pulled the blonde hair so uncommon to her people to her nose and smelled it.

Sarah couldn't help but laugh. The child laughed back and the knot in Sarah's stomach dissolved like sand on a riverbank washed away by a rushing tide.

For long minutes Sarah held the little girl while she explored Sarah's features. Soon other children gathered around her, curious. They joined the girl on Sarah's lap or sat beside her, talking and laughing. They squealed and touched her hair, shoved their little noses into it and sniffed.

And when it was time to return to her own lodge Sarah didn't want to go and couldn't wait to come back.

The next day Sarah was forced to endure another of Morning Flower Woman's basket weaving lessons before she could go to where the women and children gathered. Anxious to get there, she dragged her friend across the village to the clearing.

Soon Sarah spent more and more of her time with the mothers and their children. She watched the boys and girls, repeated their names in her head each time she heard their mother's call them.

Kangi Cikala, Little Crow, the four-year-old who always ran, forcing his mother to chase him constantly. Wikmunke, Rainbow, the little girl who had first ventured into Sarah's arms and heart, became Sarah's favorite of all the children. Only two summers old, she squealed with delight whenever Sarah appeared.

Of all those that gathered daily, only one child caused Sarah distress. Keglezela, Spotted Turtle, a boy about five who shouted and bullied the other children. Sarah glared at him, her throat tight, as he approached a younger child, pushed him to the ground and caused him to scrape his knee. She wanted to grab the boy and shake him. But in the time she'd studied Spotted Turtle and his mother, she realized no one challenged him. Not even his mother. On no occasion had she ever seen anyone correct or punish him for his actions. She perceived the mother expected the child to become a great warrior and, therefore, allowed him his aggressive conduct. Sarah understood it was the way of the Sioux, and, therefore, she didn't interfere.

Every day she grew closer to the children. She learned all their names, their personalities and who their mothers were. The women included her as much as they could and taught her how to take care of the little ones.

Spending time with the boys and girls, playing and laughing with them and being accepted by their mothers became the biggest joy in Sarah's life.

And for the first time since her capture and Ben's death, Sarah realized—she was happy.

The more Sarah interacted with the women and children, the more she learned about The People and their ways. She learned most of the men had several wives and understood the women gladly accepted other women in their lodge, as it meant less work for them.

Sarah also learned that because she lived in Man-Who-Runs' lodge she was considered his wife. But Sarah refused to accept that. She could not regard herself as Man-Who-Runs' wife. She was Ben Walter's wife and always would be. She accepted doing the same chores the other women did, but would not accept the title of wife.

And although the children had become the center of her life and she was happiest when she was with them, she went to her bed each night with the ache of Ben's absence still in her heart.

Days turned to weeks, weeks to months and the hot summer breezes gave way to the biting cold of winter. The village was struck and moved to a winter location. A fire blazed constantly in Man-Who-Runs' lodge. More buffalo robes were added to the bedding and more wood gathered every day.

Sarah was amazed at how warm the lodge stayed, despite the bitter, whipping wind and cold. She busied herself with chores of gathering wood and water while Man-Who-Runs hunted and foraged with the men.

The evening sun had set and Sarah and Man-Who-Runs sat on fur pallets in front of the fire. It was the time of day when Man-Who-Runs worked with her, when he taught her his language and customs. She was an astute student and learned quickly.

But he seemed distracted tonight, Sarah mused. All through the evening meal he'd watched her, stared at her. Although he proceeded with the lesson, his eyes drifted to her face often and remained until she cleared her throat or spoke.

His hand slid over hers.

"Sarah." His voice was a whisper.

She heard the passion in his voice; saw the desire in his eyes. Her heart began to hammer and she felt heat rush through her body.

His hand slid to her face, stroked her chin and caressed her cheek. "Sarah," he whispered again. "I want you."

Sarah pulled back. She took a deep breath, her emotions in turmoil. Ben was dead she reminded herself. *This was her life now. Could she willingly give herself to this man? A savage?*

Sarah looked deep into Man-Who-Runs' eyes, eyes full of desire. Her heart skipped a beat. *Did she want him as he wanted her? The way she had once wanted Ben?* She turned away, unable to think, unable to make a decision.

Man-Who-Runs turned her face back to his. "We are one now, you and me. You are my wife." Sarah tried to protest, but Man-Who-Runs continued. "You are my wife because you live in my lodge and have for many moons now. That is the way of The People. What I ask is my right. I have never forced you. I want you to come to me freely, Sarah. I have been patient, but I am a man."

Sarah nodded, unable to speak. Guilt paralyzed her. She was Ben's wife, not this Indian's. Just because she lived in his lodge didn't make her his wife—in her eyes or in God's. But she couldn't deny she cared for him. But could she forget about the past? Forget about Ben and the life they shared? A life she lived in another time, another place far from where she was now?

Again she looked into Man-Who-Runs' eyes. Eyes filled with hope, warmth—and passion. Her hand went to his face and traced the strong lines of his chin and mouth. Her fingers moved down his neck and across his hard chest, over his muscular shoulders and arms to the scars that marked his passage to manhood from the Sun Dance. Warmth flooded through her.

He slid closer. She didn't pull away. His lips covered hers in a hot, devouring kiss. Her arms slipped around his shoulders and drew him closer. She felt his warmth on her chest and arms and passion surged through her.

His hands moved recklessly. He tore at the ties that held her dress together. The dress slid away.

He sat back from her and admired the lines and curves of her body. Her mind spun wildly. Did passion drive her to do something she didn't want to do? He wanted her to come to him willingly. If she told him to stop, would he? Did she *want* him to stop?

He watched her. His eyes asked the same silent questions. Her hands went out to him. She drew his lips back to hers, his kiss soft, tender.

She wanted to cry, but she wanted to love him at the same time. She didn't know what she wanted.

He gave her no time to consider. His lips slid down her neck to the peak of her breast. She fought to control her breathing as he suckled and teased with his tongue. His mouth moved from one breast to the other, drove her wild with new, unleashed passion.

He was gentle as he loved her. He gave her time to accept each new touch, each new feel. Time to respond in her own way, at her own speed.

Lips caressed her stomach and she cried out his name.

## Tomorrow's Promise: Survival on the Plains     D.L. Rogers

Tears streaked her cheeks as she fought the guilt that battled her desire. She wanted this man. She couldn't deny her feelings.

She opened herself to him. He rose above her and gazed down on her face, touched the tears on her cheeks.

"Love me," Sarah managed, her throat tight. "Don't let me think anymore, just love me."

He drove into her and her arms tightened around his shoulders. Her legs wrapped around his waist and grew tighter with each thrust. Their bodies rocked in a chorus of desire, need and fulfillment. Sarah became lost in a world that included only the future and no past, only she and Man-Who-Runs.

Sarah looked into his eyes, and saw the love he had for her. She touched his face before he bent to kiss her.

Ben's face exploded in her mind. Guilt overwhelmed her and nearly sent her running from the lodge. She pushed Man-Who-Runs away and wrapped herself in the closest fur. She curled into a ball and sobbed for all she had given away. Her memories. Her love. Ben.

Tears covered her cheeks. She couldn't look at the pain in Man-Who-Runs' face and turned away. She was too confused. Over and over she reminded herself Ben was gone. This was her life now. What she and Ben had shared was gone and her life was with Man-Who-Runs. Her guilt threatened to consume her. Why, if Ben and their life together were gone, did she feel as though she was being unfaithful to him?

She looked up at Man-Who-Runs and knew she had hurt him. Badly.

"I'm so sorry," was all she could say before he stalked from the lodge.

Weeks spent in quiet loneliness passed. Alone in the lodge, Sarah added wood to the fire in the pit. She stared deep into the flames as they grew and danced before her and saw Ben's face smiling at her. She smiled back—a sad smile that bespoke her loneliness. But the image in the fire faded, replaced by the face of Man-Who-Runs. Her breath caught. She stared at the image until she could look no more.

*This is my life now and Ben is your past,* she murmured

to herself. A past that's fading like the face in the fire. A chill ran up her spine. She sat back on her heels and sighed.

"Oh, Ben. I want so much for things to be like they were. But they're not and never will be again. And I can't change it no matter how much I want to. I'm afraid of my future and of losing my past. Afraid of forgetting what we shared as I struggle to survive among these people." Between her fingers she held the treasured locket, which lay in its rightful place around her neck, the only remaining link to her past.

A tear slid down her cheek. "Forgive me, Ben. Please forgive me."

The sun rose bright and warm, a welcome break from the bitter temperatures that had battered the countryside for days. Sarah pushed out of the lodge to take in all the warmth the sun offered when the most chilling, high-pitched cry she'd ever heard shattered the quiet of the morning. She poked her head back into the lodge and looked at Man-Who-Runs for an explanation. He was standing rigid in front of the fire, his eyes dark with anger.

"What in God's name was that?" she asked, afraid of his answer. He grabbed her hand and yanked her back into the lodge.

"Do not leave here," he commanded.

"But why?"

He gathered weapons from his arsenal, then raced outside without an answer.

"What the blazes is going on?" she muttered in confusion. Other cries reverberated throughout the morning air, voices as shrill and threatening as the first she'd heard, but now melded with shrieks of terror.

They were under attack. But from who? Surely not the army. They would have attacked with bugles blaring and rifles blazing. If not them, who then? She started to shake when she realized who it must be. *Pawnee. Hadn't Andrews said they were sworn enemies of the Sioux? Hadn't they been the type of Indians they'd first encountered on the trail? The tribe One Ear had been from? Didn't they raid one another constantly?*

Her curiosity got the better of her and she pushed her way outside—and gaped in pure shock. Stretched out in front of her the men of the village were locked in combat against other Indians. Indians whose hair was spiked straight up in the air and whose faces were painted for war. Most used tomahawks or knives. Others used bows and arrows and some used long sticks with heavy stones attached to the ends. Men clashed in battle for their lives as women and children scrambled for safety inside a lodge or behind a tree.

Fear gripped Sarah like a giant vise. Murderous cries of anger and pain scorched the air and the smell of death again rode the wind. Where was Man-Who-Runs? She tried to find him among the mass of fighting Indians.

A shadow fell across her face. She looked up. A lean, sweaty Pawnee brave stood there, a bloody knife in his hand. She fell backwards into the lodge.

He stepped inside. His face was painted blue, yellow and red and his black hair stood straight up in the air. She scrambled away, scanned the lodge for a weapon. Three feet away was a tomahawk Man-Who-Runs had missed taking. She lunged and managed to grab it. She regained her balance and swung around, toward the Indian, the weapon raised over her head.

The Indian threw his head back in laughter.

She waved the weapon in a threatening manner. The Pawnee laughed harder and stepped forward.

Her hands were wet with sweat and shook with fear. Her heart raced and she wondered again where Man-Who-Runs was.

"Get away!" She slashed the tomahawk down and in front of her, barely missing the Indian's belly. He stopped and cocked his head. His eyes and mouth grew hard and he stepped toward her.

Sarah knew she couldn't hold him off for any length of time, so she let go a scream of her own. He only laughed at her wasted effort. She called Man-Who-Runs' name over and over again, but the Indian kept coming.

Sarah bumped up against the lodge wall, but continued to brandish the tomahawk in front of her. Her attempt to defend herself was futile and lasted only a few short seconds. The brave's hand whipped out and wrenched the weapon out of her hand. He twisted her wrist painfully and she cried out with the hope someone would hear her.

She wrenched her hand away, dropped to her knees and lunged around his legs. She scrambled to her feet and raced to the door but was jerked to a stop when he grabbed her braid and spun her around. He released his hold and shoved her to the floor.

He straddled her with his hands on his hips and his deep, throaty laughter sent chills of dread up and down her spine.

She kicked at his legs, but only managed to hurt her own feet through the soft leather moccasins. He merely grunted. She mustered every ounce of energy she had left and screamed Man-Who-Runs' name again.

The tent flap burst open and there he stood, breathing hard and covered with blood. His eyes went from the Pawnee to Sarah, then back to the Pawnee. He raised his arms and shouted a war challenge.

Man-Who-Runs backed out of the lodge, the Pawnee behind him. Sarah jumped to her feet after them. Outside, she stopped dead in her tracks when she saw Man-Who-Runs and the Pawnee squaring off. Each man took the end of a common leather strap that was tied around their left hand. In their right, each gripped a knife. They circled each other, their faces a canvas of rage and unveiled hatred.

The Pawnee lunged, but Man-Who-Runs jumped aside with ease. He landed, swung his knife, and ripped the flesh on the brave's left arm. The Pawnee jerked away. Blood seeped down his arm and, although it was only a minor wound, Man-Who-Runs had drawn first blood.

Sarah realized all was quiet around them. The fighting had stopped throughout camp and familiar faces were crowding around Man-Who-Runs and his opponent. The Pawnee had been beaten back, all except the one facing-off against Man-Who-Runs.

The Pawnee lunged and barely missed Man-Who-Runs, who dove left. When he landed he jerked the leather strap and pulled the Pawnee forward, almost onto his knife. But the

Pawnee managed to throw himself to the right before he was able to roll onto his back and out of the path of the blade.

Man-Who-Runs pushed up and threw himself on top of the other brave. In one motion the knife was driven into the Pawnee's heart. The brave clutched the knife and was dead before his hand dropped to the ground.

Sarah stood frozen. Her mind spun like a child's top. She gazed at the carnage around her. Around every tent lay the dead and wounded, their bodies twisted and broken. High, shrill keening cries echoed across camp as loved ones mourned their dead. Mothers cradled dead children in their arms and braves beseeched Wakan Tanka. Others wandered aimlessly, muttering, their eyes seeing nothing. Some tried to help the wounded while blood streamed from their own wounds. Sarah felt sick. Never had she seen such savagery.

All around, men lay where they had fallen, their heads smashed in and arrows in their chests. Vomit rose in her throat as she remembered her own wagon train. Had her own people been massacred like this? These people were of the same race, yet they brutalized and murdered each other. Was there no purpose in their lives other than to kill?

She watched several Pawnee captives dragged away. Sarah's skin crawled as memories of her own capture rushed into her mind.

The prisoners were thrown into a lodge far removed from the rest of the village and heavily guarded.

"What will happen to them?" she asked Man-Who-Runs who now stood beside her.

"Tonight they will die."

That evening Sarah was forced to accompany Man-Who-Runs to a clearing. In the darkness many torches burned bright in a half-circle, the faces of The People ghostlike as they chanted and danced. Inside the circle of torches stood four posts. From those posts the Pawnee prisoners were tied by their chests and waists, their arms and legs spread out away from them. A distance of approximately twenty feet separated each post. Shadows danced across the illuminated faces of the doomed as they awaited their deaths.

Three of the four prisoners mumbled to themselves, their eyes raised to the sky as they prayed to their god, Sarah assumed. But the fourth glared out over the Sioux, his eyes dark like a demon, and Sarah felt like she'd been cursed.

She watched in horror as Sioux riders, four in each row, lined up about a hundred feet in front of the prisoners.

She could only stare in mute silence at the doomed Pawnee. Man-Who-Runs stood stoic beside her, his arms crossed over his chest, his legs spread. Three of the four braves began to struggle, but the one raised his chin and shouted at the other three. He spit on the ground and began to chant. The others soon joined him in what, Sarah assumed, was the final plea to their god for strength to bravely meet their doom.

Sarah turned to the riders. Their horses stamped and snorted, the promise of death rode the air.

Then, seemingly from the depths of hell, a chilling cry rose up from the riders. The first line broke and charged, lances raised.

This wasn't happening, Sarah told herself. They wouldn't do this. It was too barbaric. They would just frighten them and release them.

Terror tore through Sarah's body. She shook violently as she watched the scene unfold, unable to look away.

The chants of the Pawnee rose, but the shrieks of the racing Sioux drowned them out. Sarah watched, mesmerized. Her heart pounded as the riders drew closer and closer to the helpless Pawnee. The villagers chanted and urged the riders forward.

Hooves pounded and dirt flew as the Sioux advanced. The Pawnee chant rose to a heightened frenzy. Sarah stopped breathing.

The riders waited in front of the posts. Lances sailed through the air and impaled the Pawnee. Pain-laced screams rent the air. The villagers cheered and danced.

The second line of riders broke toward the Pawnee.

Sarah turned away. Bile rose in her throat. She covered her mouth with her hand and tried to stumble away, but Man-

## Tomorrow's Promise: Survival on the Plains    D.L. Rogers

Who-Runs stopped her.

"Let go of me." Her throat was hoarse as she tried to keep the bile down. "Don't touch me again."

She yanked her arm out of his grip and fled to the closest bushes where she vomited until there was nothing left.

Bitter weather returned to the countryside and shadowed the bitterness in Sarah's heart. Again she'd been reminded of the savagery of her captors and what it had cost her. Ben and her existence in the white world.

She worked methodically as each day passed, doing the same thing day after day. She gathered wood, prepared meals for Man-Who-Runs, scraped hides for clothing, sewed and tended the fire. She did each task without feeling, without the joy she'd once experienced at learning the ways of these people. Her existence became as mundane and repetitive as the days themselves.

She couldn't even reach out to her friend, Morning Flower Woman, who'd been among the villagers that night cheering the riders on. She felt abandoned, rejected—alone.

Each night Man-Who-Runs reached out to her and each night she turned him away, the memory of the Pawnee raid and their torture seared forever into her mind. They were savages with savage ways. She wasn't one of them.

She saw the torment in Man-Who-Runs' eyes, but her heart had turned cold. She wanted Ben now more than ever. She wanted her old life. Wanted to be free. But the weather continued to clutch the camp and those in it with its frozen talons to keep them tight in winter's grip, forcing Sarah to stay where she was. Frozen in time. Waiting. Just waiting for an opportunity to escape.

But she couldn't think about that until the weather broke. Right now, she had chores.

The day was cold and wet and a light snow blanketed the land. Sarah left the lodge and walked to the river in search of fallen wood, as she did each morning. Slippery with ice, the bank left footing precarious and she slipped several times. Within reach a few feet up the bank she spotted a good-sized log and walked toward it. She reached out, slipped and tumbled feet first into the icy water up to her chest. The breath was knocked out of her and she gasped for air. Her lungs felt like a giant vise was crushing them. She tried to scream, but her lungs wouldn't work. She groped for something to pull herself out, but found nothing. Nothing but ice and more ice.

The weight of her clothes and the fur covering she wore for warmth tugged at her, pulling her deeper into the frozen depths. Her arms were like lead bars and dragged her down while the vise crushed her chest. Water swirled around her, grabbed and lapped and pulled her deeper against her will. She tried desperately to make her arms work, to move toward shore, but they wouldn't respond to her mind's commands. Life began to ebb away. She stopped struggling, amused at the irony she would die this way. She thought of Ben and the life they'd had together in what seemed like a lifetime ago. A fairy tale. She thought of Man-Who-Runs and the life she shared with him. How different things had become.

Too cold and too tired to fight any more, the icy depths dragged her down. She gave up her struggle and slid below the black surface.

She imagined strong hands grabbing and pulling her from the frozen waters. Those same strong hands lifted and carried her away. It was light and it was dark. She felt herself being laid upon something soft. Blankets and furs were bundled around her and more hands rubbed her arms and legs viciously. She began to shake and tried to open her eyes. Someone was beside her, held her tight as bone-rattling chills shook her body. She felt fire, more furs, more hands moving up and down her arms and legs. There was mumbling and whispering. She shook. Her teeth chattered and her breath was quick and short. Again she tried to open her eyes, but the lids were too heavy, the light too bright.

Circulation began to come back to her hands and legs. The shaking lessened and warmth flowed through her. Her breathing grew even and steady until, finally, the trembling ceased.

She opened her eyes and found herself cradled in Man-

Who-Runs' arms, an expression of fear and pain on his face.

"Sarah." Her name was whispered with such feeling it touched her deeply. She smiled and burrowed closer into his heat before she closed her eyes again.

She awakened the next morning, still enveloped by Man-Who-Runs who was asleep beside her. She studied his bronzed form, his face soft in sleep. Why had he saved her? She'd shunned him and put aside his attentions for weeks. Why was he so relieved she was still alive? And why was she glad? she puzzled as she watched him slumber.

His eyes opened and they stared at each other for several moments. She tried to read what was on his face. In his eyes. She remembered it wasn't Man-Who-Runs' arrow that had killed Ben. She no longer hated or blamed Man-Who-Runs for what had happened to Ben. She had probably lived through the wagon train attack because he had taken her away, if only because she was a prize because of her blonde hair, so unusual to these dark-haired people. And she was alive now because of him.

The Pawnee raid leapt to her mind and Sarah realized the Sioux had defended what was theirs—their children, wives and homes. They'd punished those who had savagely attacked them. She realized she'd been greatly relieved when she saw that Man-Who-Runs was unharmed.

She looked deep into the Indian's eyes and face. It was a strong face, but soft and caring at this moment. In his eyes she didn't see murder or hatred; instead she saw love.

Slowly, Man-Who-Runs leaned toward her and touched her face with his rough hand. "Sarah," he whispered.

Sarah's eyes closed at the feel of his hand on her skin. Heat raced through her body. It had been too long since she'd felt a warm, gentle touch on her face.

She sensed Man-Who-Runs moving closer until his lips brushed lightly over hers. She shuddered with fear, apprehension, guilt and yearning. Ben's blurred face flashed to her mind and she drew back. How she wished this were Ben. She missed him, wanted him, needed him. But when she opened her eyes she saw only Man-Who-Runs.

"Sarah," Man-Who-Runs said again. "Your white husband is dead. There is only me now. I will take care of you. Only me. You are mine." He moved closer and his lips covered hers again, but this time she felt his longing and passion.

Sarah's mind reeled. She knew Ben was dead. This was her life now, but...

Suddenly, the need to love and be loved surged through her. She no longer resisted. Instead, she welcomed.

## Chapter Seven

Sarah was shaken awake by Man-Who-Runs, his face a mask of concern. He spoke quickly and, although she now knew many of their words, she didn't understand what he said.

She pushed out of the lodge and was hit by the now familiar sight of lodges being dismantled. So quickly, in fact, she knew within minutes the entire village, save her own lodge, would be gone.

"What's happening?" She was still groggy from sleep. "We only joined Little Thunder's tribe here at Blue Water Creek a few days ago. Why are we moving again so soon?"

Man-Who-Runs answered her, but again spoke quickly.

"I don't understand!" she shouted in frustration.

He started to dismantle the lodge as she stood there waiting for answers. She tried to help him as much as she could, but was still inept at the task. By the time their lodge was finally struck, all the other lodges had already been packed and the villagers gone from the now dismantled camp. Sarah turned around and gaped in amazement at the empty field where the village had been only minutes before. But when she looked beyond the field, her mouth dropped open and raw fear gripped her.

In the distance sat hundreds of soldiers astride their cavalry horses. She stared in silence and her heart soared with hope. She could go home! Then Man-Who-Runs stepped in front of her. Their eyes met. She knew it meant she would have to leave him.

Her arms slipped around his lean waist. "I'll stay, Man-Who-Runs. My life is with you now." She kissed him gently. His arms circled her shoulders and she felt his warm breath on her face before he squeezed her tight. Then he stared down on her with eyes full of pain and regret.

Without words, his lips covered hers in a soft, love-filled kiss. He took her hand, led her to Midnight and helped her onto the animal's back.

"I go with Little Thunder to parley with the soldiers." He

turned the horse in the direction the villagers were fleeing and pointed. "Go with them. You'll be safe among them."

"No. I won't go, Man-Who-Runs. I'll wait for you to parley with the soldiers. I'll go with you. I can help. I can tell them what you say!" She didn't want to be sent away.

He reached up and silenced her with a finger across her lips. "Go Wi Tapeta Yuha Win." He slapped Midnight's rump and the horse bolted away.

But Sarah had no intention of leaving. She jerked the animal to a halt and spun him around in time to see Man-Who-Runs mount his horse and join the parley party, which included Chief Little Thunder, Spotted Tail and Iron Shell, who rode under a white flag to meet the advancing soldiers.

Sarah watched the Indians ride toward the Bluecoats. But the soldiers didn't stop when the Indians reached them. Instead, they kept coming, ignoring the parley party.

Sarah's heart somersaulted. She understood. The soldiers had no intention of stopping or talking. They planned to attack.

The Indians turned and raced back toward where Sarah waited. She rode up beside Man-Who-Runs and the look in his eyes caused a lump to rise in her throat.

"They're going to attack, aren't they? Why are they here?"

"I don't know, Sarah. Why they come now is the reason they have always come." He looked out over the plains. His hand came up to his chest then spread out to encompass everything around him.

"This, Sarah. The land. This is why they come and this is why we fight. We will not give them this land, our land, so they take it." His voice had grown hard. Sarah nodded understanding.

The soldiers finally stopped their advance and two riders came forward. One raised his hand and called out in Sioux.

"I must go." Man-Who-Runs' voice was gentle.

"Please, let me go with you. I can help you speak to them," she begged.

Man-Who-Runs shook his head. "I must know that you are safe." He caressed her face.

She begged him one last time to let her go, but Man-

Who-Runs turned his mount and raced to join the others.

The Indian chief, Little Thunder, stocky with a heavily creased face and several white mans' medals visible around his neck, led the parley party toward the soldiers. A long feathered headdress flapped around his sun-bronzed shoulders.

The riders halted a few feet in front of the soldiers. Chief Little Thunder extended his hand. It was refused.

Angry, frustrated voices carried on the air. Sarah's skin pricked with fear.

"...You sent for me to come and fight you or have a talk, and now you are running away," Sarah heard the officer yell as the interpreter translated to Little Thunder.

Little Thunder shook his head.

The men spoke harsh words for many long minutes. The interpreter looked around between translations, as though he were waiting for something. What was he looking for? Sarah wondered, holding her breath.

Sarah's eyes snapped back to the officer when she heard him yell. "...You must fight! I want you to come on. I have not come out for nothing!"

Sarah gripped the reins until her knuckles turned white. This soldier wanted a fight and he seemed intent to get it. Was there no end to man's foolishness?

Sarah heard more harsh words before the officer waved toward the women and children scrambling for safety in the caves and brush that lined the nearby creek. He pointed again. Sarah turned and gaped in horror as another unit of soldiers appeared over a nearby ridge. With no provocation, they rode down on the fleeing villagers.

She whirled in time to see the parley party turn and race back toward her.

A bugle sounded. The soldiers opened fire.

Rifles discharged over the dusty plain, echoed across the creek. Women grabbed their children and ran to elude the rampaging soldiers. Braves tried desperately to protect their families. Sarah couldn't believe what she was seeing. The Indians she had grown to know and care about in the last year were cut down as ruthlessly as they had killed the people of her wagon train. She watched familiar faces scream in terror and run for cover under a bush or behind a tree, only moments before being cut down by a soldiers' bullet or saber.

She sat atop Midnight, refusing to believe what she saw. Bullets slammed into the ground and trees around her and jerked her from her trance. She sent Midnight charging toward the fleeing Indians and the cavalrymen that attacked them.

"No! Don't hurt them. Don't hurt them!" she screamed as loud as she could. But the soldiers continued their ruthless attack. Midnight raced through the creek bed toward several women and children. Sarah spotted Morning Flower Woman, a cavalryman bearing down on her. Behind her a child was trying to wake up its dead mother. Sarah realized the child was Rainbow and the rage inside her burst out.

"No!" Sarah shrieked. She sent Midnight charging toward the soldier's horse then jerked the reins violently. Midnight reared and knocked the soldier out of the saddle.

"Run!" she yelled to Morning Flower Woman. "Napa! Take Wikmunke! Now!"

Morning Flower Woman grabbed Rainbow and raced away, but not before giving Sarah a grateful glance.

"Go."

Sarah whirled Midnight and raced back toward Man-Who-Runs. Anger boiled in her belly like a churning twister. She screamed for the soldiers to stop, but the sound was lost in the explosions of gunfire and wails of terror.

She felt sick.

Man-Who-Runs thundered toward her, his face a mask of rage that softened only when he spotted her.

He jerked his horse to a halt beside Midnight and ran his fingers over her face. Tears spilled from Sarah's eyes as he leaned to kiss her, the terrible knowledge in her heart he was saying goodbye.

The soldiers were advancing.

"Go, Sarah!" he yelled.

"But..."

"Go. Now!" He gave her no further chance to protest. He swung his horse around and rode directly into the path of the

***Tomorrow's Promise: Survival on the Plains***          ***D.L. Rogers***

approaching soldiers.

"No!" Sarah screamed as she watched him ride toward certain death. "Man-Who-Runs, No!"

He rode toward the soldiers, yelping and whooping, waving his bow high in defiance. His long black hair flew wildly around his shoulders.

Within striking distance of the soldiers' guns, the first bullet hit him. Blood spurted from his shoulder, but he didn't stop his advance. A second bullet tore into his leg. He slumped over the horse's neck and grabbed his leg, but rage drove him on. He regained his balance and continued forward. Man-Who-Runs drew an arrow from his quiver and placed it in his bow. Another war cry issued from his mouth. He raised the weapon... A volley of fire erupted from the line of soldiers and bullets ravaged his body. His bow slipped from his hand. He raised his hands to the heavens, lifted his eyes to the sky and slid from his horse.

Sarah gaped at his still body. She screamed out his name and sent Midnight racing toward him, directly into the line of fire.

A tall dark-haired sergeant sat stiff in the saddle and watched the scene unfold. He was besieged by mixed emotions as he watched the slaughter of Indians who tried desperately to protect themselves.

Something caught his eye and the skin on his body pricked. A brave raced toward him and his men. The Indian rode hard and fast, his bow poised and ready to fire. His men raised their rifles and took aim. The Indian rushed on.

In the distance a woman screamed. But the words were in English! His head snapped around and he searched for her amongst the chaos.

A shot rang out from beside him and he jerked his head back to see the Indian take a bullet in the shoulder. But the brave kept coming. Another shot resounded and the brave was hit in the leg. Instead of retreating, he loaded his bow and raised it to fire.

"Man-Who-Runs! No!" the woman screamed again in the distance. The sergeant tried to find her in the chaos, but before he could, a volley of fire rang out beside him. The Indian raised his arms as though praying to the heavens, then slid from his horse to the ground.

Then he saw her. She pushed her black horse at a full gallop as she raced toward the fallen Indian—and the waiting soldiers.

"Hold your fire men!" A lump rose in his throat. "Don't shoot, I said. Hold...your...fire!"

Sarah raced toward Man-Who-Runs. She jerked Midnight to a stop, dropped to the ground and knelt beside the fallen brave.

"Oh, Man-Who-Runs," she cried. She placed his head and shoulders on her lap. Blood seeped onto her dress.

"I'm sorry, so sorry." She brushed dirt off his face and wiped blood from his lips. She cradled him in her arms and smoothed his tangled hair from his face, while she rocked him back and forth. He'd saved her from death at the hands of his people, but she couldn't do the same for him.

There was movement behind her. Her back stiffened. A rider dismounted.

"How can your people do this?" She stroked Man-Who-Runs' dirty face. "I thought we were supposed to be better than them. Better than this!"

She shifted under the weight of Man-Who-Runs' still body and wiped tears from her eyes with the back of her hand. She turned to the soldier who stood over her. Her mouth dropped open and she gaped in disbelief.

## Chapter Eight

Emotions of every kind rioted inside Sarah as she paced the confines of the small tent while she awaited his return. Ben was alive. Joy, amazement and uncertainty coursed through her. But deep sadness that Man-Who-Runs and so many others were dead also filled her soul. Fear that Ben might turn his back on her because she'd lived so long among the Sioux, and obviously cared for them, hovered at the back of her mind. She knew how returning white captives were treated. They were shunned, left to fend for themselves and, oftentimes, died alone and dishonored. Or they just went crazy.

But Ben was different, she reminded herself. This was her Ben. He would take her in his arms and wipe away all the pain and horror of the last year.

Her mind returned to the events of the day and rage filled her when she thought of what lie just outside these thin canvas walls. And she was afraid. Afraid of what the future held. Minutes seemed like hours until, finally, the tent flap opened and Ben stood in its opening—tall and handsome and very much alive.

She walked toward him and searched his face. She let her eyes wander over his strong features. His dark eyes held her in their grip. She lifted her hand to touch his face, but Man-Who-Runs' face exploded into her mind and her arm dropped to her side.

"Sit down, Sarah. You're weak. You've been through hell." He helped her to the cot.

"How, Ben?" she asked. "I saw that arrow enter your back and you fall to the ground. I watched you tell me you were sorry. You were dying."

"But I didn't die, Sarah."

"Ben..."

His hard voice stopped her cold.

"Somehow I survived, but I had to use every ounce of strength I had. I'll carry the scars of that day for the rest of my life, Sarah, but I'm very much alive." He looked away then continued, his voice soft. "When I regained consciousness, the Indians had been pushed back, but you were gone. Those in the train who survived managed to patch up those of us who were still breathing, even barely, and got us to Fort Laramie where we received medical attention. I knew you were alive and I swore on my life I'd find you." He looked into her face, touched her hair.

"Once I recovered, I learned General Harney out of Fort Leavenworth was going after the red bastards who attacked our train. I had to be a part of it. I had to enlist at Leavenworth in order to ride with Harney, so I made the trip back there and joined his troops." He paused. "I used your father's influence to help me get these stripes." He pointed to his sleeve. "Otherwise, I'd be cleaning stalls at Laramie instead of riding with Harney's troops, looking for you." He paused and gazed into her eyes. "In my heart I knew you were alive and I meant to keep my promise. I had to find you. No matter how long it took." His eyes bespoke the pain and agony he'd suffered over the long last year. They were soft, but Sarah saw other emotions tearing at his mind and heart.

She leaned against his chest. She was alive and so was Ben. But so much had happened since the last time they held each other.

Ben allowed her to remain for several seconds before he pushed her away.

"That Indian. What was he to you?"

Paralyzing fear shot through Sarah. How could she explain all she'd suffered? All she'd learned? All she'd felt in the past year? Could he ever understand her feelings of abandonment, desperation, loneliness and fear? "Ben," she began slowly. "I thought you were dead. I saw you take that arrow and fall to the ground. You didn't move and your eyes didn't open. I tried to reach you that day. Oh God, how I tried. But I couldn't fight Man-Who-Runs' strength. I hated him. I thought I'd hate him forever. I tried to escape." She stopped as painful memories assaulted her. It was several moments before she continued.

"The women threw rocks and spit at me. They laughed at me. I worked from sun up to sun down beside them and never heard a kind word. My hands bled, my body ached and my pride was destroyed. I missed you so much. I was so lonely I wanted to die. I even tried to kill myself." Ben's head lifted and he searched her face.

She thrust out her wrists that bore the scars of her attempted suicide, stark white against her sun-darkened skin, and looked him in the eyes, intent to make him understand.

"But I survived, Ben, because I had to. I realized life is a gift and I reached out and took the gift that was offered to me."

The two fell silent. Laughter and shouting from outside the tent reminded Sarah of what had transpired earlier in the day and anger boiled up inside her again.

"What happened here today was a massacre. These men were no better than the Indians who attacked us. Helpless women and children were butchered." She took a deep breath. "I know these people now. I've lived with them. I've seen their savagery. I tried more than once to escape, but it did me no good. Eventually I was accepted. I learned what they were truly like and I found they only wanted to be left alone. Left alone, Ben. To live in peace. To hunt and fish and be fathers and mothers, husbands and wives, just like we are. All they want, all they've ever wanted, was to be left alone on their own land."

She drew her back up straight and proud. "After I recovered," she looked down at her wrists again, "I realized my instinct to survive is strong. I knew no matter what happened or how badly I was treated I wanted to live. I wanted to smell the flowers around me and feel the soft grass beneath my feet. To taste the snow as it fell from the sky. I wanted life, and Man-Who-Runs offered it to me. He took care of me as his property and, at first, I was. He was harsh in many ways, but I learned to live again. I never stopped wanting you. I loved you every day I was there. But I was alive and you were dead. I had to go on, to make the best of my situation."

"Did he...did he make you his wife?"

Sarah turned away. She took a deep breath then turned back to Ben and looked him straight in the eyes.

"Yes, he did."

"I see." He blinked and recoiled when Sarah touched

***Tomorrow's Promise: Survival on the Plains***  *D.L. Rogers*

him.

She pulled her hand back. "Do I repulse you?" She shook her head. "I survived, Ben. I did the same thing anyone else would do. I didn't want to die any more than you did. I fought to stay alive, learned how to become a part of their way of life and understand them. And in that process I learned to care for Man-Who-Runs. You didn't exist anymore, as much as I wanted you to. From all I knew you were gone from my life."

Ben turned his back on her and dropped his head to his chest.

"Ben, please. I love you. I've always loved you. Please turn around. Look at me."

He didn't move so she walked around in front him and withdrew the locket from inside her deerskin dress. "I fought three Indian women for this. I would've fought the entire tribe. I thought I'd lost it forever and when I found it again, I fought like a wild animal to retrieve it. Do you know why?" she asked. Ben stared at her, his expression blank. "Because it represented you, us, and what we had. I've kept this locket close to me ever since." She reached to touch him. "Try and understand. I survived."

Ben backed up and stepped around her.

"I'll be back in a little while." He stopped before the flap. "I suggest you remain in this tent. It's ugly out there."

Ben left the tent without another word.

Sarah tried to rest, but couldn't. She'd never stopped loving Ben, but could she make him understand and forgive her for doing what she had done to survive? She thrashed about in the bedroll and slept little.

"Mrs. Walters?" The voice at the tent flap brought her up straight.

"Come in." She pushed a stray lock of hair off her face, smoothed her dress and sat up. A soldier with the look and stance of an officer came inside.

"Afternoon, Mrs. Walters. I'm General Harney." He removed his hat and extended his hand. His face held a false smile.

### Tomorrow's Promise: Survival on the Plains   D.L. Rogers

Sarah inclined her head, but made no effort to take his proffered hand. "I know who you are, General. You're the barbarian who ordered today's attack."

The general's face grew hard, his cheeks flared red and his back went rigid. "I beg your pardon, Mrs. Walters. What transpired today was a necessity. A lesson to all the red devils who think they can continue to harass those who seek to journey west in an effort to civilize this country."

Sarah snorted at his flowery words. "Civilize this country?" she spat. "You call what happened today civilized?"

Harney coughed to regain his composure then pasted another smile on his face. "That, as I've said Mrs. Walters, was a necessary lesson. An example had to be made."

Sarah stared at the man and marveled at his audacity. "The only thing *necessary* about today's *lesson* was that it helped to make you feel like an important man." Sarah stared him down and waited for his response.

His eyes pinched and his jaw ticked in anger, but Sarah's glare didn't waver.

"General Harney, I don't wish to be rude, but I have nothing to say to you or the army with regard to the Indians. Your men were no less savage today than those same Indians were with my wagon train a year ago. Women and children were brutally murdered today. How dare you talk of lessons."

Harney's face turned more scarlet. "Mrs. Walters, if you would just cooperate with us. Any information you have on the Indians, which we do not already have, could be very helpful to this campaign. How many were in this camp? How many do you think got away? How many braves were there? Weapons?"

She turned her back to him, the words piercing her like a shot to her heart as she thought of all those who had become her friends who were now dead outside her tent. "I will not cooperate, General. Go back and tell your superiors I have nothing to say."

Harney crashed out of the tent. "Walters! Get me Sergeant Walters!" Harney bellowed.

"Sir?" came Ben's puzzled voice through the canvas.

"Do something with her. She's your wife and I order you

to get control of her."

Sarah walked to the tent flap and listened as the voices softened.

"Sir, she's been through a great ordeal. Please allow her some time," Ben said.

"Very well, Walters, but she's your responsibility. I've experienced this sort of thing before. Some captives come to revere these savages. Do what you can with her, but I want answers. She's your wife." Sarah heard the cold insinuation in Harney's voice.

"Yes, sir," came Ben's weary response.

Sarah stepped away from the flap just before Ben entered.

"What in blazes did you say to him, Sarah? He's my commanding officer. Show some respect."

"Respect?" Sarah spat. "How can I show respect for a man who ordered the slaughter of those women and children out there? He could have stopped it. I heard what he said to Little Thunder and the parley party. He never had any intention other than to attack! He's no less savage than an Indian."

"Than that Indian you cradled in your arms today?" Ben's voice was bitter.

Sarah stopped and let her head fall back. Her eyes closed and she breathed deep for control.

"Yes, Ben. He's as much a savage as Man-Who-Runs or any other Indian from his tribe, except for one thing. They had a reason for their attack on us. Do you want to know what that reason was?" she asked. "You may not want to hear it, but I'm going to tell you anyway. In the time I spent with Man-Who-Runs and his people I learned that the day before our wagon train was attacked the U.S. Army had visited his village. And do you want to know the reason they were in his village?" Her voice was cold and she gave Ben no chance to respond. "Because of a cow, Ben. A damned cow."

Ben remained silent as Sarah recounted the story Man-Who-Runs had related to her.

"It seems a cow broke loose from a wagon train and wandered into the Sioux village. The cow was so lame its hooves were worn through to the flesh, its body so emaciated the skin hung off it. A Miniconjou brave staying in the village killed that cow to feed his starving children, even though Chief Bear tried to stop him. But Bear was Brule and had no authority over the one Miniconjou brave.

"And do you know why his children were starving?" she asked.

Ben shook his head. "No, I don't, but I believe you're going to tell me."

"They were starving because they hadn't received their annuity of meat, dry goods and blankets from the almighty white man. They were starving, and because they were starving, this Miniconjou brave butchered that cow, what there was of it, to feed his children.

"And because the illustrious U.S. Army determined that the cow should have been returned, they went to the encampment to take the guilty Indian back to the fort and 'make an example' of him, just like your General Harney told me they did with these people today. But when the officer went to take him into custody, the Miniconjou refused to go." Sarah paused. "You see, High Forehead, as most Indians, would rather die before he allowed himself to be put into a prison cell."

Sarah stopped and took a breath before she continued. She searched Ben's face for some sign of understanding, but saw none.

"High Forehead, Chief Bear, and the soldier who had come to take High Forehead, argued. Shots were fired and when everything was over Chief Bear was badly wounded. It was then the Indians attacked the cavalrymen. They were merciless and killed every one of them."

Ben took a deep breath. "I do remember something about that. Heard about it when I was at Fort Leavenworth, before I headed back west. I believe it was a Lieutenant Gratton who went into that village and got he and his men killed. They're calling it the 'Gratton Massacre' back East."

Sarah snorted. "They would. What else would they call it when their stupidity caused it!"

Ben stared at her, but didn't speak.

"But that's not all there is to the story, Ben. Man-Who-Runs' wife and baby girl were killed, too. Chief Bear died five days later. Why? Because of a cow and the savagery of an army that believes it has the right to take whatever it wants whenever it wants!

"Perhaps General Harney would benefit from learning this story." She stalked toward the opening but was stopped when Ben stepped in front of her and grabbed her shoulders.

"Don't. You stay out of it. It's no longer your concern. He will make my life a living hell if you cause trouble. There's no telling how long we're going to have to stay at Fort Laramie. I can't leave the army now just because I want to. So you keep your tongue, Sarah," he admonished.

She looked into his stern face and her anger subsided. God, how she wished things were different! She wanted only for him to take her into his arms and hold her, comfort her, tell her everything would be okay. She wanted him to touch her lips and whisper that he loved her. But he was a different Ben, she was a different Sarah, and this was a different time.

"Ben," she began, her voice full of longing.

"I have to go," Ben interrupted. "They're making preparations to return to the fort. Remember what I said. Keep your tongue around General Harney."

She stepped forward to say something else, but he turned his back on her. "I'll be back later."

He was gone.

From atop the wagon seat Sarah sat in stunned silence. She stared across the terrain at the freshly dug graves where the men and women of Little Thunder's tribe lay, the landscape now quiet and serene, a contradiction to the sound of gunfire and terrified cries that had ridden the wind the previous day.

Bile rose in her throat as men loaded booty from what was left of these people's lives onto hers and two other wagons headed to Fort Laramie.

Sarah took a deep breath and tried to dispel the feelings of revulsion for the soldiers around her loading what remained of a people desecrated at Blue Water Creek. But she could not.

## Tomorrow's Promise: Survival on the Plains    D.L. Rogers

After a hard, silent two and a half day ride, Ben, Sarah and the company reached Fort Laramie. It stood naked against the backdrop of the dusty, desolate plains. Tall timber walls reached into the sky, sharp in contrast to the flat barren land that surrounded it. Sentries marched the perimeter and waved greetings to the returning conquering heroes.

Sarah felt nothing. She felt no joy at being back among white civilization, no comfort at being returned to her own people. She felt only a stabbing fear in the pit of her belly. She knew how people felt about white women who'd lived with Indians. Regardless of the fact they'd been taken against their will, they were ostracized and treated like outcasts.

Through the last year she had learned many lessons. Some had been hard and brutal, while others had brought her joy and revelation. She'd learned to live again, now she would have to start over—again.

Once inside the gates, still clad in her deerskin dress, Sarah felt the harsh scrutiny and whispered remarks of the people she passed. In some she felt their revulsion, in others, pity.

Although no one physically touched her, she felt that same stabbing pain, fear and uncertainty race through her that she'd felt that first day in Man-Who-Runs' camp.

She thrust out her chin and drew up her spine. Again she would have to fight to survive. But this time, it would be in her own world—among her own people.

# Chapter Nine

Ben saluted the commanding officer, then turned and ushered Sarah out of the office. Without a word he took his mount's reins and walked toward a row of shabby buildings, Sarah behind him. He stopped outside a small, weathered cabin with one window to the right of the door. Ben tied off the horse and led Sarah inside.

The room was drab with few furnishings. A single cot was shoved next to the wall on his left with a washstand and basin in the corner above it and a small, round mirror on the wall over it. A cold fireplace was directly across from the bed and a wooden chair that leaned precariously forward sat to the right of the fireplace. On the wall in front of him was a small bureau, its drawers left open as if the former inhabitant had packed its contents in a hurry. Gray curtains flapped over the grimy little window to the right of the door.

"It's not much, but I imagine it's better than what you've lived in for the past year," Ben said.

Sarah's head snapped around and her eyes flashed. "Better?" she asked. "There's no comparison."

"I didn't think so. It may be small, but at least it's clean."

Sarah laughed without mirth. "You think this is better than where I lived with Man-Who-Runs? I hate to challenge your misconception of the Sioux, but his lodge was as large as this place, much cleaner and much homier."

Anger rolled in Ben's stomach. She was defending them. Him! She even tried to make it sound more appealing than what he could offer.

"I'm sorry you feel that way," he managed, his throat tight. "This *is* the army, remember?"

"I meant nothing other than to make you realize the Indians aren't the horrible, unclean devils you all believe them to be."

She stepped further inside, surveyed the barren room and hid none of her disappointment. Her eyes stopped at the little bed pushed up against the wall and she looked up, a question in her eyes.

"I sleep in the bunkhouse with the other men."

"I'm still your wife, Ben. Don't they have quarters for the married men? Or is this arrangement by your choice?"

"I realize you're my wife, Sarah. I don't need you or anybody else to remind me of that fact." He knew his voice was hard. "I need some time. I have a lot of things to work out. It's better this way."

Sarah nodded and thrust back her shoulders. He wanted to touch her, console her, but instead he stood rooted to the floor, his hands like lead bars at his side.

"If that's what you want. Just know that whatever I did, I did to survive."

"Let's not talk about it right now. I'm exhausted so I know you must be. Why don't you rest? I'll come for you later and we'll have dinner. I'll have the cook make up something and send it to you." He turned to leave.

"Are you ashamed of me?" she asked his back.

He turned to face her.

"Well?" Her body was stiff. Her hands rolled in and out of fists.

"No, Sarah. I'm not ashamed. I just need time."

Before she could ask him any more questions, he slipped outside.

He walked to the bunkhouse trying to comprehend the way his life had been turned upside down. He tried to understand what he felt—about Sarah and himself. How could she have cared for that savage? He was angry and hurt.

He slammed into the bunkhouse, drawing the ire of the other men, and stalked to his bunk. He flopped down and threw his arm over his face. He wished he could turn back time, but knew it was impossible, so why even wish? After hours of wrestling with the bunk and himself, he drifted off to sleep, where savages and Sarah's pleas for understanding followed him.

The following morning Ben knocked on Sarah's door for the second time. He waited with no answer so he pushed open the door and entered.

A thin ray of sunlight spread its fingers across the floor, over the tiny bed and illuminated Sarah's slumbering form.

Ben walked toward her, looked down at his wife relaxed in sleep. Sun-darkened cheeks glistened in the filtered sunlight.

Once she had been his, totally and completely. But she'd also belonged to someone else. Ben's throat seemed to close at the thought. The vision of that Indian stroking Sarah's fair skin, his lips touching hers, caused a lump to form in his chest. His eyes blurred. *How could this have happened? How could he forgive her? He held such a deep hatred for the Indians. How could he overcome the paralyzing pain it caused in him each time he thought of what they'd done to him and so many others along the trail? How could he ever understand what she'd done? To survive, she said. She didn't even seem grateful to be rescued, back among her own people.*

They'd had everything between them—dreams, passion and a love bigger than life itself. He stared down at her silent figure and noticed the locket around her throat. The one she'd vowed never to take off, then fought three Indian women to get back, because it represented him and their past. *Could he ever love her as he once had? Could he ever forget?*

Sarah's eyes opened.

"I, I brought you some dresses," he stammered. "I thought you might like to get out of...that." He pointed at the deerskin dress she still wore, "and into something more acceptable." He raised two dresses in his hands.

She looked down at her dress and traced the porcupine quill beads with her fingers. She remembered how she'd fought against Man-Who-Runs to put it on. She recalled the first time she'd let it slide down over her body, amazed at its softness and workmanship. And then she saw the blood and brutality of the last few days as it exploded in her mind.

"I suppose I should get into something more, what was the term you used? Acceptable?" She looked up at him. "Acceptable, now that's an interesting word. Will I ever be 'acceptable' again?"

"Sarah, I'm trying. So many things have changed. I

don't know what to do...about anything."

"I understand, Ben. I don't know how I would have reacted a long time ago to someone in my situation, either. I'll give you whatever time you need." She looked away. "I'd like to change now; please leave."

Ben walked to the door, but paused, his back to Sarah. "Just give me time," he whispered.

"Time, it seems, I have plenty of."

Sarah spent the next several days in solitude. Ben brought her meals and she never left the cabin. It felt eerily like those first days in the Sioux camp. She knew he didn't want to be seen with her publicly, and for right now, that suited her fine. She couldn't bear the icy stares and glowering faces, even though her deerskin dress had been replaced with Ben's acceptable dresses.

Although he denied the fact he was embarrassed to be seen with her, she couldn't deny her seclusion. Each time she thought of how her life had again changed, her stomach rolled and her heart twisted.

A knock interrupted her thoughts. Ben entered, hat in hand.

"Sarah, I thought you might be rested enough to see the fort." Ben rolled his hat through his fingers.

"That would be nice," Sarah answered after a few moments of uncertain hesitation. "Would you wait for me outside?"

Ben nodded and retreated through the door.

She brushed her hair and swept it atop her head, washed her face and pinched her cheeks before she emerged from the cabin a few minutes later. The sight of Ben in the sun's light made her head feel light. His ebony hair fell below his shoulders and framed his clean-shaven face, except for the moustache he'd always worn. Dark eyes spoke their uncertainty, although his smile tried to say otherwise. She descended the step and took his proffered elbow. His mere touch sent a rush of emotion through her like a bolt of lightning.

He headed toward a cluster of buildings and gave curt

explanations of each as they walked past the mess hall, the sutler's store and the livery. While he talked, Sarah wished he would talk *to* her, not *around* her. As she walked beside him, she marveled at the desolation of Fort Laramie. It was plain and dull with nothing attractive to the eye.

Hoping to turn the conversation, Sarah said, "You've done well with the army."

"Thanks to your father."

"What?" She stepped away from him.

"When he heard what had happened to you, he snapped into action. He wanted you found and if I was the man to do it, he'd make damn sure I had the ability to do just that. If they'd allowed it, he would have had me made a general." Ben snorted. "As it is, sergeant works well enough. At least I'm not shoveling shit with the other new recruits."

"Father?" Sarah's heart leapt. "How is he? Is he well? Tell me everything you know."

"He's well, but was wild with worry about you. When I first wired him, he was hell-bent on coming out here himself. I finally talked some sense into him and he did what he could from there. He called in favors from his friends in Washington and got me my stripes and assignment with General Harney. It was enough to get me where I needed to find you." He paused and stopped walking. "I haven't wired him yet that you've been found. I, I didn't know what to tell him."

"What?" Sarah nearly shouted. "What do you mean, you didn't know what to tell him? I'm alive, what else is there?"

Ben shook his head and said nothing.

Sarah couldn't believe what she'd heard. "I'm alive, damn it. I believe he'll be happy to know that!" She felt tears threaten, but forced them back. She was through crying. Through apologizing for surviving what most people didn't. Damn them all—she was alive!

Several minutes of strained silence passed before she tamped down her anger and continued the conversation.

"What other news do you have about Father?"

"Nothing, much. Other than he was worried sick about you. We never wrote about anything else." Ben paused and twirled his hat again. "I know he blames me for your capture. He didn't say so in so many words, but I read it in his wires. If I hadn't had such wild ideas about going west, you wouldn't have been in a position to be taken by those savages."

Sarah touched Ben's face. He flinched, but didn't pull away. "I don't blame you, Ben. We made the decision together to come west. You're not responsible for my capture."

He shrugged and frowned. "Maybe not. I don't know."

"You weren't responsible, Ben. Don't let anyone tell you you were." She smiled, but he just started walking again.

He led her toward the post store. She noticed several men congregated outside who drank, played cards, smoked and chatted between themselves. Others threw horseshoes.

The lively activity stopped abruptly when Ben and Sarah walked by. Sarah tried to walk proud beside her husband, but she felt Ben shrink beneath the men's scrutiny.

Well out of voice range of the gawking men, Sarah turned to her husband.

"You are ashamed of me. I saw the way those men stared when we walked past and how you acted. I'm not blind, Ben. Does anyone around here have any idea what I lived through? Does anyone give a damn?"

"I realize you lived through a great deal, Sarah, but I lived through hell, too." Ben's voice was thick. "Once I was lucid enough after the attack to know I was alive, I nearly went out of my mind with grief when I found out you'd been taken. I thought of you constantly. I wanted to touch you, hold you and hear your voice. Know you were safe. You can't imagine the guilt I've carried with me since that day. Guilt for not protecting you and bringing you to this wilderness in the first place. I'm thankful we're both alive, and I pray to God that someday we can find what we've lost. But it's going to take time, Sarah. Lots of it."

He grabbed Sarah by the shoulders. "And I feel like a damn fool, because I worried about you all this time, when instead, you were living quite happily with your Indian buck!"

Sarah felt like she'd been punched in the stomach. Her mind snapped with pain and anger. She gulped air to regain her composure. "You make it sound like I wanted to be with them! I did what I had to do in order to stay alive, Ben. Would you rather that you hadn't found me and I were dead?"

"Of course not. I just need time to figure it all out."

"You still haven't answered my original question, Ben. We're talking about right here and right now. Are you ashamed of me?"

She shivered with the look of uncertainty Ben gave her. His face was a mask of mixed emotions. Emotions she couldn't read. She waited. He didn't answer. Instead he turned and started back toward her cabin.

"I'd better get you back. We can discuss this another time," he said over his shoulder.

Sarah stood stock-still and stared after him.

"Another time? What other time?" she yelled. "When you decide to take pity on me and allow me out of my quarters? When you feel up to it? Damn it, Ben, I have feelings. I'm confused and scared, too!"

She didn't move. Her anger gave her strength. Ben stopped but didn't turn around. Sarah waited until she could wait no longer. She turned on her heel and stalked away in the opposite direction.

"Sarah, stop," he called from behind her. She ignored him, kept walking.

"Sarah," he called again. She heard him run up behind her.

"Wait." His voice was gruff. He grabbed her elbow. "Fine, we'll talk now if that's what you want. Over here." He pointed her in the direction of a crude bench in the shade of a tree.

"I'm sorry, Sarah, I don't mean to be cruel, but there's been so much talk since we've returned. I don't know how to handle it."

"What kind of talk?"

"Talk I wasn't supposed to hear." He paused. "The men make jokes, call you names."

"Names?"

Ben looked away. "Indian lover and squaw." He turned

back, his eyes a mirror of the pain she felt. "I tried to ignore it, but..." He shrugged and continued. "I've had my share of brawls over it, too. It's always there, in the other men's faces."

Sarah placed her hand on his shoulder and felt him go rigid.

"Sarah, we've lost so much. I never should have brought you here." His voice was a whisper.

She slid closer to him. "Ben."

He pulled away before her lips could touch his cheek and pain shot through her heart like the arrow she thought had ended his life. She took his chin into her fingers and turned his face to look directly into hers.

"I love you, Ben. I've always loved you, from the first time I saw you at my father's ranch until now. You've never been far away from me, in my heart or in my mind. Please try to understand."

"I *am* trying, Sarah." His voice was gruff again and he looked away.

Sarah stared at him and neither spoke for several minutes. A soldier walked by and coughed, trying to smother the laughter in his throat, Sarah thought.

"You should get back," Ben said.

"I know," she admitted, her voice heavy with defeat. She looked out across the expanse of the desolate fort. "When will we be able to leave here? The longer we stay the harder it will be for us to put this behind us."

"I'll check with Harney as soon as I can, but you're going to have to be patient. I can't just leave when I want to. I signed up with Harney to look for you, remember, and that enlistment isn't over for more than four years. This might be all we've got for quite some time."

"Four years!" Sarah turned away and tears threatened. His words stung. He blamed her for their situation. That they might have to suffer here another four years turned her stomach to mush.

She took a deep breath. She'd be patient and wait, for as long as it took. Ben was worth it. He was different now but maybe in time, he'd become the man he'd once been. Perhaps they could even rebuild their lives, share the dreams they'd once had.

She faced him, determination in her blood.

"I'll wait." She turned and walked toward the headquarters building to ask where she could send a wire from. She was determined to let her father know she was alive and hoped at least *he* would be happy with the news she'd survived.

Several months later, Ben learned he was to ride with General Harney and his troops in search of a band of Indians that continued to harass settlers as they traveled the trail to Oregon.

In column and erect on his army mount, Ben sat ready to ride out of the fort with the rest of the men. He looked forward, but wished he could turn back the clock and feel what he so desperately wanted to feel: Love. But, the word was foreign to him now. The words that came to mind as replacements for that love were duty, guilt and acceptance. That was all he could bring himself to feel toward Sarah. His guilt for having brought her to this wilderness in the first place, his duty to remain as her husband and take care of her, and finally, the acceptance that this was now his life.

He knew she was behind him, watching, waiting and hoping he would turn around and wave farewell. Ben had no idea how long he'd be gone. It could be a week, two, maybe months. He sighed and hoped the mission would be swift and conclusive, without bloodshed. He was tired of the killing, tired of the death and destruction of human life and property. On both sides.

He wanted a normal life. But what was normal? It seemed as though all he and Sarah had known was the hardship of life on the trail, or the pain of captivity and anxiety of searching. Now he was an enlisted man and wouldn't be free for over four years. "Normal," he nearly snorted. What the hell was normal? That word was as foreign to him as the word 'love'.

The command to depart was shouted and the column headed out of the fort. Nearly to the gate, Ben felt Sarah's gaze bore through him. Perhaps just a wave. Slowly he turned in the saddle and searched the crowd. He found her, their eyes locked and a smile lit her lips, but it was a sad smile that made his heart ache.

She's so beautiful, he thought, as he gazed at her face and sun-darkened skin, stark in contrast against the blond hair that nestled around her face. Her eyes seemed to reach out to him. His hand came up, as did hers. He returned her smile then turned back in the saddle and rode with his column through the gates of the fort.

The Indians were like ghosts on the plains. Ben saw constant evidence they existed. He knew they'd passed only days or hours before he and Harney's troops, but never, ever, did he so much as glimpse one of the red men.

Ben was bone-tired and mentally weary. His company, the Second Dragoons, had been on the Indians' trail for two months and was no closer to catching those ghosts than the day the troops had left Fort Laramie.

A physical ache enveloped Ben with each day that passed. Sarah's face came to him, unbidden. Her soft features beckoned, her eyes cried out for understanding. *Why couldn't he just forget and be happy she was alive? Happy they were both alive? Why couldn't he put the past where it belonged? Behind him to begin again. They'd been given a second chance. Why couldn't he just reach out and take it?*

During the endless weeks in the saddle he thought over the year Sarah had spent in captivity and remembered how he'd agonized over what she must have lived through: Torture, constant fear and uncertainty. And yet, she'd survived, had even learned to care for the Indian who'd taken her from him. His mind rebelled each time he thought of how Man-Who-Runs had loved her and how she, in turn, had cared for him. Or had it been something else? Perhaps it had been acceptance of her fate? As he now accepted his fate?

But she'd learned to be happy and that, Ben knew, was the scab that grew thicker over his heart to leave an ugly scar that might never heal.

Day after day the morning sun greeted Ben as he bobbed wearily in his saddle. Winter was coming. The days grew shorter, the nights colder. Why didn't Harney just give up and return to Laramie? he wondered with a shiver. The man was as stubborn as an old mule. They were chasing ghosts.

The chill winds became bitter and, finally, Harney and his troops were forced to take refuge at Fort Pierre, a desolate outpost hundreds of miles from Fort Laramie. Its ramshackle buildings gave little protection from the blistering wind that constantly raked the faces and bodies of the weary men. Small in comparison to Laramie, it had little, if anything, in the way of comfort. Regardless of how little shelter the fort gave, Ben was thankful for the respite.

The weather pounded them constantly. Winds howled through the slats in the rough-hewn buildings and snow fell continually to blanket the countryside. Ben had never been so cold in his life.

Dear God, how he missed the sunshine and its warmth, and as much as he hated to admit it, Sarah and her warmth. Now that they'd been reunited and again separated, it amazed him how much he missed her, although he tried to harden himself against his feelings. Memories of her penetrated the frozen depths of his mind, her face always in front of him. Try as he might to dispel the thoughts, she was always with him.

Afraid to go to sleep and freeze to death, like private Carol who had frozen as he slept, Ben barely closed his eyes. In his exhausted state, Sarah haunted him. The feel of her skin, the moistness of her lips, the blueness of her eyes and the sweet lilac smell of her hair and body after she'd bathed, was ever with him. He missed her, no matter how much he didn't want to admit it.

He forced the unwanted thoughts from his mind with an angry grunt then jumped up to pace the confines of the tiny cabin. When would he be able to leave this barren, God-forsaken place? When would Harney come to his senses and let them all return to Laramie? The Indians weren't going to come to him asking for peace. Harney had chased them for months without so much as a second glance from them. If they wanted peace, Harney would have found them long ago.

To Ben's surprise, several bands of Indians came to the fort to ask for a treaty. They were told to return when the weather warmed, so Ben prepared himself to wait. Again.

# Tomorrow's Promise: Survival on the Plains     D.L. Rogers

Cold, bitter, lonely months passed before March arrived and the chiefs returned.

Ben snapped to attention that March day when General Harney passed by with several Indians beside him. Ben watched the Indians walk to the table, confer only a brief minute, then make their marks on the piece of paper that promised them peace.

General Harney smiled and spoke to them like dignitaries. He strutted like a peacock. Ben shuddered with irritation. The arrogant bastard had won again. But this time, he reminded himself, at least it was without bloodshed.

The treaty signed, Ben was anxious to head back to Laramie, but disappointed to learn Harney had no such inclinations.

It was another three months before the column started back to the fort. Three more months of agonizing boredom and constant, painful memories.

It was a sunny June day when the column appeared at the gates of Fort Laramie, treaty in hand. Ben searched the waiting crowd for a glimpse of Sarah. *Was she still here? Had she waited for him or grown tired and returned east?* Questions flooded his mind as he continued to search the swelling crowd. He couldn't find her. His heart slammed in his chest. *Why? If he cared so little, why was it so important she be here?*

Suddenly, there she was. Her fingers wrapped in her skirt in anticipation.

He breathed in relief, but was still unwilling to admit he cared whether she had waited for him or not. He smiled and Sarah smiled back when he rode up beside her. She seemed glad to see him.

He sat in the saddle and stared. She shifted under his scrutiny. He wanted to speak, but couldn't. He wanted to touch her, but didn't dare. Silence enveloped them like a bubble.

The leather in his saddle groaned when he dismounted to stand a foot in front of her. Her chest rose and fell with each breath and her blue eyes sparkled with hope. He could reach out and touch her, if only he dared. He stepped toward her and his hand was on her cheek.

She stood rigid, but relaxed as his hand slid along her neck. Her eyes closed and a sigh escaped her lips. She opened her eyes and Ben saw hope flicker again. *Could he give her what she so desperately needed and wanted? A return to the way things had been? To the feelings they'd shared of total trust and devotion?* He pulled away as those thoughts tumbled through his brain.

His body betrayed him. He had to have her. He'd thought too long about their reunion.

Without words he led her to her quarters. He tethered his mount and entered the cabin with Sarah close behind. The door closed and he turned to face her. She opened her mouth to speak, but Ben silenced her with a hungry, passionate kiss. He ravaged her mouth while Sarah seemed helpless to deny him. With each stroke of his tongue, she responded in kind, flaming his desires higher. His lips seared a path along her neck and she sighed as his hands worked at the buttons of her dress. She was limp in his arms. He grew impatient, tore at the material to expose her creamy-white skin. Her chemise fell away in pieces as lust shook him, his breathing akin to panting. In a few quick motions he shed his own clothing and the two lay on top of the tiny bed.

Her fingers twined through his long, scraggly hair and she pulled him closer. Her body melded to his. This was Sarah, he told himself. *His* Sarah. The woman he had loved more than life itself and she was his again. His mouth feasted on her breasts and neck while his hands sought every inch of her body. His mind remembered every touch and feel of her. He was on fire and only she could extinguish the flames.

She remained still as his eyes searched the length of her body. She reached up and touched his face, ran her fingers over his lips and ragged beard. Words formed on her lips, but were never spoken. His mouth covered hers to suck the breath right out of her. Then he was inside her.

She stiffened at his entry. He moved slowly at first but as his passion built, so did his tempo and he exploded inside her. He fell to his side, his breathing uneven. He closed his eyes and waited for his body to still, knowing she still longed for more.

Then the vision came. He saw Sarah cradling the dead

Indian in her arms, crying tenderly over his crumpled body. In his mind's eye, he saw the two entwined, as they had just been, and Sarah cried out Man-Who-Runs' name instead of his. His breathing slowed.

He turned his back to her and thought no more.

Sarah was alone when she woke later that afternoon. The sun had set, but the musky smell of their lovemaking hung in the air. She spotted Ben, fully clothed, standing across the room looking out the grimy little window.

"Ben?" she called softly. She wished he would come back to bed and hold her. Perhaps love her again.

He didn't respond, didn't move.

"Ben?" A tremor of fear rose in her stomach. Something was wrong.

His face was hard and set, his shoulders squared as though ready for battle. He strode toward her and fear tore down her spine.

"What is it?" she managed.

He started to speak, but didn't. He reached out his hand to touch her then dropped it heavily to his side, a look of defeat in his eyes.

"I'm sorry," he mumbled and left the cabin without a word of explanation.

But she knew what had happened. He'd done to her what she'd done to Man-Who-Runs. Ben had envisioned Man-Who-Runs loving her, just as she had, and it had driven him away. Would Ben ever be able to come to her without seeing Man-Who-Runs holding her? Loving her?

Sarah stared at the door Ben had just passed through. Anger and pain assaulted her. She knew he'd come to her from lust more than love and she'd taken what he'd given, gladly, willingly.

But in his need, Ben had given her something. Hope. His desire was her hope. The hope that someday she could break through the walls around his heart and bring back the man he'd been. She knew it would take time to exorcise the memories that haunted him, but she'd be patient. Perhaps his desire was the one spark that could rekindle their love until it was once again a burning flame.

    Alone in the room, she vowed to stoke that flame and bring it back to life. No matter how long it took.

# PART II

## THE WAR

*"Come with your guns of any description that can be made to bring down a foe. If you have no arms, come without them...Bring blankets and heavy shoes and extra bed clothing if you have them...We must have 50,000 men."*

*Confederate General, Sterling Price, 1861*

## Chapter Ten

Sarah sat in the rented buckboard and thought back over the last four years. She'd spent a long, lonely year at Fort Laramie where Ben, kept busy with patrols and army business, spent little time with her. The only good memory she had of the place was when her father showed up unexpectedly to bring her home—to Pennsylvania. But she dug in her heels and said her place was with her husband, even though he spent less and less time with her. Roger Reynolds spent six months at Fort Laramie badgering his daughter, trying to make her change her mind. But her love for Ben and the hope that someday their lives would be what it once was, kept her resolve from breaking and he left without her, a scowl on his face, but knowing his daughter was alive and as stubborn as always.

When Ben's orders for transfer to Fort Leavenworth finally came, she'd settled in a small cabin outside the fort. She thought about the lonely nights spent beside the fire. How she'd wished and hoped things would mend between them. Many times in her loneliness she reminisced about her time spent with the Indians. How a small fire in the central fire pit had easily warmed the confines of their lodge or how she'd gained acceptance among them.

She remembered how rarely Ben came to see her in those days. He always cited his duties as his first priority, but she'd known better. She knew he'd volunteered for most of that duty so he didn't have to spend time with her. The more she thought about it, the angrier she became. Their relationship even now was tenuous, at best. But that was going to change.

Although they'd often shared the same bed, she knew he came to her only of his own need, always to withdraw after their lovemaking, his face a reflection of guilt, anger and pain. Sarah had grown used to his rejections and took what he could give.

*But why?* she asked herself often. *Why did she continue to wait and hope and pray?* Because she still loved this man above all others along with everything that went with him. His blinding smile, when she was lucky enough to be the recipient of one. His flashing eyes, when they warmed her in his passion. And his relentless sense of duty and commitment to right and wrong that came with him, too. She would honor her promise to herself. She would wait as long as it took to win him back.

During the three long years she'd lived outside Fort Leavenworth, political tension had mounted. The state of the nation seemed to mirror the tense feelings between her and Ben and gave him the excuse needed to be away from her with his unit most of the time.

He rode with the Dragoons to keep peace along the Kansas border as Missouri slavery factions tried to force the vote of a pro-slavery delegation into power in the hope of extending slavery further west. When skirmishes erupted along the shared border with Missouri, the military, including Ben's Dragoons, were called upon to quell it.

On one of Ben's rare visits to Sarah, he talked about the strong feelings between Kansans and Missourians and how those feelings were building to dangerous levels on both sides.

He'd slammed through the door, thrown his hat on the table and slumped down in a chair.

"This whole damn country is going crazy." He rubbed his face and shoved his fingers through his hair.

"What's wrong?" Sarah's skin prickled with apprehension. Every day it seemed something new and more frightening happened.

"You remember my telling you about John Brown, the abolitionist who is riding around the country, inciting the slaves to riot? The man who raided the armory at Harper's Ferry last October?"

Sarah nodded. A lump began to rise in her throat. She'd heard all about it that day in town. It was the only thing anyone had talked about.

"Well, they finally caught him. They'll hang him, too."

"Maybe with Brown gone, things will quiet down," she said, hopefully.

Ben snorted. "If they hang him, which I'm sure they will, it'll make a martyr out of him. Every abolitionist in this country will sing his praises and hold their banners up for John Brown." He paused, sighed. "I'm afraid it won't help quiet things down. I'm afraid it'll make them worse," he'd said that night before he changed the subject to more pleasant matters.

So far it hadn't escalated. But as Sarah re-settled herself on the seat of the buckboard, she prayed it wouldn't. She had a future. Ben's enlistment was finally over. It was time to start again. She didn't need anything else to muck it up.

Ben had searched for weeks for a position on a ranch as a foreman or even as a hand, but hadn't found anything around Leavenworth City. With no other options left, they were forced to return to Westport where their journey began so many years ago, newly renamed the City of Kansas. South of town he'd found a position on a small spread through an advertisement in a local newspaper. Ben had written, given his qualifications and been told to come talk with the owner. Happy to be offered even a chance, he agreed without hesitation.

Ben climbed into the wagon beside Sarah and drew her thoughts back to the present. Now, she thought. They would put the past behind them and start over.

It was a long, silent two-day wagon ride from Leavenworth to the City of Kansas. Ben was hopeful. *Maybe the position at this farm—ranch as Sarah insisted on calling it—would be just the thing to make him forget the past? Would he ever?*

He turned the buckboard into town. They roomed that night at the American Hotel and, after a quiet breakfast the next morning, headed south toward the ranch, and, hopefully, a new beginning.

The road was bumpy and rutted and the rickety wagon threw Ben and Sarah from one side of the hard seat to the other.

"How much longer?" Sarah grumbled.

"Not much. We should come up on it real soon." The wagon crested a hill and Ben drew in the reins. Below was a shabby farmhouse with a few outbuildings and a torn up corral. He and Sarah sat mute, staring in disbelief.

Was this the ranch they were looking for? This ramshackle assemblage of buildings? The window to the right of the front door was non-existent, covered instead by a flapping oilcloth. Hand-made shutters and shingles hung loose from the walls and roof. Stairs that leaned heavily to the right, rose up to a porch where several missing boards left gaping holes in the floor. A glider swing dangled from one rusted chain and swayed in the gentle breeze.

To the right, the barn seemed to be in better condition than the main house. All its doors were intact, but the roof needed repair where Ben could see several large holes. Corral fence and posts were strewn about the ground and shutters barely clung to the windows of a small bunkhouse behind the barn.

Ben gaped at the buildings around him. No wonder the owner needed help. This place was a wreck.

"We might as well talk to the owner since we're here," he said, finally breaking the silence between them.

Ben clicked his tongue and sent the mule forward along the tree-lined drive to the main house.

At the end of the drive, Ben helped Sarah from the wagon. They walked up the stairs, careful of each step, to the front door, also crooked on its hinges.

At the door Ben sighed, shrugged his shoulders and knocked. A bent-over gray-haired woman opened the door.

He removed his hat. "Morning, ma'am. I'm Ben Walters and this is my wife, Sarah. I'm here about the foreman's position you have available. You sent me a letter telling me to come."

"Yes, yes. Come in, come in, you two," the woman said, her voice raspy. She pulled open the door for them to enter. "Have a long trip, did you? You look a little tuckered." Stiff gray hairs escaped from the tight bun at the back of her head and long wrinkles stretched across her face and down to her neck. But she moved deftly for her age as she rushed toward the fireplace to push out a chair for Ben.

"Sit here, sonny, and the missus over there." She waved at an overstuffed chair on the other side of the fireplace on the front wall of the room.

The old woman hurried to a couch at their right, sat down and folded her hands in her lap.

"I am Mrs. Emma Carter. I'm sixty-five years old, give

or take a few," she smiled and winked, "and I am recently widowed. As you can see, this ranch has seen better days. My husband, God rest his soul..." she stopped speaking, seemingly caught up in memories of her late husband, "was too crippled near the end to take care of this place any longer. Since his passing, I've thought about selling out, but I'm old and I've lived here for the last," she stopped again and calculated in her mind, "thirty years, plus or minus a few, and couldn't bring myself to leave. This place is my life. We were the first to settle this far out." She drifted again.

Snapping back, she continued, "You should have seen this place when my Jonathan and I first bought it. It was beautiful. No buildings just the land. Trees as far as you could see, but plenty of pasture. And lots of water. There's a stream that cuts through the southern portion, plenty of game and lots of room. Room to build. First off, Jonathan built me my little house, back yonder there in the woods. That's where ya'll will stay." She pointed toward the back of the house. Her eyes glistened. "That house was like a big doll house, just big enough for the two of us while we built our dream home.

"Anyway," Mrs. Carter absently waved her hand, "we built this place on our own. And I helped. I know, I know, it's not a woman's place to pound nails and dig holes, but I worked as hard as any man and was proud to do it. It took us years, mind you, but we done it. Me and my Jonathan.

"After we finished the barn and outbuildings, we bought some stock and finally had ourselves a working, producing farm. It was a long, tough fight, but we done it. And we were proud. I had me a son in that time. He only lived to be ten." Her voice caught, but the old woman forged ahead.

"Came down with the fever and wasn't strong enough to fight it. He always was a puny thing, but we loved him so much. Anyway," she stumbled on, waved her hand again, "Then we built our big house, with an upstairs and an attached kitchen so I wouldn't have to brave the cold in the winter. It took five years to build, but we did it with sweat and love.

"Enough of my sorrowful tales." She slapped her knees. "You look like a fine young couple. What brings you here? Why would you want to work for an old lady like me?" Her face might have been aged, but her green eyes snapped with the fire of a young woman and darted between Ben and Sarah as she waited for their responses.

"Well, ma'am," Ben began, "I was recently discharged from service with the Dragoons at Fort Leavenworth. I've been unable to find work in that area and read about this position in the newspaper. We want to buy our own place someday, and hoped we could work and save at the same time."

The old woman clapped her hands. "Just like me and my Jonathan. Oh that's wonderful." Her voice was clear and crisp and her eyes sparkled with delight. Abruptly, she was all business again. "And your qualifications, Mr. Walters?"

Ben chuckled at her quick change in personality. "Before my enlistment I was the foreman of several large spreads, which included one of the largest in Pittsburgh, Sarah's father's, Roger Reynolds. That's where we met, as a matter of fact."

"Yes, yes. I remember now from your response to the advertisement. Large spread back east. Ranch foreman? Good, good. I think you'll work out just fine, Mr. Walters.

"Now then," Mrs. Carter turned to Sarah. "There's another matter I'd like to discuss with you. I need someone to help me cook and clean and keep this big old place from falling down around my ears. Would you be interested?"

Sarah smiled at the older woman and paused only a moment before she answered.

"I'd like that very much, Mrs. Carter."

The woman slapped her hands on her knees again and a huge smile broke across her face. "It's settled then. You two can have the cottage out back. Oh yes," she added absently, "your wages. I can't pay you much, but you won't have to pay rent and you'll be well fed. How does ten dollars a month sound?" She waited, her face hopeful.

"With all due respect, ma'am, that's not what I hoped for," Ben answered. "I made seventeen with the Dragoons and we barely made it on that."

"Okay, okay." Mrs. Carter waved her hand again. "Fifteen, all your food and no rent, that's all I can spare. And that's for both of you. Jonathan didn't leave me much, but he left me my home. Our home. And once we get it working again, I'll raise the wages. Give you a portion of the profits. How does that sound? Mind you," she continued before Ben could answer, "getting this place to produce again is your job.

"Once it's running again, you'll have a share of the profits and a stake in the place. What do you say?" She waited expectantly.

Ben liked the sound of her proposition. He could rebuild the farm with the goal of someday gaining a portion of the profits. And in the meantime he could put money away toward their own place, since they wouldn't have to buy food or pay rent any longer on separate quarters for Sarah. He had a good feeling about the old woman. He already liked her a great deal. He looked over at Sarah who nodded her consent.

Ben stood up, crossed the room to the widow and extended his hand. "You've got yourself a deal, Mrs. Carter. When do we start?"

A week later and settled into their new home, Ben and Sarah were ready to assume their new duties. First thing, however, Mrs. Carter had Ben bring the wagon from the barn. She wanted to show he and Sarah the lay of the land.

Just as Emma had said at their first meeting, trees reached to the horizon, the land cut by tiny streams that spread out like tracings on a map. Wind blew gently through the surrounding trees while birds sang and small brush animals darted in and out of their nests in playful abandon.

"It's beautiful," Sarah whispered from beside Ben as the wagon crested a hill and she gazed out over the entire expanse of the ranch. "Everything is so green and lush."

"And this ain't even the prettiest section of White Oaks." Mrs. Carter's eyes glowed with pride. "Down yonder," she pointed, "by the south section, there's wild flowers that grow six feet tall. Sunflowers I think they call 'em." She drifted off into thought. "Anyway," she said with a wave of her hand, "they're tall and yellow with a big black face. Lots of daisies and smaller flowers grow up around those sunflowers, but none are as pretty as they are. There's a wide stream that runs beside 'em. It's where me and my Jonathan spent many an afternoon lazing in the sun of a Sunday afternoon after a long week of backbreaking work."

Ben watched the widow and felt Sarah's hand slip over his own. He looked up, surprised, and was met by a soft smile, one that warmed his heart instead of turning it cold.

Ben set to work putting the stables in order first. He patched the roof then covered it with black tar to keep out the rain. Ben and Sarah had come to Mrs. Carter with precious little. But Midnight was their most dear possession and Ben wanted to be sure the animal had a sound stable as soon as possible.

Ben worked on the corral next. He cut trees for new fence posts and rails. He dug deep holes to set the new posts and put three rails between each post for strength. Once the corral was finished, he watched Midnight race from one end of the newly built structure to the other. Ben looked out over his handiwork. Soon there would be more horses in this corral, and it would be due to his hard work, he thought with pride. He and Sarah had a stake in what became of this ranch, as he now affectionately called it, and he swore to himself he'd make a go of it.

He tackled the main house next, beginning with the porch. He replaced planks, re-nailed raised boards and reattached the porch swing so it swung evenly from the roof beams.

Sarah swept through the house like a windstorm. She cleaned cobwebs and removed what could have been several years' worth of dust. Each evening she and Mrs. Carter prepared the evening meal they all ate together.

One afternoon, Mrs. Carter and Sarah brought lunch for Ben, who was working in the stables. The widow bade Ben to take a rest from his duties and sit down.

"My, my. Everything looks wonderful, Ben." She looked at the newly replaced window frame where sun streamed through and made the barn bright and cheerful. She gazed at the rebuilt stalls and finished roof. "You've done an excellent job."

"Thank you, Mrs. Carter."

"No, no. That won't do," she said with a sharp wave of her hand.

"What won't do?" Ben was certain he hadn't missed anything.

"You needn't call me Mrs. Carter anymore. My name is Emma and I prefer you and Sarah call me by it. Mrs. Carter makes me feel old. And I refuse to get old," she giggled in her now familiar mischievous voice with eyes that sparkled with devilment.

"My, but you're sweating up a storm, Ben," Emma continued without missing a beat. "And you've already finished your glass of lemonade. Sarah, why don't you run and get him another glass?"

Sarah nodded and left the barn.

Emma waited until Sarah was well away before she turned to Ben. "That's a fine young woman you've got there. A wonderful girl. A prize for any man, and she loves you so much." Ben tried to interrupt, but the woman held up her hand. "I see it when she thinks I'm not looking. It's how I used to look at my Jonathan." Her eyes grew misty and she cleared her throat. "Anyway, I hope you don't take offense at my liberty to talk to you like this. I feel very close to the girl already. She's kind and gentle, yet she's tough as nails.

"She carries a heavy burden, though. I don't know what it is, and I'm not here to pry, but I can see it when she watches you. There's a hopeful look in her eyes." She raised her hand to stop his interruption again and continued. "Whatever is between you and her, help her to lift that burden." Her voice was soft yet firm, like a mother's would be.

She leaned forward. Her bony fingers grasped Ben's hand. "Help her with it, Ben. Help her."

## Chapter Eleven

Ben and Sarah worked through the summer. Every day after her duties in the main house were finished, Sarah went outside and helped Ben as much as she could with his repairs. Sweat poured off them like a river while the sun blistered their lips. Insects bit and buzzed at their sweat-soaked skin, but neither allowed it to deter them from their tasks. They were determined. The sooner they put the place into shape, the sooner they could start to begin saving for their own spread.

Sarah's hair grew lighter while her skin grew darker from the sun that beat down on her day after day. Her hands were rough, dry and cracked, but she didn't care. They'd set a goal and she was intent to reach it. And she was happy just to work beside her husband each day. He accepted her help gladly, and as they worked together, he seemed to soften toward her.

One evening after a brutally hot day, Ben and Sarah sat beside each other on the setee in their small front room. Sarah sewed. Ben read last week's newspaper.

Sarah lifted her eyes and gazed into her husband's face. Slowly, she placed her hand on his leg. He looked up, his dark eyes filled with something she hadn't seen in years.

Passion? Longing? Hope?

He stared at her for what seemed like an eternity before he pulled her into a gentle embrace. His breath caressed and a tingle rushed through her when he whispered, "I know these past years haven't been easy, Sarah. For either of us. Forgive me."

Sarah buried her face in his shoulder and tears flooded her eyes. She tried to wipe them away before he saw them, but couldn't. He reached up and brushed the wetness from her face and, for the first time in too many years, she saw the love they shared so long ago. Her heart leapt with hope and a shy smile turned the corners of her lips.

Ben smiled in return. Without words, he led Sarah to their bedroom. The door closed behind them and Ben guided her to the bed. He turned to face her, slowly pulled the pins from her hair allowing it to fall freely around her shoulders.

Sarah trembled at his touch, more gentle than she remembered in a long time. He was tender when he touched her ear with his lips before he moved down her neck. Her eyes closed and she sighed. His tongue teased along her shoulder. His fingers worked at the buttons at the back of her dress and she felt the material slide away from her skin like a gentle breeze. She couldn't open her eyes, afraid if she did he would disappear. Her heart fluttered with hope. His hands moved down her shoulders and arms, back to her neck and over her breasts. Air surged into her lungs as she tried to control the passion that grew inside her. Ben was *loving* her, not taking her in lust or need, but loving her, as he had in what seemed like another lifetime.

Her chemise floated to the floor. She forced her eyes to open, praying he would still be in front of her, a flesh and blood man and not a ghost that would disappear into nothingness. But there he stood, tall and handsome—and very real. Passion flashed in his eyes. His breath was ragged.

Sarah reached out and touched his cheek. He took her hand then lifted her up and placed her in the middle of the bed. He quickly removed his clothes then covered her body with his own. He was gentle, then forceful, as passion led him. Sarah responded in kind and gave him all the love she still had for him.

His hands seared a path over her body. His lips teased and tasted and Sarah thought she'd never been so happy again in her life.

Sarah nipped and teased his body. He moaned with pleasure. She ran her fingers through his hair, held him tight. She never wanted to let him go again, and wished this night would never end.

He suckled her breasts; she tickled a path up and down his back and caused gooseflesh to rise. He licked and teased her earlobes while she kissed his neck. They played and teased until Ben eased her legs apart.

Sarah gave him everything she had of herself. He moved slowly at first and, as passion claimed him, his thrusts came harder and quicker. But Sarah took in all of him. She wanted him to touch her very soul in the wish they could become one again.

### Tomorrow's Promise: Survival on the Plains        D.L. Rogers

Sarah felt as though her world couldn't be better. With a shudder, Ben relaxed and buried his face in her shoulder.

Sarah couldn't stop the rush of tears. Ben didn't move for a long time but, when he did, Sarah was sure her shoulder where Ben's face had been was wet.

One sunny, warm afternoon, Sarah stopped her dusting and sat down in a chair in the parlor of the big house. Despair washed over her. From a wooden frame on the wall the painting of a tall, husky, even handsome man, stared back at her. Emma's Jonathan. Beside Jonathan was a portrait of Emma tucked lovingly under his arm, looking up into his face.

Sarah looked back at the faces of the man and woman in front of her. Those two people had gained everything in their lives she and Ben wanted: Love. Their dream ranch. A child. Sarah's heart ached at the knowledge she'd never bear children. If she could, wouldn't she have conceived Ben's or Man-Who-Run's child long before now? She was barren. It was time she finally accepted it. Then she remembered Emma had conceived a child late in life. Perhaps she would too. It was a hope she clutched close to her heart.

She remembered the Sioux children—Little Crow, Rainbow, Spotted Turtle—and sadness overwhelmed her. *Had any of them survived the carnage at Ash Hollow? Had Morning Flower Woman been able to save Rainbow from the soldiers that day? Were the mothers she'd grown to know so well still alive, or were they among the many buried along the banks of Blue Water Creek?*

Unable to bear the possible answers to her questions, she turned her thoughts to Ben. She'd regained her husband's love. For that she was happy. Whether she ever had children or not, she had Ben. That was enough.

Roused from her self-pity by Emma's call from the kitchen, she ran down the stairs. She had things to do.

Summer passed and with it the completion of all the necessary repairs to the main house and outbuildings. One cool October morning Ben stood back and took stock of his work.

## Tomorrow's Promise: Survival on the Plains    D.L. Rogers

The house stood proud against the azure sky as gray smoke billowed from the chimney. Windows sparkled in the sunlight, doors swung free, shingles hung straight and the porch and stairs bore no reminders of the gaping holes that once filled them. Ben smiled in spite of himself and felt a satisfaction he'd never known before.

The wind had a nip to it. Winter loomed on the horizon and almost all the repairs on the ranch were complete.

Ben went into town once a week for supplies and information. Each time he returned with the same feeling of foreboding he'd experienced in Leavenworth. War talk was the predominant topic of conversation, with secession, states' rights and slavery the main issues.

On one trip into town, Ben had the misfortune to witness a slave auction. He'd never seen such a display and the whole thing made his skin crawl. The men and women for sale were treated like farm animals—worse than farm animals. Prospective buyers inspected the black men's teeth and hands. The owners made a point of showing them their strong backs and the women's wide hips, good for birthing. Ben watched in disgust and amazement as the sale progressed, yet was unable to walk away.

A dozen or so masked men suddenly flooded the street, shooting, screaming and shouting. The firing stopped as abruptly as it started when the riders rode up and halted in front of the sale platform.

"We claim this sale illegal!" one masked man shouted.

"Who the hell do you think you are?" the sale promoter yelled when he stepped to the front of the platform. "These niggers is my property, to do with as I see fit. This is a public auction and it's my right to sell them."

The lead rider leaned toward the salesman and whispered in his ear. The man's face turned ghostly pale. He stumbled backward and ran for his buggy, yelling for his men to gather the slaves back into the wagon.

"Be assured men and women of Missouri," the rider shouted, "that we will not tolerate such practices in our territory. We've stopped this sale without bloodshed—this time. But don't think we won't spill it if it becomes necessary in the future." An ominous hush fell over the crowd. "All you who hold slaves," he paused and glanced at those gathered, "be aware, we know who you are and where you live!"

A terrified rumble raced through the crowd. The riders turned and rode away, but the leader stopped and turned his horse back to the crowd. The animal reared and pawed the air.

"You have been warned!"

That night after dinner, Ben went outside to think about the events happening around him. He leaned against a tree and looked up into the sky. If Kansas came into the Union as a free state, and if war broke out, the line between slavery and anti-slavery would be the Missouri River—practically Emma's backyard. He closed his eyes, leaned his head back against the tree, and tried to push away the unwanted memories of what he'd seen earlier in town—events he hadn't shared with Sarah or Emma, already alarmed with the constant talk of war.

In the past months he'd made it a point not to voice his opinions regarding the issues of slavery and states' rights, but today had changed that. If it came to war, he knew he could never condone the institution of slavery or fight for its preservation. He'd do everything in his power to stop its spread.

Weeks later when riding out to a neighboring ranch several miles away on an errand for Emma, Ben stopped Midnight in front of the barn on his way up to the main house, not wanting to believe what he saw. Tied to a pole in the barn was one of the slaves, his chest bare, exposed to the bitter elements. Shoeless feet danced on the frozen ground and the man's lips quivered from the cold—or fear, Ben wasn't sure. Bleeding cuts streaked his face and his left eye was puffy and bruised. His nearly naked body was battered by the bitter wind and Ben held his breath at the fresh whip lines across the man's back. Other slaves in threadbare clothing looked on, their faces reflecting the pain suffered by the man strung from the pole. Horrified and angry, Ben nudged Midnight closer.

Behind the man, inside the barn, out of the harsh wind, a large white man stood in a heavy coat that shielded him from the wind and cold. From beneath the brim of his hat, Ben saw the trace of a smile on the man's lips as he raised his hand in the air—the hand that held a bloodied whip. His eyes were sharp and a wild light filled them as the whip rose in the air, again ready to find its mark. The whip cracked and the slave screamed. Blood oozed from the new tear in the already raw skin.

"Please, I won't run off no mo'," the slave begged as the whip sounded again. The slave screamed with each new slice the whip left on his back.

Ben's blood turned to ice as he watched the scene. Unable to stand by and do nothing, he nudged Midnight toward the abuser and the now unconscious Negro.

"He's had enough." Ben's voice was hard and rough as he fought to control his anger.

"You stay the hell out of this. Who do you think you are coming in here and telling me this here nigger's had enough? I say when he's had enough," the big man bellowed, raising the whip again.

"He's had enough." Ben's voice was deadly calm as he slid off Midnight's back. "I don't know what he's done, but no man deserves this kind of punishment."

The overseer dropped his arm to his side. "Listen here, mister, I'm in charge of these niggers. They're mine to do with as I see fit. This man run off, again. He's lucky he don't get strung up by the neck and hung, but Mr. Pruitt don't allow me to hang 'em. Just teach 'em a lesson they won't forget anytime soon."

"I don't give a damn about any of that."

The overseer raised the whip to strike at Ben. But Ben saw it and grabbed it from the overseer before it snaked toward him. With the whip he jerked the man to within an inch of his own face, then grabbed his neck.

"I want this man cut loose, taken to his cabin and his wounds tended. Now. Do you understand?"

Ben pushed the man backward and he stumbled before he gained his balance and stood upright. Grumbling, he walked toward the slave, then looked up at Ben.

"You'll pay for this, mister." He pulled out his knife, rolled it in his hand then glared at Ben with a challenge on his face. Ben tensed but stepped forward.

"Cut him down!"

"Who the hell do you think you are coming onto Mr. Pruitt's property and ordering me around?" the overseer shouted as the slave fell to the ground in a heap.

"I'm somebody who gives a damn about human life," Ben said. "Somebody who wouldn't treat an animal the way you've treated this man."

The overseer yelled to the other slaves to tend the man. Two reed-thin men came forward and wrapped the man in a shirt, their eyes dark with loathing, before the injured slave was carried to his cabin.

Ben looked back at the overseer, whose eyes held more hatred in them than Ben had ever seen before.

"You'll pay for this, mister. You can bet on it. I won't forget you or what you done."

His errand for Emma forgotten, Ben jumped back on Midnight, turned the horse around and raced away. His heart was as wild as the horse under him. Behind him the overseer bellowed orders for the last of the slaves to get back to their cabins.

Ben rode long and hard before he stopped to allow both he and Midnight to catch their breath. He'd been a fool. He'd believed if he turned his back and just ignored the issue of slavery, he wouldn't have to make a choice. But today had changed everything. He was sickened by what he'd seen and knew it was only one incident in many.

He continued at a slower pace and knew now he had crossed the line between right and wrong. A line that told him he couldn't just sit on the fence any longer and pretend slavery didn't exist.

He unsaddled Midnight and slammed into the house.

"My goodness. What are you doing here?" Sarah asked. "I thought you went to the Pruitt ranch for Emma? Ben, what's wrong?"

He stomped into the front room and sat down with a grunt beside the fire; the wooden chair creaked with his weight. He ran his fingers through his hair.

Sarah went to him. "What is it? What's wrong?"

He caught his breath and related what had happened.

"Dear God, I didn't know it was that bad."

But Ben knew how bad it really was, he just hadn't told Sarah and Emma to keep them from feeling the anxiety he felt. He was fully aware of the existence of the Jayhawkers, the anti-slavers. He had watched them stop the slave auction in town.

And what of the pro-slavers? He looked at Sarah's anxious face. Would the overseer hold true to his promise and some night visit Ben, Sarah and Emma to make good on his threat?

He ran his fingers through his dark hair. Sooner or later, he'd have to make a choice.

By early spring, the ranch had the appearance of a well-kept, well-run spread. A small herd of cattle, purchased by Emma with a bank loan, now roamed the property within new split-rail fences. Ben worked the herd alone and rode from morning till night.

Tonight was unusually warm while Ben rode the fence-line checking the fence and stock. He rocked in the saddle and whistled a soft tune as the moon's light filtered through a low-lying mist.

Gunfire split the silence and Ben sent Midnight racing toward the sound. He pulled the horse to a stop when he came upon a cow, thrashing and bleating in pain. The animal tried to stand, but its legs wobbled under its weight and it thudded to the ground. Ben jumped out of the saddle and knelt beside the flailing animal. He tried to calm it, with little effect. The cow thrashed and bellowed until it finally gave up and died.

That was when Ben saw the blood that oozed from a bullet wound in its neck.

He was trying to comprehend who would do such a thing when he heard a rifle click behind him. He whirled around and found himself face to face with two men on horseback with bandanas over their faces.

"Evening, Walters," the man holding the rifle drawled. "We heard some interesting tales about you taking up with the enemy," the man said, while the other murmured agreement.

"I don't know what you're talking about. What enemy? What do you men want?" Ben raised his arms to show he was unarmed.

"Listen to him. He acts like he don't know what we're talking about," the first rider scoffed. "We don't like Yankees, Walters, who stir up our slaves. We've held slaves in these parts for more years than you been around—or might be around—you interfere in our business again." Both men laughed.

"I don't hold with slavery, that's true, but I haven't run around the country stirring people up against it."

"No?" the rider who hadn't spoken yet asked. "What about that nigger at the Pruitt ranch?"

Ben recognized the overseer's voice and his breath caught.

"Damn it, that happened last winter. I'm not with you or against you. I don't hold with slavery, that's true, but I haven't gone on a crusade to stop it. I've tried to stay out of it."

"There is no stayin' out of it," the first rider hissed. "You're either with us or against us." He leaned forward in the saddle.

"It's your choice, Walters."

Ben was sure these men would kill him right here if he didn't give them the answer they wanted. But before he could say another word, another rifle cocked behind him and Sarah emerged from the trees at his back, her rifle aimed at the heart of the first rider who held his weapon on Ben.

"I suggest you men get off this land. Now!" she shouted. "Or I'll shoot you dead, right here. You'll be the first, mister," she said to the man threatening Ben. She handed Ben a handgun, who aimed it at the overseer.

"She means what she says, boys. She's a good shot and has killed before when given no choice."

The men shifted in their saddles.

"She'll do it. Take me at my word. And if she doesn't, I will." Ben shook his gun to remind them he was now armed.

The man lowered his rifle. The overseer did the same.

"You may have won this time around, Walters, but

you're damn sure gonna have to choose, and sooner than you think." The overseer jerked his horse around with the other man following, and the men thundered off the property.

"You're either with us or against us, Walters." Their voices echoed into the blackness of night. "With us or against us!"

## Chapter Twelve

The fire in the hearth blazed orange and blue and warmed the confines of Ben and Sarah's little cottage. From the chair beside the fire, Ben pulled out the newspaper he'd picked up earlier in town and groaned. Sarah looked up from her chair where she patched a pair of his trousers.

"What is it?"

"Here it is. Right here in black and white. Kansas has joined the Union as a free state."

"What, exactly, does that mean?" she asked.

"War." Ben's voice was flat. "I'm afraid that will be the only outcome. With the depth of feelings on the subject of slavery, I don't see any other solution. Since Lincoln was elected president, the South has gone secesh crazy. They shout that their states' rights are being violated, but what about the rights of the men and women they hold as slaves?" He continued to study the newspaper.

"I just pray to God that if it does come to war, it's quick," he added.

Sarah watched him and knew without question what he would do if it did come to war.

"You'll enlist, won't you?" Her throat felt tight, dry, like someone had dropped a load of sand into it. She twisted the needle in her hand as she awaited his response.

Ben looked deep into her eyes. "I've gone over that question a hundred, if not a thousand times in my mind, Sarah, and I keep coming up with the same answer. I have to. I can't just sit out a war and hope it doesn't touch us. I'm a soldier. It's my duty to fight to preserve this country."

"Oh, Ben," Sarah cried. "You've been doing your duty for years. Isn't it time to let someone else take their turn?"

Ben stared at her before he finally answered. "No, it isn't. For whatever reason, I'm a soldier and I want this Union preserved. Even without the issue of slavery, I'd fight to save this country. It's gone too far. Words aren't enough to stop the spread of hatred. Now only guns and bloodshed will finish it."

Silence filled the room for several minutes.

"Ben, I understand what you're saying." Sarah's voice cracked with her words. "I wish I could beg you not to go, but I won't. But promise you'll come back to me." She rolled the material she was mending in her hands. "I've lost you once already," she barely whispered, "I couldn't bear to lose you again."

Ben's eyes met hers. "I'll come back, Sarah. I promise."

It was mid-April several months later, when Ben slammed through the back door of the main house and into the kitchen.

"Ben? Didn't your momma teach you any manners?" Emma chastised over her shoulder. "That's no way to enter a house." She turned from the cook pot and stopped stirring.

"Whatever is wrong, Ben? You look like you've seen a ghost."

Sarah entered the room, following Ben's loud entrance. "What in tarnation is all the noise? Ben? What is it?"

"It's happened. After a two-day siege of Fort Sumter, Major Anderson surrendered to the Confederates. It's all right here." He slapped the front page of a newspaper with his hand. "The Confederates asked him to surrender the fort two days ago. But Anderson wouldn't and they opened fire." It's all here." He raised the paper in front of him again.

Sarah grabbed the paper and began to read. Emma dropped the wooden spoon into the pot and walked toward her.

"Read it out loud, dear," Emma said. "My eyes aren't what they used to be and I'll never see over your shoulder." Her hand came to rest on Sarah's back as the younger woman began to read.

### *ANDERSON SURRENDERS FORT SUMTER!*

*Following the dispatch by General Beauregard of Confederate Colonel James Chesnut (formerly a U.S. Senator); Colonel A.R. Chisolm (Governor Pickens' representative), and Captain*

## Tomorrow's Promise: Survival on the Plains        D.L. Rogers

*Stephen D. Lee, formerly of the United States Army, to request the surrender of Fort Sumter, and subsequent refusal by Major Anderson to do so, the sky around Charleston Harbor was lit with a full day of bombardment to finally force Major Anderson to surrender Fort Sumter to the newly formed Confederacy.*

Sarah's eyes widened with each word and the realization of what was happening gripped her. She dropped the paper to her lap.

"What happens now?" Her voice trembled and her hands began to shake.

"War. Lincoln has called for 75,000 volunteers."

"And?" She looked at Ben and knew.

"I leave in the morning."

Sarah drew a deep breath to keep her composure. How could it be happening all over again? Her world was spiraling out of control, and she could do nothing, absolutely nothing, to stop it. Ben was to be snatched away and taken into war where he could be killed and lost to her again. This time forever.

Tears formed in her eyes and she ran from the kitchen, leaving Ben and Emma to stare helplessly after her.

Again. It was happening all over again.

The sun rose bright and cheerful, unaware of the pain it brought with its arrival. Sarah rolled over and slid her hand across Ben's back.

As the sun rose, Sarah looked into the face of the man who slept beside her.

"Please come back to me," she whispered.

Ben's eyes opened. "I will. I promise." He grabbed her and kissed her full on the mouth before he worked her nightgown over her head. Gently, yet with a sense of urgency, they made love for the last time before he went to war.

Later that morning Sarah watched from the porch as Ben saddled a new horse Emma had given him, to leave Midnight for Sarah. The saddling finished, he strode up the stairs to where she stood.

"I'll come home, Sarah. I promise. President Lincoln is

sure this will be a quick war and I have to agree with him. The South doesn't have the weaponry or the men to last in a long war. The Southerners are peacocks, afraid to get dirty. We'll give them what-for and be home before you even realize I've gone."

She forced a smile and tried to believe his words. Tried to be brave. "I hope you're right, Ben. At least it's spring and I'll have plenty of work here to keep me busy. And there's Emma. She'll keep me strong."

Ben smiled and nodded. "I'll miss her. Where is she by the way?"

"She'll be right out. She said not to leave before she says goodbye."

"I wouldn't leave without saying goodbye. She should know that."

"Know what?" Emma emerged through the front door with a bulging white sack.

"Know that I wouldn't leave without saying goodbye to you." He reached out and drew her into his arms. "You're a wonderful lady, Emma, and you've given Sarah and I a lot to be thankful for. And a lot to hope for."

The older woman blushed. "You've been the son I lost so many years ago, dear Ben." She drew him closer. "And Sarah has become the daughter I never had. There's so much love in her heart. Come back to her," Sarah heard Emma whisper into his ear. She stepped back and dropped the sack into his hands.

"Here. Sarah and I baked some cookies for your journey. There's also chicken and cornbread, in case the trip is long." Tears glistened in her eyes. She brushed them away and hurried back into the house.

Ben watched Emma disappear through the door then turned to Sarah. He took her hand and bent to kiss her. It was a long, emotional kiss. One that would have to last for a very long time. "I love you, Ben Walters," Sarah managed through a tight throat. "Don't you ever forget it."

"I won't forget it. And don't you forget I love you."

He stepped back and without further words jumped off the porch and pulled himself onto his mount.

He whirled the horse around and sent the animal racing down the drive. He waved sadly as he rode down the drive and away.

"I love you, Ben." Sarah shouted, waving to his retreating form. Her tears flowed freely now. "Come back to me," she whispered. "Please come back to me."

## Chapter Thirteen

After eight days of hard riding, Ben reached the camp of General Nathaniel Lyon in eastern Missouri. He saluted the general as he entered the command tent. Lyon briskly returned the salute then tugged on his dark red beard. Ben sensed deep anger in the man as he paced back and forth, his hands rolling in and out of fists.

"Walters, I understand you served five years with the Dragoons under Harney." Ben attempted an answer, but Lyon waved his hand and continued abruptly. "I need seasoned officers, Walters. Men who have seen battle. Men who won't run away from a fight. Men who know what the hell to do when they find themselves looking down the barrel of the enemy's rifle." Lyon's voice had risen to a nagging bellow. He continued to pace and Ben remained silent. "Were you commissioned when you left the Dragoons?"

"No, sir. I left as a sergeant."

"A sergeant. hmmmm. As I said previously, I need seasoned men. Most of the men I command here are mere boys. Green and young. I need a man with experience to lead them. Might that man be you?"

Ben snapped to attention. "I'd do my best, sir."

"Very well. I have it in my power to promote you to lieutenant. Congratulations." Lyon saluted, stuck a cigar in his mouth and turned to his maps spread out on a table in front of him. "Dismissed."

Ben left the tent, his head spinning. It had happened so quickly. He was now an officer in the Union Army.

The following morning a private plodded his way through the rain-soaked ground to Ben's tent.

"Lieutenant Walters! Lieutenant Walters! General Lyon wants to see you, sir." He saluted Ben, huddled under his tarp in a futile attempt to keep the heavy rain from soaking everything he wore.

Ben returned the salute, adjusted his gun blanket against

the rain and trudged toward General Lyon's tent.

"Walters," Lyon's voice boomed when he entered, "I'm sending out a contingent of men, mostly the German Home Guard, to try and cut off the retreat of that renegade son-of-a-bitch Governor Jackson. I want you and your men among them." He strolled the confines of the cramped tent and pulled absentmindedly on his beard. "I plan to stop that traitor before he reaches the safety of Arkansas. If we stop the link up between Sterling Price and Jackson, we stand a better chance of defeating them."

"You'll move out at dawn. Report to Colonel Siegel." He saluted in dismissal.

Ben returned the salute and exited the tent. Excitement coursed through him as he searched for Colonel Siegel and his Home Guard, men of mostly German decent. He came upon the man watching his troops drill in the pouring rain. From one side of the muddy field to the other they marched. Back and forth, over and over again they raised their rifles, aimed and pretended to fire. They were quick and efficient, seemingly unhindered by the downpour.

"He drills them all day, every day," an awe-filled voice from beside Ben said. "They're the best."

Ben nodded his agreement then walked toward the colonel.

Ben's hand snapped to his forehead. "Lieutenant Walters reporting, sir."

Siegel saluted in return. "Come. I have been waiting to meet you." Ben studied the man who still carried a heavy German accent. A look of strength and confidence radiated from him.

"Our mission. You have been informed?" Siegel asked.

"Yes, sir, I have. We're to block Jackson's retreat into Arkansas and split his and Price's forces."

"Yah, Walters. For a short time you become part of the Home Guard. The best. We will hammer those Confederates into the ground. Teach them a lesson they won't soon forget!" He clapped Ben on the back.

"Yes, sir," Ben answered.

"We head south by rail to Rolla then move toward Springfield on foot. We leave at first light tomorrow. That is all." Ben saluted and Siegel snapped one in return before he went back to watching his men drill.

Every day following Ben's departure Sarah had to force herself out of bed. She replaced her cumbersome dresses with Ben's trousers and shirts and bound her hair tightly to her head. She pulled on riding boots and donned one of Ben's old hats and rode the property day and night, as Ben had done.

Emma often chastised her for working so hard, but Sarah wouldn't be deterred.

"Ben and I have a stake in this ranch, too, Emma, and we're going to make it work. I can ride as well as any man and I've a strong back. I'll be all right, you'll see."

She fell into a blissfully busy routine that kept her mind so occupied, she didn't have time to think about missing Ben or the turmoil tearing the country apart.

From a hill, Sarah surveyed the vast land around her. As far as she could see there was tall, swaying grass, bountiful trees filled with chirping birds, and below, the brook that ran through the southern section of the ranch. Someday, she and Ben would have a place like this; just large enough for them to take care of, but big enough for them to spread their roots.

Although it was toward the end of June, the oppressive heat had subsided slightly. Midnight, tethered to a tree five feet away, lifted his head and snorted. He swished his tail and swung his head back and forth to dislodge a multitude of flies that had gathered on his neck and hindquarters.

"Isn't it lovely, Midnight?" Sarah asked. As she surveyed the beauty around her, she thought of Ben. She'd received only one letter since he left. He was with Nathaniel Lyon's troops and had been promoted to Lieutenant, but more than that, she didn't know. She assumed he didn't have time to write because he was kept too busy.

Gunfire to the north shattered her musing.

She ran to Midnight and pulled herself into the saddle. She picked her way through the trees and brush then swung the black in the direction of the shot. When she reached the edge of a small clearing beside a grove of trees, she reined Midnight to an abrupt stop, able only to stare at what she saw.

"Let's string him up." A short, stocky white man gave the order.

"No!" the taller man argued. "We get more for him alive than dead."

Sarah stared at the black man being held up between the two men. His eyes were swollen nearly shut and blood flowed from several long cuts on his arms and face. Spittle oozed from his lips. He was tall, yet reed-thin, his eyes full of pain and dread.

"Please. Don't bring me back. Just kill me here," he begged. "Please..." His voice trailed off when a rifle butt slammed into his stomach and he doubled over.

"Shut up! Don't you be tellin' me what to do, Boy," the tall man said, the word *boy* drawled like a dirty word.

Sarah reached into her saddlebag and pulled out the handgun, then tugged gently on Midnight's reins so the horse would back up. She held her breath as he picked his way back into the cover of trees. Just as Sarah thought she would be clear to turn and run, the horse stepped on a fallen branch. It cracked like a gun blast and alerted the two men hovering over the now unconscious salve.

They jerked upright and grabbed for their guns.

"I wouldn't do that." Sarah's voice was deep. She pulled the brim of her hat low over her face, raised the gun and clucked Midnight forward. In Ben's baggy shirt and pants, she prayed the men wouldn't realize she was a woman.

The men put their hands in the air.

Midnight stopped twenty feet from the men. "Get off this property," she growled, her voice as low as she could make it. "And leave him." She gestured toward the unconscious man.

"But mister," the tall man protested. "We been chasing this buck for three days. It's a powerful lot of money you're asking us to walk away from if we don't bring him back to his master."

"I don't give a damn about any of that. Get off this

property. Now." She swung the handgun away from the ranch.

The short man started to back away, but Sarah noticed his hand moving toward the back of his belt. His hand snapped down then out with a gun.

She fired.

The man dropped to his knees, a surprised look on his face before he fell to the ground. The other man stared for only a moment before he turned and jumped onto his horse.

"You'll pay for this, mister. Mark my words, you'll pay!" He threw himself into the saddle, dug his heels into the horse's belly and galloped away.

Stunned, Sarah let him ride away. Her heart pounded like a mallet then skipped several beats when she looked down at the still form on the ground. She had killed again, but this time to save herself. Again, she had had no choice. Shaking now, she glanced at the unconscious Negro. His hands and feet were bound together.

She nudged Midnight toward him. His eyes were closed and he looked dead. She dismounted and walked closer.

His eyes flew open and he tried to crawl away. "Please, please don't hurt me no more. And don' take me back to da masser," he pleaded.

Sarah stepped closer and squatted beside him. "You poor man."

His face took on a look of puzzlement. He stared at Sarah then looked around.

"Where them two slave catchers?"

"They won't bother you again." She took a deep breath. "One's dead and the other rode off."

"Dead?" He asked, incredulous. "One is dead? How?"

"I shot him." She leaned to untie the cords that bound him.

"You, miss?" he asked in disbelief. "You? They was real bad men, how you shoot one dead?"

"I just pulled the trigger and he's dead. Now we need to get you away from here and back to the house where we can dress these wounds."

He tried to scramble away again. "Where you gonna take

me, miss?" Fear was strong in his voice. "You ain't gonna send me back, are you?"

"No," she answered quickly. She thought of Emma. What would that dear old woman say when Sarah appeared at the ranch with a runaway slave? Oh well, she'd find out soon enough. She would not send this poor creature back to his former master.

"What you gonna do with me then, miss?"

Sarah looked at the man in front of her. He was tall and rail thin, but looked as though he could hold a fair amount of weight on him if he were fed properly. He carried the scars of previous beatings on his arms and legs and his eyes were filled with haunting pain. And hope. She couldn't turn him away; she knew that. He was a man and deserved his freedom.

"It may take a bit of doing on my part, but I'm sure Miss Emma will let you stay at the ranch. You can wait in the bunkhouse while I smooth things over with her."

"Miss Emma?"

"The widow who owns this place. She's a fine, understanding lady. I'm sure she'll agree you should stay."

Sarah watched the man relax. His head lifted in strength. She sensed pride, regardless of the beatings and uncivilized way he'd been forced to live. Sadness filled her. She'd grown up without slavery. Any help her father kept was paid wages. But she was aware, too, that a large percentage of slave owners were not cruel to their slaves. She knew most slaves in the south were well taken care of, were almost considered a part of the family. They lived with their families most of their lives and many even helped raise the master's children. There were only the few that abused their slaves. But it was those few that made Sarah's stomach turn.

She looked back to the man who was watching her closely, waiting to learn his fate.

"In return for our taking you in, you can help around the ranch." Sarah hoped her offer would convince the man to let her help him. "Emma is old, and care of this ranch has fallen to me, so we both have something to gain if you stay. But you'll have to stay out of sight. What I'm doing could get us all killed."

He sat wide-eyed, massaging his bruised wrists.

"I know that, miss. Thank you, miss. Thank you. I swear I'll work hard for you. Just say the word and I'll do it for you. Just don' send me back."

Sarah smiled and nodded. She looked toward the dead man lying in the pasture. "Once you're all patched up, your first duty will be to bury him."

"Yes, ma'am. First thing," he agreed. His smile showed no regret the other was dead.

With great difficulty, Sarah helped get him onto Midnight and led the horse and rider toward the ranch. They walked in silence for several minutes before she asked his name.

"Caleb, miss. My name's Caleb." He winced from the pain in his lip when he spoke.

"Well, Caleb, I'm Sarah Walters."

"And Mr. Walters? What he gonna say about you bringing me back to your ranch?"

"Mr. Walters isn't here. He's with Nathaniel Lyon's troops."

Caleb tensed again. "Which army is that?"

"The Federals, Caleb. You have nothing to fear."

When they reached the bunkhouse and with more difficulty, Sarah got Caleb inside.

Once he was settled on a lower bunk, she asked, "Why were those men beating you so badly, Caleb? Was it only because you ran away?"

"Yes, Miz Sarah, I run away. I couldn't stand bein' beat no more. The masser works us like dogs an' treats us worse. I couldn't take it no more." He averted his eyes from her sorrowful gaze.

"And those men?"

"They was slave catchers. They work for whoever pays them to find us. They enjoys their work. They hunt us down and beat us before they bring us back to our owners so they can beat us again. Lots of times the whippings kill the weaker ones," he added, his eyes distant.

Immense shame gripped Sarah.

"It's time I let Emma know you're here," she said to

change the mood. "You stay here, I'll be back in a few minutes with some food and linens to dress your wounds."

She saw worry creep back into Caleb's eyes.

"Don't worry, Caleb. She may protest, loudly at first, but I know she'll see the rightness of letting you stay. It'll be fine, I promise."

Caleb nodded then lay down on the tattered cot and closed his eyes.

Sarah left the bunkhouse and walked toward the house, rehearsing over and over what she would say to Emma. She was talking to herself when she ran smack into the woman on the porch.

"Humph!" Emma clucked. "Sarah? What are you doing? And what on earth are you mumbling about, child?"

"Emma. You startled me." Sarah's heart was in her throat.

"You're as jumpy as a bride on her wedding night. What's got into you?"

Sarah took Emma's hand and led her to the porch swing. "Sit down, Emma. We have to talk."

Emma sat, her face full of concern, and waited for Sarah to begin. Sarah paced nervously as she searched for the right words until Emma shouted, "Spit it out, girl! The faster the better. Just do it. I could drop dead by the time you find the right words." Her voice was firm but held a hint of laughter.

Sarah couldn't contain her smile. "You are a kind woman, you know."

"Yes...?" Emma drawled and cocked her head.

She took Emma's hand. "Emma, I killed a man today. Shot him dead."

Emma's hand jerked out of Sarah's and went to her cheek. "Good Lord, child. I heard gunshots earlier, but I never imagined..."

Sarah's chest rose with the deep breath she took. Now or never, she thought, and plunged ahead.

"He was a slave catcher, Emma. An evil man who would have killed me if I hadn't killed him first."

"On my land? A slave catcher? Here? On my property?"

## Tomorrow's Promise: Survival on the Plains    D.L. Rogers

Emma nearly came out of her seat. "Why would a slave catcher be here? I don't hold any slaves." Her gnarled hands shook and she looked at Sarah for an explanation.

"They had chased down a runaway and beaten him half to death, Emma."

"Oh dear, oh dear," Emma muttered.

"But there's more."

"This is going to get worse, isn't it?" Emma whispered. She looked at Sarah, then at her hands whose knuckles were white they were twisted so tight in front of her. She took a deep breath. "What else?"

"I heard a gunshot so I went to see where it came from. I couldn't believe what I found. Two men were beating a slave senseless. He was bleeding and almost unconscious. I didn't intend for them to see me, but they did." She spoke quickly now to get the words out. She felt her face drain of blood when she looked at Emma's frightened expression, but forced herself to continue.

"Midnight stepped on a tree branch and it snapped so loud it alerted them that I was there. I disguised my voice like a man and hoped that, in Ben's baggy clothing with my hat pulled low, they wouldn't know I was a woman. I told them to get off the property and leave the slave. One man went for his gun. I knew he would have killed me, so I shot him." Her heart was pounding when she stopped talking."

"And...?" Emma's voice prodded? "Finish it."

"The man is dead and...the runaway is here."

Emma sat in stunned silence. Sarah waited.

"A slave, here," Emma finally mumbled. She twisted her handkerchief tighter in her hands. "A runaway, no less. My poor Jonathan would turn over in his grave. He didn't hold with owning slaves, but I'm sure if he had a chance, he'd help one if he could. Dear Lord, what is this world coming to?" she asked, weary. She sat in silence a few moments before she slapped her knees and stood up. "Come, show me this poor soul you've rescued."

The women went to the bunkhouse. Caleb had given in to his wounds and was asleep. Emma walked to the man and touched his forehead.

"He's still alive, but not for long. He's burning up and, if we don't tend to those lacerations soon, they'll become infected and he won't make it."

"Yes, ma'am," Sarah said. Great respect for the older woman flooded her. She knew what risk Emma would take by allowing a runaway slave to stay on her property.

Emma's words, "Go on, child, be quick," snapped Sarah back to the task at hand.

Sarah hurried to the house and gathered food, clothes and medicine. When she returned to the bunkhouse, Emma was watching over the slumbering man.

"I'll take over now," Sarah whispered.

At that moment, they heard the rumble of a wagon as it entered the drive. Both women paled with the thought of discovery.

"Be calm, Sarah. We'll go see who it is together," Emma said quietly.

A buggy stopped at the end of the drive when the two emerged from the bunkhouse.

"Mornin' ladies." A balding, graying man tipped his hat. Sarah and Emma greeted him and waited for him to state his business.

"I'm lookin' for Mrs. Emma Carter. Would either of you be her?" he asked.

Emma stepped forward. "I'm Mrs. Carter."

"Doc Hansen sent me to fetch you, ma'am. It appears your sister, Hattie, has taken sick and is in need of your assistance."

Emma's face went white with fear. "Hattie? Ill?"

Sarah stepped forward and rested her hand on Emma's shoulder. "You go. I'll stay here and watch over the ranch."

Emma whirled on the younger woman and pulled her out of hearing distance of the driver.

"Sarah, we don't know what kind of man that slave is or what he might do when he recovers from his wounds. I can't leave you here alone."

"Emma, I have a good feeling about him. I've looked

145

into his eyes and I don't believe he'd hurt me. I saved his life." Sarah turned Emma toward the house. "You're needed by your sister. I'll watch over things here. Pack and go to her, I'll be fine. I promise."

Emma cocked her head. "You're sure?"

"Yes, Emma. Go. Be with Hattie."

It took little prodding to convince Emma to accompany the driver back into town.

After she'd packed a few necessary items in a carpet satchel, Emma climbed into the buggy beside the driver. She turned for a last, unsure look at Sarah, who closed her eyes and nodded for her to go.

A whip snapped, the buggy lurched forward and in minutes Emma was gone. Sarah walked back toward the bunkhouse. A twinge of fear gnawed at her spine. She was alone. Again.

Sarah had just laid a cool, damp cloth on Caleb's forehead when his eyes opened.

"Welcome back," Sarah said from her perch on the stool beside him.

"Miz Sarah," he croaked. "The missus. What she say? Can I stay?"

"Yes, Caleb, you may stay. I told you, she's a fine lady."

"Yes, ma'am," he agreed and closed his eyes again. When they opened again a moment later, they were filled with gratitude.

"Don't you worry, Miz Sarah, I won't forget what you done. No, sir. You ain't like them others. You is a good person, I see that by what you done for me, and I'm beholding to you. I won't forget. Ever, Miz Sarah. And don't you worry, I'll protect you from now on. You won't never have to worry about killing no man again while the mister is gone. I'll take care of you."

Sarah smiled and nodded. God how she wished she'd seen the last of the violence. Hoped she'd seen the last of the remaining slave catcher. But no matter how much she hoped, a shiver ran up her spine when she recalled his promise as he'd ridden away. He'd be back, and they'd better be ready.

She knew in her heart today was just the beginning.

### *Tomorrow's Promise: Survival on the Plains*     *D.L. Rogers*

They'd only survived the first battle.

## Chapter Fourteen

Ben was snapped awake by the movement of the train that rumbled toward Rolla, but his heavy eyelids closed quickly and he was once again in a dream-filled sleep. Although out of the rain and warm for the first time in days, he shivered.

He was on the farm on which he grew up. It was a small spread by most standards, but it was his kingdom and all his subjects lived together in harmony. The horses, the cows, the pigs and chickens all bowed to his wishes. He had been king of that little kingdom, well, perhaps only a prince, for his mother and father ruled with an iron hand. His father's stern, yet kind face flashed to the fore of his mind. A strong man with huge hands and the strength of two men, he pulled little Ben into his arms then swung him up over his head and onto his shoulders. Ben laughed with glee and held tight to his father's forehead until the sturdy shoulders suddenly became soft and slumped under him. The earth spiraled toward him and Ben was tossed to the ground. He found himself staring at the shell of the man he had once known as his father, now pale and thin with the sickness that ate away at him. His large hands were now bony and gnarled and limp hair fell across his drawn, ashen face—a face contorted with pain.

"Papa!" little Ben yelled as tears streamed down his face. Another set of hands, small, sun-darkened and rough from hard work, took Ben's hand and led him away. For what seemed like forever, he watched his mother's tenderness as she nursed his father. She fed him, bathed him, read to him, but still he continued to wither away, and with him the strong, vibrant woman who was Ben's mother. She didn't eat and didn't sleep as she cared for her husband.

He wondered how she had the strength and why she kept taking care of his father, even though he continued to fail, until one night the curiosity of youth got the better of him and he asked her, "Why do you do it, Mother?"

"Because it's my duty," she said. She paused in thought,

then added, "And because I love him," before she turned back to tend his father.

He woke with a start, his mind in a whirl, the word *duty* bouncing around in his brain. Duty had eventually killed his mother, who sat beside his father until the day he died, then followed him in death not six months later. He thought about the war and what was happening around him. That same sense of duty had made him join the fight. Would that same sense of duty get him killed? He pushed the thoughts from his mind and looked out the window. He watched the hills and valleys fall away outside and he tried not to think anymore.

Hours later, the train rolled to a stop in Rolla. Ben grabbed his gear, forced himself from his seat and followed the other men out of the train car.

"Lieutenant Walters?"

Ben nodded and a clerk handed him a packet. He opened the envelope and read the contents.

"We're to start the one hundred and twenty mile trek to Springfield," Ben informed his men several minutes later. "Gather your gear and be ready to move out in one hour."

A week later, sore and desperately tired, they reached Springfield, Missouri, the first leg of their trip toward the Arkansas border.

After a day's rest, Colonel Siegel's troops, inclusive of the Home Guard and Ben's men, started toward the Arkansas border to check troop strengths and search for Governor Jackson's army. Near Carthage, Siegel sent several civilian-clothed officers into town to gather any information they could about the elusive Confederates.

Ben was in the command tent with Siegel when the officers returned, highly agitated with the news they carried. They reported that Governor Jackson's forces were encamped by a little farm just ten miles outside of Carthage.

They were close. So very close. There was a long, heated discussion between officers. And although they were outnumbered, the decision was made to engage the enemy in the morning.

After a night of little sleep, Ben set out with his and

Siegel's troops to meet Governor Jackson's forces. Anticipation and excitement raced through him. Today he would meet the enemy. Today he would fight for what he believed in. Would he see tomorrow?

Ben and the other soldiers reached the edge of a stand of trees and looked up at the top of a hill at the men that lined its ridge. Those men looked just like the men he rode with. But they were the enemy. They weren't clad in buckskin or have feathers in their hair. They read the Bible, had wives and families just like he did. He watched as Siegel's seven cannons were put into place, and waited. A cold chill swept through him when in unison, the guns opened fire on the line of Confederates across from him. There were shrieks of pain as the artillery fire shattered men and horses in its path.

Ben could only watch in silence. The war, for him, had begun.

Artillery pounded back and forth for two hours, but with no results. The order was given to march forward. Siegel's troops advanced on the Confederates and fired steadily as they went.

Ben's heart raced and his palms sweat as he fired and reloaded his carbine with expert swiftness. His arms grew weary and heavy like fence posts, but still he loaded and fired. His life depended on it. Ahead of him he could see the Confederate lines starting to buckle. On he went. Bullets buzzed and whizzed around him. Sweat poured off his brow. Beside him he heard a strangled cry. He turned and saw the frightened eyes of a young boy clutching his throat as blood poured through his splayed fingers and down his neck. Ben grabbed the boy just as he fell. He lowered him gently to the ground. His eyes were wild with fear and the strangled cry in the boy's throat brought bile to Ben's own.

"Shhh," Ben whispered. "Don't try to talk."

The boy tore at Ben's coat, ripped and grabbed at the sleeve.

"I...I'm..." The boy's voice broke off in a gurgled sob before his eyes closed and his hands went limp on Ben's arms.

Ben laid the boy on the ground and placed his arms across his body. A frigid wave washed over him as he looked down at the boy, although it was already hot under the July sun.

The thunder of hooves drew his attention. What little Confederate cavalry there was burst out in front of him in a flurry of horses and men. They were everywhere, closing in on all sides. Then just as quickly they disappeared into the woods across the field of battle. In the distance he heard the call for retreat.

"Pull back!" he yelled to his men. One at a time, he watched the cannon move back giving cover fire as the men retreated back toward Carthage.

Ben slowly worked his way from the field of battle. What he had seen and heard today sickened him. And it had only been a skirmish. But the dying boy's face would be seared into his memory forever.

The war had truly begun and he had an ominous foreboding it wouldn't be as short-lived as everyone believed.

Later that month after Siegel's troops had rejoined the main body of Lyon's forces, Ben tried to rest. They were headed back to Springfield and camped for the night.

Ben rolled over and was about to doze off when he heard a horse and rider thunder into camp. His rest forgotten with his curiosity, he watched the boy in the blue Federal uniform lean over the neck of his horse and ask one of the soldiers where General Lyon could be found. The man pointed. The young man jumped off his mount and headed in the direction of the command tent. Ben watched and listened as the boy hurried to find General Lyon.

"General. General, Lyon, sir!" The young soldier snapped to attention when Lyon stepped outside the command tent.

"What is it, soldier?" Lyon replied gruffly.

"I have word, sir. About Bull Run."

"Continue," Lyon drawled, his attention captured.

"It appears, sir, Beauregard and McDowell met at Bull Run Creek in Manassas, Virginia. Intelligence reports the Rebs sent our troops fleeing. The harder we hit them, the more they came on. They're calling the Reb General Thomas Jackson "Stonewall" because of the way he stood like a stone wall against the Union forces." The soldier stopped and took a breath. Ben watched Lyon's face grow hard and red with anger.

"Any word as to who finally took the day?" Lyon asked.

"Word has it those Rebs sent our boys to scurrying, sir." The boy shuffled nervously from foot to foot while he twisted his hat in his hands. "They're giving the day to the Rebs, General."

"Damn!" Lyon howled. "Goddamn it!" He rushed into his tent shouting commands.

"Corporal, I want a list of all men whose ninety day enlistments expire soon. I need to know how many men with experience I'm going to lose when their enlistment ends."

Ben grew tense. He knew one name that would be on that list. His.

Twenty minutes later, Ben was summoned by General Lyon.

"Walters, I understand your ninety days are up soon."

"Yes, sir. That's correct."

"I'll get right to the point, Walters. I need seasoned men, just like I did early on. I need men who've seen battle before. Good men, like yourself. Looks like this damnable war won't be as quick as we all thought it would." He paused and gave Ben time to absorb his words before he continued. "I need for you to remain with the troops until we've met the enemy I seek. I need you to give the men encouragement and direction. And leadership." He looked directly into Ben's face. "Don't desert our cause when the battle looms so close."

For an instant Ben thought of home and of Sarah. He looked at Lyon who watched him expectantly. He knew Lyon was right. He was a soldier and they were at war. It was his duty. His sworn duty. He had to stay.

Ben pulled his back up straight and saluted the man in front of him. "Yes, sir. I believe you're correct. I'll stay until the battle has been won."

Lyon's face relaxed and he clapped Ben on the shoulder.

## Tomorrow's Promise: Survival on the Plains     D.L. Rogers

"You've made the right decision, soldier. I knew I could count on you." He pulled on his red beard and nodded his head as if pleased with the results of his and Ben's talk. "Dismissed, Lieutenant." He returned Ben's salute before Ben exited the tent.

Ben's mind swam. He'd agreed so easily to stay. But he had to. He was a soldier. Duty demanded it. But how the hell was Sarah going to take it?

*My dearest Sarah,*

*I hope this letter finds you well. How is Emma? As ornery as ever? I expect she keeps you busy enough to keep you from worrying. I can only hope.*

*I write today with bad news, Sarah. General Lyon came to me personally and requested I remain in his service until Price and Jackson are caught. He's in desperate need of seasoned men, officers who are willing to lead. I'm afraid it didn't take much to convince me I must stay. Perhaps it is from some deep desire to prove myself to your father. He has such little regard for me; perhaps I must show him I am worthy of his daughter's love.*

*I struggle within myself, knowing it's my damnable duty to stay, but I long to be with you. Every day I envision your face, your smile and eyes and my heart swells with love. I don't know how much longer I will be needed, but know that I think of you every day I'm here.*

*I must go. Don't worry over me. I'll be home as soon as possible. And I will come home. Remember that, Sarah.*
*All my love,*
*Ben*

Lyon and his men were camped outside Springfield to await further orders, as well as to allow the men to recuperate from a bout of diarrhea and vomiting caused by their constant diet of beef and more beef.

Several days later Ben learned Lyon's troops would move to intercept Price in a surprise attack. In camp, Ben prepared to again meet the Confederates in battle. His mind lingered on thoughts of home—the knowledge deep down that he should be there. His ninety-day enlistment was, in reality, over. But he was an officer now and had a responsibility to his men. Mostly young green men that he had to try and mold into battle-smart soldiers.

He thought of Sarah. Of her smooth skin and long, silky hair. He remembered the scent of lilacs she carried after her bath, the smell lingering on her skin and hair. He envisioned her beside him, working as hard as he, to rebuild the ranch that might soon give them the chance to have a place of their own. He thought of Emma and smiled at the memory of her strong character and loving ways. God, he missed them both terribly.

Lyon appeared to address the men and pulled Ben from his reverie.

"I want you men to hold your fire until your target is close. Aim low and above all, do not be frightened!" His voice rose as he continued. "It is no part of a soldier's duty to get scared."

Ben looked at the young faces around him. Scared faces.

Following Lyon's address, Ben and his men finished packing their gear and began the march toward Wilson's Creek, a deep, gnawing fear in the pit of Ben's belly.

Near midnight, it began to rain. By the time Ben and his men reached the outskirts of the creek, saddle-weary and anxious to rest, the rain came down hard enough to limit visibility. From the crest of a hill, Ben looked out over dismal Wilson's Creek. Tall hills rose up and ravines cut sharply between them. The small area below was covered with heavy croppings of bushes and scrub oaks.

It was desolate, uninviting and eerie as the rain pelted the earth and fog crept over the creek and up the hills. But he and his men made themselves as comfortable as they could. In less than five hours, the order would come to attack. Ben pulled his hat down over his face to ward off the soaking rain and tried to remember what it felt like to be dry.

And he waited.

Cannon fire exploded at dawn. Ben and his men marched with Lyon's forces toward Bloody Hill and the Confederates led by Colonel James Cawthorn. Rifles and muskets smoked with each round they fired.

# Tomorrow's Promise: Survival on the Plains       D.L. Rogers

"Push them back!" he commanded. "Push them back!"

They advanced; they moved back. They fired into the brush not three hundred yards ahead of him but were met by constant fire that drove them back to the cover of bushes they'd just come from. For hours the battle raged as both factions surged forward, only to be pushed back again minutes later, the gunfire so close you could almost reach out and touch the man shooting at you.

Ben was on the ground on his stomach. He hadn't advanced in hours. He was exhausted. If only he could have slept last night. But he'd been too wound up, knowing he'd fight for his life today. Another round of gunfire shook him from his thoughts.

He rose up on his elbow, shouted the order to charge, then forced himself up ahead of his men. A barrage of bullets flew. Pain exploded in Ben's left arm and drove him to the ground on his belly. He tried to grab at it, tried to stop the burn. His hand came away red with blood. Men shrieked all around him as bullets stopped with a dull thud in someone's body. He rolled onto his back and tried to see how bad he was hit. His head reeled from the pain.

A man bent over him to check his arm. Another burst of rifle fire came from the trees.

"I don't think it's too bad," the man said. "Looks like it just got the..." The man jerked, his voice trailed off and his eyes glazed over.

"Harris. Harris!" The man fell over on top of Ben. More blood soaked Ben's shirt and Harris' weight pinned him to the ground. Too much weight for him to move in his weakened state. His wound burned like a hundred fires. He was dizzy and cold, losing strength as blood drained from his body. Cannon and gunfire continued to explode all around him. Sounds became muffled. Voices ran together and the sky turned black.

Unaware how long it had been, Ben forced himself back to consciousness. He was still pinned under Harris' lifeless body. There was movement beside him and he called out for help.

A heavy-set man pulled Harris off him. Ben sucked in a deep breath and filled his lungs. The burly man swung Ben's right arm over his shoulder and helped him back to the safety of their own lines. There Ben slumped to the ground in front of a tree, pulled off his neckerchief and wrapped it around his arm to stop the flow of blood from the hole where the bullet had passed through the meat of his upper arm. Using his right hand and teeth, he pulled it tight. He knew medical attention was many hours away.

Ben watched the two sides continue to battle. Back and forth they went without gaining or losing anything more than a tiny strip of ugly land. They'd been fighting for nearly five hours and he could see the exhaustion on both sides. The Union lines were beginning to buckle. General Lyon ran on foot from one end of the line to the other. He raised his saber and shouted orders and encouragement to the men. Ben marveled at the strength of will of the man.

He was admiring that strength when a bullet grazed Lyon on the side of his head. Another struck his leg.

Ben sat slowly upright and stared at Lyon. His arm screamed in pain. The general stopped his forward motion, momentarily stunned, then walked on, his sword still waving in the air. Ben breathed again, but saw blood ooze from the side of Lyon's head when he turned and limped in Ben's direction. Pale, shaky and dazed, Lyon dropped down beside him.

"The day is lost," Lyon muttered. He sat for a moment before he forced himself up again to rally his troops along the battle lines.

Ben gaped at the wounded man. Although his arm hurt mercilessly, he grabbed his carbine and scrambled toward the front lines. If Lyon could keep going with a head and leg wound, so could he.

It was a ghastly scene. Dead men from both sides were strewn so deep a path had to be cleared to move the cannon. The sight almost made Ben physically sick. Instead he drew and fired.

"Come on!" he yelled, each time he awkwardly reloaded. "Come on!" Sweat poured off his head and chest, his clothes were soaked, but still he kept on.

He suddenly heard Lyon's voice boom behind him. Ben

turned just as a bullet slammed into Lyon's chest with such force he was thrown from his horse and lay still where he landed.

Ben slumped to the ground as men raced to pull Lyon behind the lines. A feeling of defeat enveloped him.

Men scrambled all around. Mass confusion broke out within the ranks. Someone called a full retreat. The men hurried back behind the lines. That was the end. Lyon was dead, and with him gone the battle was lost. He was their rallying force and without him, the men had no encouragement to continue the fight they knew was already over.

Ben turned for one last look at the field of battle. His heart ached for the dead men strewn one on top of the other across the land.

Across the battlefield, his eyes met those of the men he had fought. They breathed as heavily as he did and looked as ragged and exhausted. But they smiled. Some even waved goodbye.

He caught up with his own troops, their retreat watched by the exhausted Confederates, who gladly let them go.

## Chapter Fifteen

"Dear child, I do wish you'd change your mind and come to Hattie's with me. My sister's home will accommodate both of us. Won't you reconsider?" Emma begged Sarah from beside her on the porch swing.

Sarah touched the old woman's arm. "I can't go into town, Emma. There's a great deal of work to be done here. What would happen to the ranch if we both left?" Sarah asked. "We've all put too much time and effort into rebuilding to let it go again."

"But..."

"I'm staying and that's final." Sarah shook her head. "I can take care of myself." Sarah stopped and reflected back to her run-in with the slave catchers. A ripple ran along her spine. She had been lucky that day, but what if the other man returned as he'd promised? She forced the thought from her mind.

"Caleb is here. Besides, I have to be where Ben can find me when he comes back." She sighed as she remembered the letter she'd received telling her his enlistment would last longer than the original ninety days.

"I've got to go. The driver is getting fidgety. Make sure you keep Caleb out of sight and for goodness sake, take care of yourself."

"Yes, ma'am," Sarah managed, her throat in a knot. "I'll miss you, Emma, like I've missed my own mother for so many years." Their tears flowed freely now and neither Sarah nor Emma made any attempt to brush them away. "I love you, Emma."

"I love you, too, child."

The two embraced and held on for several moments before the driver cleared his throat. "We'd better git, Miss Emma. We don't want to be on the road after dark. No telling what no accounts might be on the road these days after the sun goes down."

Emma pulled away snuffling and rushed to the buggy. She settled herself on the seat beside the driver and waved for him to proceed. In minutes they were down the tree-lined drive and out of sight.

Sarah watched them disappear and tried to heed Emma's words. But no matter how hard she tried she couldn't put aside her worries about Ben. She thought of him constantly. His was the first face she saw in the morning and the last she envisioned at night.

She heaved a heavy sigh and turned back to the house. Day by day. That was how she lived her life now, just as she had with the Indians. Only now instead of escape she wished for Ben's return.

The Fall day was gloriously sunny when Sarah and Caleb saddled up for their morning ride of the perimeter. Sarah shoved the Colt handgun and canteen into her saddlebag before she mounted. Caleb slid a pistol into his belt and mounted.

"It's going to be another hot one." Sarah groaned, and with a kerchief wiped the dampness already accumulating on her neck.

"Yes, ma'am. It sure is," Caleb agreed, already wet with sweat, too. "We need to ride quick and hope there's no fence down this morning."

Sarah smiled and nodded at the man who had become a dear and trusted friend, as well as laborer and protector. She was grateful to have him with her while Ben and Emma were gone.

She pulled her hat down over her golden hair, woven tightly at the back of her neck. She always wore it like that these days, propriety out the window with comfort now her only concern.

At the north section of the ranch, several lines of fence were down.

"Damn!" Sarah cursed. Caleb looked up at her, his face tight with disapproval.

"Oh, Caleb. Don't be such an old priss," she chastised. She dismounted and walked toward the torn fence. Caleb chuckled behind her.

The morning sun had risen high and full and the two were soaked, the droplets on Caleb's brow as big as bullets. He stopped pounding and stood up then wiped his forehead with the back of his gloved hand and peered off into the distance.

"What is it, Caleb?" Sarah shaded her eyes and followed his gaze.

"Don't know, Miz Sarah. See them horses? See how they keep looking over there in them trees? And their noses are flared? It's probably just an animal. No need to worry." He replaced his hat and returned to his work.

Sarah went back to her own hammering and barely heard the shot over the pounding. She swung around—and screamed. Caleb was face down on the ground, a red stain of blood on his side.

"Caleb!" She ran to him. His eyes were closed. But he was still breathing, although with great difficulty. She looked around, trying to find the gunman. Leaves and branches crunched in the distance before he emerged on horseback from the woods. He was stout with a full beard and his hat was pulled low over his eyes, but Sarah knew that form. She'd seen it before.

Instinctively, she ran toward Midnight and the Colt hidden in the saddlebag. She fumbled wildly at the ties and was just about to pull open the flap when the rider descended on her.

He jumped out of his saddle and whirled her around to face him. His eyes went wide with surprise when her hat fell off and he got a look at her face.

"Well I'll be a son-of-a-bitch," he hooted. "A woman. A damn flesh and blood woman!" He stared at her face and touched her cheek. Sarah tried to jerk away. "Well, well, well. I've done a powerful lot of thinking about what I was gonna do to you when I came back, but I never dreamed you was a woman. Or of all the fun I can have with you now...before I kill you," he drawled. His eyes sparkled with hate. "You cost me my partner and a lot of money. And now I'm back to collect. I'll bring that buck back to his master, too. Dead or alive, I don't rightly care, but I'll take him back just the same. But you, now you're another matter."

His eyes glinted in the sunlight and caused a cold chill to race down Sarah's sweat-soaked body.

"When you was just a man, I dreamed of how I was gonna kill you. Slow. Painful. But now..." His eyes gleamed with the prospects as he stroked his bearded chin.

Sarah seized the opportunity and kicked him in the groin. He doubled over, yelling obscenities as she ran. She ran as fast as she could. But the man was quick, regardless of his size and the pain he was in. He was on her in a matter of seconds. His huge hands dragged her down to the ground in a heap.

He jerked her up like a rag doll. She summoned every ounce of inner strength she possessed and punched him square in the face. He howled in pain and anger when his nose spurted blood. His grip relaxed long enough for her to break free again and she raced toward Midnight.

He was on her again before she could swing herself into the saddle.

"Damn you, woman! I'll teach you a lesson you won't forget," he yelled. He pulled her from the saddle and threw her back to the ground on her back.

She kicked at him as he approached her. "Stay away from me," she yelled. Her boot connected with his knee.

He reached down and yanked her to her feet. "I'm going to enjoy this." He laughed hollowly and grabbed both of Sarah's wrists in one hand. He dragged her toward his horse where he pulled a leather twine from his saddlebag.

She fought against him, but he was too strong. He turned her back to him and with no little effort on his part he bound her hands behind her.

Sarah jerked when a gun exploded and the man's grip suddenly relaxed. She whirled around to see his mouth gape open and a queer look cross his face. Another shot resounded. He lurched backward and fell to the ground.

Sarah stood stock-still. She looked away from the man and saw Caleb, bloody and weaving on his knees, the smoking gun in his hand. She ran to him at the same time she worked at the cord binding her wrists. When she had loosened it enough, she slid her hands out and helped Caleb to his knees then onto his back. She sat down beside him, lifted his head and placed it gently on her lap.

"I told you I'd take care of you, Miz Sarah. I meant what I said..." The gun fell from his hand and his eyes closed.

"Caleb. Caleb!" She prayed out loud that he was still alive, tore off a section of her shirt and placed it on the wound under his shirt to stop the blood flowing from his side.

She ran to Midnight, threw herself into the saddle and, in a wild fury, spurred him toward the house. She returned as quickly as was possible with the wagon and wrapped Caleb in the blankets she'd brought. Then she tried to move him. It was impossible. He was just too heavy. Sweat poured into her eyes.

"How am I going to get you into the wagon, Caleb?" she asked the semi-conscious man.

"Don't know, Miz Sarah. But I think I'll rest now..."

She looked around her and tried to think of a way to get the big man into the wagon. There was no way she could lift him. She needed another way.

She closed her eyes and her mind filled with the image of Man-Who-Runs. She smiled.

"You are a smart woman, Wi Tapeta Yuha Win. Remember in our village how a rope was used to ease the weight of our heavy burdens? Use the strength of your animal, the cunning of your brain. You can do this, Sarah." His image faded and Sarah opened her eyes.

She looked around again, thought only a few minutes more before she unhitched the mule, pushed several big rocks under the wagon's wheels to keep it steady, then wrapped Caleb's chest in an extra blanket. She pulled a rope from under the seat and tied it around him before she ran it through the wagon and around a tree to finally tie it off to the mule's harness.

"Pull, mule. Pull." She prodded the animal forward with a switch. Slowly, the line grew tight and Caleb's body moved. He was barely conscious now and Sarah prayed the jarring wouldn't injure him further as she pushed the mule forward. When Caleb's head reached the end of the wagon bed Sarah ran to guide him inside.

The mule stopped.

"Damn, mule," she cursed. "Come on, mule. Move!"

She left Caleb's side and went back to the mule to prod

him back into motion. After much cajoling, the animal finally complied. When Caleb's head reached the bottom of the wagon bed she ran to guide him over the edge and inside. Once his upper body was inside the wagon, she grabbed his legs and swung him in the rest of the way.

In the wagon, Sarah took the rope off his chest and placed another blanket under his head.

"Stay with me, Caleb. Don't die," she whispered and jumped from the wagon to re-hitch the mule.

With a quick look behind her at the dead man she'd left behind, Sarah clucked the mule toward the ranch house as quickly as she dared, the wagon swaying and creaking as she went. She couldn't figure a way to get Caleb into the house and into a bed. He was too heavy and she'd never get him up the front steps. She thought of the bunkhouse but decided she wouldn't even be able to get him into a lower bunk. She decided the barn was her only option and drove as far into a pile of hay as she could get. From the wagon bed she pushed and pulled Caleb around so that his head was at the foot of the wagon. She jumped down and placed a blanket on the pile of hay then grabbed Caleb under his arms. Slowly, she guided him out. He nearly crushed her when he fell free to land on top of her in a heap. She was soaked, exhausted, and breathing hard when she finally managed to roll him off her.

She rested a moment then grabbed him under the arms again and pulled. She groaned with his weight. Finally, after several attempts she got him settled on the blanket.

Caleb was still warm, but barely breathing. Sarah raced to the house for bandages and alcohol. She tore the bloody shirt away and examined the hole in his side. Her initial examination showed the bullet had passed right through the only meaty part of his body. When she cleaned away the blood she could see the bullet had entered just above the top of his hip and below his ribs in the meat of his side.

She said a quick prayer and set to work.

After an hour of cleaning and dressing the wound, she sat back on her heels.

"I've done all I can for now. The rest is up to you. Fight,

Caleb. Fight."

Caleb's head swung from side to side as fever ravaged his body. He shook with chills one minute then threw his covers off the next.

"Hang on, Caleb," Sarah pleaded. She dabbed a wet cloth at his head. "Hang on."

She had sat with him day and night for three days; left him only for fresh water and bandages and when she felt weak from hunger.

"Try and take a little water." Sarah soaked a clean cloth with fresh water. She placed it on his cracked lips. He made a slight movement to suck the liquid from the cloth.

"That's it, Caleb. Taste it. There you go." She soaked the cloth again, reapplied it to his lips and squeezed a few drops into his mouth.

"Come on, Caleb. A few more drops. A little more."

His eyes opened.

"Caleb?"

He managed a weak smile before his eyes closed again.

"Sleep now, but I believe now you will wake up."

"Pssst, Miz Sarah. Miz Sarah," the weak voice summoned.

Sarah raised her head from her knees where she'd fallen asleep. She looked around. Where was she?

"Miz Sarah?" the soft voice called again.

"Yes?" she whispered, still disoriented.

"Miz Sarah. It's me, Caleb." The voice jolted Sarah's memory.

"Caleb! You're awake!" She scrambled to him.

"Yes, ma'am. Thanks to you."

She felt his forehead.

"Thank God. Your fever's broken. It's a good thing you're a strong man, Caleb. That gunshot wound, let alone that kind of fever, would have killed most men." She pulled the blankets up around his neck.

"Most men wouldn't have someone to tend them like

you did."

"Caleb, the only reason I'm alive at all to care for you is because you killed that horrible man. If you hadn't he would have had his way with me and left us both to rot until Ben came home to find us."

"I know that, Miz Sarah. I promised to watch over you and keep you safe. And that's what I done." A weak smile lit his face. "I guess it's a good thing that man thought I was already dead," he said. "Else he never would've turned his back on ole Caleb."

## Chapter Sixteen

  Ben and the men of the 13th Missouri relaxed, smoked, napped, wrote letters, and chatted amongst themselves in the Union camp that overlooked the Missouri River at Lexington. The camp, which housed the garrison of Colonel James A. Mulligan of the Irish Brigade to which Ben and his men had been reassigned after the debacle at Wilson's Creek, was to the north of the town. A rampart of sod and earth twelve feet high and twelve feet thick surrounded the three-story high, brick Masonic College. Beyond this fortification was an irregular line of earthworks and rifle pits, protected by ditches, stakes, trip wires and more ramparts, which housed seven cannon. Inside these lines, Ben lounged in the unusually hot September heat and began a letter to Sarah.

*My Dearest Sarah,*
  *We've been immobile for days. Waiting. Just waiting for the Rebs to arrive. We wait for word that reinforcements will come at any time. But none do. The days pass and with them our boredom grows, along with fear as we learn of the swelling numbers that advance toward us. The sun bakes us by day and bugs and mosquitoes bite by night and cause me wistful memories of nights spent on the trail with you so long ago.*
  *I wish the pending battle would begin, if only to shatter the insipid boredom that surrounds us. I'm restless and anxious, as are my men. I find myself constantly breaking up fights and arguments because of the irritability that grows with each second that passes. With each shot fired, I tense and jump and my weary mind wishes only for respite.*
  *I think of you often, miss you more than I could believe possible. Why, after all we've been through, did this war have to separate us again? I fear our lives have been spent mostly searching or waiting for one another. It tears at my heart and soul with each sunrise as I wonder how you fare. How you manage in my absence.*

## Tomorrow's Promise: Survival on the Plains    D.L. Rogers

Ben stretched his legs out in front of him, laid the letter aside and picked up a discarded newspaper. Minutes later he threw it down in disbelief and grabbed up the letter again.

*It's extremely difficult for me to fathom that General Freemont has declared martial law throughout all of Missouri. Any man who bears arms against the Union will be executed and all his property forfeit, his slaves released. Missouri is, by most accounting, a southern state with southern sentiments, even though many of her people don't even own slaves. And although the Union forces hold many strategic positions here, we're not on home soil here. We're the invaders, a well-known fact to those of us in the field. To declare martial law in such a state is ludicrous, at best. President Lincoln is up in arms about it, a recent newspaper account says, and rescinded the order himself. I pray you fare well through all of this.*

*I have a very bad feeling about the ensuing battle. It's said nearly ten thousand Rebs march in this direction, compared to our meager three thousand. They may be a ragged bunch, but their determination and mere numbers are enough to frighten any man.*

*I still pray this war will be over soon and I'm on my way home to you in due haste...*

An alert sounded throughout camp and interrupted his writing.

"Price is on his way! The Rebs are coming."

Ben shoved the letter inside his jacket and scrambled for his gear. He shouted orders and he and his men prepared to meet the Rebel force.

Time ticked away as the Union forces met the attacking Confederates. Cannons exploded and rifles discharged. Ben fired again and again into the front lines, but the numbers of men seemed to swell and reproduce with each man that fell. His men fired into wave after wave of attacking Rebs, while Ben shouted encouragement, if only to hearten himself. Sweat poured down his face and into his eyes, stinging. He swiped at his face, tried to clear his blurred vision. The line of Rebs seemed to have multiplied.

"Keep firing, men!" He raised his rifle and took aim. "We can't let them break through. We have to hold Lexington at any cost!"

His men continued to fire and managed to keep the Rebel advance at bay. But for how long? They were outnumbered at least three to one. How long could they hold their position?

The Rebs came on endlessly, hour after hour, their numbers seeming to swell with the passage of time. And as their numbers rose, the Federals dwindled. Ben and his men grew more exhausted with each new attack.

"We're surrounded," a man beside Ben grumbled. "They're everywhere. The more I shoot, the more they come on."

Ben nodded agreement, his eyes and body heavy with fatigue. He continued to fire while he prayed for a miracle. But by the time the sun set that night, no miracle had come.

Sentries were posted and the bone-weary men bedded down, hoping their miracle would come with the sun.

But by evening the next day, the only miracle Ben and his men got was that they'd survived the day. And so it went.

For days the battle continued with little relief in sight. The sun beat down mercilessly on the Federal troops, who were cut off from the river, their main source of water.

They were ordered to recapture the Anderson house, a large, two-storied building. Yellow flags declared it a hospital, but regardless of that declaration, the Confederates attacked and took it. Ben and his men moved in several times to try and recapture the building, but each time they were met by heavy rifle fire and were forced to pull back. And when they did finally recapture the building, it was only to be driven out again hours later. And so it went in an endless tug-of-war for control of the Anderson house.

While the Rebs held the house, Ben's troops dodged sniper fire from over the rise and inside while they tried to recapture the building. When his own Union forces occupied the house, which had changed hands so many times he'd lost count, they got a short rest from the continual sniping.

"We need fresh troops," Ben muttered to himself. "Where in hell are they?"

He picked up his rifle and fired at a Reb guard who took a smoke at the rear of the Anderson house. The shot missed and Ben leaned back for a momentary rest when the man ducked back inside.

The days passed in a flurry of constant skirmishes. Water became non-existent. Days ran one into the other and heat scorched Ben's tired, dehydrated body while the Rebs took pot shots from every direction. He'd never been so beaten down or thirsty in his life.

Ben rolled onto his back and looked up. He shaded his eyes from the rays of the rising sun that had beat down on him for the last nine days. It was only 8 a.m. and he could already feel the heat on his face. His lips were cracked and bleeding. Sniper fire always popped in the background. He closed his eyes against the feeling of helplessness that threatened to overwhelm him. Shooting had been constant and there was no relief in sight. And there were no troops coming. He knew that now and felt abandoned and alone.

A commotion across the field drew his attention. He glanced out over the field and his mouth gaped open in disbelief.

"Dear God in Heaven." He pushed himself up off the ground. "What the hell is that?"

Several other men gathered around him and watched a long line of hemp bales being pushed toward the Federal lines. Three, sometimes four, unarmed confederate soldiers rolled the bales with poles or by crawling on their hands and knees, butting the giant rolls with their heads or pushing with their backs. And as the bales were placed in strategic positions just out of rifle range, they were soaked with water from the river, precious water the Federals hadn't had in days, to keep the hot shot and cannon fire from setting them ablaze, Ben assumed. Once soaked the men began to shove them up the hill again. But now, a line of soldiers behind them fired into the Federal lines.

"Fire!"

Ben and his men fired. Artillery flew, but nothing penetrated the thick rolled hemp that moved closer and closer. Bullets thudded dully into the thick hemp. Even cannonballs couldn't destroy the moving barricades. They merely rocked in place a little with each ball that stuck before they were pushed closer.

"How the hell are we supposed to stop them?" Ben groaned aloud, stunned by the sight. He pulled himself together and yelled to his men.

"Keep firing, men! Don't...stop...firing! We can't let them get close enough to break our lines! If we do, we're done!"

The battle raged for hours and ammunition dwindled, along with morale and the lack of food and water for the battle-weary men.

At one point in the day all firing stopped and a lone white flag was hoisted above the Union troops. Ben watched a courier ride from the Confederate lines and deliver a message to Colonel Mulligan. Had they really surrendered? Ben wondered as he watched the exchange. After a few minutes, the rider returned to his own lines. Shortly after the order was given to resume firing.

Ben didn't learn until later that day that the flag of truce had been raised unknown to Colonel Mulligan. When Price had sent the courier to question if the Union forces truly meant to surrender, it was rumored Mulligan had written back, "General, I hardly know, unless you have surrendered."

When the attack resumed it was relentless, the sun brutal. The lack of water drove the men to the brink of insanity. But still the Rebs continued their advance, repelled only when they got close enough to be driven back by a flurry of gunfire.

It was mid-afternoon when the attack finally stopped and the field grew quiet. Ben spotted Colonel Mulligan and his staff, erect on their cavalry mounts, riding toward the battlefield. A white flag flapped above them.

Ben's head dropped to his chest and his eyes closed.

Cheers erupted from behind the huge bales when the rag tag army spotted the officers. They raced back to their own lines, whooping and jumping like children.

Ben stared at the officers. It was over. After nine days of constant fighting and baking in the sun, it was over.

What now? he wondered as he watched Colonel Mulligan ride toward the Confederate lines. The battle was over and, although the officers would concede Lexington to the enemy, he was still alive.

It was 2 p.m. on September 20, 1861, when Colonel Mulligan and his officers stood in front of the confederate general Sterling Price to await terms of surrender.

Ben watched the rest of the garrison march out onto the field and lay down their weapons. Mulligan raised his sword, as did Ben and the other officers, and offered them to General Price. But to their surprise, he declined.

"You gentlemen have fought so bravely that it would be wrong to deprive you of your swords. Keep them. Orders to parole you and your men will be issued, Colonel Mulligan, without unnecessary delay."

Ben's head swam. They were to be paroled? What, exactly, did that mean? Did it mean he'd be released to go home? What were the terms? He was almost giddy with relief, relief that would be short lived.

The Irish Brigade, inclusive of Colonel Mulligan and his officers, lined up to await their fate. They baked in the sun and learned Claiborne Jackson himself would address them.

Hands clasped behind his back, his knee-high boots polished to a high sheen, the governor strode toward the captured men.

"Men, today is a proud day for Missouri and the Confederacy. We have shown the Union Army we are a force to be reckoned with. We will not turn tail and run, as so many of you Yankees predicted." Jackson scanned the men in front of him and smiled.

His secessionist speech dragged on until the men were sweat soaked and ready to fall down. Finally, Jackson said his farewells and a major stepped forward.

"Unfortunately, there are no facilities in which to hold

you as prisoners of war. Therefore, we are forced to release you."

Confusion broke out amongst the captives. Ben sighed with relief. The major had restated what Price had offered the officers earlier. Parole.

Whistles blew. "Silence!" the major bellowed.

"There are stipulations to your release, however. You will sign an affidavit swearing you will not raise arms again against the Confederacy until a formal exchange has been made for you and Confederate prisoners being held. Private for private, sergeant for sergeant and so on. Only with your signature on this document, will you be released."

The major scrutinized his prisoners. "Believe me, sirs, this is not done out of kindness, but only because the war effort is so new we have no place to confine all you blue bellies."

Ben's heart soared. He could go home to Sarah. For him the war was over.

A heavy hand came down on his shoulder. "You. The general wants to see you," a Rebel guard said. Ben's heart pounded and his head spun as he was led toward a command tent and left under guard in the broiling sun—again. He was told he awaited the arrival of Sterling Price himself.

Ben's mind ran wild. What the hell did they want with him? Why, of all the other men, had he been singled out? Sweat ran down his face, into his eyes and mouth. He waited nearly an hour before Price and another lieutenant arrived.

"Lieutenant, Colonel Mulligan informs me you're a career military man," Price said.

"Not exactly, sir. I served with the Second Dragoons under General Harney out West, but left when my enlistment was over. I reenlisted only when the war broke out."

"I see." After a thoughtful pause Price continued. "During that time with the Dragoons you spent a lot of time on patrol, traveling the western roads?"

"Yes, sir?" Ben's response was hesitant.

"In that case, Lieutenant, I'm afraid I must detain you."

"Sir?" Ben's heart ricocheted in his chest.

"You will be sent east for interrogation of your

knowledge of the western roads. Of the entire garrison only you and Colonel Mulligan will be detained."

"Colonel Mulligan, sir?"

"Yes, he's refused to be released with the rest of his men. He shall accompany me until other arrangements are made. Unfortunately for you, that will not be the case. As I stated earlier, because of your knowledge of the western roads, you will be kept as a prisoner."

Ben stood stock-still. His body tingled with fear and apprehension. He wasn't going home with the rest of the men. Instead he was going to prison.

Ben stood in the rain in front of a long, rectangular three-story brick building. Droplets formed on the tip of his nose and ran off the brim of his hat and he heard little of what the man pacing in front of him said. His mind was back in Richmond where he'd been beaten, starved, and threatened for information on the western roads. But in the end he'd withstood their tactics and divulged nothing.

"...Libby Prison," the man's voice droned. Ben looked up at the three-story building in front of him. The upper half of the building was natural color brick, while the lower half was whitewashed but dirty. Rows of windows lined the ominous-looking upper brick walls and armed guards ringed its perimeter below. Shivers of dread raced down Ben's spine when he finally looked at the man who belonged to the voice penetrating his weary mind. The man walked back and forth in front of him, striking the palm of his hand with a riding crop. The man stopped in front of Ben and his steel-gray eyes bore into him.

"You men are prisoners of war, so do not expect to be treated with kindness or compassion. You may have been officers in your army, but you're in our army now." He laughed, a dead, hollow sound.

"You will be fed and given shelter. Nothing more. Should you try to escape you will be hung—or shot—whichever comes first." He strode past Ben, again bringing the crop down into the palm of his hand. He stopped before a frightened young soldier who quaked beneath his heavy glare.

The man smiled. "Before I have finished with y'all, every man here will cower before me!"

He stepped away from the frightened soldier and continued his deliberate march.

"I am Major Thomas P. Turner, commandant of this facility." He waved his crop to encompass the walls of the prison. "Do not forget my name or the respect you will associate with it. Move them inside," he commanded a soldier who herded the men away.

The room Ben entered was bare, except for the fifty or sixty men already strewn about the floor with no blankets, no bedding and very little clothing to cover their dirty, emaciated bodies. Ben was led through the men toward another door and he nearly retched when the smell of urine and body odor hit him square in the face.

He entered a smaller bare room, where twenty or thirty men huddled close together, trying to ward off the cold dampness of the rain that fell outside, a wetness that seemed to permeate the walls and bodies of those housed here.

Ben shuffled toward a corner and sat down along the wall. The cold immediately seeped into his body through his already wet garments. He shivered, pulled his knees to his chest, dropped his head onto them and closed his eyes. A feeling of complete despair washed over him.

"Dear God," he prayed in silence. "Give me strength."

It was nearly morning. Ben shifted stiff, sore arms and legs and the chill of the air pierced his body like a knife. Around him men labored to breathe in the damp, frigid room. Small, white clouds billowed from their mouths when they exhaled. Ben sucked in a deep breath and tried to refill his brittle lungs, but coughed when the cold hit them.

Down the hall he heard the familiar shuffle of feet. It was beginning all over again.

"Get up you lazy sots!" The guard's voice boomed when he strode into the room. He kicked and shoved the men as he made his way in. Prisoners jumped out of his way as quickly as they could in their weakened conditions. Ben stared at them.

They seemed to have aged tenfold since their initial arrival only four weeks ago.

"If'n ya'll want breakfast this morning," the guard drawled while he picked at his pimpled face, "you'd better raise your lazy carcasses up and move out."

Across the room an old man tried to pull himself up. Ben couldn't recall having seen him before. Such an old man. *Why was he here?*

Ben walked toward the man to offer assistance. He stopped in his tracks when he was only two feet away and realized the man was, in fact, no older than himself. He'd grown sickeningly thin and pale. Ben blanched when he looked into the sunken, dead eyes.

"Here let me help." Ben put his arm around the other.

"Thank you," the man barely whispered with fetid breath.

Ben pulled the man up and grabbed him under the arms. Although what remained of the soldier was feather-light, he weighed heavy on Ben in his own weakened state. His head bobbed as Ben helped him out of the room.

"How long have you been here, soldier?" Ben asked.

The man looked up at him, his eyes blank, but he finally managed to speak. "What's the month?" His voice was raspy and so low, Ben had to strain to hear.

"October," Ben answered.

"Only October?"

Ben nodded and waited for a response.

The man's gaze dropped to the floor and tears formed in the corners of his eyes.

Ben dragged the man a few steps forward. Suddenly, he rose up straight as a nail.

"We can't hold, sir!" he shouted. "They're breaking through. We've got to run. Save your life!" He yanked free of Ben's grasp and ran, his arm raised above him like he was wielding a sword.

"Wait!" Ben yelled, racing to catch him.

As suddenly as it had begun, the man stopped and slumped to the floor. Ben grabbed him just before he hit the cold, hard planks.

The soldier's eyes were again blank and emotionless. After regaining his composure and getting a grip on the lifeless man again, Ben dragged him to where they would get their morning meal.

The walk was hardly worth the effort. Each man received a stale piece of bread and a piece of rancid meat, so tiny even the smallest of children wouldn't be satisfied. Ben took his plate then reached for that of the man he carried. His own plate almost clattered to the floor when he jerked his hand away when the guard with a club cracked it.

"Man's got to take his own plate, Yank," came the gruff response.

"But he's not able. Can't you see that?"

"Don't give a damn whether he's able or not. Rules are he's got to take his own plate, otherwise you might eat his and yours."

Ben hoisted the semi-conscious man to his feet.

"You've got to try, soldier. I can't do it for you. Just reach out your hand and take the plate. Once we're out of sight, I'll carry it the rest of the way for you."

The man stared, his eyes blank, for several seconds before he drew in a deep breath. His back straightened a fraction and his arm went out toward the plate of food.

"That's it," Ben prodded. "Go on. Take it."

White, spindly fingers curled around the edge of the plate. Ben watched the man pull the plate away from the table—and crash to the floor.

"Next!" the guard yelled as he pushed Ben and his burden down the line.

Ben dragged the man back to their room. Others watched, some with blank stares, some with pity in their eyes. He sat the man down against a wall and tried to make him comfortable.

"Wouldn't bother much about him, Lieutenant," another man beside Ben said. "I seen it happen before. Once they get this far it's only a matter of hours or days."

Ben whirled on a skinny blond-haired boy he'd heard

others call 'Miller'. "So that means we shouldn't care? Shouldn't try to help him?" he lashed out, drawing the attention of several other prisoners. A few shrugged their shoulders then went about finishing their meager meals.

"Listen, Lieutenant. I'm just telling you the way it is. Once their mind goes the rest is close behind. It happens a lot here," Miller said.

Ben turned around to fully face the man with the face of a boy, and settled on the floor. "How long have you been here?"

Miller did a quick calculation in his mind. "Three months, near as I can figure."

"And what about him?" Ben motioned to the unresponsive man beside him.

"Same time. Some of the men just can't cope. Their minds just disappear. Saw a few of them at Bull Run just load and fire, load and fire into the air over and over again, that same blank look in their eyes. When they were brought here they just starved to death." Miller leaned forward and looked at the man.

"Won't be long. He'd been sitting in the same spot for days until you moved him. He tried to get up, but just didn't have the strength and always fell right back into the same spot."

Ben turned toward the frail man and watched him for several moments. Fear suddenly overcame him. Would three months in this place do that to him?

"No," Ben breathed. "I'll survive, or I'll find a way out."

"What?" Miller asked.

"I said I won't die like him. I'll survive this hellhole or I'll escape."

"Or you'll die trying. These here guards take great pleasure in outright killing a man who tries to escape, or make an example out of him," Miller said. "If you plan to escape, don't fail." The boy absentmindedly licked his fingers, trying to taste the last morsel of food.

"What's this man's name?" Ben asked.

"Adams, I think. Don't know for sure. We've all just called him Adams for lack of something better."

Ben spoke to the lifeless man.

"Here, Adams. Take a bite of this." He broke off a small

piece of his own stale bread. "It'll make you stronger." He tried to shove it into the man's mouth, but his teeth were clamped shut. Ben tried again then gave up.

"Hey! If you don't want that food, toss it over here," came a muffled voice from within the crowd of prisoners.

Ben shoved the small piece of meat and bread into his mouth, chewed and swallowed then licked his fingers as though he'd just eaten the best meal of his life.

Later that evening after a routine day of roll call then nothing but interminable boredom, Ben watched the sun set until a mere arrow of sunlight split the room. He tugged at what little clothing he had on and tried to suppress the shivers that racked his body. He couldn't decide if he shook from the cold or from an inner fear of death. He'd looked death in the eye many times in battle, but had never experienced eyes that haunted as much as the blank ones beside him. They gnawed at his entire being. He'd faced death in the form of Indians, but had never felt the helplessness he felt now. He thought of Sarah. Her face rushed to the fore of his mind's eye and gave him comfort.

He exhaled with a groan, pulled up his knees, put his arms around them, dropped his head, and drifted into a restless sleep.

When Ben awoke the next morning, the sun was already bright; its light glowed eerily in the death-like stillness of the cold chamber. He turned toward Adams who still stared off into space, but his mouth had fallen open and spit dribbled from the corner. Ben touched Adams' arm. The man's head rolled to his shoulder.

"I told you," Miller said.

Ben looked down at the dead man and his flesh crawled.

"What now?" he asked Miller as he slid away from the body.

"They'll pick him up during breakfast. They wait till we're gone and anybody left behind not breathing is taken away."

The space on the wall was empty when Ben returned with his breakfast. Fear stabbed at him as he took his place. He thought about Adams the whole time he ate his stingy fare. *Would he die like that? Cold. Alone. Brittle, used up and unaware of what went on around him? No. He'd be damned if he would. A bullet in the back trying to escape would kill him before he'd die like that.*

Ben finished his meal but his stomach continued to rumble in discontent.

Miller leaned toward him. "It'll do that for a long time. You'll get used to it."

Ben nodded understanding. His stomach continued to roll and buck for more. He laid his head against the wall and closed his eyes.

"Miller? Have you ever felt like you've been cast from earth down into the bowels of hell?"

He opened his eyes in time to see Miller nod agreement.

Ben looked around the room. These had once been strong, able-bodied men. Now they were skeletal broken pieces of flesh.

Ben heard whistling down the corridor and Miller went rigid beside him. Sheer panic swept over the soldier's face when a guard entered the room. Ben's eyes darted between the guard and Miller who was looking at the floor, his breath quick and short.

The guard walked toward them and Miller pushed up as far as he could against the wall.

"Mornin' boy," the guard drawled.

Ben looked up at the man's face. It was a nondescript face that wouldn't stand out in a crowd. He had dark eyes and sandy hair that fell to his shoulders and a smile curled his lips. The guard stood just under six feet with wide shoulders. But it was what Ben saw in the man's eyes when he took the time to look that made his spine tingle with dread. They gleamed with anticipation.

Miller squirmed when the guard bent down and touched his arm.

"No, Dobbs. Please, no." There was desperation in Miller's whispered plea.

The big man threw back his head and laughed before he

leaned down to Miller. "Yes, Miller," he said through gritted teeth.

Ben watched terror sweep over Miller's face.

"You lookin' at something?" the guard snapped at Ben. He moved to within inches of Ben's face and Ben nearly retched from the foul stench of the man's breath.

Ben looked away. "No."

"No, what?"

"No, sir," Ben responded. He felt like a coward, but he didn't want a fight, not in his condition.

"That's better. Me and Miller got business. Ain't that right, Miller?" There was laughter in his voice.

Miller's face was wild with fear but he nodded anyway.

"Good. Let's be on our way then," the guard said, his smile wide.

Miller stood up on unsteady legs. The guard shoved him to the door. He turned for a last pleading look at Ben, the only man in the room who even acknowledged the guard's presence then he disappeared through the door.

## Chapter Seventeen

Water for the morning coffee was boiling in the kettle when Sarah heard the riders' approach.

"Stay calm," she reminded herself. She walked to the front room to receive her visitor.

She waited for the knock, counted to ten and swung open the door.

"Morning, Sheriff. What brings you out today?" She put on her brightest smile.

The older man tipped his hat. "Mornin' Miz Walters. Sorry to bother you, ma'am, but a rather rough fella is missing." He shifted his feet. "The man's a slave catcher. He told his present employer he was going looking for a runaway near this place." He paused and peered around the inside of the room. "You seen him or the runaway, ma'am?"

Sarah gasped in real shock. "A negro slave? On Miss Emma's property?" she asked. "Why, Sheriff. She doesn't hold with slaves, you know that. And since I'm in charge of the place while she's in town, I can tell you I haven't seen or heard anyone on the property that would fit the description of either of them." She shook her head.

The sheriff seemed unsure. "Mind if I have a look around the property?" he asked. "Just in case that black buck decided to hide somewhere on the property and you haven't found him yet."

She took a sharp intake of breath. "Certainly, Sheriff. You may look around if you like. I'll feel much safer knowing you've searched the whole place. Since my husband and Emma are both gone, it's been rather lonely here and sometimes, although I hate to admit it, I've been a little frightened. Perhaps I could stroll with you as you search?"

She stepped through the doorway and led the man toward the barn. From the barn they searched the bunkhouse, corral and cottage in the back before they headed toward the house.

"There's no need to check the main house, Sheriff. I'm

sure there's no one on this property. Perhaps the runaway went in the other direction and the slave catcher is well away from here. Let's do hope so," she said, her voice coy.

Again the sheriff looked uncertain. He nodded his head and turned to his horse tethered in front of the porch. "I'll be on my way then, Miz Walters. I thank you for your time." He mounted, tipped his hat once again and turned his horse down the drive and out of White Oaks.

Sarah calmed her racing heart and stepped back into the house. She walked to the rear bedroom and opened the door.

"Is he gone?" Caleb asked.

"He's gone, but I'm sure glad your fever broke yesterday and we were able to move you from the barn. I couldn't bear to lose you after all this."

"Don't worry, Miz Sarah. As soon as I'm up to it, I'll be puttin' up in the bunkhouse again, able to warn you if someone's coming onto the property."

Sarah nodded. She'd taken care of the last detail of her ordeal with the slave catcher only earlier this morning. She'd buried the man a foot from where he fell. Thank God the Sheriff hadn't ventured deeper onto the property and found the freshly dug grave.

Several weeks later, Sarah busied herself in the kitchen. Often she envied Emma living in town, away from the harsh duties of the ranch. But Emma was an old woman and Sarah was more than able to handle this household. Caleb's knock on the back door interrupted her thoughts.

"Morning, Miz Sarah."

"Morning. You're looking fit today." Sarah's voice was weary. She pushed the door open for Caleb to enter.

"Something the matter, Miz Sarah? You seem a might put out."

Sarah looked into her friend's concerned face. "I dreamt about Ben again last night, Caleb. I haven't received a post from him in several weeks. I'm getting concerned. It's not like him to go so long without writing. Anything could have happened."

"You can't think that, Miz Sarah. You got to stay strong.

For yourself, Miss Emma and Mr. Ben. Besides, I'm sure that husband of yours is too wiley to catch a Reb bullet. He's fine, I'm sure of it." He nodded his head with certainty.

"So am I," Sarah agreed. She handed Caleb a plate of thin oatmeal and one strip of fatty bacon.

Sarah scooped up another plate of the same and followed Caleb out of the house and onto the side porch. There they ate and chatted about the chill in the air and the imminent arrival of winter.

"I hate to see winter come, Caleb. It's such a dismal season with its bitter wind and ice."

Caleb's head moved up and down. "You know, Miz Sarah, any time you want me to take over full care of them cattle, all you has to do is ask."

Sarah smiled. "There's plenty for the both of us, Caleb." She looked out over the buildings. It was definitely enough to keep her mind occupied while Emma was away. But her thoughts went back to Ben. *Where was he and was he all right?*

The sun rose high into the early November sky and warmed Sarah's face. Caleb whittled on a piece of hedgewood while Sarah kept her hands busy with needlework.

The sun reached toward noon and birds chirped in the trees that surrounded the main house.

A blood-curdling scream broke the sweetness of their song.

"Dear God, what was that?" Sarah cried, the hair on the back of her neck on end.

"I don't know, Miz Sarah, but I think we should get the rifles." He ran from the porch to the bunkhouse to retrieve his rifle and Sarah dashed into the house and grabbed hers from beside the fireplace.

Sarah was trying to place where the scream had come from when another shriek reverberated from behind the house.

Caleb jumped back onto the porch, his face lined with worry. "Miz Sarah, I think we should get into the house, bolt all the doors and lock all the shutters. I got a bad feeling." His words were lost as shots erupted from everywhere.

Horses and riders thundered into the courtyard from all

directions around the house. Jerked to a stop, the animals danced with excitement, their ears raised, snorting and throwing their heads and feet into the air. Sarah assessed the dozen or so heavily armed men.

"What do you want?" Her voice quavered, although she tried to appear unruffled. She was shaking, but held her rifle steady.

"Haughty one ain't she?" one rider asked.

"Awfully upitty for one who keeps niggers what obviously ain't slaves," spat another.

Sarah drew up her back. "I'll ask you again. What do you want?" She held the rifle steady, but didn't point it at anyone—yet.

Silence hovered over the group for several seconds before a lone rider spurred his horse toward Sarah and Caleb. Reddish-colored hair flashed beneath his wide-brimmed hat and his pale eyes looked angry. He reined-in, laid his arm across the saddle horn, then sat and glared at them for several moments.

Sarah's legs shook. She tried to regain her composure and shouted, "I've asked the question twice. I should like an answer. Who are you and what do you want?"

The man had light eyes, a thin-lipped mouth and unshaven chin. He leaned forward and greeted Sarah.

"Mrs. Walters, isn't it?"

"Yes, I'm Mrs. Walters."

"The wife of Ben Walters who fights with the Federals?"

Sarah stood her ground. "Yes, Ben fights for the preservation of the Union, and..."

"Save your sermonizing, woman. Your sympathies lie with the enemy, therefore, I declare we will take what we need from here to clothe and feed ourselves in the name of the Confederate States of America." The men hooted and cheered behind the light-haired man.

"How dare you!" Sarah shouted. She raised the rifle, putting the light-haired man clearly in its sights. "I am not the owner of this property, but widow Carter has entrusted its care to me. I will not allow you and these ruffians to take what is not yours, or mine, to give," she announced.

Several men inched their horses forward.

"I'm warning you. I'm as fine a shot as any man. Don't press me or this man will bear the full load of my rifle."

Caleb stepped beside her and raised his rifle.

The reddish-haired man laughed heartily. "There's hellfire in her veins, men!"

Sarah stood poised on the porch, the rifle still trained on the reddish-haired man.

"I'm telling you all right now, get off this land. I live here in peace. I don't bother anyone. I wish to be left alone." She swung the rifle toward the gate at the end of the property.

"Perhaps we'd like to stay, just to gaze upon your lovely features, Mrs. Walters," one of the men shouted, drawing chuckles and catcalls from the others.

Sarah was furious. "Just get off this land and leave us alone!"

"I regret, pretty lady, we cannot do that. We've set out for food and supplies and intend to return to camp with a rich bounty. I've many mouths to feed. Men look to me for their food and shelter."

"You're nothing but a band of thieves!" She kept her eyes fixed on the man who spoke.

Annoyed, he sat back in his saddle and eyed her. "Madame, I am forced to provision my men the best way I can. You see it your way, I see it mine." In one motion he slid from the horse and stepped toward Sarah.

"Stop right there, mister." The rifle was trained squarely at his chest.

He came to an abrupt halt, swept off his hat and bent in a low bow before her. "May I introduce myself, Mrs. Walters. I am William Clarke Quantrill, better known as Charley to my friends."

Sarah felt the blood drain from her face. Fear rose up sharp in her belly. She knew that name. Knew about his infamous raids on the countryside, as well as garrisons of troopers. He was fearsome and sly and slipped endlessly out of the grasp of the army that sought to have him and his band of raiders destroyed.

"Ahhh, you've heard of me."

"Yes, I've heard of you."

Without warning he surged forward and grabbed the barrel of her rifle.

Sarah's finger tightened around the trigger and the weapon exploded. Dust swirled in the air where the bullet slammed into the ground a few feet away from Charley and caused the horses to dance nervously in the yard. Sarah's heart raced wildly.

Before Caleb could make a move someone from behind jerked the rifle out of his hands. He was left as defenseless as Sarah.

"I'm tired of this game," Quantrill growled. He yanked the rifle barrel, which pulled Sarah toward him. He caught her as she fell down the porch steps. The men hooted. Pure hatred shook Sarah as she looked up into his face, filled with unconcealed mirth.

"I see you'd like to make a closer acquaintance," Quantrill joked. Sarah struggled but couldn't free herself. And even if she did manage to break free, men ready to take his place surrounded her. Sarah stopped fighting.

"Let go of me," she said in a controlled, even voice. Quantrill complied and she stepped back. Powerless to stop them, she watched the men dismount and head toward the different buildings of the ranch. Several men walked toward the barn at her left and others ran to the bunkhouse behind it. The sound of crashing furniture and breaking glass made Sarah cringe. She looked on helplessly as men raced behind the main house to her own little cottage and listened to her own precious few belongings being shattered. Two men strode toward the big house.

Sarah ran up the steps and blocked the door. "Please, not Miss Emma's home," she protested.

The men laughed and looked toward Quantrill.

"Mrs. Walters. I do not know how your Miss Emma holds with this war, but be assured if she's a good southern lady, she'll gladly relinquish any and all goods that might help our cause. If she's not then we gladly relieve her of her burdens,"

Quantrill finished with a flourish of his hand.

He mounted the stairs and stepped beside Caleb, restrained by two men. Without warning Caleb lunged at Quantrill, pushing him aside. Another of Quantrill's men slammed the butt of his rifle into Caleb's stomach, then into his head, before he went limp.

"Tie him up!" Quantrill bellowed. "I'll deal with him later." He turned back to Sarah who struggled with two other men.

"That black buck just made what could have been the biggest mistake of his life. How dare he touch me?" Charley glared at Sarah then looked down with distaste on Caleb's prone form on the porch. "He's lucky I'm feeling amicable today, else he'd have had a bullet in his head instead of the stock of that rifle." He paused before he addressed Sarah again. "Seems he's willing to die for you, Mrs. Walters. Not many a slave is ready to lay down their life for their master. Why is he?"

Sarah was taken aback by the inference and loathing in his words.

She lifted her chin. "He is not my slave and I'll ignore your insinuation, Mr. Quantrill," she said, her voice cold. "He is a friend."

Quantrill, his face a mask, gazed at her for several seconds before he waved his hand in dismissal and stepped toward the door of the house. Sarah fought the men who held her, but to no avail. They simply picked her up and moved her out of the way for Quantrill and the others to enter.

The house, out buildings and stock were ravaged. Sarah's heart broke as the two milk cows, chickens and finally Midnight were led from the barn.

Raw, raging anger swept through her. She kicked the man holding her left arm and bit the other one. Both howled as Sarah broke away and ran to Midnight and grabbed him around the neck. The horse, who had been stamping and snorting when led from the barn, quieted immediately.

"Oh please, not him." She fought tears.

"Sorry, ma'am," the man who led the black replied.

"Charley said take everything of value. I'd say this is

one pretty valuable chunk of horseflesh."

"Please," she whispered one last time in the hope the man might change his mind. She looked into the bearded man's face and thought she saw a trace of regret, but he sighed heavily and shook his head.

"Charley would skin me alive if I didn't take this horse. Maybe I can talk him into letting me handle him, but that's the best I can do. I promise if he does, I'll take good care of him for you."

Deep down she knew no matter how much she begged or pleaded, Quantrill would never ride out of here and leave a prize like Midnight behind. She nodded, kissed Midnight on his nose, turned and walked away, her back straight, her eyes clear, her heart filled with rage.

She spotted Quantrill watching her from across the courtyard. Shoulders squared, she thrust her head up in defiance and walked toward him.

"Mr. Quantrill, know that someday you will get your just due."

Quantrill grabbed her arm and yanked her toward him, his face only inches from hers.

"Don't push me, Mrs. Walters. I've been relatively kind to you and your nigger. I've even decided not to give him the lashing he deserves because I'm pressed for time. Unless, of course, you push me further." His eyes gleamed with hatred and Sarah shrank away from him.

"I didn't think you'd pursue the matter any further. We've gathered all we can. We're through—for now." He left the words hanging in the air.

He turned toward Caleb, guarded on the porch by two of his men. "Your buck was lucky today," he said over his shoulder before he turned back to face Sarah. "The next time he may not be. The next time I'll remember today and he'll be dead. *You* remember that." He pushed her away and swung himself onto his horse.

His men's shouts pierced Sarah's eardrums as they raced from the grounds of the ranch. Chickens squawked as they hung upside down from rider's fists and the cows bellowed, pulled behind the horses. Helpless, she watched Midnight led away by the bearded man.

A deep sob caught in Sarah's throat when she turned and saw Caleb's still form on the porch.

She ran into the house and returned moments later with water for him. He stirred slightly at the water on his lips and forehead. His eyes fluttered open.

"Miz Sarah..."

"Don't talk, Caleb. Can you stand?" She used her body as a crutch and led him inside the house. They weaved like two drunks before she dropped him face down on the couch.

"I's sorry, Miz Sarah," he whispered before Sarah disappeared into the kitchen. "I wanted to protect you from that man. Like I promised I would."

Sarah returned and put a wet cloth on the wound at the base of his neck. Caleb's eyes closed. He gritted his teeth at the apparent pain, but didn't cry out.

"I thank you for what you tried to do, Caleb. But I would sooner have them strip this ranch bare, as I'm sure Miss Emma would, too, than to lay a hurtful hand on you."

"Yes, Miz Sarah."

Did Caleb feel more toward her than she imagined? He was a dear friend to her, but had she become more to him in his eyes?

She stepped away and sadness filled her mind. She righted a chair, sat down and pushed a stray hair out of her face.

"He's my friend," she whispered to the four walls. "And I am his."

Sarah read by the firelight when she suddenly recalled the last time she had sat vigil for her friend. It was the day he had saved her life by killing the slave catcher. She'd sat with him for three days, hoping and praying he'd survive his wounds. He had, and from it a greater friendship had grown—as would from this, she told herself.

Caleb moved, grabbed his head, and groaned. He rose up on his elbow and tried to focus on Sarah.

"How long I been here?" His voice was a mere whisper.

"A few hours."

He forced a smile.

She averted her eyes as Quantrill's accusations resounded through her brain.

"I've righted the house while you slept." She was anxious to talk, but not about what was really bothering her. "They made a fine mess of this place. But they could have done worse and burned it to the ground. Instead they busted everything they laid their hands on. Dishes, glasses, and furniture. Anything that wasn't nailed down they broke or took. I re-hung Emma's few undamaged pictures, picked up broken glass, righted chairs and tables and threw out everything they destroyed, which was considerable. They did a thorough job. Nothing of value is left. Emma's treasured vases and irreplaceable tintypes are ruined, either shattered into a thousand pieces or crumpled and bent." She stopped and stared, remembering the portrait of Emma and her husband, now a shredded mess.

As she spoke she looked around Caleb, not at him, but she felt his eyes on her. When she did finally look at him, he was staring at her, his head cocked in bewilderment. She looked away and continued her nervous prattling.

"Miz Sarah?" Caleb's puzzled voice broke in.

"Yes?"

"Is something wrong? Has I done something to make you uneasy with me?"

She gazed into his expectant face and all her fears surged to the surface.

"Oh, Caleb! You could have been killed. Why would you even think to touch Quantrill? He would just as soon shoot you as look at you?" She jumped up from her seat.

He looked deep into her eyes.

"Miz Sarah, you don't care that my skin is black or that I been a slave all my life. You sees me as a person. I guess I didn't think." He looked away. "I just knew them men was gonna hurt you and I couldn't stand by and do nothin'." He raised his head, his eyes filled with tears.

"That's all?" she asked.

He nodded his head, confusion in his face.

"Of course. What else is there? We friends, ain't we, Miz Sarah? You saved my life and I told you a long time ago I don't forget a kindness. Besides, I made you a promise, one I'll at least try to keep, as long as I draw a breath."

Sarah smiled sadly and nodded. They were friends and that was all there was to it. No matter who tried to make something else of it, they were just friends.

Caleb recovered quickly and within a few days he and Sarah were working together side by side as they had before. Life was now a constant state of readiness and for weeks they prepared the house against another possible attack.

Together they hooked extra shutters onto the windows that could be bolted from inside. A small opening was cut out in the center so a rifle or handgun could be fired through it. An extra bolt was attached to both doors into the house and guns and rifles were strategically placed throughout. Caleb and Sarah moved into the main house to keep their forces from being divided should the band return at night. Caleb was in a small room at the back of the kitchen, and Sarah was in Miss Emma's room. Both slept lightly and wakened easily to the sounds of the night.

Several days before Christmas Sarah hitched the wagon to an old sway-backed mule, the only animal Quantrill's men had left, and drove into town to purchase some much-needed supplies. She walked into the general store and noticed a carved wooden-handled knife for sale on the counter. She ran her fingers over the hilt and recalled an ivory-handled knife she'd given Ben one Christmas, in what now seemed like forever ago. A smile touched her lips. So much had changed. She had changed. She'd grown and learned and survived a great deal. She wondered about Ben. Had he changed? Was he even still alive? It had been too long since she'd gotten any word from him.

Afraid thoughts of Ben would turn her mood worrisome, she turned her attention back to the knife. It was the perfect gift.

She purchased her supplies, the knife, a newspaper and left the store. Climbing into the wagon, she pulled out the newspaper and scanned its contents. **PROVISIONAL CONGRESS AT RICHMOND FORMALLY ADMITS MISSOURI INTO THE CONFEDERACY!** the bold headline read. Her head started to pound. She now lived in a confederate sanctioned state. She grabbed the reins and slapped them against the mule's rump and headed toward home.

During the trip back to White Oaks, Sarah worked herself into a frenzy.

When she reached the ranch she jumped from the wagon and shouted for Caleb.

Caleb emerged from the barn. "Yes, Miz Sarah?"

"Well, Missouri is now officially part of the Confederacy." She flipped her hand at the newspaper.

"There's nothing we can do about it, Miz Sarah," Caleb said. He walked with her toward the house. "It's almost Christmas. Let's don't ruin the days with war talk. This is supposed to be a happy time."

"I know, Caleb, but I'm just not in a very happy mood. I'm tired of wishing things were the way they used to be. I'm tired of working from sun up to sun down only to fall into bed completely exhausted to get up the next day and do the same thing all over again."

She thought of Christmases past. Of the night she and Ben had planned their journey West, and of the Christmas that came and went, unknown, while she was with the Indians.

She took Caleb's arm. "You're right. It's Christmas, and it's time I got into the Christmas spirit." She forced plans of holiday baking into her head.

Christmas arrived and Sarah chose to be merry. She butchered and roasted a skinny chicken she had managed to buy in town and baked two potatoes. After their sparse dinner, she and Caleb went into the living room.

"I have something for you, Caleb." Sarah's smile was warm as she picked up a long box from a side table.

His eyes went wide. He took the box and ran his fingers over the brown paper.

"You'll never find out what's inside if you don't open

it," Sarah teased after he'd held it, unopened, for several moments.

He removed the paper and opened the box to reveal the knife. He stared at it, but didn't touch it. When he looked up at Sarah his eyes were moist.

"Miz Sarah. I can't take this. You can't afford to buy me no present like this."

"It's too late. It's already done. You're my friend and you deserve it. I hope it will come in handy around the ranch."

He picked up the steel knife and rolled the carved wooden handle in his hand. The eyes of a hawk stared back at him.

"Thank you, Miz Sarah. This means a whole lot to me. More than you can know."

His eyes were still moist when he jumped up and fled to his tiny room behind the kitchen. But he returned quickly with something in his hand.

"Miz Sarah, I know this can't compare to this here knife, but I want you to have this as a gift from me. It was my momma's. She give it to me before they sold her away from me and my brothers when I was a small child. It's the only gift I ever got from anybody, besides this here knife you just give me." He cleared his throat and handed Sarah a tiny cross that was carved in white birch and dangled from a thin leather thong.

"I can't take something so precious to you, Caleb," Sarah whispered as she admired the cross. "Your mother gave it to you."

"No, Miz Sarah. I want you to have it. Besides my momma, you're the only person ever cared a whit about me. I want you to have it. Please." He closed her hand around it.

Sarah gave in. She smiled and placed it over her head to settle just above her own treasured locket.

## Chapter Eighteen

The prison walls gave little shelter against the bitter January winds that whipped through cracks and seeped through floors.

Ben ate whatever morsel of food he was given and hoped for what little strength it might give him. The smell of death permeated the air as men, in a desperate attempt to free themselves of their prison, gave up the struggle for life.

Ben curled up in the darkness and tried to ward off the frigid air that filtered through the shabby clothes he wore, as hunger gnawed at the pit of his belly. He hugged himself and pulled his knees up below his chin. A chill shook his body, but his mind continued to work on a way to escape this prison.

He woke to the usual sounds of bellowing guards and dragging feet. He rose slowly and made his way to get his food.

Ben grabbed a plate of grits and stared at it.

"This slop is moving." The plate fell back to the table with a clatter. "Jesus, it's filled with weevils! I can't eat this."

His stomach screamed in revolt.

"You'd better eat it, Yank, cause that's all you're gonna git." The guard rubbed his chin in thought. "Just think of them little critters as extra meat!" He howled at his own joke then scooped up a plate for the next man.

"I wouldn't feed this slop to pigs!" Ben yelled, his mind in reckless rebellion.

The man stopped filling the next plate. "Why, you ain't equal to pigs. You're lower than the dung of pigs. You're prisoners!" A contemptuous smile covered the guard's face.

Ben's mind snapped. He lunged over the food table at the man, caught him with a fist in the middle of the jaw and knocked him to the floor. Dazed, he looked up to find Ben over him, ready to strike again.

"I'll teach you, you lousy blue belly!" the man screamed. But before he could regain his balance, Ben was on him again. He slammed his fists into the man's face while cheered on wildly by the other prisoners.

More guards rushed in and Ben was dragged away and shackled.

He was hauled outside, stripped to the waist and hung by his wrists between two posts and left to wait, his body numb within minutes from the brutal cold. His teeth chattered uncontrollably, but his eyes darted from one guard to the other with unconcealed hatred.

The guards around him grew silent. From his left he could see Major Turner's approach. The major stopped in front of him and assessed his prisoner.

"I see we've had a bit of difficulty," Turner drawled. He reached out and grabbed a handful of Ben's hair and jerked his head back. Ben grunted, gritted his teeth, but said nothing.

"So, you think you're tough, blue belly? Well, we're going to beat some of that stubborn Yankee tough right out of you." Turner's voice grew soft, his face within an inch of Ben's.

"This is one lesson you'll never forget, Yank."

His riding crop laced Ben's face like a bolt of lightning. Blood beaded and dripped down his cheek and burned like hellfire itself. But he didn't give Turner the satisfaction of crying out. Instead, Ben grinned and spat on the ground to barely miss Turner's highly polished boot.

"Finish him. And do a proper job," Turner yelled. He turned away and strode back into the building, crop slashing across the palm of his hand.

Ben braced himself. He hoped because his body was numb it might take away the bite of the whip. He was wrong. The first lash sent his mind reeling with unequaled pain, while his back burned with white, hot fire. Again and again the whip found its mark until, after what seemed like hours, it finally stopped.

Ben's wrist bindings were cut and he fell to the frozen ground. Barely conscious, he felt himself dragged back into the building and dumped in a corner. His legs curled up under him and his arms hugged his chest. Everything went black....

It was daylight when he woke. He moaned every time he

moved and dried blood clawed at the lacerations on his back.

"Be still," Miller hissed as he dabbed Ben's back with a damp piece of rag. "I'm doing the best I can with what I've got to work with. Don't make it worse by moving around."

"Do what you can," Ben managed. Sweat beaded on his forehead, despite the bitter cold.

"I am, I am, you lunatic. Whatever possessed you to hit that guard?"

Ben shrugged then groaned with the pain it caused. His body jerked when Miller dabbed again at his exposed back.

"Damn fool," he heard Miller mumble before darkness enfolded him again in its warmth.

Ben floated in and out of consciousness. When he finally opened his eyes, Miller was beside him, a smile on his face.

"Welcome back, Lieutenant. I thought you were a goner."

"How long?" Ben grunted.

"Two days. Appears you'll live, though. With an added collection of stripes."

Ben smiled at the young man's humor and tried to reposition himself to a more bearable spot. Pain shot through every fiber of his body.

"Damn!" he cursed. "Did a sound job, didn't he?"

"Yes, sir. That he did," Miller answered.

As comfortable as his wounds would allow, Ben closed his eyes.

*Strength. I have to regain my strength if I'm going to get out of here. I won't die here like so many already have. I swear on my life I won't. I'm going to get out of here, alive. No matter what it takes.*

Ben fought to regain his strength. He ate every stingy morsel of food he could get his hands on, drank every drop of water at his disposal. When his lacerations scarred over, he worked his body. His mind was always in a quandary thinking of then discarding, plan after plan to escape his hell on earth. The days turned to weeks and Ben's mind burned with regret and yearning. Regret for having allowed himself to be so easily talked into staying with Lyon's command because his damnable duty demanded it, and yearning for Sarah. She was the first thing on his mind each morning when he rose to face the challenge of living, and was in his dreams when his mind and body finally succumbed to his exhaustion. Only one other thought occupied his mind—escape.

He regained as much strength as was possible, but knew it would be futile to try and overpower the guards. Even if, somehow he were to take one, the prison was a veritable fortress. Guards ringed the perimeter day and night and just waited to get a man in their sights for the sheer joy of killing him. The prisoners dared not even venture near a window for fear of being shot by one of the overzealous sentinels outside.

Men continued to die around him and, as abhorrent as it was, Ben stole their clothes then bartered what he didn't need for extra food or water. He would do what was necessary to escape. No matter what.

Ben woke to the sound of shuffling feet and soft whistling outside their common room. The low, melodious whistle grew louder as it echoed off the cold, barren walls in the hall as it drew closer. A key rattled in the door. Ben waited. Someone slid up beside him. It was Miller, trembling with fear.

Ben thought back to the previous time Miller had become so scared when a guard had approached. He had been gone for hours and was quiet and withdrawn when he'd come back. When Ben tried to touch him, he'd wrenched away like he'd been stung. There were no cuts, no bruises, so Miller hadn't been beaten. Ben suspected the truth. He saw the shame in Miller's eyes before he turned away and mumbled that he'd be all right.

Now Ben watched again as the guard entered the room and advanced on Miller who kept his eyes on the floor and whose body shook like a leaf on a tree in a November windstorm. Ben saw raw terror in the man's face before he looked away.

The guard stepped directly in front of Miller then looked over at Ben. A cold chill tore up his spine before he turned away.

"Hey, Miller, you an' me got business."

Miller shook his head. "Please, no, Dobbs."

"You gonna come quiet or do I have to drag you?" the guard asked.

Ben couldn't help but look up. His skin crawled at the anticipation he saw in the man's eyes.

"You lookin' at something you mangy scum?" Dobbs snarled at Ben.

Ben looked away. "No, sir."

"Good. Me and Miller got business. Don't we, Miller?"

Ben felt Miller go rigid before he stood up and shuffled out the door in front of the guard like a prisoner being led to the hangman's noose.

That night Ben waited hours for Miller's return. When he did, his eyes were glazed and lifeless. Dobbs led him to the wall and pushed him to the floor, a smile of conquest on his face.

"Till next time," the guard chuckled.

Miller drew himself as far away from Dobbs as he could and hid his face in his knees. Dobbs left the room, kicking any unfortunate man in his way as he went.

Ben leaned over and put his hand on Miller's shoulder, who jumped as though stabbed.

"Shhh, Miller. It's me."

Miller looked up, his eyes red and hollow. Tears streamed down his face. A face full of shame. Ben wanted to kill Dobbs with his bare hands. Wanted to watch him squirm and die slow.

He put his hand on Miller's arm.

"This won't happen again, Miller. I promise."

Miller looked up with more hope in his eyes than Ben had ever seen before in his life. "But..."

"Don't ask, Miller. Just believe me, it won't happen again."

For days Ben watched and learned. He followed Dobbs with his eyes and noticed how the other guards excluded him from any activity. Whenever Dobbs walked by, the other guards went silent. They kept their distance, never looked him in the eye and only nodded in passing.

The man was an outcast. It was only a matter of time till

Ben would use that fact to his advantage.

Weeks passed. Every night Ben waited for the keys to jingle and the whistling in the hallway.

The room was dark, the men's snoring the only sound in the inky blackness before Ben snapped awake at the jingle of the keys in the lock and the soft whistle that accompanied it. He sat bolt upright. Miller was beside him, still asleep.

The rattle of the keys stopped and the door creaked open. A sliver of light crossed the room over the slumbering figures. Ben waited, his heart pounding, his body tight with anticipation.

The guard walked straight toward Miller. He reached the boy and nudged him with his boot toe.

"Hey, Miller, rise and shine."

"No."

The guard swung around to face Ben. "What the hell do you mean, no?"

"I mean Miller's too sick to move. He's been curled up in a ball all night, moaning."

Dobbs's eyes came alive. An odd smile crossed his face.

Ben waited as the guard looked between himself and Miller, curled up in the corner. He felt sweat bead on his brow, despite the bitter cold. His heart raced, his blood pumped.

Dobbs inspected Ben as though he were a prize chicken at a country fair. His skin crawled.

Dobbs finally pointed toward the door.

"You'll do instead, I s'pose."

"And if I refuse?" Anger rose like an uncapped well inside Ben at the thought of what this man intended.

Dobbs raised his stick high over his head.

"I've broken many a head with one swing of this here club. Don't s'pose you'd want me to try it out on you?"

Ben closed his eyes and prayed for strength. He'd promised Miller and now it was time to follow through. The guard nudged his shoulder.

Ben grumbled, but stood up and let Dobbs push him toward the door then down the hallway.

He walked in front of Dobbs down the few stairs to the

basement. It was dark and smelled musty, the passage lit only by a small candle the guard carried. Eerie shadows danced on the walls. The cold seemed to follow them down the stairs. Or was it just the cold surrounding Ben's heart?

Dobbs opened a door with his keys and shoved Ben inside. Ben went stiff when the door closed behind him and the keys rattled in the lock.

The room was dank and smelled of old sweat. To Ben's left was an old, tattered cot with so little ticking inside it was nearly flat. This must be where Dobbs brought Miller. *This is where it will stop.* He had to conjure up every ounce of strength he had to keep himself from whirling on the man and breaking his neck. *The plan*, he reminded himself. In due time it would all be over, one way or another. But right now it was too soon. *Just a little longer*, he reminded himself.

He turned around and looked at the guard who stood with a sly smile on his face, an evil glint in his eyes.

Dobbs hooked the keys onto his belt, put the candle in a holder on the wall and then dropped his hands to his sides.

"I figure it's time for a change from Miller's sniveling every time I touched him." His eyes bore into Ben. "Or are you gonna fight me, too?"

Ben's mind revolted at the prospect of Dobbs pawing at him, but he had to make the guard believe he would allow himself to be taken instead of Miller.

"I won't fight. I won't like it, but I'd rather be a live prisoner than a dead one." He cast a glance at Dobbs' club, which rested a short distance from his feet.

The man smiled to expose jagged teeth.

Ben's fingers shook as he worked at the buttons of his thin shirt. Dobbs watched with obvious anticipation; his eyes followed every motion. Ben's mind worked overtime to keep from screaming out loud and trying to overpower the guard. He had to finish the part he'd created.

Dobbs removed his shirt and started to work at his trousers.

"Don't you get no ideas. I can knock you out colder than a stone before you even finish thinking about grabbing that club," he threatened.

Ben's heart was pounding, his throat so tight he could barely breathe, but he continued the charade.

Ben gazed into Dobbs's expectant eyes and wanted to retch. With every ounce of effort he possessed he stepped forward. Disgust and dread welled up inside him, but he tamped it down. Not yet.

Dobbs took a step closer and touched Ben's face. Ben shuddered with revulsion, yet stood solid. Dobbs smiled an evil smile then placed his hands on Ben's shoulders. The man sighed and his breath became quick and short.

Almost.

The guard's hands slid down the length of Ben's arms and up again.

Dobbs never knew what hit him.

Ben punched the guard in the face a second time. He fell to the ground. But Ben gave him no chance to regain his senses or his feet. Ben's boot slammed into Dobbs's chest. Ben heard air explode from the guard's mouth, but kicked him again.

Ben leaned down and grabbed Dobbs by the hair. "You son-of-a-whore, bastard," he hissed.

He dropped the man's head back to the floor and kicked him again and again with every ounce of fury he'd withheld, until the guard lay motionless, his head twisted unnaturally, his sightless eyes open. Blood oozed from a deep cut in his cheek, from his mouth and nose.

Ben stood over him and glared down at the abomination.

"That's for Miller and all the other poor bastards you've taken against their will."

He stripped the rest of the guard's clothing off and, within minutes, Ben became Dobbs. He pulled the grimy hat down over his eyes, took the keys off his belt and opened the door. Outside, he closed the door and relocked it before he slipped out of the basement and up the stairs.

He heard voices ahead. Time to finish the game. He took a deep breath and stepped into a room where several guards played cards. He shoved his hands into his pockets, hung his head in the same manner he'd observed Dobbs do, then walked toward the exit. Behind him, he heard the familiar snicker of the other guards.

Almost there. Almost there. There it is. The way out. The way to freedom. Only a few more steps. Just one more guard at the door. His heart was hammering so loudly in his ears, he was certain the other guards could hear it.

Ben continued toward the door. He kept his head low and his hands deep in his pockets. At the door he reached for the knob, but was stopped by a harsh voice five feet away.

"A little late for a midnight stroll, ain't it, Dobbs?" There was contempt in the other guard's voice.

Ben forced himself to chuckle deep in his throat like Dobbs. "Need some air," he mumbled.

The guard hesitated. Ben tensed.

"Somethin' wrong with your voice?"

Ben coughed then rasped, "Cold." He pounded his chest and coughed again.

The guard hesitated again before he motioned Ben through the door. "Go ahead."

Ben nodded and opened the door. Fresh air assailed his senses and he stood frozen in the doorway. Slowly, he walked forward, toward the ring of men that lined the perimeter of the prison. He pulled his coat up tighter around his face and nodded as he passed; the men moved out of his way like the Red Sea parting.

Slowly, Ben made his way through the guards.

"Where do you suppose that son-of-a-bitch is going?" Ben heard one of the men ask.

"Where do you think?" another responded. "Probably tired of the poor selection inside." The guards howled with laughter as Ben walked away, head lowered, shoulders hunched.

On the road outside the prison, he noticed a weathered sign with arrows pointing this way and that. He was on Carey Street. To the left was 20th Street. He peered up into the black night sky. The North Star was over his left shoulder. He headed north on 20th Street.

Well outside the perimeter of the prison and just within the buildings that marked the town, he heard the first alarm sound from inside. Damn it! Someone must have discovered Dobbs' body in the basement, Ben reasoned. His walk became a run.

"Prisoner escaping! Prisoner escaping!"

Ben heard yelling and running behind him. He recognized Turner's familiar voice.

"Get him. Don't let him get away! Take steady aim, men! I want him dead!" the commandant yelled. "I want him dead!"

Although weak, Ben forced himself to run like he'd never run before. He weaved between buildings, ran through backyard gates, hurried behind any cover he could find. He could be no more than a shadow in the distance to those who pursued him, but they fired anyway. Bullets slammed into the structures he ran past and he cursed his luck. He ran in a jagged pattern, back and forth, back and forth, down alleys, between shops and houses. A shot barely missed his cheek and ricocheted off the building in front of him. He covered his face when wood splintered around him. Another shot exploded behind him. He stumbled and grabbed his leg, suddenly on fire and bloody at the thigh.

*Got to go on. Can't stop!* his mind screamed. *I'm a dead man if they catch me. Won't let them get me.*

They were still behind him, their voices faint, but there nonetheless. His mind screamed. How was he going to outrun his pursuers? He was weak to begin with and now he was injured and bleeding. Luck. He just needed some damn *good* luck!

The hopeful thought had no sooner crossed his mind when he realized the building he was running toward was the livery. His heart thumped and hope swelled. Maybe, just maybe, he'd have enough time to grab a horse and get out of town before they could catch him.

"Goddamn it!" he heard Turner's angry voice. "Find that son-of-a-bitch! I want him caught and punished. Or dead! No one escapes Libby. No one!"

Ben crouched in the shadows and ran toward the huge barn. He pulled at the livery door. His heart sank when he realized it was locked. He wanted to scream. He ran to the shadowed side of the building and looked for a window, rewarded when he spotted one slightly ajar. Pulling an overturned bucket underneath the window, he boosted himself up and through. Inside, he located a pitchfork and, using a crate he found, pushed himself back up, leaned out the window and shoved the bucket away with the handle of the fork. Breathing heavily from his exertion, he dropped back inside and latched the window quietly behind him, just as the voices became clear at the front of the livery and in the alley outside the window.

His thigh burned like hell itself, but he couldn't acknowledge the pain. If he did, he would die. He worked his way among the stalls that held several horses. Some nickered at his approach and his mind screamed with caution. "Shhhh, my friends. Please be quiet," he whispered, desperate.

At the end of the row he spotted a bay mare that had remained quiet with his intrusion. This one, he decided.

He dropped to the ground when the livery doors rattled behind him. "Locked from inside, sir."

"Check around back. Over there." Again, Turner's voice was unmistakable.

Ben trembled as he lay in the hay and manure and waited to be discovered. The window he had entered through rattled. "This is locked, too, sir."

"He must have gone farther down the alley. Find him, damn it. I want that man found!"

Ben took a deep breath to gather his senses. His leg burned like fire and was getting stiff as he lay there on the cold ground. But he didn't move until all was silent around him.

When he thought it safe, he stood up. His leg screamed in rebellion, but he forced himself to step into the stall with the bay. The horse tossed its head and nuzzled him but made no sound. He threw a saddle, draped over the top board of the stall, over the horse's back and cinched it. He put the bit in its mouth and secured the bridle.

Ben took a deep breath and stepped out of the stall, leading the horse behind him. The other horses stamped and moved around, anxious to be out with the other. He prayed no one was close enough to hear their noises.

His mind screamed with caution. The only way he could leave the livery was to open one of the doors far enough for the horse to get through. He took a huge breath, unlatched the bolt, slid it away and pushed one door part way open. It moaned and squeaked like the dead being brought back to life.

He led the horse into the moonlight—and all hell broke loose!

"Here! He's here!" someone yelled from not far down the alley. "I've found him. Over here! Stop, or I'll shoot!" the shadowed voice shouted at Ben.

Ben ignored the order, threw himself into the saddle and kicked the horse into an immediate gallop.

Men charged out of the alleys and from between buildings in every direction. Shots rang out all around him.

There were two men in front of him ready to fire. He charged the horse toward them. They screamed and threw themselves out of the path of the racing horse and their guns discharged harmlessly.

The last thing he heard as he raced out of town was Turner's bellow to "Catch that man! I want him caught, damn it. I want him dead!"

Ben kicked the horse wildly, although the pain in his leg nearly blinded him. He slapped the reins across its neck.

Shots continued to buzz from behind him as he raced down the street. He was going to die. A searing pain tore through the lower part of his left arm, which grew warm in the cold night as blood soaked his shirt. He slumped over the horse's neck as the new pain gripped him.

He struggled to pull himself upright and keep the horse going. He saw woods a fair distance from the end of the road and headed the animal in that direction. Minutes or seconds later, Ben couldn't tell in his state, the mare fairly flew into the trees. Limbs slapped at Ben's face and injured arm and leg as they charged forward.

"Kill him, damn it! I want that man dead! Keep firing!" Turner's voice shrieked behind him, but from a good distance now.

Ben rode blindly and without direction. He just kept

going and didn't stop until he realized he didn't hear voices or men behind him any longer. No more shots were being fired and bullets weren't whizzing by. Relief washed over him. Only then did he allow himself to feel the pain of his wounds. He stopped and tore off a piece of his shirt and wrapped it around his leg with his right hand, barely able to use his left to tie off the material he was so awkward in the saddle. He tore off another piece of his shirt and wrapped it around his arm. The material was soaked with blood in minutes.

What the hell was he going to do now? He had no idea where he was or in what direction to head, other than to follow the North Star. At this rate, he was going to bleed to death and he wouldn't have to worry about finding anything. Or worry about anyone finding him.

It was at that moment a raccoon popped out from under some bushes to Ben's right. The horse spooked and jerked violently to the left. Ben lost his balance, fell off and landed on his injured thigh.

Pain exploded in his leg. He gritted his teeth to keep from screaming out as he lay there and watched the horse race off into the darkness. He almost passed out, but reminded himself he was in the open and could be easily found once the soldiers mounted and came after him.

He forced himself up, forced his feet to move. They dragged, but he went on until he could go no further. He fell against a tree. Where to now? He was outside the city, but it was still enemy territory. There would be no smiling faces to take him in and tend his wounds. He had to find a place to hide. And fast.

He somehow managed to walk through the night. When the sun began to rise he could go no farther. He found a thicket of bushes, crawled under, curled up and tried desperately to stave off the torturous pain that blazed through his arm and leg. The wound in his leg gaped open, but had stopped bleeding and was crusted with black, hard blood. He pulled the shirt away from his arm—and gagged. Blood oozed out of the jagged wound and dried clumps of darkened blood and tissue dotted just above his wrist. Pain rushed through his mind and body. He closed his eyes, pushed the unbearable pain away and finally drifted into unconsciousness.

He awoke stiff and nearly frozen. He didn't know how long he'd been out but it was dark around him. His arm was numb and his leg throbbed.

*Got to get moving,* his mind prompted. He tried to sit up. His body railed at the attempt. He flopped back to the ground and tried to make his mind work.

*I'm lost in the woods in Virginia. What the hell do I do now?* As though in answer, his arm writhed with uncontrollable pain. It was all he could do to keep from screaming out loud. He bit down on his lip so hard he drew blood.

He floated in and out of consciousness. *Survive, Ben. You've got to survive.*

"I had to survive. No matter what. I wanted to live. To smell the flowers around me. Feel the soft grass beneath my feet. Taste the snow as it fell from the sky. I wanted life, Ben—I had to go on..."

Sarah's words hit him with more power than Turner's whip. He understood. Understood completely now Sarah's overwhelming desire to live. To survive.

He finally understood. But now was it too late?

## Chapter Nineteen

Ben floated in and out of consciousness. The voices of angels floated above him. He felt himself lifted, higher and higher, until he drifted without mind or body.

He cried out, "I'm ready God. But please, give me one last chance to tell Sarah I love her and understand everything she tried to tell me."

His voice drifted into the distance as he was carried away and blackness consumed him.

Heat surrounded his body. Warm for the first time in months, he snuggled deeper into the blankets. Slowly, his eyes opened. Sun streamed through a window covered with lace curtains to his right. He scanned the rest of the room adorned in flowers and frills. A long dresser filled with tiny bottles and powders stood against the opposite wall. Lace-edged towels were beside a small pitcher and bowl on the dresser. Several pictures of Christ, on the cross and rising to Heaven, hung on the wall next to a fireplace on his left. He was in the middle of a warm, comfortable bed. He moved and excruciating pain tore through his entire left side, causing him to grit his teeth to keep from crying out.

The door to the room opened and a dark-haired woman entered. She drew back when she reached the bed to find Ben staring at her.

"Oh, you're awake," she stammered.

Taken by her youthful beauty, Ben continued to stare. Her dark brown hair swirled in gentle curls around her head, with a pink bow in the middle on top. Green eyes flashed with gentleness and her smile offered kindness. Her cheeks flared red under his lengthy scrutiny until he realized his bad manners and looked away.

He opened his mouth to speak, but it came out in a dry croak.

"Wait." She rushed from the room but returned a moment later with a glass of water. "Here, drink this." She held the glass to Ben's dry, cracked lips.

Once he tasted the refreshing liquid, he tried to drink it too quick and it spilled out of his mouth and down his chin and neck.

"Slowly," she ordered. "Drink it slow." Her voice was soft and gentle.

He finished the water and she placed the glass on a small table beside him. "You might be able to talk a little easier now."

He saw no hatred or deception in her eyes, but he still couldn't be sure.

"I...," came out hoarsely. "Wh...where am I?" he managed.

"You're on the Dugan farm." She sat down in a chair on the right side of the bed.

"How did I get here?" The last thing he remembered was hiding under the bushes, bleeding and hurt.

"My brother found you four days ago when he was out hunting. You were almost dead and we brought you here."

"Four days ago?"

"Yes. You've been unconscious and feverish since we brought you in."

He felt a throbbing ache in his left arm and remembered what it'd looked like that terrible night. His eyes settled on the bandage that started just below his elbow and covered the rest of his arm and included his hand. He trembled.

"How bad is it?"

"When my brother, Hal, and I, brought you in, your arm was no longer bleeding thanks to the bitter cold, but the damage was already done. The muscles were badly mangled and several bones were shattered. The bullet went through your hand, but..."

She looked down at her lap and wrung her hands.

"But what?"

"We don't know how much use you'll have once it heals. We did the best we could. We're not doctors." She looked up at him, sadness in her eyes.

Ben drew in a deep breath and tried to grasp reality. He'd escaped Libby Prison, but at a cost. His heart skipped a beat when he remembered the wound in his leg. His eyes fixed on the lower part of his body, blanketed in the coverlet. He wanted to move his feet, to see if he still had two legs. Two legs that worked. But his mind wouldn't let him. He was paralyzed with fear. He glanced at the young woman who smiled with reassurance.

"We had more luck with your leg. We were able to get the bullet out and cleanse the wound completely. You're a lucky man. The bleeding slowed after you put the tourniquet on it, and the bitter cold helped to keep you from bleeding to death. It'll heal, but you'll have a nasty reminder for the rest of your life."

"It seems I'll have a few nasty reminders." He thought of the scars on his back and touched his cheek.

He moved his toes, happy to watch the blanket move back and forth. Relief flooded his senses. He closed his eyes and let his head fall back against the pillow. Tears escaped his closed eyelids.

Several minutes of awkward silence passed before he looked at her again.

"Thank you for what you've done. I would have died out there."

She nodded and smiled in return.

"I have a million questions, but I can hardly keep my eyes open. Can we talk later?" he asked.

"Of course. And when you're better able, we'll scrape some of that extra hair off your chin and see what you look like under there," she teased. She helped him get comfortable then tucked the cover under his chin. He was swept away in a warm slumber where he rested peacefully, without intrusion of war, pain, death, or even Sarah.

Shadows filled the room when he next woke. A bright fire danced in the hearth. On his right the dark-haired woman read in the soft glow of an oil lamp. When he stirred she raised her head and smiled.

He smiled back and, although this woman looked nothing like Sarah, hers was the face he saw. God how he missed her! Needed to get back to her.

"Good evening," the woman said, reminding him of where he was.

"Evening."

"You must be starved. I'll get some food."

She left the room and Ben tried to move. Pain shook his body. He grabbed at the fresh bandage around his left arm and hand and again, pain tore through him. It was a bitter price to pay for his freedom, he thought, but at least he was alive.

"Thank you, God," he whispered.

Sarah re-entered his thoughts. She must be worried sick about him, even wondering if he were dead by now, without word from him for so many months. He knew as soon as he was able he'd have to find a way to post a letter to her, but not until he was sure about the motives of these seemingly kind people.

The door opened and the woman came back into the room, a tray of food and drink in her hands. She placed the tray on the table beside the bed and his mind rolled with questions. *Who was this woman? Would she nurse him, only to send him back to Turner when she was done? Was she a spy, sent to learn all she could from him before he was sent back?* He didn't think so, but he had to be sure before he exposed anything of himself.

She pulled a napkin from the tray and placed it across Ben's chest. She dipped a spoon in a bowl of soup then raised it to Ben's lips. He stopped her arm in mid-air.

"I can feed myself."

She dropped the spoon back into the bowl, a hurt expression on her face. "You'll need to sit up more if you intend to do this yourself." She helped him resettle then picked up the tray and placed it over his lap while he refused to admit how painful it had been for him just to reposition.

His stomach began to roll when he smelled the soup. A sick feeling settled in his throat and he had to force himself to keep from vomiting. His head dropped back to the pillow and he took several deep breaths to recompose himself.

"It's been a while since you've had any real food, hasn't it?"

He barely nodded, the ill feeling still with him. Several minutes passed before his stomach stopped churning and he lifted his head. He took another deep breath, picked up the spoon and sipped the soup.

He ate little before his stomach felt like it was tied in

knots and he pushed the tray away.

The woman removed it to the other room then sat back down beside him.

"Where, exactly, am I?" Ben asked.

"You are in Virginia."

He stiffened, but she quickly reassured him.

"We may be in Virginia, sir, but there are many of us who do not hold with this war." There was stern dignity in her voice. "My brother and myself, for a few. Hal and I are the only thing that keeps this farm from falling into ruin. He doesn't fully comprehend what this war is about. He's very young." She paused and sighed. "Heaven knows, it's difficult enough for both of us to keep this place running. God forbid he run off to fight a war we don't believe in and leave me with this responsibility alone." Her voice sounded incredulous that anyone should expect such a thing. "My brother is only fourteen. He's still a child and I will not allow him to take part in this war." She paused again. "Besides, we promised our father only moments before he died that Hal wouldn't join either cause in this war. I pray every day this senseless war will end before foolish men destroy the world around us."

Ben was impressed by her honesty and her words, but still couldn't trust her completely. He was in the South. In Virginia. Enemy territory. He couldn't take any chances.

"What's your first name? Miss...Dugan was it?"

"Mary. Mary Dugan. And yours?"

"Ben Walters."

"And where are you from, Ben Walters?"

He paused, unsure of how much to tell her.

"The City of Kansas in Missouri."

His mind flew to memories of White Oaks. And Sarah.

"And your people? Are they there, too?" she asked.

His eyes met hers. "No. No family. Just me." He chose not to mention Sarah. He didn't want to give her anything of himself that could in any way be used against him.

"You fought for the Union?"

"Yes, ma'am. That's how I wound up in Libby," he said, the words bitter in his mouth.

He heard her gasp at the mention of Libby.

"Ahhh, you've heard of the establishment?"

She nodded. "I know of it," she whispered. "And I am ashamed when I hear of the evil that rages throughout that vile place." She looked away, her hand at her throat.

Ben sensed sincerity in her words, but he still wasn't completely convinced he could trust her.

"Is that where you got your many scars from?"

Ben nodded and let his head fall back into the pillows. He shuddered when he remembered the hell he'd lived through. But, he reminded himself, whatever the result his freedom was well worth the cost.

In the weeks that followed, resentment and anger surfaced often and grew heavy in Ben's chest. He would lash out, throw the clay ball he squeezed in his hand to regain his strength and wish with all his heart the ball would land in the middle of Major Turner's forehead and kill him dead.

He wanted to go home to Sarah. He couldn't post a letter to her because enough time had passed and now he was ashamed to admit he hadn't trusted the Dugans enough to tell them about her. But it was more than that, too. He didn't want to hurt Mary.

In the time he'd been there he knew she'd grown to care for him.

More than once during his lowest times, she'd reminded him to be thankful he was alive. "Many men weren't as lucky as you and are buried on the battlefield," she chastised when his anger revealed itself.

Ben watched her face, full of warmth and concern when she spoke. He tried to tell himself she was just a kind woman, but deep inside, he knew more was happening. And he realized how easy it would be to care for her. Just as easily as Sarah had learned to care for Man-Who-Runs, perhaps?

Each day Mary made excuses to spend more and more time with Ben. She dressed his wounds or walked the grounds with him and her growing feelings for him were plain on her face.

One evening while Ben, Mary and Hal sat in front of the

fire in the front room, Ben picked up a newspaper Hal had brought in from town. He unfolded it and his skin went cold as he glared at the bold headline.

"UNION FORCES SHELL FORT HENRY ON THE TENNESSEE RIVER."

"Read it out loud, Ben," Hal prodded, his green eyes alive with the curiosity of his fourteen years. A chill passed over him. How many boys, some barely older than Hal, had Ben seen left on the battlefield?

"Come on, Ben. Will ya read it?"

Ben nodded and began to read.

*Fort Henry Surrenders—After two hours of constant bombardment our illustrious Confederate troops at Fort Henry under Brigadier General Lloyd Tilghman were forced to surrender to Union Flag Officer Andrew Hull Foote. The early gunboat battle began with the deafening boom of the cannon as the Essex pounded the fort and the fort counter-fired. The Essex approached up river and gradually shortened the distance until their shells were fused at five-second intervals. The elevation of the guns was depressed until every shot went straight home. None from the Essex seemed to fall short. But the wind blew quickly across her bow and the big guns under General Tilgham sent a direct hit straight into her center boiler. It was reported by those inside Fort Henry that they could see men throwing themselves from the portholes into the water from the blast of steam that must have come from such a boiler. One report was that of the Essex's commander, Captain John Porter, who was scalded by a direct blast and threw himself into the water to be held by the waist by another seaman until rescued. It is also reported another of the gunboats, the Cincinnati, sustained extensive damage as well. She took 31 hits and suffered the most damage in her unarmored areas...*

Ben dropped the paper, unable to continue. He could see and hear the battle in his mind's eye. Smell the powder. Hear the thunder of the cannon, the screams of the wounded. See the blood run red like a river. He closed his eyes.

"Come on, Ben. Finish it." Hal's voice was expectant.

Ben looked up. Hal wanted to hear stories of glory and

great battles on the front. But that was something Ben wouldn't do. He wouldn't glorify war. It was an evil institution that he wished he'd never had to be a part of.

"Hal, don't press. I imagine Ben doesn't want to talk about the war any more."

"But Mary, I want to know. How will I ever know anything, me stuck here on this old farm?" Hal's voice was almost a whine.

Ben felt his heart thud and his blood ran cold.

"Hal, that's enough. Can't you see you're upsetting Ben?" Mary's voice had become stern, one the younger Dugan would no longer question.

Hal's lip curled up. "I'm sorry, Ben. I just want to know. And I'll never know stuck here."

"Be glad you're stuck here, Hal. And pray to God you never have to find out what it's like out there. Pray, Hal. Pray."

After Mary and Hal went to bed, Ben finished the newspaper account of the surrender at Fort Henry. The Union forces had emerged victorious, but at what cost? More good men. Both Union and Confederate. He closed his eyes and tried to force the unwanted thoughts from his mind.

He drifted to sleep in the chair. And as he slept, his mind waged its own war. He knew he should return to the front. He was a soldier and it was his duty. But he also wanted to go home. He needed desperately to return to Sarah. To tell her he was alive and everything he'd learned.

He woke the next morning, stiff and restless, but with a decision made.

He forced himself out of the chair. The scent of coffee led him to the kitchen where Mary stood by a table pouring the nearly clear, brownish liquid into a cup.

"Good morning." Her eyes sparkled with warmth when Ben walked into the room.

"Morning," he responded, his mind still spinning.

"Did you sleep well? I didn't dare disturb you. You seemed so quiet and peaceful."

"I slept fine." His voice was curt and he saw the hurt jump into Mary's eyes. She turned away and went about her chores, the room painfully quiet for several moments before she turned back to him.

"Have I done something?"

He felt rotten. "No, Mary. You haven't done anything but be kind and caring. I'm the one who's done something wrong. I've lived here for weeks, eaten your food, enjoyed yours and your brother's company, but given nothing in return." He stopped, tried to decide on the right words before he continued.

"But I've been happy to do it, Ben."

He turned away from her sad, questioning eyes. "It's time for me to go, Mary. Home to my wife in Missouri."

Mary stiffened. He rushed to finish his explanation.

"I didn't tell you when I first got here because I didn't know you. I had to protect certain things about myself." He ran his fingers through his hair. "I felt like I had to protect that part of me in order to keep her safe—just in case."

He looked into Mary's eyes, now welled with tears. She didn't move as she waited for him to continue.

"I'm sorry, Mary. So very sorry. I love Sarah and I have to try and get back to her. I have a lot to tell her. I never meant to hurt you. I just, well..." He couldn't finish. The pain in Mary's face stabbed him like a saber.

"Please. Try to understand. I had just escaped from prison, was in an unfamiliar place in the middle of enemy territory with people I knew nothing about. I had to be sure. And, by the time I was sure," he stammered, "I couldn't bring myself to tell you. I didn't want to hurt you. I saw what was happening, but I didn't do anything to discourage it, and for that, I'm truly sorry."

Mary closed her eyes and hung her head. "I understand, Ben. I suppose I just fell in love with the wrong Yankee." She raised her eyes to meet his then left the room, her back straight, her head high.

Ben felt miserable, but he knew what he'd done was right. It was time to go home.

He left that day after the midday meal. Mary packed as much food as he could carry and insisted on giving him one of three horses they'd managed to keep. Ben tried to decline, but

Mary insisted.

"Call it a loan, Ben. Call it whatever you want. You'll never make it back without it."

"You'll take good care of Nellie for me, won't you Ben?" Hal slapped the horse's belly to tighten the girth.

"I will, Hal. I promise." Ben walked toward the young man and clapped him on the back. "I want you to know how grateful I am for everything." His eyes flashed upon Mary who stood silent on the porch, watching.

"Have a safe journey, Ben." Hal extended his hand and the two shook.

Ben released Hal and walked to Mary, her face ashen.

"Goodbye, Mary. I can't thank you enough for all you've done. I'll never forget you." He touched his lips to her cheek.

Tears filled her eyes and her lips quivered. Her arms flew around Ben's neck and she kissed him full on the mouth. A warm, desperate kiss.

"I love you, Ben Walters. Always remember that," she whispered only loud enough for him to hear. As quick as she had flung her arms around his neck, she drew away, stoic, her hands folded in front of her. "Goodbye, Ben. Be careful."

He stepped off the porch and walked toward Hal and the horse. He grabbed the saddle horn with his right hand and awkwardly pulled himself onto the horse's back. He took the reins and spun the animal around to face Hal and Mary who stood together watching him from the porch.

He waved.

"Stay off the main roads," Hal called. "There are a lot of Virginians who would relish the idea of turning in, or outright shooting, a stranger as a spy. Hopefully, those clothes you're wearing won't attract attention," Hal said of his father's old work clothes. "Just stay in the brush and head West." Hal raised his hand and waved. Mary only smiled. The sadness in her face tore at Ben's heart as he nudged Nellie forward.

"Goodbye and thanks again." He turned Nellie westward toward home and never looked back.

## Chapter Twenty

Ben rode long and hard each day. Thoughts of Sarah drove him onward. His arm throbbed mercilessly, but the pain reminded him he was alive and going home, to Sarah and White Oaks. More often than he was comfortable with he felt the pangs of guilt for, in essence, he was a deserter. But for all the army knew, he was still in that hellhole, Libby. Or dead. Once he got home and spent some time with Sarah, he'd eventually ride back to Fort Leavenworth and let them know he was alive.

But for now, his only goal was his wife.

The horse foraged in the woods when they rested and he ate sparingly of the food Mary had packed.

He'd been in the saddle for five days and was deep in the western half of Virginia, or was it Kentucky? He didn't know for sure. He just rode west toward home.

While resting along the roadside behind some thick bushes, the echo of hooves in the distance brought him alert. Sunlight splintered his view so he couldn't see who was riding toward him, and it wasn't until the detachment of men was almost on him that he saw the blue uniforms that marked them for a Union company.

Concealed by the bushes he took a minute to decide what to do. Should he hail the troops and travel with them? They were headed west. It would be safer. But if he did, would he be free to leave when they reached their destination, or would he be pressed back into service? He was still a soldier, he knew that, but he needed more than anything to reach Sarah.

The snap of a twig behind him gave him only a second's warning before the cold muzzle of a gun on his temple took the decision out of his hands.

"Wait." Ben said. "I'm a Union officer."

"And I'm Abe Lincoln hisself," the soldier hissed. "If that's true, why the hell are you hiding in these bushes like a damned Reb spy?"

"I'm not a spy. I'm Lieutenant Ben Walters," he said in a rush. "I was captured at Lexington last September while serving under Colonel Mulligan with the 13th Missouri. I was taken to Libby Prison, but managed to escape several weeks ago." He looked down at his hand. "I came away with a souvenir for my time spent there." He raised his useless arm.

"Don't move, mister. At least not until I'm sure who you are."

Ben lowered his hand and remained frozen.

The soldier looked Ben over with suspicion. Several others joined him. A sergeant stepped up and told Ben to continue his story.

"After I escaped, I was found by a family who nursed me back to health. I'm on my way home to Missouri right now."

The sergeant grew thoughtful. Ben knew Missouri was still a hotbed of southern sentiments, but he had to convince these men he was, indeed, a Union officer.

A captain approached and reined in his horse. He spoke to the sergeant then turned and addressed Ben.

"Why should we believe your story?" His voice was even and cold. "We find you crouched in the bushes, ready to strike, and we're to believe you're a Union officer who's escaped from Libby Prison?"

"It's the truth, sir," Ben answered quickly. "If you search me and the area around me, you'll see I have no weapon."

The captain nodded and pointed the sergeant to the bushes. "Search it well, gentlemen."

"Nothing here, Captain," the sergeant reported minutes later, "but that still don't prove nothing. How do we know he ain't a spy, or a rebel sympathizer?" He cast a dark glance at Ben who remained frozen.

Several other soldiers grumbled and Ben felt his composure beginning to slip. How was he going to convince these men he was a Union officer? He had no identification. No papers. No uniform with his rank. He had only his word.

The captain stared down at him and took in his mangled arm and the scar on his cheek.

"Where'd you get those?" he asked.

"Libby. Compliments of Major Turner, the prison's commandant." Ben was unable to keep the contempt from his voice.

"The captain looked thoughtful. "What engagements have you seen, Lieutenant?"

"I was at Carthage and Wilson's Creek, sir. I was with General Nathaniel Lyon when he died." Ben remembered the courage of the man. "After that, I was assigned to the 13th Missouri at Lexington, where I was captured when Price took the city. I was taken to Libby for my knowledge of the western roads because I served under General Harney out West before the war." A bead of sweat rolled down his forehead as the captain mulled over his words.

The captain and sergeant moved away and heatedly discussed Ben's situation for several minutes before the captain returned to Ben.

"I'll take you at your word, soldier. You may join us, but be aware, you'll be watched at all times. You may be who you say you are, but I'll not risk my men solely upon your word. Not until you've proven yourself."

"I understand, sir. Be assured, you won't be sorry. I'm no spy."

"Collins, keep a watch on him." The captain saluted the sergeant then turned his horse and rode to the front of the waiting column.

"Don't you pull any funny stuff mister. I get the least idea you're a Reb and I'll shoot you dead just as quick as look at you," Collins promised.

"You have no need to worry, Sergeant. I'm who I say I am and only time will prove it." The prickling sensation in Ben's bones started to subside.

The trek westward turned into days of hard riding and Ben had no idea where they were going. During discussions with the other men about Wilson's Creek, Lexington and Libby, he knew he was beginning to win their trust, but still no one would tell him where they were headed.

The weather turned unseasonably warm for early February, and Ben welcomed the tepid air on his worn body and the sun on his face as the column rode long and hard each day.

He kept mostly to himself, but a feeling of helplessness hovered over him. Overheard bits and pieces of conversations told him the company was on its way into battle.

Would he be forced to accompany them, or would he be allowed to continue his journey home? If he were forced to fight, he would do so with an almost useless hand and no passion. He just wanted to get back to Sarah. He ached to hold her, touch her and explain all he'd learned.

Dozing in the saddle, his mind swam with memories of the past year. He saw Miller, curled against Dobbs in the darkness of the prison walls. Mary hovered high above. Her soft green eyes beckoned and pleaded. He watched himself thrown to the ground as a bullet exploded into his arm. And as he watched, his fingers detached from his hand and crawled away.

He woke with a start, a cold chill throughout his body.

"Catch a few winks?" the soldier beside him chuckled.

Ben nodded and forced a smile, unsettled by his dream.

"Won't be long now."

"Till what?" Ben asked.

"Fort Donelson," the man said.

"Fort Donelson?" Ben was fully awake now.

"Yep. Should git there in the next few hours. Captain says we'll hook up with General McClernand's troops and take that fort in no time."

Ben nodded. At least his destination now had a name. Fort Donelson on the Cumberland River.

Several hours later the company forded the Tennessee River. Once on the south side, a Union scout led them to General McClernand's encampment. There, Ben learned they were to wait for General Ulysses S. Grant and his forces coming from Fort Henry.

Why was he still here? he asked himself over and over again. In all reality, his enlistment was over. He'd have to go to the commanding officer and ask to be released from duty before he could go anywhere, but he'd done his time. More than his share. He'd stayed with Lyon at Wilson's Creek because it was his duty. Damn! If he left now without being formally discharged, he could be chased down as a deserter.

General McClernand's adjutant led Ben to the general's tent. He snapped to attention. "Lieutenant Ben Walters reporting, sir."

General McClernand returned the salute and offered Ben a chair.

"What can I do for you, Lieutenant?"

Ben took only a few minutes to explain his situation. He referenced on several occasions that, technically, his enlistment was already finished.

General McClernand rubbed his chin. "Lieutenant, I am sorry to be the one to refuse you, but battle looms on the horizon. I need every man I have, and many more I don't."

"But, sir. My enlistment was over long before now. I've served more than my share."

"I understand and appreciate that. But things are different now. That was the beginning of the war, Walters. Men were hurrying to volunteer, certain we were going to whip these damnable Rebs in no time. But those same men have learned war isn't as glorious as it's made out to be in books—is it?"

"No, sir." Ben's heart slammed in his chest. He wasn't going to be discharged. General McClernand was going to make him stay. He almost smiled at the irony. He was no longer a prisoner of the Confederates, but one of his own army.

"I'm sorry, Walters, I can't grant your release." McClernand stood, saluted and turned away.

Ben sat for another minute while he absorbed the fact he'd been given no choice but to stay. He knew what happened to deserters. And regardless of the fact he'd volunteered for only ninety days, he would not be discharged. He'd heard the Confederates were considering the use of conscription; the right to force a man into the army against his will. Was his being forced to stay any less than being conscripted by the army he'd already done his time for?

Unable to change the general's mind, Ben accepted the fact he had no recourse but to make the best of being among McClernand's troops. While the other soldiers finished setting up camp, Ben relaxed against a huge oak tree and soaked in every warm ray of sunshine that stroked his face. He began a letter to Sarah, but quickly put it aside. "I'll finish later," he thought, uncertain how to tell her, yet again, he wasn't coming home.

He soon drifted off to sleep. Sarah came to him in his dreams. She begged and pleaded for him to come home, but he shivered and tried to explain he had no choice but to stay.

He woke later that afternoon, shivering at the bitter cold that had settled in. The wind whipped and a frigid chill gripped the air. The sun had disappeared behind a huge bank of clouds and a cold drizzle had begun to fall. By nightfall, the drizzle turned to sleet and the temperature plummeted.

Weapons and artillery froze to the ground. Men shook in the bitter cold, having discarded their coats at the earlier false promise of spring.

Ben clapped his hands and feet, trying to keep warm, while the other men struggled to do the same. His mind flashed back to the frozen time he had spent at Fort Pierre. He thought of Libby, where the gnawing cold had been a constant every day and night he had been there. He shook involuntarily at the vivid pictures that assaulted his mind. Dobbs. Miller. Had he killed Dobbs? And what had happened to Miller?

He was snapped back to the present when a bullet whizzed past his head. He dropped to the ground out of the sharpshooter's line of fire.

Throughout the night the Rebels took potshots at the Union men and made it impossible to light fires to warm themselves.

To the rear in the dark Ben was, at least, able to move around. He paced, blew on his hands and stamped his feet in his attempt to stay warm. His nose was numb and he couldn't feel his ears or fingers. He'd been smart enough to hang onto his coat earlier in the day, regardless of the warm temperatures, but in the bitter cold it brought little comfort.

When the sun rose, Ben slid to the edge of a ridge above the river and watched the Union gunboat flotilla arrive, along with twelve army transports and a reported additional 10,000 men. Word came down the lines General Grant was among the newly arrived troops, fresh from his victory at Fort Henry, to join the effort to take Fort Donelson.

Ben studied the flurry of preparations on the four vessels in the flotilla, which helped keep his mind off the bitter temperature. Men piled chains, lumber and bags of coal on the upper decks of the steamers to keep them from being damaged by plunging fire, catapulted from inside the fort. By late afternoon the gunboats were ready and headed upriver toward the fort and battle.

At a range of less than 2,000 yards from the fort, the *St. Louis* opened fire. The shells exploded against the thick earthworks around the fort, but the confederates held their fire.

The Federal boats steamed closer. The Confederates held their fire, but the fort remained silent. Ben knew their plan; they'd wait until the steamers got in closer before they pounded them with everything they had. And so it went. When the ships got to within four hundred yards of the fort, the Rebs opened fire with their twelve big guns.

Cannon from the fort pounded the Federal boats. Black smoke billowed into the air as the Confederate guns ravaged the ironclad gunboats. The *St. Louis* took a direct hit through the pilothouse, injuring Flag Officer Foote, Ben learned later. Smoke stacks fell into the river; anchors exploded into fragments of iron and steel, wheelhouses were destroyed. The roar of cannon was deafening and continued without cease. The *Louisville* took several direct hits that left it out of control as it floated back down river and out of site, the now powerless *St. Louis* right behind it. When the *Pittsburgh* tried to turn, it ran into the *Carondelet* and took off her starboard rudder to send both steamers floating helplessly down river, also.

In the midst of this chaos, the barrage from the fort stopped and silence enveloped the surrounding areas. Ben's heart sank. He knew the battle was lost. All the gunboats were severely damaged and gone from sight.

Now it would be the men's turn to try and take the fort. Tomorrow, he would face the enemy again.

An eruption of cheers from inside the fort broke into his thoughts. But this was today and the Rebs had won the day...and they were damn sure letting the Yanks know it.

That night the wind blew in discontent and brought with it more frigid weather. Temperatures dropped even lower and snow started to fall.

Ben shivered and tried to keep warm. His mind flashed to Sarah's face, smiling and soft, and he felt a real ache in the pit of his stomach he missed her so much. He missed her tenderness, her laughter, and her love.

He stared into the blackness of night remembering, wishing and hoping. Coldness crept over him. He got up and walked in circles, jumped up and down, stamped his feet to keep the circulation moving in his frozen body. It was going to be a long night.

After a restless night, at the first sign of light, campfires were lit to warm frozen hands and feet. Coffee boiled and sparse rations were distributed.

Wild screams broke the quiet of the morning. Ben looked toward the fort and watched hundreds of Confederates swarming out from inside.

He scrambled for the weapon they had finally given him; aware he was in serious trouble.

Ben felt as though he was looking straight into the fires of hell as the sea of gray-clad men raced toward him, his imminent death their quest. He shivered from the cold and dread. His knuckles were white he gripped his handgun so tight.

He fired. Fired again. The weapon discharged continually until its chamber was empty. Reloading was awkward at best as he used his crippled hand to steady the gun. A burst of Union fire dropped the first wave of Confederates and they broke from formation to regroup. But within minutes they charged again.

Ben raised his gun and squeezed the trigger. A Reb was sprawled in front of him, his eyes staring up at heaven, his mouth agape. He fired into the gray mass until his gun was empty again. He rolled onto his elbow, reloaded and sat up just in time to ward off another attack. He fired without thought into an approaching soldier's chest. A red flower of blood burst onto the soiled gray uniform and the Reb fell with a strangled gurgle to the ground.

The Confederates came quicker. Ben raced between

rocks and trees. His bullets spent, he grabbed a fallen soldier's rifle and used the bayonet while his arms grew heavier and less effective with each thrust of the weapon.

"Behind you!" someone yelled. Ben whirled in time to force the blade into the stomach of an oncoming Reb. His mind screamed for retreat, but he fought on while he encouraged other men to do the same. In their faces he saw fear and courage as they continued the struggle to save their lives.

Horses burst onto the hill and Confederate cavalrymen flooded the woods.

Ben pulled a cartridge box from a dead soldier and reloaded his gun. He fired and reloaded again and again. The Union forces were being pushed back foot by foot, rock by rock, while he and the other men tried to hold their positions.

"Dammit," Ben growled. "I'm out of ammo again."

Another soldier slid up beside him. "Need more powder?" There was a strange gleam in the man's eyes.

Ben nodded.

"Wait."

The man slid toward the oncoming line. He raised his rifle and took aim. A baby-faced boy fell without a sound when the rifle shot slammed into his chest. The man scrambled toward the boy, pulled the gun from his hand and searched the body for the cartridge box. He returned a few moments later and presented Ben with the gun and ammunition while Ben stared at the dead eyes of the fallen boy.

Firing erupted behind him. Ben swung around and watched in horror as the men fell from rifle fire from their flank.

"What the hell is going on?" he screamed. "We're in a cross-fire! Get down and stay down," he yelled to any man who was listening. A volley of mini balls flew above his head. He crouched behind a rock, jumped when balls slammed into the trees and rocks all around him. He could do nothing but wait and hope the Rebs didn't attack again from in front.

It seemed like hours before the firing stopped. And when it did, the Rebs didn't wait long before they came on again.

Ben rolled back and forth firing and reloading as the Rebs continued to swarm his position. Men fought behind any tree or rock and sprawled on the frigid, unyielding ground.

Suddenly the firing stopped. He peeked out from behind the tree he was using as cover and noticed that there were no more Confederates coming over the hill.

"Where are they?" Ben yelled to a private in front of him hiding behind a rock. He was certain the Rebs were regrouping to strike again, harder and stronger than before. They waited, but nothing happened. His curiosity got the better of him. He slithered to the crest of the hill and was amazed by the sight that greeted him.

The Confederates were in complete retreat.

"They're high-tailing it back to the fort," a private shouted. The Rebs were kicking the tar out of McClernand's forces, so why in hell would they retreat? Ben wondered as he watched them in full withdrawal.

Cheers erupted along the embattled Union lines and Ben understood.

To the west, fresh Union artillery and rifle fire resounded throughout the countryside. A death knell for the exhausted Confederates.

## Chapter Twenty-One

Ben watched as the dead from both sides were buried. The carnage at Fort Donelson was overwhelming and he felt numb while he and the others waited for word to move out. But every day the order was delayed, yet again.

Word was General Grant was furious over General Halleck's continued delays.

*We should have chased those rebels right into the earth,* Ben thought. But instead they cleaned their weapons and awaited orders to depart.

So instead of allowing his time here to be a complete waste, Ben scavenged some paper and the stub of a pencil and wrote a letter.

*My darling Sarah,*

*I am alive! I know I haven't written in months, and for that, please forgive me. I know you must be wild with worry by now. When you hear my tale you'll understand, but for now, just know that I am alive and making my way home.*

*How can I begin to tell you the horror I've experienced since I saw you last? Good men die on both sides of this war in bloody battles for fields and forts.*

*We fight men such as ourselves, who have families and believe in the same God. Why, then, do we kill and maim each other as we do?*

*I cannot bear the moments until we are together. There is so much I must say. Firstly and above all else, I must beg your forgiveness. I have learned life is sacred, as you did in your ordeal with the Indians, and now I fully understand the torment you suffered because of me for so long. I've stared death and privation in the face. I've seen men die quickly and mercifully, slowly and grotesquely. I've done things I'm not proud of, and never dreamed I could or would ever do. But I was forced to, as you once were, in order to survive. And even though we mended the rift between us before I left, there was always a hole in my soul where I knew you'd cared for that Indian. Now, at least, I can sincerely say I understand it. I can't wait to be with you and*

## Tomorrow's Promise: Survival on the Plains      D.L. Rogers

*talk of all these things, so you will truly know my thoughts.*

*I fear this war will drag on forever and feel as though I've aged tenfold since we were last together. I pray daily I live long enough to say these things in person.*

*Until we're together, I remain forever, your loving husband.*

Ben sealed the letter in a ragged envelope and stuffed it in his breast pocket to post as soon as he possibly could.

Orders finally came to depart and the men marched to Pittsburg Landing, on the Tennessee River. Buoyant once again from the victory at Fort Donelson and happy to be on the move, the troops set up camp on a plateau four miles inland on the western side of the river in what was deemed "enemy territory." And again, they waited.

Ben scanned the area from the front of his tent. All around there were orchards and forests cut by deep, winding ravines. Several creeks and rivers guarded the camp to the north and south and the river to their rear. The position deemed secure by Grant and his advisors, no barricades were erected against the enemy and listless guards walked the perimeter without conviction.

Ben walked onto a wet road and took a deep breath of the strong smells of the surrounding woodlands, of the camps with brewing coffee and lit cigars. He walked aimlessly, wanting only to be moving, tired of the unending wait. He ambled from one encampment to another and listened to the excited talk of green soldiers anxious to be in battle—to stomp the Rebs into oblivion. He shook his head while he gazed into the faces of children. Boys, barely old enough to shave, fighting for—what? The preservation of the Union? Freedom for the black man? States' rights? Or because they rallied to the cry for war, not realizing the true horror that would confront them on the battlefield.

He stopped in front of a little white building that looked like a church where heavily armed men guarded the door. Inside he could see men moving quickly and purposefully. He spotted General Sherman and assumed the building to be his headquarters. He glanced up at the dull, decaying sign that swung over the door of the building's weathered exterior.

Shiloh.

A thunderous explosion shook the ground.

Ben jerked bolt upright. It was still dark, the middle of the night. "What the hell was that?"

He scrambled from his tent out into total chaos. Men ran in every direction, screaming and yelling.

"What the hell is going on?" He grabbed the sleeve of a soldier who ran past. The sound of gunfire popped all around.

"Firing to the south!" the soldier yelled. "The 53rd has been attacked."

Ben looked up to see Federal soldiers running toward him from the direction of the gunfire.

"Where are you men going? Turn and fight!" Ben commanded.

"There's too many, sir. The Rebs are everywhere!" one of the retreating soldiers cried. "Save yourself!"

Ben stood rooted to the ground, unsure of what to do next. Then he saw them. Like a hoard of angry ants, hundreds of Confederates marched right toward him.

"Form battle lines!" he yelled. "Hold your ground!" Some of the men were beginning to reform lines when there was a barrage of bullets around them. Ben threw himself behind the cover of the closest tent and watched the army in gray advance. His body shook and sweat beaded on his brow. His breath came in short gasps as he fought for control. He checked his carbine and looked down at his waist to make sure his handgun was still tucked tight into his belt. His ammo box was full and he prayed it would last.

"Here they come!" someone yelled.

Ben stepped out from the cover of the tent and fired. The men around him fired and the night sky exploded into brilliant orange and yellow fireworks. Gray-clad men staggered and fell like rag dolls under the heavy barrage.

The assault continued for hours. He was tired beyond imagination, but he held his ground and fought back wave after wave of confederates as best he could. When the sun rose, its rays glinted off both Confederate and Union rifles that lay unmanned beside dead owners. And still the Rebs came on.

"Fall back!" came the call from the embattled Federal lines. "Fall back!" Ben repeated.

Inch by inch, foot by foot, Ben and his newly assigned company withdrew, firing as they went. He was exhausted, soaked with sweat, but still the Rebs came on.

A shadow moved across Ben's face. A Confederate soldier was beside him, bayonet poised to strike.

Ben threw himself to the right and landed heavily on the ground a split second before the bayonet plunged into the tree he'd been standing in front of.

"I'll kill you, you damn Yankee!" the Reb yelled. He thrust the bayonet a second time. Ben rolled to his left. The blade missed his ear by a mere fraction. He scrambled to his feet, raised his rifle, pulled the trigger, and shattered the face of his attacker.

He dropped to his knees holding what remained of his face and slid to the ground, silent and dead. Ben was shaking and knew he had to compose himself.

He stood up. His chest heaved and sweat poured down his face. He looked down at the dead man until his thoughts were interrupted by silence. He looked up, turned in every direction—and saw no one.

He'd been in the midst of battle and now he was alone. Everyone was gone.

He listened for gunfire in the distance and headed in its direction.

The woods were quiet except for the crackle of leaves and twigs under his feet. Streaks of early morning sunlight filtered through the trees and cast an eerie glow on the world around him, littered with dead men. It was ghostly still, with not even a wisp of wind to disturb the fallen bodies.

Several Confederate stragglers came toward him from the direction of the gunfire. The men stopped and stared, then turned and ran.

Ben breathed again.

He wandered for nearly fifteen minutes before he came

onto the flank of a company of Federal troops.

He quickly identified himself and joined the men in blue.

"Better get your head down, Lieutenant. The Rebs are having a grand time taking pot shots at us," one of the soldiers yelled.

Ben dropped to the ground and slithered up behind a rock. He poked his head up and saw a line of gray uniforms that was slowly closing in around the company. They were in front, to the left and right! If they weren't stopped, they'd soon have the Union boys completely circled.

Cannon shells exploded and sent debris flying in all directions. Ben ducked, covered his head and waited for the flurry to end. Another explosion, only twenty feet away, left his ears ringing a wild tune. Wave after wave of gray uniforms inched forward in the attempt to circle the Federals.

The Rebs were relentless, but the Federals were as determined not to be surrounded and the battle became a stalemate. Positions surged back and forth for hours as the Rebs pounded the Union troops and the Federals answered before the order was finally given for them to fall back.

As the Federals retreated toward the river and out of the line of fire, Ben searched for his lost company. Once located, he rejoined them and rested, thankful not to have been caught in the horseshoe the Rebs had tried to close around him. He'd never allow himself to be taken prisoner and put in a rebel prison again. Never. He'd die first.

Ben had just curled up against a tree to rest, when cheers erupted across camp. Buell's army had been spotted crossing the Tennessee to relieve Grant's exhausted men.

Ben smiled, laid his head down on a little patch of earth and closed his eyes, thankful for even a few minutes respite.

The night sky was filled with clouds. It turned cold again and the men huddled together for warmth.

The engagement had raged for hours after Ben's company retreated, and the field of battle moved closer to camp.

But as darkness descended the battle was given up until daylight. From where Ben and his company bedded down for the night he could hear the strangled cries of wounded and dying men in the distance—men who had fallen earlier that day and left on the field of battle.

Though cannons and guns were quiet in the darkness, the cries of the wounded rode the night air like wraiths. Unable to sleep, Ben walked instead. Before he knew it Ben had walked to the edge of the day's battlefield, and what he saw in the occasional moonlight that slipped through the scudding clouds, made him want to wretch. He rubbed his eyes to make sure he wasn't hallucinating. To his horror, the scene was real.

Hundreds of men lay where they'd fallen, dead and wounded alike. They were piled one on top of the other, some with their faces to the sky, others buried in the dirt. Pitiful pleas for help floated on the night air and pierced him to his soul.

"Why doesn't somebody do something?" he asked no one.

But he knew the answer to his own question. There was nothing anyone could do. There was no way to transfer the injured behind the lines. Nobody would even try or the snipers would add them to the casualties already on the field.

He stared out over the dead and wounded and his skin began to crawl like an invasion of lice. Unable to stand any more he stomped back to his men, a feeling of helplessness enveloping him like a glove.

Hours later when full darkness had descended, the wretched voices faded and a cold, heavy rain began. Frigid wind whipped from the north and lightning flashed in the sky to light up the ghastly sight on the battlefield.

"Sweet Jesus," Ben whispered as he stared out over the grisly visage. Blood from the battlefield flowed like a red river as rain pounded the earth and the bodies that littered it. Pools of water mixed with blood stood crimson in the moonlight. Horses stamped and snorted, anxious to get away from the red, oozing stench of death.

Ben stared in anguished horror and nearly choked on his own bile when, in the flashes of lightning, he saw packs of wild hogs feasting on the flesh of the dead.

Unable to stand the sight any longer, Ben staggered away, his head spinning like a child's top. A feeling of sheer helplessness threatened to crush him. Would he survive this damnable war or would he, too, end up like those men, forgotten and left as fodder for the pigs?

Determined to survive, Ben slid to the ground. He pulled his hat down over his face, wrapped his arms around his legs and curled up against the cold knot of anger and fear growing in his stomach and forced himself to sleep.

After a fitful night he and his men woke with the order to march. Grant was ready to counterattack.

Amidst a sea of mud and rain, Ben ordered his men into formation and fell into step with the rest of the troops that marched back into battle.

At the first line of gray-uniformed men, they fired. The Confederates were a raggedy lot, maybe even more exhausted than the Federals, Ben thought, and gave way to the Union forces with little effort. Ben fired constantly as the unit made its way back through their original encampment and toward the little white church called Shiloh.

Near the building, he and his men were met by bitter resistance. All day the Rebs charged. And all day the Federal lines held.

The smell of blood and death saturated the air, Ben's clothes, and the countryside around him. He thought the fighting would never end. Every ounce of his body screamed for rest. Real rest. He checked himself routinely, unable to tell whether the blood that soaked his uniform was his or someone else's.

He readied himself for another Rebel charge. Fired. A boy fell in front of him. The Reb's mouth twitched and his eyes rolled in his head. He coughed and blood dribbled down his neck. This was the enemy Ben had to remind himself, even though he wanted to run to the boy, cradle him in his arms and comfort him in his last seconds before death.

Another charge brought Ben back to reality and he fired into the mass of attacking troops, their Rebel yell preceding them.

The day proceeded relentlessly. It was one attack after another in the effort to push the Rebels back a little farther and reclaim Shiloh church. Ben prayed only to live through the day.

Finally, the Rebel yells became akin to a croak and by late afternoon had all but died away.

The Confederates retreated. Ben dropped to the ground, exhausted and thankful to be alive. He watched the Rebs stagger away, their faces dirty and bitter.

Ben jumped upright and saluted sharply when General Grant and his aide rode up beside him. Grant surveyed the defeated rebel troops through his field glasses.

"Shall I pass the order to pursue them, General?" the aide asked.

Grant lowered his glasses and glanced back over his own bloody, exhausted men.

"No, Major. These men have seen enough action today. We shall reserve our strength for yet another day."

It had been days. Or was it weeks? Ben rocked in his saddle, more tired than he'd ever been, the feeling his constant companion these past years. He looked up at the afternoon sky and wondered if they'd ever reach Corinth, on the northern border of Mississippi.

General Halleck, who had replaced General Grant in charge of all Federal troops after the near debacle at Shiloh, was following the retreating Confederates—but at a snail's pace. He was a wary general and every day became an exercise in tolerance for his men. They rode a mere mile a day of the twenty-three mile distance to Corinth. The soldiers were restless and irritable. They'd been traveling for weeks on what should have been a hard one-day ride.

Ben shook his head at the caution being exercised by General Halleck and nearly chuckled. *The Rebs would be long gone by the time they reached Corinth. Why even bother?*

Finally, after nearly a month in the saddle and a few minor skirmishes, Halleck's troops reached Corinth. Ben prodded his mount forward for a better view. It looked like any other city, with wooden buildings that lined a main street, sidewalks and stores. Except this city was deserted.

Of course it was deserted, he nearly shouted out loud. It had taken them weeks to make a trip that should have taken one day. *What was Halleck thinking? That the Rebs would sit around and wait for the Union Army to arrive?* They must have had a good laugh at the expense of all these weary men thanks to the general's caution.

Ben was leaning forward on his saddle, gazing out over the deserted city, when an explosion rocked the ground. Then another. Black smoke billowed into the sky as building after building ignited until the entire city was one giant fireball.

By the time the rubble cooled down enough for the Federal troops to enter, all that was left of the city was a smoking blackened skeleton. The Rebs had destroyed all provisions they couldn't take with them and left the Federals with nothing but the city's charred remains.

Ben gazed out over the blackened town, deserted and destroyed. But in the destruction of Corinth he understood the ramifications of what it meant. The Confederacy was now split in half and unless an incredibly brilliant counter-offensive was struck, the desperate Confederate bid for the Western states was all but lost.

A year had passed since Ben witnessed the destruction of Corinth and his company was now attached to General Hurlbut's troops. They'd done little more during the last year than wait, with the exception of a few guerilla excursions to break up enemy communications and, basically, harass the Rebs. Now they were being sent to reinforce Grant's troops at Vicksburg. And again, they would wait.

It was July 4th, Independence Day, 1863, and from atop a hill that overlooked Vicksburg Ben gazed at what had been the site of the forty day siege. His heart ached as he watched thousands of beleaguered men march out of the city. It was rumored the inhabitants had eaten every cow, dog, cat and rat to be found during the siege. The men were haggard and beaten and looked like walking scarecrows. Ben's heart went out to them. He knew how they felt. Uncertain of their future. Of life itself. At least they'd get some decent food in their bellies, he thought, as he watched the Union stores brought out to feed the hungry prisoners. He stared in silence from the hilltop as men attacked the food ravenously. He looked away, a heavy sadness overwhelming him. He thought of Miller and wondered if he was still alive in that hellhole of a prison. Ben had wished over and over he could have somehow gotten him out, but knew if he'd tried they'd both be dead. At least he'd kept his promise, he reminded himself. Dobbs would never hurt Miller again.

Ben was shaken from his melancholy thoughts by uproarious cheers of the Union troops. Curious, he joined a crowd surrounding a courier.

He tapped a soldier on the shoulder. "What's all the commotion?"

"Gettysburg! That's what's all the commotion, Lieutenant," the soldier answered, a silly smile on his face.

"Well? What happened?"

"This here courier brought word Gettysburg fell yesterday. We sent those damn Rebs retreating! Again! Yesterday, Gettysburg. Today, Vicksburg. We've all but got those Rebel dogs whipped!" The man danced away into the crowd of revelers.

Ben's spirits soared. With the victories at Gettysburg and Vicksburg, maybe the tide of the war was finally changing. The Confederates were low on everything. They had few horses, little food or ammunition for their rifles; they were so bad off, many of the men didn't even have shoes. They couldn't last much longer.

*But,* he thought, *they've held on like a tick on a dog for this long without giving up, without giving us a rest. Why should these victories change anything?*

## Chapter Twenty-Two

It was a typical Missouri summer day—hot and muggy—and Sarah fidgeted in the heat. She'd come into town to visit Emma and her sister, but had decided to visit the general store for some needed supplies while she was there. She laid the newspaper down on the bench outside the store. She was so tired of war news, more tired of reading about the battles and seeing lists of the dead. She rubbed her eyes and laid her head back against the wall. *When would it all end?* She leaned forward, picked the paper back up, and read an article about the Rebel bushwhacker activity that continued to disrupt the mail service and taunted the local Federal garrison. She wondered if there might be a lost letter from Ben in those sacks of mail stolen by the guerillas, and clung to that hope. Fear gnawed at her every day that he could be dead or a prisoner, but she refused to allow herself to dwell on it, afraid she'd lose her sanity. Although she hadn't heard from him in so long she couldn't even remember the last letter, she had to believe he was alive, but unable to correspond or his letters lost, and would return to her as soon as he could. Focusing on that got her through each day.

Shouting erupted down the street as an army wagon rumbled toward her. Eight or ten women were huddled in its bed and looked like frightened does. They held onto each other for support as their eyes darted from one side of the wagon to the other. The wagon rolled past and Sarah stared into the women's eyes. In them she saw fear, but she also saw determination. Surrounded by Federal soldiers the wagon clattered past. Who were they? she wondered.

Her curiosity piqued, she followed behind with the swelling crowd until the wagon stopped in front of a brick building on Grand Avenue. The women were led inside, still clinging to each other for support. One soldier took up guard outside while several others followed the frightened women inside.

Sarah wanted to know who they were, if only to ease her

curiosity. Something important was happening, and she wanted to know what it was. The army didn't make a practice of parading women through the center of town and imprisoning them.

She pushed her way to a nearby soldier and tapped him on the shoulder.

"Excuse me, soldier. Who are those women? Why are they being held?"

The soldier was more than happy to answer, a wide grin across his face.

"These here women are kin to them guerillas, Quantrill and Bloody Bill. They's part of the system that keeps gettin' supplies to 'em so's we can't catch 'em." He paused and ran his sleeve across his nose. "We'll catch 'em now. Now that they won't have nobody feedin' 'em and givin' 'em shelter."

Sarah thanked the soldier and hurried away. Fear gripped her like a claw. Quantrill and Bloody Bill wouldn't stand by as their friends and loved ones were imprisoned. There would be hell to pay. Retaliation. Sarah hurried to her wagon and sped home as quickly as the old mule could go.

Several weeks later, while Sarah was mending a shirt in the bright, afternoon sunlight of the front room, a wagon clattered up the long drive. She dropped her stitchery on a table and stepped onto the porch to await her visitor. Emma sat beside the driver of the wagon, her face ashen and drawn with worry, obvious even from a distance.

The wagon stopped and the driver helped Emma to the ground. She met Sarah at the bottom of the porch stairs.

"Emma, what's wrong?" Sarah knew something was terribly wrong as she went to help her friend up the steps.

"It's terrible, dear girl, just terrible," the older woman mumbled. She pushed past Sarah, up the steps and into the house. To Sarah she seemed more frail than she had several weeks ago on her last visit to town.

"Come here, child," Emma commanded. She sat down on the sofa and patted the seat next to her. Sarah sat down.

Emma took Sarah's hand. "Child, I bring dreadful news."

Sarah's heart pounded. Had Emma heard something about Ben?

"Do you recall some women?" Emma began. "Friends and family of some of those raiders? Oh, what were their names?"

"Quantrill and Bloody Bill?" Sarah recalled very well the women brought into town by wagon several weeks ago.

"Yes, dear. Those are the very ones. Anyway, the building they were being held in collapsed." Sarah gasped. "Five of those women were killed and many of the others were injured," Emma continued. "One of the dead girls was a cousin of Cole Younger, who rides with Quantrill, and another was a sister of Bloody Bill himself." Emma paused. "The men swore revenge."

Sarah went cold. Her mind raced. "And?" she managed, certain there was more.

Emma took a deep breath. "Four nights ago Lawrence, Kansas, was attacked. Authorities say the men rode into town chanting about the murdered girls before they killed a hundred and fifty men and boys. They burned most of the businesses and some of the finer residences. Only the women and small children were spared." The words caught in Emma's throat and Sarah hurried for a glass of water for her friend.

"There's more, isn't there?" Sarah handed the glass to Emma.

The older woman nodded. "Of the hundred and fifty dead, only a small number were Federal recruits or soldiers. The rest were civilian men and boys." A sob racked her frail body. "Will this war never end?"

Sarah grabbed Emma by the shoulders and hugged her.

Emma composed herself and looked at Sarah with tear-filled eyes. "That's not the worst of it, Sarah."

"You mean there's more?" Sarah's voice was weak.

"That general, Thomas Ewing, the Federal Commander at Fort Union there in the City of Kansas, he's issued something called General Order Number 11."

"What, exactly, is that?" Sarah asked. Her skin crawled with foreboding.

"The way I understand it, all civilians that live more than a mile from any military post in the counties that surround the City of Kansas have been ordered to move from their farms into town within fifteen days. They have to be inside the city by September 9th. Once inside, they're to take an oath of loyalty to the Union. If they refuse to come into town they'll be forced out of their homes one way or another."

"Are you saying I have to leave the ranch?" Sarah was incredulous. "What about Caleb?"

Emma shook her head. "As far as the ranch goes, we'll just have to leave it go and hope for the best. Hope it survives the war without being burned to the ground, by either side. As for Caleb, he'll come into town with us."

Emma took a breath and continued. "The Federals are sending troops out all over the countryside to bring people in. Those that won't come, their homes are being looted and burned." Emma coughed again. "One way or another civilians are being forced out of their homes. Some have even been murdered for refusing to comply with the order." The woman wrung her hands with worry, her knuckles white from the pressure.

Sarah's heart skipped a beat. She was a loyal Federal in this damn war and wanted the preservation of the Union. She prayed for the abolishment of slavery. And now she was to be thrown out of her home! She jumped up from the couch and paced the floor; her hands balled in and out of fists.

"Damn!" Sarah shouted. "Damn, damn, damn. It seems no matter what we do, we're damned. We support the Union in this damnable war, yet we're to be forced out of our home? If we acknowledge our support of the Union the pro-slavers will come in and burn us out. If we *don't* leave the ranch and run into town like we've been ordered, the damned Federals will burn us out. What the hell are we supposed to do?" She was ranting now, stomping her feet as she went from one end of the room to the other.

She whirled. "And where, exactly, is Caleb supposed to go when we get into town?"

"From what I understand, they're using an old

warehouse to house Negroes who seek refuge. He'll stay with the others who come in. He'll be fine, Sarah. You must worry about yourself."

"She's right, Miz Sarah."

Sarah spun around to see Caleb standing inside the kitchen door.

"We has to go into town. If the army don't come and get us, Quantrill and his men still might. We ain't safe here no more. And don't you worry about me. I'll be fine. You worry about yourself, Miz Sarah. You gots to go."

Sarah ranted and raved most of the night, but finally managed to pack a trunk of clothes. Caleb was throwing the case into the back of the buckboard the next morning when fifteen Union soldiers rode up the drive.

They pulled their mounts to a halt and jumped from their horses, the sergeant shouting orders.

"Bates, check the barn. Lewis, check the house. Marshall, take the rest of the outbuildings and beyond."

Sarah charged out the front door and stopped dead on the porch.

"You men stop right where you are!" she shouted. "By what authority do you come onto this property with intent to do damage?"

The men halted and turned to the sergeant. "By General Order Number 11, ma'am." The sergeant strolled toward her and slowly pulled off his cavalry gloves.

"And what right does that give you to send your men into my home with the possible intent of doing harm?"

A hard look came over his face. "The right of the Union Army, ma'am. You see," he stepped closer, "you people are to come into town where we can keep an eye on you." He turned toward Caleb who stood by the wagon.

"Exactly what kind of people do you mean?"

"Slavers." The word was drawled like it left a bad taste in his mouth.

It was all Sarah could do to keep from slapping him square across the face. "You ignorant fool. My husband is off fighting for the Union Army. We're loyal Federalists!"

He cocked his head. "All due respect, Ma'am, there's no proof your husband is fighting with our troops."

"What kind of proof would you like, Sergeant?"

The man didn't speak, just scratched his head. "Well, I don't rightly know," he said. "Guess I'll just have to do what I think is best."

Sarah's heart pounded.

"What's happening?" Emma whispered from inside the house.

Sarah waved her hand behind her. "Stay back, Emma. I'll take care of this."

"Well?" Sarah asked.

The man rubbed his chin in thought then straightened his back. "You men heard what I said," he yelled. "Check the barn, house and outbuildings! Do it, quick," he shouted to Sarah's horror.

It was like Quantrill and his men all over again. She heard furniture being upended and thrown across the room. She ran to the sergeant.

"I told you I'm a Federal, you damn fool. And so is the woman who owns this place. Why are you doing this?"

He leaned over, his face within inches of hers. "Because I don't believe you."

He turned and strolled away. And laughed. Sarah spotted Caleb out of the corner of her eye inching toward him.

"Caleb!" Both men turned and Caleb walked toward her.

"Don't do anything foolish," Sarah said under her breath. "You barely made it without getting yourself killed when Quantrill visited. This time you might not be so lucky."

"But, Miz Sarah..."

"No, Caleb. I won't discuss it. Just let them have their way."

Emma's shouts made Sarah turn.

"You dare to touch me?" the elder woman shouted.

Sarah raced back up the porch steps. "Get your hands off her you vile man," she screamed.

The man removed his hand and stepped away. "Nothing inside, sir," he shouted to the sergeant.

"Same here," called another of the men who had gathered in the courtyard.

"You all can get in your wagon now. We're through. But we'll make sure you go directly into town," the sergeant said to Sarah, laughter in his voice.

Sarah stomped over to him. "Don't you think you've done enough?" she hissed.

He surveyed the house. "Not really. You've managed to survive our visit quite well, in fact. Many others don't. So don't give me reason to show you what happens to those who defy me." His eyes chilled Sarah to the bone.

She bit her tongue then whirled to get Emma and Caleb. They climbed into the wagon and Caleb took the reins. He clucked the old mule forward. The men remounted and fell in behind the wagon and followed them all the way into town.

After being left by the soldiers, the trio entered town. Caleb stopped the wagon in front of the warehouse, handed the reins to Sarah and jumped off.

"I'll come visit, Caleb," Sarah promised.

Caleb shook his head. "It won't be right, Miz Sarah."

"You think that matters to me?" Sarah asked.

Caleb smiled and shook his head again. "I suppose not." He wiped his nose and turned away.

"I'll see you, Miz Sarah, and you, too, Miz Emma," he called over his shoulder as he strode away. "Don't you worry none. I'll be just fine."

Sarah watched her friend hurry away and disappear inside the building.

"I'll miss him, Emma."

The older woman nodded agreement. Sarah clucked the mule, and the wagon that carried everything they owned in the world rumbled away down the dusty street.

## Chapter Twenty-Three

Time passed slowly for Sarah as she settled into a new routine of loneliness and boredom. Humming to keep herself cheerful, she placed her folded laundry in the small bureau in her room in the little house she had shared with Emma and her sister, Hattie. But Hattie had died six months ago and the house now seemed quiet and empty.

The door burst open and Emma hobbled in, her face white with anger.

"What is it?"

"Let me sit first." She gasped for air as she shuffled to a chair.

"It's those Rebs again. They captured Centralia, near Jeff City, stopped a train and murdered twenty-two Federal boys who were on it! Just lined them up and shot every one of them. What's this world coming to?" she wailed. "I'm so angry I could just spit!"

Sarah put her arms around Emma's hunched, shaking shoulders. Fear swept through her as she held Emma's frail body. The woman was a shell of the one Sarah had so admired only a few years ago. Gone was the strong, arrogant, self-assured lady. In her place was a broken old woman who begged only for this senseless war to end.

"Who did it?" Sarah asked, afraid to hear the answer.

Emma took a deep breath. "They say it was that Bloody Bill Anderson riding ahead of that no-good rebel, General Price. Word is they're heading for St. Louis." Emma stopped and took a breath to compose herself.

When she breathed easier, she continued. "I heard the 39th is going after him. Maybe they'll get lucky and catch him this time. And string all of them up by their necks!" Emma's tiny fist shot up in the air and her eyes gleamed with anger.

"Emma!" Sarah chastised. "Is that how you really feel?"

Emma shook her head and waved her hand. "Listen to me. I don't know what I feel anymore. About anything. I'm just tired. I'd be happy to go to sleep and never wake up again so I wouldn't have to be a witness to all the ghastly things happening around us."

"Emma, don't talk that way," Sarah berated softly. "The war will end soon."

*How many times had she said those same words in the last few years?* Sarah wondered. *And how much closer was the war to ending now than it had been when she'd first said them?*

The two women sat in silence for several minutes, each lost in their own world of thoughts and fears. Finally Sarah broke the silence.

"We've got to be strong, Emma. The Rebs can't hold out much longer. They're running low on everything. We have to be strong. We just have to."

Sarah cradled her friend in her arms and wished she believed her own words.

Later that week when someone knocked on the door of the small house, Sarah found Caleb, his hat brim rolling nervously between his fingers, before her.

She nearly threw her arms around him, but restrained herself. She hadn't seen him in months, except for an occasional glimpse here and there when he did odd jobs for some of the women left behind by the war.

"Caleb!"

"Miz Sarah." A nervous smile broke across his lips.

"Come inside, Caleb," Sarah invited.

"No, Miz Sarah. We should talk out here."

Sarah heaved a heavy sigh, but agreed. She stepped onto the porch and waved her hand to a bench beside the door. She sat down, but Caleb stood in front of her, his eyes darting from side to side and shifting from foot to foot.

"What is it, Caleb? You're as tense as a mountain lion ready to pounce on his dinner. And you're making me nervous. Get on with it," she chided.

"I got something to tell you, Miz Sarah."

Sarah waited for him to continue, her heart in her throat. This was not going to be good news.

"I...I want you to know, Miz Sarah, that I'm thankful for

everything you done for me." He paused and looked into Sarah's face.

She nodded. "And...?"

"I been doing lots of thinking and," he paused again, shuffled his feet then looked directly at Sarah. "I wants to go North."

Sarah went stiff and her breath caught in her throat, but she waited, silent, for him to continue.

"I need to go where folks won't look at me like a...nigger." He had to compose himself after he said the word. "I's a man, Miz Sarah, and I want to be treated like one."

"But..."

"Let me finish, Miz Sarah. You know I don't include you with the white folks what didn't give me no chance. You've always treated me with respect. But I need to find my own worth. Make my own way. You got to understand that, Miz Sarah." His voice pleaded for her to understand. "If I's gonna be free, I need to be truly free. Up north where people will see me as a man and not a no account slave."

Unable to speak, Sarah nodded. She forced back the need to reach up, grab him and beg him not to go. But she knew this was something he had to. She'd go if it were her.

She stood up and stared into his face, unable to stop the tears that gathered in her eyes. Caleb turned away, as though seeing a mirror of his own pain in her face.

She touched his arm. He spun back around, his eyes brimmed with tears. He bent over and pulled out the knife Sarah had given him from his boot. He rolled it between his fingers, stroked the carved handle. Its blade glistened in the sun.

"This here knife is the most special thing I own, Miz Sarah. Every time I look at it or use it, I think of you and what you done for me."

Sarah saw a tear slip from the corner of his eye before he abruptly bent over, replaced the knife in his boot and swiped his face with the back of his hand.

He straightened up. "I gots to go, Miz Sarah," he whispered. "I thank you for all you done for me. I truly do."

Sarah touched his arm again. "I'll cherish our friendship

forever, Caleb." Her throat hurt in her effort not to cry and her fingers caressed the wooden cross that hung around her neck.

"You're a fine man and a dear friend. I'll never forget you. I'll pray for your safe journey and, if it's possible, please get word to me you're all right."

"Yes, Miz Sarah. I can do that." Caleb stepped away.

With a backward glance he left the porch and walked from the house, his head hung low. She watched him leave and felt as though her heart would burst inside her chest. They'd been through so much together. She'd saved his life and he, in turn, had saved hers. They owed each other a debt far greater than just friendship.

Perhaps he would find what he was looking for up north. She prayed he would, at least, find happiness.

The days dragged for Sarah. Emma's health continued to deteriorate, as though she had no desire to keep living. Sarah tried to keep Emma's spirits high, but when Hattie had died, something in Emma seemed to have died, too. She was failing, and Sarah could do nothing to stop it.

Emma grew thinner than Sarah would have believed a person could get. Her hands were skeletal and her glazed eyes were sunk deep into their black-ringed sockets. When she could walk, it was stooped over, as though unable to carry her own frail weight. Sarah wanted to cry at the sight of her, helpless to do anything except watch and wait. Without question, Emma was dying.

A low fire burned in the hearth to ward off the evening chill when Emma summoned Sarah to her bed.

"Child, this is the last I will see of this world." Emma's voice was raspy and bony fingers grabbed Sarah's hand. Sarah shook her head, but Emma closed her eyes and nodded.

"Yes, dear. You must face the truth. Tonight I will join my Jonathan. I've waited a long time to see him again and now that the time is near, I'm anxious to go."

A fit of coughing and wheezing sent Sarah hurrying for a pitcher and water. She helped Emma drink, then helped her lean back to rest.

Several minutes later Emma continued, her voice barely above a whisper. "Sarah, you have come to mean as much to me as the daughter I never had. And Ben, even though gone so long, like a son. Although he has been far from you for so many years, you must have hope. You must believe the good Lord will bring him back to you." She stared off into the room, her eyes ablaze, more alive than Sarah had seen them in weeks.

"Yes, Jonathan. Very soon," she whispered before she focused back on Sarah.

Tears filled Sarah's eyes. This woman meant as much to her as the mother she'd lost as a child. She admired Emma's inner strength and goodness.

Sarah felt the bony fingers tighten around her hand. Emma's face contorted with pain and the old woman gasped for air. Sarah pulled her hand free, wrung a cloth from the bowl beside her and stroked Emma's forehead.

"Thank you, dear child," Emma whispered when she could speak again. Her eyes closed and her breathing grew even. She opened her eyes.

"Faith and patience. You must have both, dear Sarah. Believe Ben will come home and things will be as they were before. Better."

Sarah prayed Emma was right. She had waited so long already. But war changed a man. Made him see life and death in a different way. Maybe it would change Ben enough to help him understand.

*If he's still alive.*

Emma's fingers tightened again and she sucked in a deep breath. "Sarah, I have something for you. There's a letter in the desk over there." She pointed across the room.

Emma was taken by another fit of coughing, this time spitting up blood. Sarah wiped her friend's face with the wet cloth until she calmed down, then retrieved the letter.

She gaped in amazement as the words on the page came into focus. It was Emma's Last Will and Testament. White Oaks with all its property, buildings and livestock, were to be left to Mr. and Mrs. Ben Walters, along with the small house and its few meager possessions.

Sarah shook her head and took both Emma's hands into hers.

"Emma, you're going to be fine. In a few months, when this war is over, we'll both return to White Oaks."

Emma shook her head slightly. "No, dear. I'll not see the end of this dreadful war and I'll never see my beloved White Oaks again. My time on earth is nearly spent. I'm reconciled to that and I'm ready to meet God. And my Jonathan..." More coughs shook her frail body and left her barely able to catch her breath between spasms.

Sarah dipped the cloth into the water and dabbed Emma's head, gently soothing until her friend was finally able to rest. Thinking Emma had lapsed into sleep, Sarah tried to pull away, but Emma's fingers grabbed tight and her eyes opened.

"This is what I want, dear Sarah. For you and for Ben. I want you to take what Jonathan and I built and carry on. Love the land the way we did. You're both young and have many years left to enjoy it and each other. Take those years and rebuild your lives, and my farm, into something strong and indestructible. Please," she rasped, her eyes intent on Sarah's face.

Sarah looked deep into the eyes of her friend. Emma was dying; there was no way she could deny that fact. Sarah couldn't refuse her last wish, couldn't refuse her the joy of letting her give what meant so much to her.

"Yes, Emma. We'll take the ranch. And I want you to know," the words caught in her throat, "that I love you. With all my heart. As much as I loved my own mother. Thank you."

Sarah bent over and kissed Emma's sunken cheek.

"I know and, as I've said, I feel the same for you. And Ben."

Emma gazed into the distance. The haze returned to her eyes. Again, she was taken by a fit of coughing that left blood trickling down her chin and neck. Sarah rushed for clean water. Emma was gasping when she returned.

Sarah pounded her on the back and with great effort Emma finally sucked in a huge gulp of air and filled her lungs.

Sarah held her tight. She felt Emma's life ebbing away.

The old woman looked up, her eyes filled with tears.

"Stay hopeful, for I know your hope has sustained you all these years." Emma managed a ragged breath. "Don't give up. Someday you and Ben will look back on these years with understanding and a new bond of love..." Her grip went slack and her eyes closed.

With one last wheezing breath, Emma died.

Sarah held on tight to her friend and wept bitter tears. She wept for Emma and for herself, alone again in a world still out of control.

Vicksburg and Gettysburg had fallen, both great victories for the Union cause. The tide of the war had changed and Ben, along with his troops, rode the wave of victory toward the sea.

The sun was high in the sky as Ben gathered his gear for the long march to Savannah. But he had a bad feeling.

After Vicksburg fell, he and his troops had moved to Atlanta and spent ten weeks doing little more than destroy the old city and everything around it. He surveyed the once beautiful place and saw only a wretched tapestry of the travesty of war.

Buildings stood like skeletons against the sky, their remains charred and black. Rats scurried from one pile of debris to another while dirty, ragged women and children lined the streets and begged for scraps of food. Ben turned away, unable to look at the pain in their faces.

What he heard and saw sickened him. His men were wild, like unleashed savages, bent on destruction.

He thought about the Indians who had attacked his wagon train in what seemed like another lifetime. These men were worse than the Indians. Indians weren't supposed to be civilized. These men were.

Thousands of miles of railroad tracks, communication lines and personal property had been destroyed, and he knew the devastation was certain to continue on the march south. Sherman himself had given the men license to burn and loot if they met any resistance along the way.

The soldiers moved out, wild with joy—save one.

Sherman's troops left a path of destruction as wide as sixty miles in some places. Ben struggled with his conscience every day as he watched farms burned to the ground, livestock butchered then left to rot, fields trampled after being stripped of bounty, and entire families of women and children left homeless.

The Federal soldiers were like animals. They ravaged everything in their path and mocked Ben because he refused to join in that destruction. But he didn't care. He gladly withstood their abuse. What they were doing was unconscionable in his mind.

By late afternoon of the third day out, the troops reached a knoll that overlooked a little farm. Alone, Ben checked the outer property.

He heard a woman's scream of terror in the distance. He raced toward it to burst through a stand of bushes, nearly falling over a Union soldier who was clawing at a squirming, screaming girl, possibly no more than thirteen years old. The man stopped groping and the girl whimpered pitifully when Ben burst through.

The girl pulled at her dress to cover her exposed breasts and tears streamed down her face. Leaves and debris were scattered in her hair and her dress hiked up around her waist. Anger tore through Ben.

The soldier grinned. "You want some of this?"

"Get off her you disgusting leech!" Ben grabbed the soldier by the collar of his uniform and threw him from the girl.

The soldier scrambled up, ready for a fight, but noticed Ben's newly replaced lieutenant bars and stopped.

"Aw, come on, Lieutenant, have a heart. I was just having a little fun. Just following orders." A crooked smile curled his lips. An evil smile that made Ben's skin crawl. A smile that reminded him of Dobbs.

"Following orders?" Ben yelled, amazed.

"Why sure, Lieutenant. You know, to put down the rebel spies like General Sherman said."

Ben looked at the cowering girl struggling to keep her dress together. Her eyes were wild with fear and her small body shook. Ben leaned over and offered his hand, but she scrambled backward, her eyes wide with mistrust.

"Don't worry, I won't hurt you." Ben offered his hand again and after a few moments she accepted it. He glared at the soldier.

"Spy? Does this child look like a spy to you?" Ben was trembling with rage.

The soldier backed away and cocked his head.

"Maybe. Maybe not, Lieutenant. But this is war. Maybe this little girl has sold information to them Johnny Rebs, I don't know. She was hiding in the bushes like a spy," he said. "Come on, Lieutenant, I just wanted a little fun." Ben heard no remorse in his voice.

Ben turned to the girl.

"I offer my profound apologies, miss," Ben whispered, his emotions so inflamed he wanted to break the man's face. *What had this army come to?*

He whirled on the soldier. "Get the hell out of here before I have you court-martialed."

"Not likely," the man snorted. "I'll git, Lieutenant, but only because I ain't itchin' to fight no officer. And there wouldn't be no court-martial anyway. Not anytime soon."

He strutted away, the arrogance in his step infuriating.

Ben turned to the muffled sobs of the girl behind him. He put his arm around her shaking shoulders until her trembling stopped. When she'd calmed down, he took her to her grateful family, his heart like a lead weight in his chest.

The Union Army marched on and continued to ravage the countryside as they went. Ben tried to stay detached, but every day his stomach churned in disgust as he watched the daily rape of the once beautiful South.

Ben's dark hair swirled around his head in the warm air. He dismounted and tied his horse to a branch in a patch of woods beyond a cornfield. He sat down with a thud, rolled to his belly and wished only for a cool bath, a real bed and a razor. Raucous hoots and hollers erupted in the distance. It had started again. The plundering. The destruction.

He was outside the perimeter of the farm the men were

searching, content to stay as far away from the lunacy as possible. How could these men continue to get pleasure from the destruction of human life and property day after day?

His mind turned to Sarah. He'd been able to post several letters to her in the last year, but hadn't received a response to any of them. He'd poured his heart out to his wife in the letter he sent from Fort Donelson, but there'd been no answer. He'd tried to explain it away that they just couldn't find him to deliver a letter from her, but other men received letters all the time.

Perhaps she'd forgotten him. No, he told himself, there must be an explanation. Sarah would never abandon him. There had to be some other reason. So he went about his business, trying to stay detached from the other men and their looting, and the only thing that got him through each day was the hope of his return to Sarah soon.

He was lost in these thoughts when a rifle clicked behind him.

"Get up, blue belly." The voice was ragged, thick with emotion.

Ben drew up his knees and slowly stood up.

"Turn around."

An old man as thin as a forgotten scarecrow and ancient-looking as Methuselah gave the command. His hand shook on the rifle aimed at Ben's chest.

"Wait, mister." Ben raised his hands.

"Don't wait me you yeller-bellied, Yank!" the old man spat. "Look what they're doin' to my farm. I ain't done nothin' to nobody," he wailed. He raised the rifle when it drooped.

Ben backed up with his hands in the air.

"Listen, mister," Ben tried to reason. "I don't hold with what they're doing. That's why I'm out here alone, away from all that." The old man's eyes ran with tears and his hands shook in his impotent rage. He seemed not to hear Ben's words and swayed on his feet. His eyes closed. He sniffed then swiped at the tears on his face with his shoulder.

"I ain't done nothin'," he cried again. He glanced at the farmhouse in the distance where men ran to and fro, laughing and shouting while they broke and stole the man's possessions.

"I'm just an old man waiting out the end of this war. I only want it to end. I don't even care who wins anymore. But look what they're doin'!"

The rifle drooped again and Ben leaned forward, but he raised it back to Ben's chest and his eyes became clear.

"You lousy vermin are destroying everything I have left," he screamed. "Already took Emily and all my stock. There ain't much left, but what there is is mine!"

Ben tried to stay calm. He'd faced the enemy many times in many forms, but never in that of a broken, bitter old man. His heart ached over the devastation, but he was powerless to stop it. He gave orders, but they were countermanded by a higher power. He tried to control his men, but short of stepping into the path of destruction and welcoming his own death, he couldn't stop what was happening.

"Mister. I told you I don't agree with what those men are doing. That's why I'm out here alone. I wish I could change it, but..."

"I don't want to hear none of your words, sonny. Not a word." The man's voice had grown as hard as steel. "Not a damn one."

"Mister, listen to me..." Ben stepped forward.

The rifle exploded.

## Chapter Twenty-Four

Sarah stood over Emma's grave and reflected on the past years of her life. From the start of her journey with Ben, her time spent with the Indians and through the ravages of war, she thought about how she'd been forced to accept so much death in those years. The senseless deaths of those in her wagon train and her belief that Ben had been killed in that attack. The brutal death of Man-Who-Runs. Hattie and now Emma.

She felt empty, like the day she'd slipped beneath the black waters of the Niobrara River beside the Lakota camp. Her life seemed like a dream with separate parts that didn't quite fit together. *Where did she belong in this scheme of life? She and Ben had been happy, but that happiness had been sucked away by her capture. She'd been content to live with Man-Who-Runs, but that, too, had been torn away. Now she'd lost the woman she'd come to love like her own mother. Even Caleb was gone.* She was as alone and lonely as she'd ever been.

The days passed, the war dragged on and Sarah felt utterly useless. She tried to keep busy by rolling bandages and packing war supplies, but she wanted to do more. She wanted to find a more worthwhile way to contribute.

Hearing Rebel forces were said to be heading toward Westport and fearful of what might happen when they got there, Sarah decided to bury what few precious belongings she owned.

The sun low on the horizon, she slipped outside to the rear of the cottage and dug a hole the size of a small book. Her task complete, she sat back on her heels and stared down at the small burial pit.

Her arms felt like lead weights when she lifted them to her neck and unclasped her treasured necklace. Tears streamed down her cheeks as the locket slipped into her hand.

"Forgive me, Ben," she whispered. "Once a long time ago I swore I'd never take this from my neck as a symbol of my love for you. I lost it once and, I vow, I won't lose it again." She took a deep breath to gather control of her emotions. "Only because I have no choice, Ben, do I again remove it from my neck to preserve it and all it means to me. Strength, hope, but most of all, my ever-enduring love for you."

Unable to control her mounting fear, she began to sob. She felt as though her heart might break. Carefully, she lowered the locket into a white linen pouch. Once the locket was safely inside the pouch she untied the crude birch cross that still hung upon her chest.

"And this, Caleb, will always signify our friendship." It followed the necklace into the sack.

She stared down at the gold ring circling the third finger of her left hand. Her symbol of hope, of all she'd endured to regain Ben's love. She twisted the ring and watched it slide free of her finger through eyes blurred with tears.

"Come back to me, Ben. Please, come back." She kissed her wedding ring then tucked it inside the bag with the other items, pulled the drawstring and laid it inside the hole.

Her heart aching, she covered the pouch with dirt. She smoothed it over, stood up, squared her shoulders and brushed the dirt off her fingers and knees.

The Rebs would not get her precious jewelry, she promised herself. They've taken everything else; they won't get my memories, or my hopes, she promised.

Within days, soldiers wounded in skirmishes with the advancing confederates began to enter the city and Sarah was given a way to help. Every morning she left the warmth of the small house and went to help with the wounded. From morning till night she read, soothed the wounded and helped the doctors in any way she could. She never left until well into the night, her hair a tangled mess and exhausted beyond anything she'd felt before.

The first few days she shed hundreds of tears for the broken men that came in. But she forced herself to be strong, for herself and for the men she nursed, and now she didn't cry at all.

She spent a great deal of time writing letters to the men's sweethearts, mothers and wives. Once, she finished the note only moments before the soldier died, his hand holding Sarah's in gratitude for her kindness.

Difficult as it was, she went back every day. The men watched for her and begged her to stay long into the night. Some nights she was so tired she could barely walk the short distance home.

Each day she looked into the face of war and searched for Ben with the hope he was, somehow, among the injured. But each day she was disappointed.

It was late October and Sarah was on her way to the makeshift hospital when she heard the Rebs had crossed the Big Blue River and were getting closer.

When she reached the hospital, the stench of death and mutilation assailed her senses the moment she stepped through the door. Men were everywhere. Bloodied, screaming, writhing in agony. Men with limbs barely clinging to mangled bodies, others who held their stomachs to keep their insides from spilling out.

She was frozen to the floor, trying to take in everything around her and regain some semblance of composure, when a hand grabbed her and snatched her out of her daze. Warm and covered with blood, the hand left her own red and sticky. Bile rose in her throat, but she forced the acid down and bent over to hear the soft whisper of the soldier who held her in his grip.

"Talk to me, ma'am, please," he managed. "Just talk."

Sarah knelt beside him. Her stomach rolled and gorge rose again. The man had been gut-shot and the bandages around the wound grew redder with each second that passed.

Sarah watched him. His mouth worked, but nothing came out. Tears welled in his eyes. She squeezed his hand and spoke.

"What's your name, soldier?" She forced herself to sound cheerful to grant this man his last wish in life.

He opened his mouth again, but a mere croak escaped. He tried again. Sarah leaned closer.

"Tom? Is that your name?" She put on her best smile. His hand trembled and held hers in a death grip.

He nodded his head then grimaced as pain shook him. Held in his death grip, Sarah could only watch and try to soothe him. She called for a doctor, but none came. She held the man's hand. His fingers nearly crushed hers when he had another spasm of pain. After a few moments, he relaxed and she managed to pry her fingers loose.

"I'll be back," she promised when she saw fear leap into his eyes.

She ran for a towel and some water. She'd heard about being gut-shot. It was hopeless. That was probably why he wasn't being tended to. He was a lost cause. Whether he was a Yank or a Reb, there was nothing anyone could do.

Chills raced down her spine although she was wet with sweat. She grabbed a bowl of water and a towel and hurried back to the injured man. The least she could do was make him as comfortable as possible before he died.

Sarah resumed her spot beside him, dipped the towel in the water and sponged his forehead. He gazed into her eyes and smiled like a contented child. His smile faded, he sucked in a deep breath and his face contorted. His body bucked and jerked, then stopped. He exhaled.

Sarah waited. The man didn't move again. She finished sponging his forehead and face, and as she cleaned the sticky redness away the face of a child emerged. Barely more than sixteen. A sob caught in her throat and anger rose in her chest. So young! She turned away, unable to look at the boy's face.

Emotions of every kind hit her with the force of a cyclone. Anger, fear, regret, doubt, and hatred. She stared at the boy who gazed, unseeing, at the ceiling. A single tear clung to the corner of his eye. A cold calm enveloped her. *What terror had he experienced before the ball slammed into his stomach and stole his life? Had he been afraid or brave?*

*What of his mother and father, brothers or sisters? A lover? Did he leave a special girl behind to grieve for him? Would they cry bitterly or accept his death as a casualty of war?*

Those words, "casualty of war," stuck in her mind like paste. *Was Ben one of those casualties, lost among so many others already dead and forgotten?* She almost sobbed out loud with the realization that if Ben were alive, somehow he would have let her know.

She felt her emotions drain away like a bottle being uncorked. Her heart went cold like the dead boy beside her. She would never feel again. Never love or trust. Never hope. Everything inside her died, as she now realized Ben was probably dead.

A gentle voice startled her.

"Leave him. It's too late for him, but there are many more we can save."

Sarah nodded to the other woman and pulled herself away from the boy. The woman was right. There were too many others here who could still be helped.

Sarah administered to the wounded throughout the day and night. She cleaned and read to them, held their hands as they died. But now coldness surrounded her like a shroud. She covered the dead and carried on; offered whatever comfort she could, but felt nothing.

## Chapter Twenty-Five

Ben woke in darkness. There was moaning all around him; voices that echoed through the inky blackness that surrounded him. Agonized cries begged for mercy. He opened his eyes and focused on his surroundings. He was inside a white tent, not very large. Men were moving around shouting orders. He tried to move and cried out at the pain that tore through his leg. He grabbed at it; tried to make it stop. His pant leg was bloody and he could feel a bandage. Then he remembered. The old man. He'd tried to reason with him, had tried to explain he wasn't like the others.

But the old man wanted none of it. Ben remembered stepping toward him, trying to soothe him. When he wouldn't listen Ben had grabbed for the rifle. It exploded sending white-hot pain through his left leg just above the knee. Now he was here, in what appeared to be a hospital tent. How long? And how bad was his injury? He dropped his head back down on the cot.

A man stepped up beside him and Ben turned. The face was gaunt and tired, the eyes red-rimmed with exhaustion. The man smiled a tired grin.

"How bad is it, doc?"

"Not as bad as it could have been. If the shot had been a few inches lower, that knee would have been shattered and you would have probably lost your leg. You're lucky the bullet only went through the meaty part of your lower thigh. My prognosis is that you'll walk, possibly with a limp, but walk nonetheless."

Ben breathed a sigh of relief. "Thanks." He paused. "What happens now?"

"Well, son, it looks like you've seen the last of this war. I'm sending you home."

Ben tried to absorb the man's words. He'd fought for so long that he suddenly felt as though he were in a dream. He was going home. He shivered, but not from cold or fear, but from excitement and happiness. He was finally going home.

An oil lamp in the parlor glowed in the last light of the late fall day. It had been weeks since the Union victory at Westport outside the City of Kansas. Sarah heard footsteps on the porch outside, then a knock.

She opened the door. A squeal of delight exploded from her throat as she rushed outside and threw her arms around Caleb's neck.

"Caleb! You're home!" Tears of joy instead of sadness streaked her face for the first time in years.

Caleb smiled that strong, crooked smile she had grown to love. "Yes, ma'am. I'm home."

"Come in, Caleb. Come in."

"Now, Miz Sarah, you know it ain't proper," he chastised before he stepped inside. A grin of mischief lit his face. He suddenly stopped, turned around and stepped back outside. Sarah looked after him anxiously. When he came back through the door, a slender, dark-eyed Negress was with him. Ebony hair curled tight around her head and her lips were pursed with worry. Slender of build, Sarah thought she was the most beautiful woman she'd ever seen.

"This here is Prudy, Miz Sarah. My wife." Caleb had a lopsided grin on his face as he gazed down at the woman beside him.

Sarah's heart skipped a beat. "Wife!" she squealed for the second time in so many minutes before she hugged Caleb again. "You two come in here, right now," she ordered. "I'll get something for us to drink and you're going to tell me all about your travels."

She returned from the kitchen with a pitcher of weak lemonade and glasses, poured them each a drink then sat down on a chair across from where Caleb and Prudy sat perched on the couch.

"Tell me everything, Caleb. What happened? You went north didn't you?"

Caleb drew a ragged breath.

"Yes, ma'am, I went up north. But people there ain't what I thought they'd be, Miz Sarah. They look down on us black folk just as bad, sometimes worse, than the southerns do. I tried to find work, but they don't want to give no jobs away to niggers. I was living worse being free than if I'd stayed here with the rest of my people in town, waiting for this war to end." His voice was hard, bitter.

Sarah's heart ached for him.

"Now, don't you go feelin' bad, Miz Sarah. Ain't none of that you're doing. I tried and it weren't no good. Now I'm back. We're gonna put that ranch back in shape for Miz Emma and things are gonna be just fine. Where is Miz Emma, anyway?"

Tears formed in Sarah's eyes before she could stop them. Although so much inside her had died, she still mourned every time she thought of her friend.

"Miz Emma passed on, Caleb. Just wasted away. I don't know if it was disease or just plain not wanting to go on in these hard times. She was little more than a skeleton when she went, so frail and weak. It tore my heart out to watch her waste away like that."

Caleb bent his head and nodded agreement. Prudy put her hand on his shoulder and he reached up and covered it with his larger one.

Sarah gazed at the two people on the couch. It was obvious from their mere touch and the looks in their eyes how much they were in love. Her heart ached with pain and longing. *God, how she wanted Ben.*

"Caleb, tell me about you and Prudy. How did you two meet? How long have you been married?" Sarah asked in a rush. "Tell me everything!"

Caleb's face brightened. So did Prudy's.

"I was heading north when I come upon a small camp of freed slaves. I joined up with them and, well, me and Prudy found out we liked each other real nice." He grinned and patted Prudy's hand.

"She used to be a house slave, so she knows how to speak real proper. And she can cipher, too, even though she ain't supposed to know how. After the plantation she lived on was burned during a Union raid, Prudy and the rest of the slaves took north. That's when I met up with them."

He turned and smiled at his wife whose dark eyes sparkled with love for her husband, and whose lips were fixed in a smile of happiness.

Sarah stared at the couple as Caleb spoke again.

"What about Mr. Ben? What you hear from him? Is he back?"

Sarah sighed, looked away and shook her head.

"No, Caleb, I haven't heard from him in a very long time. If he were killed, I should have been notified by now, so I keep hoping he's still riding with the Federals—somewhere. Or is even a prisoner, but still alive. I even try to convince myself I've had letters in the bags of mail that were lost when Quantrill and his men disrupted service.

Sarah jumped to her feet like a nervous cat. "I don't know anymore, Caleb. I just know I'm worried sick and wish I knew where he is. I'm scared to death he's rotting away in one of those filthy southern prison camps and my blood just goes cold at the thought."

"This war can't last much longer, Miz Sarah. He'll be home soon. You'll see. Even though I ain't never met the man, I know he's good, else you wouldn't have had him in the first place. Trust me, Miz Sarah. I feel it in my bones. He'll be back."

"Thank you." Sarah took Caleb's outstretched hand, not quite as certain as he. "We'll see."

## Chapter Twenty-Six

Sarah packed her few belongings for the return to White Oaks. She touched her neck where her treasured locket hung again, Caleb's cross just above it. Absently, she twirled the ring on the third finger of her left hand, her symbol of hope that Ben would come home to her. She kissed the ring and whispered, "Come home Ben, please come home."

The city now safe from Rebel attack, and General Order Number 11 no longer being enforced with the zeal it once was, Sarah decided it was time to go home.

A feeling of loss descended on Sarah as she thought of her return to White Oaks. The ranch she and Ben had rebuilt for Emma was now theirs, where she had spent so much time with the dear lady who was now gone. Sadness swept over her, but she pushed the dreary thoughts away, anxious to be off. It was time to move forward, not back, and that meant getting to the ranch and putting things in order.

She looked through the tiny rooms of the house for anything left behind, then walked out the door and left the house to be sold to new tenants.

Sarah met Prudy and Caleb out front and handed him her suitcases. He dropped them into the bed of the wagon and finished hitching the mule.

"It's time to go home," she said. Although she had no idea what she'd find when they reached the ranch, she was anxious to be on her way. She wanted to start putting things back in order, begin to get things ready for Ben to come home. *If* he came home. Her heart sank, but only momentarily. She forced the melancholy thoughts from her mind. She was going home to White Oaks and she was glad. And when this damnable war ended and Ben came home she'd be there waiting for him.

Sarah settled herself on the seat next to Caleb with Prudy in the back. Caleb clucked the mule forward.

Soon they were far from the city. The November day was warm, the countryside quiet, basking in the warm rays of the sun that filtered between the bare-limbed trees. Prudy sat silent in the bed of the wagon and studied her new surroundings. Caleb hummed and Sarah enjoyed the sights and smells of the land, realizing how much she missed the ranch, far from the bustle of the city.

But the birds weren't chirping in the trees, and Sarah thought it odd that on such a beautiful day they weren't singing their praises at the top of their lungs. Something rustled in the bushes beside the road and she turned.

Horses and riders exploded from the trees lining the trail. Prudy screamed. Caleb jerked the mule to an abrupt halt as horses suddenly blocked their way. Sarah was thrown forward when the wagon stopped, circled by a dozen masked riders.

She trembled and felt Caleb tense beside her. Prudy grabbed Caleb's arm and held on tight, her eyes wide like a frightened doe. Sarah knew these men and cold dread swept up her spine.

Quantrill. She spotted him right off. His auburn hair billowed out from under his hat and his steely eyes pierced her like an arrow. He prodded his horse toward the stopped wagon, jerking the animal to a halt beside Sarah.

"Afternoon, ma'am." He tipped his hat and there was amusement in his eyes.

"Mr. Quantrill," Sarah managed. Caleb shifted to stand, but Sarah put her hand on his arm to keep him still.

"No, Caleb," she whispered.

"That's right." Quantrill leaned forward in his saddle to address her. "You keep your black buck under control. We wouldn't want him to get hurt." He eyed Caleb, whose breath was quick and short as he restrained himself. Prudy pulled at his arm, her face lined with worry.

"Why have you detained us?" Sarah demanded.

Quantrill leaned back in the saddle and pushed his hat off his forehead.

"Still as feisty as ever," Quantrill drawled. "I have my reasons, Mrs. Walters. It is Mrs. Walters, correct?"

"You know damn well who I am!"

Men's laughter boomed through the trees. Sarah drew

her back up even straighter. "What do you want with us?"

Quantrill studied Sarah before he spoke. "There is no 'us'. Only you, Mrs. Walters. I've need of an escort."

"Escort?" Her heart raced with fear. "What do you mean?"

"I've need of a lady's company on a journey I intend to make very soon."

Sarah jumped up. "I'll not accompany you and these, these scoundrels anywhere, Quantrill!" She grabbed the reins. The mule reared, but one of the men snatched the animal's bridle and stopped it before it could bolt. Caleb jumped up beside Sarah, but every man had his gun on him. He froze.

Sarah grabbed a whip from under the seat and threatened to use it on the man holding the mule.

"I wouldn't do that if I were you, Mrs. Walters," Quantrill growled. "Some of my men have rather bad tempers, and I don't know that I could control their actions if they were to be on the receiving end of a whip. A whip yielded by a woman, no less." He chuckled under his breath.

"Perhaps, then, I'll use it on you instead, Mr. Quantrill."

His eyes turned hard and all humor disappeared from his face.

"I wouldn't recommend that, either, Mrs. Walters. It might very well be the last thing you do, regardless you are a woman." His voice was as cold as a January wind.

Sarah threw the whip on the floor and sat down. "What, do you want, Quantrill?"

"I need a woman. Certainly, I'm not distressed that woman will be you, Mrs. Walters." His eyes gleamed and he tipped his hat in a gentlemanly gesture.

Sarah looked around at the men around her, then back to Quantrill.

"You won't be troubled by them, Mrs. Walters. You have my solemn word on that," he said before she could voice her silent question. "On my honor, if a man touches you it will be under the penalty of death. Do I make myself clear?" He eyed the men who quickly shouted their understanding of the order.

She snorted unladylike and mumbled under her breath,

## Tomorrow's Promise: Survival on the Plains          D.L. Rogers

"Your honor."

Quantrill scowled then glanced behind her and nodded. A man jumped onto the wagon and hoisted a screaming Prudy into his arms, her hands and legs flailing wildly. He put her into the lap of another man on horseback who rode away and dropped her to the ground like a sack of potatoes on the side of the road some distance away.

Caleb jumped off the wagon to run to her. The butt of a rifle in the back of his head stopped him cold. He went limp and crumbled to the ground.

"Caleb!" Sarah screamed. Prudy's cries echoed from down the trail.

Sarah glared at Quantrill. The man in the wagon climbed onto the seat beside her and jerked the reins from her hands. A look of delight sparkled in his eyes.

Sarah reached out to strike Quantrill, but the wagon jerked forward and threw her back onto the seat.

"You'll pay for this, Quantrill," she screamed. "I swear, someday you'll pay!"

The men whooped and hollered and disappeared from the trail leaving Sarah and her driver on the road. Sarah's mind raced. The other men were gone, maybe she could catch the man beside her off guard and escape. She turned her head and groaned. Behind them and to the left side of the wagon rode Quantrill himself.

He smiled with arrogance, inclined his head and tipped his hat. "Miz Walters."

That afternoon after a long, tedious ride, Quantrill, his men and Sarah entered a camp of about twenty men who greeted the riders with loud cheers. She was reminded of her ride into the Indian camp so long ago, in what seemed like another lifetime. Where all eyes were fixed on her. Where the women and children laughed and taunted and poked at her exposed legs. Only this time, those who taunted and laughed were men of her own kind. The thought drew a derisive snort from her. Her own kind. When the Pawnee had raided the Sioux camp, she'd wondered how they could war on each other. They were of the same race. Yet men of her own race warred with each other. The

Indians suddenly seemed so much less barbaric.

Exhausted and grateful to be allowed some privacy, Sarah entered a small tent she was pointed to. She declined the evening meal offered her in order to rest. And plan.

Her mind was wild with the events of the last few hours. Again she'd become an unwilling captive. But this time, she'd use what she'd learned from Man-Who-Runs and do everything in her power to escape. She'd bend to Quantrill's will, even if it wounded her pride, to make him believe she'd give him no trouble. She'd bide her time and wait for the right moment. She wouldn't stay a captive for long, she promised herself.

She would, once again, become Woman with Fire Like the Sun. Become the Indian she'd once been. To survive.

Sarah woke the next morning to the sound of men's voices and poked her head out of the tent. A short distance away men were squatting around Quantrill, who spoke from the middle of the circle.

Curious, Sarah stepped out of the tent and walked toward them. Her guard followed.

"We've fought long and hard, men, and I'm damned proud of what we've accomplished. We've caused those Yankees more than a few sleepless nights these past years."

Quantrill threw his head back and laughed, which brought immediate agreement and laughter from the men. He held up his hand for silence and continued. "I've formulated a plan to let them know we're not through with them yet." He leaned over and pointed to what Sarah assumed was a map. "This is where we are now...and this is where we'll end up. In between," his voice thundered, "we'll cause those Yanks a few *more* sleepless nights."

Amidst the cheers of his men, Sarah's mind whirled. *Where did he plan to end up? What was his plan?* Her curiosity drove her closer.

"Richmond," Quantrill said shortly. "The capital of our illustrious Confederacy."

Sarah looked behind her. Her guard was no longer watching her, his attention now on Quantrill. Maybe she could slip away without his realizing.

"But," Quantrill's voice boomed, "more importantly, it is only a stone's throw away from Washington. And Abe Lincoln himself."

Sarah turned back to the circle.

"What's your plan?" one of the men asked.

"We make our way East. We do as much damage as we can along the way until we reach Richmond. Then, on to Washington." He paused and caught the attention of every man in the circle. And Sarah.

"My goal is to assassinate Abraham Lincoln and end this war with a victory for the Confederacy."

A blood curdling Rebel yell erupted from the men.

A scream caught in Sarah's throat and shivers ran up and down her spine. How was she involved?

Once the men had quieted, Quantrill continued. "As you all know, we've taken a hostage. She'll be my ticket into the city. No one will be looking for a man *and* a woman. They're looking for Charley Quantrill and his band of raiders."

Quantrill laughed then swung around and stared directly at Sarah.

"Morning, Mrs. Walters," he drawled.

"I will not be a party to such a scheme!" Sarah shouted as she stomped toward him.

"Mrs. Walters," he chuckled, "I don't believe you have a choice."

## Chapter Twenty-Seven

The sun seemed to fall like an orange ball over the roof of the main house of White Oaks. From atop his weary cavalry mount, Ben stared at the welcome sight. Home. He was finally home. After four years of brutality and devastation, for Ben, the war was over.

The ranch looked abandoned, as though no one had been there for a long time. He prodded his horse forward and dread descended.

He rode to the barn and dismounted. He winced at the pain that rushed through his still tender leg. He opened the door and entered. The sun cast long shadows across the barn walls and floor as he led his horse to a stall.

A gun cocked behind him. Ben went stiff.

"Who are you?" a deep voice asked. "What you want?"

"I'm Ben Walters. I live here. I've just returned from the war."

Ben heard whispers behind him, the addition of a woman's voice to the man's. "This here's the man I tole you about. The one who stopped Masser Pruitt's overseer from beating me to death before this war started. That's him, I's sure of it." The gun uncocked. Silence.

"Mr. Ben?" the man asked. "Miz Sarah's Ben?"

Ben turned and found himself staring at a tall, unfamiliar black man with strong features and dark, penetrating eyes. A small woman stood beside him, her shoulders covered by one of the man's powerful arms.

Ben nodded, wary, unwilling to take his eyes off the man who still held the gun. Although it wasn't pointed at him, Ben knew it could be raised and fired fast enough.

A wide, blinding smile crossed the black man's face and revealed several broken teeth.

"Mr. Ben!" he shouted. He handed the gun to the woman, strode across the barn and clasped Ben's hand in his own.

"Mr. Ben, my name is Caleb. It's a long story about who we are, but I sure enough know who you are, Mr. Ben. I's the slave you stopped the overseer from killing at Masser Pruitt's before the war. I can't believe you the same man Miz Sarah talked about all the time."

Ben stepped forward and clasped the man's hand. "I'm glad to see you've survived the war. And you know Sarah?"

Ben listened as the man rambled on, gave his account of how Sarah had saved him from slave catchers and the two had become friends. He listened intently, until Caleb went silent.

"What is it, Caleb?" Fear gnawed at his gut. "Where is Sarah now?"

"When we come back from the North, me and Prudy, we went straight to Miz Sarah. We was on our way back to the ranch, when..."

"What?" Ben almost yelled when Caleb stopped speaking.

"That dirty, no good, thievin' Quantrill. Two days ago he stopped us on the trail and took Miz Sarah with him. I don't know where they gone, but I'll be right beside you when you go to git her." He rubbed the back of his head, "I'm sure we can pick up their trail easy enough. They was at least fifteen of them." His voice was strong with determination.

Ben went rigid with anger. He'd withstood four years of war to come home to this! He threw back his head and screamed.

"Damn you, Quantrill! Damn you Rebels to hell!"

Days blended together as Sarah, Quantrill and his men rode further east. She pondered an escape over and over in her mind, but never came up with a viable plan. They seemed to know her every move. Someone was always watching her. Whether she saw him or not, he was there, especially the bearded man named Billy. He always watched, always stared, with eyes that bore deep into her.

She recognized him as the man who'd taken Midnight in Quantrill's raid on the ranch and had promised to take good care of him. He had, at least, been true to his word. The horse appeared healthy.

Billy molested her with his eyes every time she glanced at him, every time she went to visit Midnight. He was careful never to touch her, as Quantrill had ordered, but his presence, nonetheless, caused her great discomfort.

By late afternoon of the fourth day, exhausted, she dozed in the saddle as they trod relentlessly east. In Sarah's dreams Man-Who-Runs came to her. He stood before her, tall and majestic, arms crossed over his chest, his voice stern when he spoke.

"You are a smart woman, my Sarah. A beautiful woman and you must use that beauty to gain your escape from these men. One looks upon you more than the others. He is the one you must focus on. Do what must be done. You survived capture with my people. Survived the cruelty among your own when you went back. Now it is time to do what you must to survive this. That is who you are, Wi Tapeta Yuha Win, Woman with Fire Like the Sun. Do what you must to survive."

Sarah's head snapped up like she'd been shot from a slingshot. Her answer had been right in front of her all the time. Billy. He was her way out. And he rode Midnight, so hopefully she could escape with the horse, too. She looked up into the sky.

"Thank you, Man-Who-Runs. Thank you."

It was another two days before Billy was posted outside for the late night watch over Sarah. She'd seen him before she closed the flap and blew out her candle.

Impatient and anxious, she waited several hours in hope the rest of camp would be deep in sleep before she set her plan in motion. When the moon was high in the sky she took a deep breath for courage and pushed out of the tent.

Billy jumped in front of her and blocked her way.

"Hello, Billy." Sarah's voice was soft, almost a purr. She smiled.

"Mrs. Walters, you know you can't be out here," he whispered.

"I know, Billy, but I just had to. You see," she looked away coyly then forced the rest of the words out. "I've been waiting for you to be my guard..." She let the words hang. Gave him time to think.

Sarah turned and gazed up at the sky, sighed and turned back to Billy. She lowered her eyes, fluttered her lashes.

Sarah stumbled on her words as she spoke. "I, I've seen you watching me, Billy. I see you during the day when we ride and at night when we camp. Always." She toyed with a lock of her hair. "At first it unsettled me. It's been a very long time since a man looked at me—you know, that way." She brought her eyes up to meet his and sighed.

"I must confess," she continued, "I'm somewhat embarrassed to say this, but I find myself thinking about you, too. I've been alone so very long..." She continued to look at him then glanced away. Inside, she felt ill.

Billy shuffled on his feet. He was grinning when she looked back at him.

"I sure think about you a lot, Mrs. Walters."

Sarah smiled, reached out and ran her finger down his cheek. He swallowed hard and moved nervously under her touch.

"Isn't there somewhere more—private we could go?" She slid her fingers along his rough beard.

Silence.

"Do you know what I would really enjoy?" she asked.

Billy shook his head. Sarah traced her finger along his neck and the man nearly cried out.

"A late night ride. We could be very quiet, you and I. I'm sure Midnight wouldn't make any noise if we rode together. Close together. We could steal away and have some, well, you know..." She ran her fingers through his hair. Her skin crawled.

Billy looked around. "You know I can't do that, Mrs. Walters. Much as I'd like to. Charley would skin me alive and leave my carcass for the buzzards if I did. He doesn't hold with that kind of stuff," he said, his eyes hot with desire.

Sarah demurely dropped her eyes to the ground before she let out a heavy sigh.

"Oh, Billy, I so hoped tonight would be special. I'm so afraid of what the coming days will bring..." She let the words hang. When she looked up his body was tense. Again, he looked around camp. Sarah waited. She didn't want to press too much too fast, but she couldn't lose him, either.

Billy's eyes came to rest on Sarah's face and she feigned despair. "Oh, Billy..." She touched his cheek again and his eyes closed in longing.

"Maybe just a few minutes." The words hung in the air as he opened his eyes and looked around camp one last time. "Seems like everyone is asleep. But we can't be gone long." He grabbed Sarah's hand and led her toward the tethered horses.

Sarah's heart was racing and her nerves were as tight as a bowstring. She thought of Man-Who-Runs and a serene calm came over her. She'd learned much from him. Now she would use that knowledge.

The horses were tied to a long rope stretched between two trees. Sarah stepped beside the tree to the right. She watched Billy untie Midnight, soothe him, and back him away from the other horses.

Almost. Be patient. Just a few more seconds.

Billy was beside her, a smile of anticipation on his face. He turned to slip the rope over Midnight's head, his back to Sarah.

There was a sickening thud when the two-inch thick branch Sarah had hidden earlier hit him square in the head. He crumpled to the ground in a heap.

Sarah stared at the still form. She'd vowed she would escape at any cost. She'd done what was necessary. He was a criminal, a murderer, on his way to assassinate President Lincoln.

A small pool of blood formed at the base of Billy's neck. Was he dead? She didn't have time to find out. Her own life, and maybe even Lincoln's, was at stake.

She walked Midnight away from the other animals, whispered to him to keep him quiet.

She was fifty feet outside the perimeter of the camp, ready to mount, when a match flared to life beside her.

To her left stood the wraithlike form of Charley Quantrill. His face glowed in the light of the match, eerie and angry.

She tried to throw herself onto Midnight's back, but

Quantrill grabbed her ankle before she could.

"Damn you!" She kicked her foot, tried to break free. "Damn you all!"

He didn't make a sound, but Sarah sensed his deep anger. Suddenly, she was on the ground. Quantrill stood over her looking down, pure venom in his eyes.

"Billy's most likely dead. You laid him out good, Mrs. Walters. Took that tree branch and broke his skull."

Calm and determined she looked into Quantrill's face.

"Just a casualty of war, wouldn't you say, Charley?"

The crack of flesh on flesh sounded like a thunderclap in Sarah's ears. She fell onto her back. Her cheek burned like fire, but she didn't cry out.

"He was a good man. Stupid and lovesick maybe, but a good man," Quantrill ground out.

Minutes later, Sarah landed with a thud on the cot in her tent. Quantrill towered over her, his hands on his hips, anger in his eyes.

"Damn you, woman. You've cost me a good man with your foolish attempt to escape." He paused and strode within the confines of the little tent.

"Don't you realize someone is watching you? Always!" His face was red with rage.

Sarah's heart hammered and blood raced in her ears. Her eyes closed against the wave of fear that threatened to suffocate her. She took a deep breath. She was Woman with Fire Like the Sun.

Her composure returned. "We're at war, Mr. Quantrill. This war has made me an unwilling captive. It is my duty to escape."

Quantrill's head snapped back and laughter burst from his chest.

"You speak like a damn soldier, lady."

"When one is captive, one must think like a soldier. It is my duty to escape," she reminded him again.

"Point taken, madam. Well taken." He tipped his hat and turned to exit the tent. His hand on the flap, he stopped. He didn't turn around but said, "Be assured, Mrs. Walters, if you attempt another escape, you had better succeed. For if you do not, you will pay with your life, regardless you are a woman."

His tone was as sharp as the tip of a saber and Sarah was certain he meant what he promised.

He left the tent, his words floating like a challenge behind him.

The next morning Sarah watched as they dismantled the camp. Tents were taken down, fires swallowed up by the earth and any remnants of the men who had stopped there disappeared. She recalled how the Sioux, within minutes, could strike an entire village and leave only the land behind.

When the men were ready to ride, she gazed out over what had been camp for thirty men. There was nothing.

No wonder the soldiers could never find Quantrill and his bunch, she thought. They were like the Indians who disappeared in the morning vapor to leave no trace of their existence. But, she thought as an idea formed in her head. That was because they *didn't* want to be found. She, on the other hand, did.

"Move it, Mrs. Walters." The harsh voice startled her, and she nudged her horse forward.

Wind bit at Sarah's face, but her mind was hot. All through the day she mulled her chances of being able to leave something behind. Some clue that she had been there. She was watched constantly. Even at night as she slept there was an armed guard who sat outside her tent, and another guard watched him. She never had a moment's privacy. Except when...

She reined the horse to a halt when the idea struck. They did, at least, allow her the smallest privacy. If only she could leave behind some kind of clue. Something that couldn't be missed. Of course! A small smile broke over her lips.

Later that day she pulled the horse to a halt.

"What are you stopping for? Keep going," her guard growled.

"I must." She feigned embarrassment. "I must—you know..."

The other riders rode around her and her guard and left them at the rear of the group.

"Please," she begged. "I can't wait much longer."

"Women," the man mumbled. "You got three minutes. You got me? Three minutes, not a second more."

"Yes. Three minutes." Sarah slid off her mount and hurried behind a stand of bushes, watched closely by her guard.

"Do you mind?"

"Don't you do nothing stupid, you hear?" he yelled when he turned his back to her.

"What can I possibly do?" she asked. "If I were to try and run away, you'd just pluck me up like a chicken, so why bother?"

The man snorted his agreement. "You best believe I'd pluck you up like a chicken, missy. Don't even think about trying to run off," he shouted. "Billy was my friend. He was stupid and lovestruck, but he was still my friend."

"I'm sorry about Billy. I really am," Sarah called from behind the bushes as she wrestled with her clothing. "I never meant to—to kill him. I was desperate. You must understand that. I truly never meant to kill him."

"Yeah. I guess I can. I've felt kind of desperate a few times myself over these last years." The man sighed then fell silent.

Sarah placed a torn section of her slip on the backside of the bushes, away from the guard's view, but in plain view of anyone coming up the trail. It would be like a beacon in the night for anyone who came looking for her. She had to stifle a chuckle. She smoothed her skirt down and walked out from behind the bushes. Within minutes they were back with the rest of the men.

*Now, God,* she prayed. *Please let someone be looking for me. But who?* Sarah wondered.

## Chapter Twenty-Eight

The door of Federal Headquarters was nearly wrenched off its hinges Ben slammed it so hard.

"Who's in charge?" he demanded.

"I am," answered the man behind the desk. "What may I do for you?"

"I need information. About Quantrill."

"Quantrill?" The man chuckled. "You and about three thousand other men hereabouts."

Ben placed his knuckles on the desk and leaned forward. "I don't give a damn if I'm one of ten thousand," he snarled. "The bastard has taken my wife and I intend to get her back. Now, are you going to help me, Captain...?"

"Reed. The name is Captain Reed. Please, do sit down," he said. "You realize what you ask is very near impossible. That son-of-a-bitch has run us ragged for over four years."

Ben started to speak, but was silenced by the commander's hand. "Sit down and let me finish," the officer snapped.

Ben sat down and forced himself to listen.

"We've been informed Quantrill and his men are headed toward Kentucky. A Negro, Caleb, reported two days ago that Mrs. Ben Walters had been abducted by Quantrill and his men. I assume, sir, the lady is your wife?"

Ben nodded. "Get to the point."

"We have information as to his possible whereabouts and have a unit preparing to strike out as we speak. We leave at dawn."

"I'll be ready. I have more at stake than just finding Quantrill."

"Yes, of course." The captain's brow arched, his voice condescending.

"My wife was kidnapped, Reed. She is not with them of her own will," Ben reminded him, his temper about to explode.

"Of course, of course, I didn't mean to imply..." Reed

paused in thought. "You realize, Mr. Walters, the lady is your responsibility. Solely. I am going to find Quantrill, and find him I will. I will not bargain and I will not make trades. And I will not allow you to jeopardize this operation with sentimentality. Is that understood?"

"Sir." Ben tried to keep his temper, but was about to lose the battle. "Isn't it the responsibility of the army to protect civilians? May I remind you my wife is a civilian and needs your protection. It's my hope..."

"I don't give a damn what your hopes are, Walters," Reed snarled. He stood up and leaned across the desk. "My mission is to come away with Charley Quantrill. Dead or alive. It doesn't matter to me, as long as I return with him. Your wife is your responsibility. Is that understood?"

"Completely!" Ben slammed the door behind him when he left the building, the rage inside him like a living creature.

A knot formed in Ben's stomach. He knew Reed was going to be trouble. The captain was cocky with stars in his eyes, Ben was certain. This was the man's chance at fame. He was going to catch Charley Quantrill and his band of raiders, regardless of the price. Ben knew Reed would be as much of a hindrance in finding Sarah, as a help.

Ben met Caleb on the street and related his conversation.

"We leave tomorrow, Caleb, and I pray to God that single-minded, cocksure bastard doesn't get Sarah killed in the process of trying to save her life."

Dawn broke with an eerie stillness. Ben rode beside Caleb at the rear of the column led by the boisterous, young Captain Reed.

The column rode long and late every day and trackers were sent out to pick up the trail. On the sixth day, a scout raced back into camp.

Ben, Caleb, Reed and the rest of the unit circled the man to hear what he said.

"Captain Reed. I found this along the trail tied to some bushes like a white flag." The scout held out a long section of what looked like woman's undergarment.

Captain Reed took the material and turned to Ben. "Your

wife's?"

Ben's heart leapt. It had to be Sarah's. Who else would have left it so obvious for someone to find?

"It's got to be hers. She left it so we could follow their trail," Ben said.

"Well then, gentlemen, I suggest we get a good night's rest and be ready to ride at daybreak," Captain Reed stated.

The next day the tracker rode back into the column with another piece of white linen, left in plain sight for someone to find. They were on the right trail, Ben was certain, and he praised Sarah for her resourcefulness.

They were close. Very close. He could feel it.

Ben slid on his belly until he could see down into the valley. Below, a fire lit ghostlike figures that moved to and fro in the encampment. Horses were tethered to a rope to the right of camp and numerous tents ringed a large fire in the center. Ben counted twenty men, but assumed there were more inside tents and on guard. It had to be Quantrill and his men.

He and the tracker scooted backwards until they were far enough from the ledge to stand up without being seen.

Ben took off his hat and wiped sweat from his forehead. The thought of Sarah with that bunch of cutthroats made him feel like a knife was being driven into the center of his heart.

"Thanks for letting me see firsthand, Joe. You and I both know Reed isn't going to lift a finger to get my wife out of there. All he cares about is Quantrill and the fame that'll go with capturing him. It's going to be up to me to get Sarah back."

"I know." The tracker clucked his tongue. "Ain't too much love lost between me and that young 'un. He's gonna get us all killed with his quest for fame. You have any idea how many others have gotten killed trying to find, much less catch, Charley Quantrill? I get goose bumps just knowing how close we are to the man."

"I know, and I appreciate your help." Ben sighed. "I guess it's time we let Reed know what you've found."

The two men rode back to camp and informed Reed of what the scout had discovered. The captain was incensed the scout had told Ben before informing him, but there was nothing he could do except fume, sputter and stomp back and forth.

"We go in at first light," Reed commanded.

"Go in at first light! Damn it, Captain! What the hell do you mean by that? Do we just charge in? Surprise them so they can shoot Sarah in the back before she blinks? Damn you, I want my wife freed before there's any bloodshed!" Ben yelled.

"And what do you suggest, Walters?" the captain asked smugly.

"I suggest we pretend to make a deal. Pretend to trade Sarah for their freedom, but while you're negotiating, Caleb and I sneak into their camp, ready to grab her when the firing starts."

"What!" Reed exploded. "Under no circumstances. I told you at the outset, Walters, there will be no deals. I intend to return with Quantrill. He's within my grasp. Do you actually believe I'd let him get away by trading his freedom for some woman I don't even know?"

Ben grabbed Reed by the front of his shirt and pulled his face to within inches of his own. "But she is someone I know very well and care very much about," Ben ground out. "Besides, if you'd listened to a word I just said, we *pretend* to make a trade. You just negotiate to keep their minds off us and we sneak into camp and grab her when the shooting starts. Very simple."

Ben pushed Reed away and he staggered backwards.

"Walters, don't press me. I'm in charge of this operation and you will do as you're told or I'll put you under arrest and you'll have no chance to obtain her freedom. Is that understood?"

Ben didn't answer. He wouldn't. His temper was about to burst. Then an idea came to him.

"I told you, Walters, no deals."

Ben's temper snapped. Caleb grabbed him a split second before his hand would have closed around Reed's throat.

"Damn you, Reed! You don't think I've come all this way to let something happen to her? I won't let you. I'll kill you first." Ben lunged, but Caleb held him back.

Reed retreated and adjusted his clothing. "Perhaps pretending to negotiate a deal with Mr. Quantrill will work. But I guarantee, the moment I think your wife is clear, Quantrill is mine."

"I don't give a damn about Quantrill. He's all yours. All I want is Sarah."

"Very well." The captain turned and stalked away.

Ben was certain Sarah's life would be in jeopardy from the mealy-mouthed Reed. But he was at Reed's mercy. There was no chance in hell he could get into that camp and rescue Sarah without being seen unless there was a diversion of some kind. Guards were posted all around the perimeter. Men with guns just itching to use them. He had to depend upon the strength of the army behind him and hope it would scare Quantrill and his men into submission.

At least long enough to get Sarah out.

## Chapter Twenty-Nine

"A trade, Reed. Don't forget to negotiate a trade," Ben growled from his vantage point that overlooked Quantrill's camp. "Caleb and I will make our way into camp while you're negotiating."

Reed glared at Ben and it was all he could do to keep from attacking the pompous ass.

"Do it!" Ben snarled, his teeth clenched.

A sergeant slid up beside Reed and whispered in his ear. Ben leaned toward the captain and listened, certain he was up to no good. He heard the word sharpshooter and fear tore through him like the arrow that had nearly cost him his life so many years ago.

He reached over and grabbed Reed by the collar. "You intend a double-cross you slimy, little bastard," Ben bit out. "Where is he? Where's the sharpshooter you intend to kill Quantrill with while you're negotiating for my wife's freedom?"

It was all Ben could do to keep from tearing Reed apart. He'd known all along this son-of-a-bitch would do whatever he deemed necessary to take Quantrill, regardless of the fact that it might cost an innocent woman her life in the process.

Reed scrambled back from the ledge, stood and stared at Ben. Ben saw no remorse, no guilt, not even the slightest bit of doubt in Reed's eyes and a cold wave rushed through him.

"Where?" Ben asked, his voice so low only Reed could hear him.

"In those trees over there." Reed pointed left toward a small patch of trees.

Ben glanced at the trees on a slope just above the valley. Within those trees was Sarah's possible death, Ben thought with anguish.

"Damn you to hell, Reed."

"I told you from the beginning, Walters, I will come away with Quantrill. At any cost." His words were strangled in his throat when Ben wrenched him off his feet.

"It will not be my wife!" Ben snarled before two men

dragged him off the captain.

"Five minutes," Ben said in desperation. "Just keep him talking for five minutes before all hell breaks loose or you give the signal for the sharpshooter."

Reed strode to Ben, hatred in his eyes.

He contemplated Ben's words. "Five minutes. That's all you've got. And so help me, if you alert that camp I will fire at will at the first thing that moves. And that includes you or your wife."

"Deal." Ben tore himself free.

"Let's go, Caleb." They ran toward a copse of trees that lined the opposite slope of the hillside.

When they reached the stand of woods they slipped behind some trees and began working their way downward. Neither said a word. They moved in hurried silence as they worked their way toward the guard.

They came upon him stretched out beside a tree, twirling a twig in his mouth. Ben stepped up beside him and snapped his neck before the man even knew he was there.

Reed's voice suddenly broke the stillness of the early morning.

"William Clarke Quantrill! You and your men are surrounded. Don't anyone move!"

Ben frantically searched the camp. His spine stiffened when he couldn't find Sarah. Where the hell was she? All of a sudden he wished he didn't know.

A tall man with reddish hair pushed his way out of one of the tents that ringed the dying fire using Sarah as a shield. His left arm was tight around her waist and his right hand was clenched in a fist in her hair. Ben watched helplessly as Quantrill tugged her hair. Her face contorted in pain, but she didn't cry out, she grit her teeth instead.

Ben's breath was quick and his heart pounded like a mallet. He was close. So very close. He could see the contours of her face, the rise and fall of her chest, a strange calmness in her eyes. *But was it calm or something else?* he wondered as he remembered Sarah's spirit. A chill raced up his spine as he realized it was anger.

"Don't do anything foolish," he heard himself whisper as he watched the scene unfold, unable to do anything to help her.

"You have three minutes to decide your fate, Quantrill," Reed shouted. "Release the woman, surrender and return with me to be tried for your crimes, or die here. Be assured, you will return with me dead or alive. It makes no difference to me. No difference at all."

Ben's mind raced. He had only three minutes to get to Sarah before the shooting started. Reed didn't give a damn about her. One way or another he was going to take Quantrill and his men. He felt sure Reed would kill Sarah or anyone else for that matter to get him.

Quantrill's laughter floated up the hill. "Do you think for one minute I'm going to let her go and let you have a free shot at me?" he yelled. "Be assured, blue-belly, that if me or any of my men are fired upon, this woman will die before the first ball strikes dirt!"

Ben nearly rushed out of the trees, but Caleb grabbed him and held him firm. Instead they waited and watched. For anything. Any opportunity to rescue Sarah.

Ben searched the faces of Quantrill's men, a shaggy lot, most clad in the blue uniforms of Union soldiers. *No wonder they wandered the countryside unmolested. They probably carried phony Union papers, too.*

Sarah cried out, drawing Ben's attention. Her head was cocked at an odd angle by the way Quantrill had her hair wrapped around his fist. That look was in her eyes again. The look of anger and sheer determination.

"Don't do anything stupid," he whispered. "Please, don't do anything stupid."

Reed yelled again from the ledge and in that instant, Ben made up his mind.

He charged out from the copse of trees, his hands high above his head.

"Quantrill!"

Ben heard guns cock and he braced himself for a volley of gunfire to rip through him. But it didn't come. He stepped closer.

"That's close enough. Who the hell are you and what do you think you're doing?" Quantrill yelled.

"I'm that lady's husband and I want a trade. Me for her."

"Why should I trade her for you? I got no reason to care whether she lives or dies. Or you for that matter. I could shoot you both right here, right now."

Ben knew he had to get Sarah out of there. Somehow. Tension rode the air like gunpowder ready to ignite with the smallest spark.

"Quantrill! I know harming women is not in your code. Let her go."

In that instant Sarah lifted her leg and kicked Quantrill square in the knee. He howled and shoved her so hard she stumbled and rolled to the ground.

The morning exploded with gunfire. Men scrambled, yelled and dove for cover.

Everything seemed to move in slow motion to Ben, although men shouted and scrambled for their lives. Bullets whizzed past, slamming into tents, men and the ground. Sarah pushed herself up and Ben started to run toward her. But someone grabbed him from behind. He heard Caleb's voice, cold and deadly, and a gun discharged behind him. The hand fell away. More guns exploded. Ben ran toward Sarah, her face lined with fear, her eyes wild.

"Sarah!" he shouted. But her name died on his lips when her smile faded and turned to a grimace of pain.

She collapsed ten feet in front of him.

When he reached her, her back was covered with blood. The earth beside his foot exploded with the impact of a bullet. He spun around and shot wildly.

He turned back to Sarah, now cradled in Caleb's arms. The two men raced with her to the cover of woods and safety.

Ben heard Quantrill's voice as he taunted, "Did you think I would be caught without an alternate escape route?" he yelled. "Better men than you have tried to capture me, and failed, Captain Reed! Until we meet again!"

Quantrill disappeared between two adjoining hills, his

men close behind, their laughter following.

Horses thundered from the top of the ledge and crashed down on what remained of Quantrill's band. They raced past, guns blazing, before the cavalrymen disappeared in pursuit of the bushwhackers.

Minutes later all was quiet and Ben knew, without question, Quantrill and his raiders had escaped. Again.

Ben smoothed the hair off Sarah's face. Her eyes were closed, but she was breathing. Barely. He looked down at the hole in her left side and winced at the thought of her pain. The bullet had passed right through her side, just below her rib cage.

He studied her features and wiped the dirt off her face. She was so beautiful and he had so much to tell her. She couldn't die. He'd waited too long to tell her he was sorry. To actually say the words. To tell her he loved her with all his heart.

His breath caught at the thought he might lose her. She'd suffered so much. She had to live. Had to.

A man entered the tent.

"Can you help her?"

"I'll do my best," the soldier replied. "A lot will depend on her. If she's strong, she's got a chance. If not..." He looked into Ben's eyes and his sentence remained unfinished.

Ben shoved out of the tent. The air inside threatened to suffocate him. He walked toward a row of horses tied on a tether between two trees, left behind by Quantrill's men. He stopped and turned when an agitated horse kept nickering behind him.

"Midnight?"

A sad smile broke his lips. He walked to the familiar animal and stroked its snout.

"Hello, boy. How'd you get here?" he wondered out loud, unaware that he'd been taken from White Oaks so long ago. He gazed over at the tent where Sarah fought for her life.

"She's had a tough time of it. But she's strong and we have to believe she'll make it."

His last words came out in a gruff whisper. He drew in a heavy breath to keep from crying out. Why? After all they'd been through, did she now lie in that tent, close to death, with

him unable to ease her mind?
    And his own.

## Chapter Thirty

An azure sky surrounded Man-Who-Runs. He sat before Sarah, a smile on his face, and pulled the sinew tight on a new bow. His face was serene as he continued his task. Behind him loomed another figure. Tall and dark. A fine figure, with strong shoulders and lean hips. It moved into the sunlight and the face became visible. Ben. Sarah tried to speak. But couldn't. She wanted to ask him why he hadn't come home. Why he'd left her to take care of herself for so long. He smiled and reached out to her.

"Come on, Sarah. Fight," he whispered. "You're a fighter and this is one battle you can't lose."

She wanted to answer him, but couldn't form the words. Pain. She felt red-hot pain, but didn't know where it came from.

Ben smiled and continued to offer his hand.

"Fight, Sarah. I love you. Fight, so I can tell you so," he said.

She forced her eyes open. Everything was a blur. She blinked several times and tried to clear the haze from her eyes, but she just couldn't focus.

She waited, closed her eyes hard, then tried again. This time she saw where she was. A ceiling was above her and four drab walls surrounded her. A mirror, some pictures. And Ben.

Ben! He had come. She had run to him and then...

She closed her eyes, shook her head, and winced at the pain the movement caused. When she opened her eyes again she saw her husband, heard him speak.

"Don't move, Sarah. You've been shot."

Sarah gazed into his dark eyes and wondered if she was still dreaming. Her mind was clouded, but she forced herself to remember.

Quantrill. She'd been with Quantrill. And Ben had come just before the paralyzing pain struck her. He'd come for her!

"Ben?" she barely whispered.

"Don't talk. Save your strength."

"How?" she managed.

"It's a long story. Once you're more rested we'll talk and I'll explain everything. From the beginning," he promised.

She felt her eyes droop and had no power to stop them from closing. Within seconds, she was asleep again.

Sarah floated in and out of consciousness for several days. Whenever she woke, she was groggy and in great pain, but Ben was always there. She had so many questions, but didn't have the strength to ask them. He was with her and that was all that mattered. He was alive and he'd come for her.

After four days of semi-consciousness, Sarah finally came fully awake, her mind clear and ready to ask questions. She opened her eyes and looked around the room. It was empty. Had she dreamed Ben was with her all along? Had he been a vision in her delirious state of mind?

Tears were forming in her eyes when the door opened and there he stood. It hadn't been a dream. He was here. He was real.

She'd waited so long for him it was hard to accept that he was really there. Could there be an explanation as to why she hadn't heard from him in all the time he'd been gone?

She studied the man. He'd changed much. Lines etched his handsome face and gray streaked the temples of his long dark hair. He was thin and gaunt with a haunted look in his eyes.

"Welcome back." Ben smiled and stepped toward her.

He grabbed her hand and squeezed it; gazed into her face.

"Sarah, my darling Sarah. How I've missed you." His voice was hoarse with emotion.

"How would I know?" She was suddenly angry. *Why hadn't he let her know he was alive? Why had he made her go mad with worry?*

Sadness filled his eyes at her harsh words. "I was constantly on the move, before..." His words broke off and that haunted look came back into his eyes. He seemed to push the unwanted thought from his mind and continued. "I posted a letter after the siege at Fort Donelson. But you never wrote back. I posted others, but never got any answers. I thought you'd turned your back on me."

"I never received any of your letters. They must have been among those lost with Quantrill's raids." She paused a minute. "And why would I turn my back on you?"

He shook his head. "I was cruel to you for so long, Sarah. I thought maybe you'd finally given up on me. I was afraid you wouldn't wait for me after so long with no word." He clicked his tongue. "I should have known better." He leaned forward. "Sarah, you must listen to me. I've learned a few things in the past four years."

"Such as?" Anger made her voice gruff.

"That I must ask your forgiveness of my terrible treatment of you before I left."

"But we worked that out, Ben." Sarah was confused. "Unless it was just words?"

Ben shook his head. "No, no. That's just it. There never were any words. No words to tell you how sorry I was for the way I treated you. No words to tell you I understood why you did what you did. I'm here because I love you and need to beg your forgiveness."

Sarah was barely able to comprehend his words. *Beg her forgiveness?* She thought they'd reconciled their differences before he left for the war. She just didn't understand.

"I have so much to tell you," he began, his voice soft.

He ran his fingers through his graying hair. "I don't quite know where to start." He took her hands into his. She gasped at the sight of his mangled arm.

"As you can see, I've suffered a great deal. I've been trying to get back to you for years. To let you know I finally understood what you did and what you lived through."

Sarah tried to speak, but Ben wouldn't let her.

"Please, let me finish. I have to say it all and you have to listen." He took a deep breath and continued.

"I was captured at Lexington, way back at the start of the war and shipped to Libby Prison." Sarah gasped, but Ben continued. "There I nearly lost my life. But it was there, Sarah, I finally understood what you'd suffered and what you did to survive. I realized how sacred life is and to what lengths I would go to save it."

Sarah felt tears threaten, but she forced them back.

"I managed to escape Libby, but at the cost of nearly losing the use of my hand." He looked down at his arm. "I was fortunate enough to be taken in by a family who nursed me back to health. As healthy as I could get," he added.

"Once I was on my way back to you I met up with a Union detachment on their way to Fort Donelson and was pressed back into service. From there the rest is almost a blur. From Fort Donelson to Shiloh to Vicksburg and finally Atlanta and Sherman's March to the Sea.

"It all runs together now, but through it all, all I ever wanted was to get back to you. To tell you I understood and beg your forgiveness. But we were always moving. And the few letters I did manage to post must not have made it through."

He fell silent. His eyes pleaded for her to understand. Her heart nearly burst from her chest. Her prayers had been answered. He'd come back to her.

"And now I've come home to tell you I love you. To tell you I've always loved you and always will."

Sarah was rocked by his words and she tried to calm her racing emotions.

She gazed into Ben's hopeful face, bounded by weariness. He understood. Understood everything. All she had done and cared for in her pursuit of survival. And he loved her! *Really* loved her. She touched his cheek, traced her finger along a white scar that ran from his cheek to his jawbone.

"A souvenir from Commandant Turner," he said. "With a few more that match on my back."

Sarah flinched at the tortures he must have endured.

"I promised myself that no matter what I had to do, I would escape that hellhole. And I did, Sarah. How I escaped makes me sick inside, so sick I can't even speak of it, but it was necessary and I'd do it again to win my freedom. To survive, just as you did."

Sarah stared at the man who was her husband. A much different man than she had married. Different than the one who'd gone off to war.

She couldn't breathe. Ben leaned over her.

And kissed her.

It was soft and warm and full of tenderness and love. Warm shivers rippled along Sarah's body. Memories of long ago flooded her senses. She was in his arms, enfolded by his strength.

Her insides tingled. Her arms were weak and her heart fluttered like a hummingbird's wings. If she were standing, she was sure she wouldn't be able to hold up her own weight, her body liquid like water.

The kiss was gentle. A kiss Ben Walters, the man she had married, would have given her. All she needed to know was in that kiss.

Although her body ached, she put her arm around his neck.

She'd lived through capture with the Indians and had learned to live and love again. She'd returned to her own people, only to be ostracized. But she'd learned. Always learned. She felt the pain of her husband's rejection, the dull ache in her heart constant. And from that rejection, she'd learned to be strong.

But now the only thing in her heart was joy. More joy than she'd known in her entire existence. The man she loved with all her being was alive and had come for her. And told her he loved her. Her joy and relief consumed her and tears flooded her eyes. Ben was back and he was hers. He'd come for her when no one else could. Her arm tightened around his neck.

She'd known the bond between them was inseparable. Now it was forever.

Sarah, Ben, and Caleb returned to White Oaks. Sarah recovered slowly with much tender care from Ben. Weeks turned into months and Ben and Sarah began a new life together.

They gave Prudy and Caleb their little cottage to the rear of the main house. Caleb worked side by side with Ben and earned wages, while Prudy helped Sarah with the house and garden. They rebuilt their lives with the bricks of peace, added and fortified as each day passed. They were part of the rebuilding of a nation devastated by war.

On a gloriously beautiful day in June, Ben and Sarah

rode to the crest of a hill overlooking White Oaks. They dismounted and gazed out over the land. Their land.

"It's so beautiful." Sarah sighed. She shaded her eyes from the warm sun that beat down on her face. "I still can't believe it's ours. After everything we've been through, we've got our ranch. I only wish it had been some other way, but through us, Miss Emma's legacy will live on."

Ben nodded agreement, but didn't speak.

Sarah thought back over the last eleven years. Of the great anticipation she and Ben had felt at being part of the discovery of a new country. The world of the Indian. The world of hate. The world of war and the horrific suffering that went with it. She thought of the present where she was again safe and warm in the comfort of Ben's love.

Absently, Sarah caressed the golden locket that rested against her neck. The symbol of her past—and her present. She ran her finger over the wooden cross that rested above it, a token of friendship.

Her view swept the expanse of land around her. This was her destiny. Tomorrow's promise that her future was here, with Ben.

Ben's arm circled her waist. Happy and secure she looked out over White Oaks, whispered goodbye to all that was and welcomed all that would be.

## The End

## Afterword

Although this novel and its characters are a work of fiction, the story itself is based in fact. In order to enhance this story, it was necessary to slightly alter some historical facts.

In the summer of 1854, within eight miles of Fort Laramie, three tribes of Sioux Indians were encamped together. When a Mormon wagon train passed by the encampment of the Brule. Miniconjou, and Oglala, a lame cow broke loose from its tether and wandered into the Indian village. There, a lone Mineconjou brave butchered it and fed his starving family.

When word reached Fort Laramie of the incident, a young, brash officer went to the village to demand compensation. Lieutenant Grattan was intent on bringing the brave back to Fort Laramie for his "crime." The brave refused. Firing erupted and the Brule chief, Conquering Bear, was mortally wounded. The Indians retaliated and all thirty soldiers that had accompanied Lieutenant Grattan were killed. Conquering Bear died five days later. The actual event occurred in August, but to be used as a catalyst for this story, it happens earlier in the year.

The "Battle of Ash Hollow" at Blue Water Creek, where Sarah is rescued by Ben, is a factual event. There, the Indians were brutally murdered in retaliation for the Grattan massacre, as described above.

The question has arisen in history as to whether or not William Clark Quantrill actually plotted to assassinate President Lincoln. He and his men were travelling east out of Missouri in early 1865. In May of '65, Quantrill was mortally wounded in Kentucky and died a week later in prison.

## Sources Consulted

The following books, although many more were studied, constitute a list of primary reference materials that were consulted to verify facts such as accurate depiction of an Indian battle/attack and movements of our characters as our story and history developed around them. They were also consulted for; a natural language usage; accurate dress of the era; military events transpiring; accurate terminology usage in description of history event; Indian customs of the era; Civil War era prison conditions; proper verbal military commands; attack/assault formation: descriptions given by diary authors of animal reactions; food preparation; Indian camp mannerisms; adornment, jewelry, etc; weapons; horses; fires; camp design; songs/music; Inner Tribal customs of Indian; pioneer customs; Landscape features; and many cross references between the titles were checked for accuracy and original sources.

*Lakota Belief & Ritual.* Written by James R. Walker. 1991, U. of Nebraska Press. p 270

*Everyday Lakota.* General Editor, Joseph S. Karol, M.A.; Asst. Ed. Stephen L. Rozman, Ph.D.

*The Massacre of Lt. Gratton* – Paul Hedrer, Arthur H. Clark Co.

Brochure for Lexington, Missouri
*A State Divided: Missouri and the Civil W*ar. Missouri Department of Natural Resources; Division of Parks & Historic Preservation.

Time-Life Books. The Civil War – *The Road to Shiloh* (1983)

*Historical Times Encyclopedia of the Civil War.* Patricia L. Faust, Editor, 1991, Harper Perennial

*We Rode With Quantrill.* Donald Hale, author. 1992

*Tomorrow's Promise: Survival on the Plains*     *D.L. Rogers*

## About the Author...

Diane was born on "The Jersey Shore" and spent much of her youth on the beach, but for the past 20+ years she's lived in the Kansas City area. She currently resides south of Kansas City with her husband, horses, and a multitude of cats. She has two grown children and five grandchildren. She's always loved the old West and history of the Civil War period. Her favorite movie is Dances With Wolves, an inspiration for the first book in the White Oaks Series. Having parents from both the "North and the South" and a cousin whose parents were reversed, they called each other "Yebels" as children and imagined themselves, as children will do, 150 years ago fighting different sides of the war.

As a kid, Diane played "Cowboys and Indians" more than she did Barbie, and it comes through in her writing, as she relates stories of the struggle of common people and what made this country great.

When Diane isn't working on her next book in progress, one can find her curled up on the sofa engrossed in a good book or watching and old western movie. She currently is employed as a legal administrative assistant at a major law firm in Kansas City.

Diane would love to hear your comments on the books... e-mail her at dlrogers2@peoplepc.com.

*Tomorrow's Promise: Survival on the Plains*     **D.L. Rogers**

Electronic books Published by Awe-Struck E-Books, Inc.
Copyright © 2007
ISBN: 978-1-58749-648-6

Electronic rights reserved by Awe-Struck E-Books, all other rights reserved by author. The reproduction or other use of any part of this publication without the prior written consent of the rights holder is an infringement of the copyright law.

This is a work of fiction. People and locations, even those with real names, have been fictionalized for the purposes of this story.

To learn about other books Awe-Struck publishes, go to the Awe-Struck E-Books website at http://www.awe-struck.net/

CPSIA information can be obtained at www.ICGtesting.com
Printed in the USA
LVOW10s1650020616

490978LV00012B/128/P